Twin Alphas

ABUSED MATE

PART ONE: OMEGA

Twin Alphas Mate; Part One: Omega

Copyright © 2021 Jamie Craig.

Printed in Australia

Cover design by Shawline Publishing Group Pty Ltd

First Printing: November 2021

Shawline Publishing Group Pty Ltd

www.shawlinepublishing.com.au

Paperback ISBN- 9781922444646

Ebook ISBN- 9781922444653

A catalogue record for this book is available from the National Library of Australia

For My Family, thank you for supporting me in my journey as a writer.

And to those who dare to be different, never stop being yourself.

More Love, Less Hate

*Thank you to Shawline Publishing Group for giving me a
chance to achieve my dream of publishing a book.*

In the year 2020, different supernatural creatures exist in the world, hidden from humans. For each supernatural, life can vary from good to bad.

For Levi, life has been nothing but hell. His pack abuses him, treating him as no more than a slave simply because he is considered different. With his eighteenth birthday still a year away, Levi has some time to wait before he can find his mate and escape his hell. When he finds his mates early and they turn out to be the twin Alphas of the second largest pack in the world; Levi will find out if he will be accepted or if he will be rejected.

Twin Alphas, Kyro and Kaiden, have always been close, and that hasn't changed since they became joint Alphas of their pack. However, will things change when they find out that they are mated to the same wolf? And will they protect their mate from those that wish to harm him?

In this story, the Covid-19 Pandemic does not exist.

Warning this story contains mentions of the following:

- Sexual, Physical and Mental Abuse
- LGBTQ People and Couples
- Sex Scenes: Heterosexual and LGBTQ
- Mpreg: Male Pregnancy
- Violence

Things To Know Before Reading

Communication:

Throughout the story, there are different forms of communication between the characters.

Normal conversations:

- Conducted out loud between characters or a character talking to themselves out loud

- 'Written like this,'

Conversation over71:

- Conducted in the characters mind, unless in the link other characters won't hear what's being said

- **Written like this**

Conversation with Inner Shifter:

- Conducted between a character and their inner shifter creature. Can involve one or more people and their inner shifter creatures.

- ***Written like this***

Pack Ranks and Roles:

All pack ranks and roles are gender neutral.

Alpha: Head of the Pack

Luna: Mate of the Alpha

Beta: 2nd in Command of the Pack

Beta's Mate: Mate of the Beta

Gamma: 3rd in Command

Gamma's Mate: Mate of the Gamma

Head Warrior: most senior pack warrior

Warriors: protectors of the pack

Senior Pack Doctor: most senior member of the pack's medical staff

Medical Staff: includes doctors, nurses, midwives, medics, etc. They take care of the pack's medical needs.

Twin Alphas

ABUSED MATE

PART ONE: OMEGA

JAMIE CRAIG

ROYAL SAGA

TWIN ALPHAS

ABUSED MATE

PART ONE OMEGA

JAMIE CRAIG

CHAPTER 1: LEVI'S POV

'GET UP AND make breakfast for everyone right now you fucking runt,' I groaned, getting up from my bed. Well, if you could call a mattress on the floor and a thin sheet a bed. My Alpha yelling at me was nothing new. I was used to it, besides yelling was the least of what he and the rest of the pack would do to me. As I sat on the edge of my bed thinking, I heard heavy footsteps thunder down the stairs and into the dingy basement that was my room. 'Did you fucking hear me, you little bastard? I said get up and make breakfast right fucking now,' the Alpha yelled as he grabbed me by the throat and punched me in the gut, causing me to double over in pain. He threw me across the room, towards the stairs.

Before he was able to hit me again, I scrambled up the stairs and into the kitchen. I quietly made breakfast for the entire pack; it consisted of cereal, toast, bacon, eggs, juice, coffee, and tea. Once breakfast had been made, I brought everything out to the dining room and placed them on the tables. As I was finished putting breakfast onto the tables, Jake, the son of our pack Alpha, came into the dining room with his friends Future Beta Howard, Future Gamma Mick, Trainee Warrior Oba and two others.

'Looky here guys. It's little Omega Levi,' Jake and his friends said before laughing. Before I could leave the room, I was grabbed and spun around, so I was now facing them.

'What'd you make for breakfast you pathetic little Omega?' Jake asked.

'Yeah. What ya make? It better be good or you know what will happen,' Oba said in his usual gruff tone, he cracked his knuckles which made me flinch.

'I-I-I m-made cereal, t-t-toast, b-bacon a-and e-eggs to e-eat and j-juice, c-coffee and t-tea to drink s-sirs,' I stuttered out. I was very scared of Jake and his friends and for good reason. After a couple of minutes Jake decided to let me leave, so I ran out of there and went straight back to my room. I looked through the few clothes I had, trying to find the cleanest set. I ended up finding a pair of black skinny jeans which had numerous holes in them and a thin light blue shirt to wear. Once I had them on, I put my sneakers on, grabbed my school bag and raced up the stairs and out the front door of the pack house, making my way to school on foot. The pack grounds were bleak and unimpressive to look at but I did like the forest that surrounded it.

When I got to school, I was a bit early so I decided to go to an empty classroom and wait there until the first bell rang. The classroom I was waiting in was one of the art classrooms, there were paintings drying on the racks and clay models sitting on one of the benches at the side of the classroom. I spent the time until the first bell drawing in my sketchbook. When the first bell rang, I left the classroom and headed off to my first class. When I got to my first class, I made my way to my desk at the back of the room. Slowly my other classmates made their way into the room, with several of them making their way towards me and I flinched, wishing they would leave me alone.

'Hey boys, look what we have here. The little runt showed up,' Jake said as he pushed me off the chair. Jake and his friends laughed at me but before they could do anything else, we heard the teacher coming, so they made their ways to their desks and sat down. As I got up and sat back into my seat, our teacher walked into the classroom. Goddess, this lesson is going to take a long time. Mr Elmers, a fellow pack member, was one of my least favourite teachers at school. Firstly, because he taught my least favourite subject, maths, and secondly, because he always droned on and on. I was always tired by the time his class ended and had to force myself to stay awake. When the bell rang for the next class, I groaned as I got up, I was stiff from sleeping on the floor all the time. I quickly made my way to my next class as I wanted to get a seat before anyone else showed up. My next lesson was sports, I groaned at the thought of having to do sports. I absolutely hated doing sports, almost everyone in my sports class was bigger and fitter than me. When the teacher said that today we were playing dodgeball, I could feel my palms start to sweat as panic set in. I always ended up with new injuries when I played dodgeball, I was always the first one to get out as Jake and his friends targeted me. After splitting into two groups for dodgeball the teacher had us each grab a ball and then move to our respective sides of the room. Once he blew his whistle all hell broke loose as students tried to hit each other. I looked over to Jake's side and saw him and his friends' smirk at me. Before I could react, they all threw their balls at me. I was knocked to the ground and could feel blood gush from my nose. The teacher blew his whistle, causing the class to stop playing. He walked over to me with a scowl on his face, I always seemed to annoy him. Even though I'd never done anything to him.

'Levi get up and take yourself to the nurse's office. I don't need you bleeding all over the court,' he huffed, while the rest of the class laughed at me.

'Aww Levi has a boo boo and needs to go to the nurse,' I heard Jake say. Goddess, I hated him so much, I thought to myself as I got up off the ground and left the gym. I headed down the hallways and eventually made it to the nurse's office. I knocked on the door and a woman's voice called for me to enter.

'Oh, my Goddess, Levi. What happened to you?' Diomika Lang, the school nurse, rushed over to me, gently took my face in her hands and looked me over.

'It's nothing Diomika. Just had an accident in class, we were playing dodgeball,' I told her as she led me to the bed and made me sit down.

'Levi, there is no need to lie to me. You can tell me anything, you know that right?' She looked me straight in the eye as she spoke.

'I know Diomika. It really was an accident in class,' She sighed and went and grabbed some things to clean me up.

'How was your weekend Levi?' Diomika asked as she cleaned my face up.

'It was fine. Just did some cleaning and hung around the house. You know the usu—' I was cut off when Diomika applied a little too much pressure to my nose, causing me to wince in pain.

'Oh, my Goddess, Levi. I'm so sorry,' she said, trying to soothe me.

'It's ok Diomika. I've had worse.' And I had, which Diomika knew. She was probably the only one outside the pack who knew what happened to me. Though not a member of my pack, Diomika was a wolf. She wasn't a member of a pack, instead she was a lone wolf. My pack didn't like rogue wolves or lone wolves. The only reason my pack did nothing about her working at this school was that it was on neutral territory and therefore she was free to be here. I knew Diomika wished she could help me but I also knew that there wasn't anything she could do against an entire pack. After she finished cleaning my face up, I said goodbye and went back to class.

Thankfully, the bell rang a few minutes later and I was able to leave again. After I left, I made my way to the library, where I sat down and read several books. Technically it was lunch time but I knew that the other members of my pack, especially Jake and his friends, would make sure I didn't get anything to eat. I was only allowed to eat a couple of times a week and even then, it was just enough to stop me from dropping dead. Throughout the rest of the day, I did my best to avoid Jake and his group as all they did was insult me and abuse me. However, seeing as Jake and his friends were werewolves, avoiding them was near impossible. Actually, to be honest, all students at this school were werewolves, as this was a werewolf only school, so no humans attended. The other students at the school either ignored my presence, bullied me, or turned a blind eye to what was happening. I had no friends at school and didn't bother trying to make any, as I didn't want anyone to suffer because of me.

My next lesson of the day was history, one of the few lessons I actually enjoyed. Today's lesson was about Ancient Greece, particularly, Ancient Greek Gods and Goddesses. By the end of the class, I decided that my favourite Goddess was Athena, as she was both smart and strong. After history, I had science and then after that was lunch, which I again spent in the library. My last lesson of the day was probably my favourite lesson, cooking. My cooking teacher, Mrs Le Beau, a plump motherly woman from a different pack always came up with interesting things for us to do in class. She would allow the class to eat what we made but I never did as I feared what would happen if my pack found out I had something to eat without permission. When she asked why I never ate, I told her that I wanted to save it for when I got home so I could share it with my pack's Alpha family. She just nodded and accepted my response. What I told her was only partly a lie, I was taking the food I cooked home for the Alpha family, I just never got to have any of it. Once the lesson was over, I packed my things up and left class. I didn't have any food to take home today as we made things for a staff luncheon that afternoon.

I made my way to my locker, located on the other side of the school. Once at my locker I took the books I didn't need and returned them to my locker. Just after I finished grabbing that night's homework, I felt people approaching me from behind. Before I could do anything, I was grabbed and thrown to the ground.

'Look at this Jake. Here he is looking ready for a beating,' Mick laughed as he spoke and then kicked me in the stomach.

'You're right Mick and it'd be bad if we didn't give him the beating he was waiting for, wouldn't it boys,' replied Jake. The group laughed and then they all started kicking and punching me, insulting me as they did. I was in so much pain and knew that I had several new broken bones, was bleeding on the outside and definitely had internal bleeding. I didn't fight back as I knew it would prove futile. As they continued to beat me, I felt myself starting to slip in and out of consciousness. All of a sudden there was a loud growl. The growl caused me to whimper as I could feel the power radiating in it. The power from the growl was similar to that of my Alpha, if not even stronger, so I knew that whoever growled had to also be an Alpha. Jake and his group stopped beating me and turned to face the person who had growled. I could hear Jake say something but I couldn't quite make out what he said. But whatever he said obviously offended the Alpha that was present as all of a sudden Jake went flying and the Alpha let out another deep growl. This time instead of staying, Jake and his group left as soon as the growl happened. As they left, I sensed someone kneel down beside me and felt them put their hand on my neck. I felt sparks go through me when the person touched me and I was confused as to what caused it. Suddenly, I was gently picked up by a strong pair of arms, arms I felt oddly safe in. But before I could say anything, I fell unconscious.

CHAPTER 2: KYRO'S POV

MY TWIN BROTHER Kaiden and I were sitting at our desks in the Alpha office, both of us reading yet another report sent to us by another pack. We have been joint Alphas for the last three years and it seemed like all we do is read reports from other packs.

'Goddess, what the hell do these people expect us to do? It's like they can't even run their own damn packs,' Kaiden said, his agitation rising as he continued reading the reports.

'I don't know brother but they are an ally of ours.' My twin harrumphed at my response and then went silent. Half an hour later there was a knock at our door and at my invitation Beta Jaden walked into the room.

'Alphas, how goes the reading?' The smirk on Jaden's face indicated he knew exactly how the reading was going. I shook my head at my Beta and so did my twin.

'Keep it up Jaden and I'll make you read every new report that comes in for the next year,' My twin threatened. Jaden held his hands up in surrender but a smile played on his face.

'What brings you here Jay? Besides annoying my brother and I that is,' I asked setting down the report I was reading.

'I came to remind you we were going to pick up your brothers and my sister from school in an hour. If we don't leave now, we will be late getting back for the video conference with the Alpha from the Amber Sky Pack,' Jaden replied. I nodded, I had almost forgotten that I was picking my brothers and Jaden's sister up from school. I sometimes get so focused on work that other things slip my mind.

'While you go pick up the kids from school, I'll get everything ready for the video call,' Kaiden said as I stood up.

'Sounds good. I'll see you when we get back,' Jaden and I left the room and made our way to the garage. We went to the garage and got into my car that I had only gotten a couple of months ago; I absolutely loved this car. While driving through the pack lands, we passed by the many different pack buildings. Such as houses, workshops and several other buildings. After we left the pack lands, we headed along the highway that led to the town where the school was located. It took us around half an hour to reach the school and as we arrived the school's bell rang. After parking and getting out of the car, we headed towards the front of the school and through the front doors. As we made our way through the front doors, there were a lot of students coming out of the classes. The students parted ways to allow Jaden and I to pass by. Though most of the students we passed weren't from our pack, they could recognise from the auras that Jaden and I gave off, that we were an Alpha and Beta and as such they would avoid offending us. When Jaden and I found his sister Sakura and my brother Kode, they were sitting together, murmuring to each other. They were so engrossed in their discussion that they didn't notice us until we stood directly in front of them.

'Hey big bro,' Sakura said as she stood up and hugged Jaden, squeezing him tightly.

'Damn sis you are getting strong,' Jaden laughed out as he returned his sister's hug.

'So, what were you guys just talking about?' I asked once Sakura had detached herself from her brother. Sakura and Kode blushed and looked away, not answering my question.

My they are cute aren't they Kyro? Jaden asked me on a private mind link.

They are cute. I really hope they are mated together one day, Jaden nodded at my statement. Their closeness indicated that Sakura and Kode could be mated one day. None of us would be bothered by it if they were, in fact we were all kind of hoping they would be. 'Do you guys happen to know where Kaito is?' I asked.

'No, we haven't seen him,' Kode replied as he and Sakura both shrugged. Damn they seemed to mirror each other at times, more reason for us to believe they would be mates one day.

'Ok you two take my keys and go wait in the car for us, while we look for

Kaito,' I said as I handed my keys over to Kode. After Kode and Sakura left, Jaden and I went to go and look for Kaito. I sniffed to see if I could detect Kaito's scent but due to the scents of all the other students and staff at the school, I couldn't find Kaito's. So, looks like we will have to do this the hard way.

'If you were Kaito, where would you be?' Jaden asked as we walked around.

We looked at each other before smiling and in unison we said, 'library'.

When we got to the library, we found Kaito with his head stuck in a book.

Hey, let's scare him, Jaden said after nudging my shoulder. He had a smirk on his face and his eyes twinkled with humour. Sometimes Jaden and our pack Gamma Rowan acted like big children, well so did Kaiden and I. Sometimes you just needed to let go and relax.

Let's do it, I replied. We quietly walked over to Kaito and stood right behind him. Once we were close enough, we both yelled out his name. Kaito let out a high-pitched scream and jumped from his chair. I could have sworn he was about to shift but he managed to stop himself from doing so.

'What the fuck guys? You fucking startled me,' Kaito said as he clutched his chest and brought his breathing under control.

'Is that any way to speak to your Alpha and Beta?' I asked my brother, a serious look on my face.

'No, that's how I speak to my annoying older brother and his equally annoying friend,' Kaito raised an eyebrow at me as he responded. Jaden gasped and placed a hand on his chest in mock surprise at my brother's response.

'Equally annoying. I like to think of myself as being more annoying thank you very much,' Jaden said sarcastically. Kaito and I shook our heads at Jaden.

'What are you guys doing here? You're not supposed to be here until 3. The last bell hasn't even gone yet,' Kaito asked, causing Jaden and I to laugh at him. He must have been very focused for him not to have noticed the bell had gone off.

'It is three-fifteen Kaito,' Before Kaito could respond, an older man walked into the room a concerned look on his face.

'Is everything ok? I heard a scream,' The man asked.

'Everything is ok sir. Just startled my brother who had his head stuck in a book,' I replied.

'Kaito sure is a bookworm,' The man said as he nodded at my response.

'That he is,' I said as I ruffled my brother's hair. Kaito swatted at my hand before turning to pack his things into his bag.

'Well, I shall leave you be,' the man said. 'Alpha de Luca, Beta McCallister, Kaito.' The man nodded and then left the room. It was strange being addressed by my last name, instead of my first name.

'Don't know if I will ever get used to being addressed by my last name,' Jaden commented.

'Same here. You ready to go Kaito?' I asked. After Kaito nodded, the three of us left the library and headed back towards the parking lot. As we walked through the school, I was suddenly hit with the most alluring smell of cinnamon and hot chocolate.

Oh, my Goddess. Follow that smell right now, My wolf Shadow said, encouraging me to follow the smell and I gladly did so. I was confused as to why I found it alluring but I wouldn't let that stop me from finding the source of the scent.

'Kyro what's going on? What are you doing?' Jaden and Kaito both asked as I continued to track the smell. I ignored them as I was too focused on finding the source of the smell and nothing would stop me from doing so. Growing up if I was focused on something not much could break that focus, and now as an Alpha it was even harder, if not impossible, for someone to get through to me when I had become this focused on something. After wandering through the school for several minutes, I turned down a hall where I saw several guys beating up a much smaller boy. I could see that the boy on the ground was barely conscious and that he was bleeding badly. After a quick sniff, I realised that the smell I had been tracking was coming from the boy on the ground.

Mate. He's our mate, Shadow whimpered. I felt my heart break upon realising that the young, beat up boy laying on the ground was my mate. I had been searching for this little wolf for the last three years. I released a loud threatening growl upon knowing that these wolves in front of me had hurt my mate. My growl had unfortunately caused my little mate to whimper. My mate's soft whimper caused me to feel sad, especially knowing that I had caused it. One of the guys that had beaten up my mate, moved to stand in front of the group. By his aura he was most likely the son of an Alpha, not that I cared as I knew I could easily take him out if needed. 'What the hell is your problem asshole? This has nothing to do with you so why don't you just fuck off?' The guy said. Shadow growled at the guy's words, before we snarled out loud.

Who the fuck does this pup think he is, speaking to us like that? We should rip his fucking head off right now. See if the bastard is feeling cocky then, Shadow had been on edge ever since we first caught the scent, he became more on edge when we realised the injured young boy was our mate and now because of this boy's attitude, Shadow was seeing red. *We are an Alpha. How dare he speak to us like that?* Shadow added.

Calm down Shadow, we can't kill him. Not yet at least, we are on the neutral territory, I told my wolf. Shadow huffed but calmed down as I had told him to do. I decided that even though I wouldn't kill him, I would still hurt him. I quickly moved in front of the guy, quickly grabbed the front of his shirt and threw him as far as I possibly could. I released another growl towards him and his friends as the guy came crashing to the ground. Jaden and Kaito moved to stand quietly either side of me, ready to help if the assholes decided to try anything.

'If you ever come near this boy again, I assure you that I will make you feel so much pain that you will be begging me for death,' I threatened.

'You can't do anything to us,' the asshole responded, his voice wavering slightly.

'Oh yeah. Just keep going and see what I'll fucking do to you,' I threatened again, my voice steady. The asshole I had thrown scrambled to his feet and left with his friends, as quickly as they could. I knelt down beside the smaller boy and felt for a pulse. When I touched the boy, I felt sparks travel through my body.

That feels really good, Shadow said, with a light purr. Though I felt happy to have finally found our mate, I was sad to see him in such a terrible condition. I felt my anger rise and I had to stop myself from chasing after the assholes who had hurt my mate.

We have to get him to the pack hospital; he needs a doctor now, Shadow said and he was right, our mate needed a doctor and fast.

'Jaden help me pick the boy up. We have to get him to a doctor and fast,' I growled out.

'Yes Alpha,' Jaden responded before moving to do as I had ordered. As soon as the boy was securely in my arms, I turned and headed to the parking lot, Jaden and Kaito following behind me. At the car, Jaden helped me to put the boy into the middle seat.

'Jaden, you drive. Get to the pack hospital as quickly as you can,' I said as I hopped in beside my mate. Jaden didn't question my order, instead he got in the driver's seat, while Kaito hopped in the front passenger seat.

'Who is the boy, brother?' Kode asked from the back seat where he and Sakura were sitting. I was too focused on my mate's smell and also his heart beat, which was very slow, especially for a werewolf.

'Who is he?' Kode and Sakura asked at the same time. I growled; I didn't want to talk to anyone right now.

'The Alpha will tell us who the boy is when he is ready to. Until then we will leave our Alpha be,' Jaden said in his Beta voice. Kode and Sakura sat back in their seats after Jaden spoke. I could tell they wanted to ask more questions, but they wouldn't go against Jaden, especially since he had used his Beta voice. Jaden and Kaito did not know who the boy was or what he meant to me, but they didn't bother asking because as Jaden had said, I would tell them when I was ready. Thanks to the fact that Jaden was speeding, we managed to get back to our pack in just under fifteen minutes.

Kaiden, I need you to get to the pack hospital and fast, I said to my twin as soon as we crossed our pack's border. I didn't wait to hear my brother's response as I immediately mind linked our senior pack doctor. **Doctor Veracruz, I'm on the way to the pack hospital now with a seriously injured wolf. Have people waiting for us when we get there.**

Of course, Alpha. I will have people and a stretcher waiting for you, Doctor Veracruz responded. As we approached the hospital, I saw Doctor Veracruz waiting out the front of the hospital with several of our pack's medical staff. Once the car came to a stop, Doctor Veracruz opened the car door and leaned in to give the boy in my arms a quick exam.

'Oh, my Goddess. He is going to need surgery right away. Morgan, Luke, help get the boy out of the car. Azalea, get the stretcher ready,' Doctor Veracruz said as she got out of the car. Morgan and Luke, who were two of our pack nurses, carefully took my mate from the car, while Trainee Doctor Azalea moved the stretcher closer. Azalea happened to be my sister in-law; she was mated to my younger brother Kingsley. After my mate was placed on the stretcher, Doctor Veracruz and her team, made their way into the hospital. I made my way into the hospital behind them but was stopped when they entered the pack hospital's surgical ward. I wanted to follow but I knew that I couldn't do so. As I stood there staring at the doors of the surgical ward, I felt myself starting to become weak. My vision started to blur so I shook my head in an attempt to clear my thoughts. Unfortunately, it didn't work and I collapsed.

'Oh, my Goddess, Kyro. Come on, let's get you to a seat,' Jaden said in a concerned voice as he caught me before I hit the floor. Jaden then helped me to a seat before turning and telling my brothers and Sakura to return to the pack house.

CHAPTER 3: KAIDEN'S POV

MY BROTHER AND Jaden had left several minutes ago. While they were gone, I was setting up the video call for the meeting with Alpha Lucas Caldwell of the Amber Sky Pack. The meeting was supposed to have taken place in person but Alpha Caldwell's mate, Luna Sophie Caldwell, was due to give birth to their first child any day now, so the meeting was changed to a video call. As I went through the plan for the meeting in my head, I grabbed the laptop from its place in the cupboard and placed it on my brother's desk. I then set up all the screen and made sure the cables were all connected correctly. Once everything was ready for the video call, I moved to sit back down behind my desk. I stared at the paperwork sitting on my desk. There sure was a lot of it.

This paperwork is going to kill me one of these days, Storm. Seriously, one day they are going to find my dead body hunched over a stack of paperwork, I said to my wolf Storm. My wolf huffed at that, he hated paperwork even more than I did. He usually hung out in the back of my mind while I had to do paperwork. I grabbed the first file off the pile of paperwork in front of me. It was a request from one of our pack members, they were asking for permission to travel to another pack. I read through it and signed off on the request before grabbing another file. After a while I sat back in my chair and took a break from the paperwork, thinking back on times before I became Alpha. My twin brother and I had begun training to become Alphas of the pack from a young age. We were taught diplomacy, fighting, and the many other things we needed to know for the day we took over the pack. Our father was a great and well-respected Alpha and my brother and I hoped to be like him. We wanted to make him and our mother proud, so we had trained hard for our future roles. In the times we weren't learning to become Alphas, we had fun with our friends. We would go to the movies, go on runs, play pranks on each other and just did our best to relax and have fun while we could. Our best friends growing up were Jaden, the son of our father's Beta and now our Beta and Rowan, the son of our father's Gamma and now our Gamma. The two of them had been trained alongside my brother and I in order for us to be able to work together more easily when we took over our respective roles. Being best friends with each other was an added bonus, as some Alphas, Betas and Gammas didn't get along well and this created problems within a pack. Since taking over our pack three years ago, time to ourselves was a rare occurrence but a welcome one. Knowing I had a few moments to myself; I leaned back and closed my eyes for a second. I hadn't realised that I had fallen asleep in my chair until a knock on the door woke me up from my sleep. Shaking my head to wake myself up I called for the person at the door to enter. When the door opened, in strode Rowan with a big smile on his face. I was always wary of Rowan when he had a smile on his face like this. It usually indicated that he was up to something and it usually ended with us getting into some sort of mischief.

'Why hello Alpha Kaiden. What's up man, you seem tense?' he asked in a weird voice. Ok now I knew he was up to something.

'What are you up to Rowan? And don't try denying anything, I know you too well,' I said, looking straight at him. The expression on his face made me laugh.

Goddess, his expression is priceless, Storm chuckled out. Rowan was trying to look innocent and shocked at the same time.

'I'm shocked that you would think that I'm up to something. Can't I just be here to see my best bud? Can't I be here to make sure you are ok?' he replied with a pout. I raised an eyebrow at that and smirked at him. 'Ok, ok. I'm here to ask if you want to come to the new club in town. Tonight is the grand opening and it is said that it's going to be an epic event,' he added. I sighed. 'You know I don't like clubs Rowan,' I said to him.

'But if you don't come who will keep me company? I'll be lonely,' Rowan responded. I smiled at my friend; he had no trouble attracting company. Nothing ever happened as he had a wonderful mate that he loved and would never hurt like that.

'You never know, if you come with me, you might meet someone. Who knows, you might even meet your mate,' I looked down at my lap when Rowan mentioned meeting my mate. 'Aww man I'm sorry. I didn't mean to bring up a sore spot for you,' Rowan said as he came over to me and gave me a hug.

'It's ok, I know you mean well. Why don't we go to that club you mentioned, it might be good to unwind for a while,' I said kindly. When I looked up, I saw the biggest smile get plastered on Rowan's face and I knew I would be in for a very long night.

'Awesome. I already spoke to Tansy and let her know I was going to the club with you, Kyro, and Jaden,' he said happily as he sat down on the chair in front of my desk.

'I'm surprised that you didn't ask your mate to go with you to the club tonight,' I said to Rowan.

'I did ask Tansy to come but she said she was going over to the pack orphanage to read to the orphans tonight,' he replied and I smiled. We currently have nine orphans in our pack at the moment. Three of them were between eight and fifteen years old and were the children of pack members who had died. These three orphans had been taken in by family members after the death of their parents. The other six orphans were not born into the pack and were all under two years old. The pups had been found after we had tracked down several rogues who had attacked our pack a couple of months back. When we had found the pups, they were being held in cages. The sight of these horrid conditions angered myself and the other warrior wolves with me. We killed every rogue present, freed the captive pups and returned with them to our pack. Despite our best efforts we were unable to find the families of the pups, so Kyro and I took the pups into our pack as full members. They resided in a home near the pack hospital. It wasn't really an orphanage but that is what it came to be called when the pups moved in there with their caretaker. Their caretaker was an older she-wolf named Lauryn Gardner; her mate had been killed by the same rogues that had taken the pups. Lauryn's own children were all grown up and had families of their own. As Kyro and I didn't know the names of the pups, our mother Maevis and Lauryn decided on names for them. Lauryn also told us that the pups could all have her last name. My brother and I would go and visit Lauryn and the pups whenever we could to spend time with them and to make sure they had everything they needed.

I heard someone clear their throat and realised that while thinking about the orphans I had spaced out for a few minutes. I looked at Rowan and he smiled, knowing that I was thinking of the pups. 'Well, it's going to be several hours until the grand opening, so why don't we do something productive until then? It seems like you have a lot of paperwork that you might need help with,' Rowan said. I handed him a few files and he quickly looked them over.

'Well, this is definitely going to take a while,' he said as he settled into his seat. I smirked, knowing that it will definitely take us a couple of hours to complete. After working on the paperwork for a while I felt someone mind link me, so I let the link open.

Kaiden, I need you to get to the pack hospital and fast, Kyro sounded scared on the mind link and it didn't sit well with me, for my brother to be scared something bad had to have happened.

What's wrong Kyro? You sound scared. Is everything ok? I asked him over our private link. I got no response, instead I felt the link close, which only caused my fear to spike. Something bad has definitely happened for Kyro to close our link off like this.

What the hell happened? He only went to the school with Jaden to pick up Kaito, Kode, and Sakura. Storm asked scared.

'Rowan, we need to get to the pack hospital right now. Kyro just mind linked me, saying to meet him at the pack hospital,' I said as I got up and headed straight out the door.

'What on earth happened?' Rowan asked as he followed me out the door, concern in his voice. 'I don't know but Kyro sounded scared,' I replied. I felt Rowan hot on my heels as I raced through the pack house and out the front door. As we raced through the pack grounds towards the pack hospital, we passed by several pack members who looked at us strangely. Confused as to what could have caused one of their Alphas and their Gamma to act in a frantic manner.

When we got to the hospital, I followed my brother's scent to the waiting room near the surgical ward. When I entered the room, I saw my brother with his head in his hands and the front of his shirt was covered in blood.

What the hell happened to him? Storm asked with fear in his voice. Jaden stood just beside Kyro, a blank expression on his face. Neither my brother, nor Jaden, reacted when Rowan and I entered the room, which was surprising. After a quick look around, I realised that Kaito, Kode, and Sakura should have been here, but I didn't see them. Oh, my Goddess. What the hell has happened to them? I raced to my brother and knelt in front of him.

'Kyro what happened to you? Where are Kaito, Kode, and Sakura? Are they hurt? Are they here in the hospital?' Kyro didn't answer me, he didn't even react in any way. Instead, he remained in the same position he was in when I first came into the room.

'Jaden, what the hell happened?' I asked as I turned to look at my Beta.

'We should talk outside,' Jaden responded in a flat tone. I nodded and then Jaden, Rowan and myself left the waiting room.

'What the hell happened Jaden? You just went to the school to pick up Kaito, Kode, and Sakura. What happened to them?' I asked as soon as the waiting room door closed behind us.

'Sakura, Kode, and Kaito are fine. We sent them to their rooms at the pack house as soon as we got here,' Jaden responded and I looked at him quizzically.

'If nothing is wrong with them, then why is my brother covered in blood and in such a state?' I growled out. Jaden and Rowan bowed their heads slightly after I growled. Jaden bit his lip and I felt his nerves grow before he answered me.

'When we got to the school, we found Kode and Sakura almost immediately. Kaito wasn't with them, so after sending them to the car, Kyro and I went to find Kaito. We eventually found Kaito in the school library with his head in a book. Once we found him, we made our way back towards the car when all of a sudden Kyro started off in another direction. Kaito and I were both confused and we asked him what was going on but he didn't answer and instead kept on his path. We tried to get him to open up, but you know how hard that is to do. So, instead we just followed to make sure nothing went wrong. Eventually Kyro came to a stop and when we saw what had caused him to stop Kaito and I were both angered. We saw a group of boys beating up a smaller guy who lay bleeding and barely conscious on the ground. Kyro was angered by this and growled at them,' Jaden said before taking several deep breaths and then continuing. 'The head guy, who I realised was the son of an Alpha, stood in front of the group and told us to fuck off. As I'm sure you can understand, Kyro didn't take that very well. He threw the guy several metres and then growled at the group again, this time causing them to run away. Kyro asked me to help pick the smaller guy up and after doing so we headed back to the car. After the boy was safely secured in the car, we all hopped in and Kyro ordered me to drive here as fast as I could. Kyro mind linked you to tell you to get here and then mind linked Doctor Veracruz to let her know we were coming in with an injured wolf. When we got here, Doctor Veracruz checked the boy, had him placed on a stretcher and then taken straight into surgery. Kyro collapsed after the boy was taken into surgery but I caught him before he hit the ground and brought him to the waiting room. I then ordered Sakura, Kode and Kaito to return to the pack house,' Jaden took a few more deep breaths.

'I will talk to my brother in private now. I want you two to stand guard at the door and let no one inside until I say otherwise,' I told Jaden and Rowan. The two of them nodded and I walked back into the waiting room, while Jaden and Rowan stood guard outside as I had instructed them to do.

Chapter 4: Kyro's POV

IT'S BEEN SEVERAL minutes since Jaden helped me to a seat in the waiting room after I had collapsed. Most of my time since then was spent trying to rub my mate's blood off of my hands. During this time Jaden had stood quietly to my side knowing that what I needed right now was silence and time. While I waited, I prayed to the Moon Goddess that my mate would be ok, that Doctor Veracruz and her team would be able to save him. I couldn't lose my mate, not when I had only just found him.

We need him. Please, Goddess, let him be ok, Shadow pleaded in my head before curling up and whimpering. I could feel tears building up in the corner of my eyes, so I quickly wiped them.

'Did you want me to grab you anything Kyro?' Jaden asked as he kneeled down beside me. I could see a sad look in his eyes as Jaden looked at me gently. He could see that I was in pain but knew there was nothing he could do about it. Kaiden, Jaden, Rowan and I were best friends, none of us liked seeing each other in pain. 'I could go and get you something to clean yourself off if you wanted me to. Or I can go and get you something to eat and drink,' I simply shook my head at Jaden's offer. I didn't trust myself to speak without breaking down. Jaden went to say something else but stopped when the door to the waiting room opened up and my brother and Rowan walked into the room. I could hear Kaiden approach me and then kneel down right in front of me. I was vaguely aware of my brother talking to me but my brain was unfocused and I didn't register a thing he said. A few seconds later I heard the door open and close and then I was alone in the waiting room.

What are we going to do Shadow? How can we help our mate? I'm scared he won't like us Shadow, I asked my wolf; I couldn't stop the fear seeping into my voice as I talked with him.

I don't know what we are going to do. But the Moon Goddess gave him to us as our mate, so we will love him and treat him with the respect and kindness he deserves, Shadow replied. *You are right Shadow,* I said softly. Thanks to the short conversation with Shadow, I was able to focus my thoughts a bit better. We both need to focus on something other than thinking about our new mate potentially dying on the operating table. I lean back in my chair and put my head against the wall. I started to think about how I would bring up the mate bond with my new mate. I was worried about how he would react to our mate bond; from his injuries I doubted he was comfortable around powerful wolves. Seeing as I was an Alpha, I was worried that he would have trouble trusting me. I heard the door open again and looked up to see my brother walking into the room. He then walked over to the seats and sat down beside me. From what I could hear, Jaden and Rowan were waiting just outside the door.

'Kyro what's wrong? I can feel your pain,' I could sense the concern Kaiden had for me when he spoke. When I turned to look at him, I could see the concern in his eyes as well. Seeing his concern, I lost control and broke down. I was in so much pain after seeing my mate getting hurt by those assholes and then seeing the injuries that he had suffered because of them. Some people underestimated the impact that the mate bond can have on someone. People didn't understand that one can fall so quickly after meeting their mate. Kaiden pulled me to his chest and hugged me tightly while rubbing my back. 'Shh brother, everything will be ok,' he said soothingly. 'Please tell me what's wrong. Maybe I can help you,' he added. I shook my head and took several deep breaths in order to gather my thoughts. I then sat back up, looked at Kaiden and then took a few more deep breaths.

'I suppose when you went outside before, Jaden told you about everything that happened at the school,' I said to my brother.

'He told me about what had happened and that you seemed to be focused on something rather intently. He said you tracked something and you eventually found a young boy being beaten up. He said you were very angry about the boy's condition and after getting rid of the assholes hurting him, you brought the boy back here to be treated by Doctor Veracruz,' Kaiden replied and I nodded at his response.

'There was a reason for why I was so focused but I am afraid to say why,' I told him.

'What are you afraid to say Kyro?' Kaiden asked.

'I'm worried about what you will think,' I said honestly, before looking away from my brother. 'Nothing you say could ever make me think badly of you. You are my brother; I love you and I will never judge you,' Kaiden said before grabbing my hand and squeezing it.

Tell him Kyro. He is our brother; he can help us, Shadow said softly. I took several deep breaths and then turned back to face my brother. 'The reason I was drawn to the boy is because he is my mate,' A shocked look passed Kaiden's face when I said the boy was my mate.

'Your mate? You have found your mate,' Kaiden sounded happy when he spoke, but a moment later his face fell. 'Oh, my Goddess. You found your mate and he was badly hurt,' I nodded my head at his words.

'I don't know what to do. I'm worried that he won't accept me,' I told Kaiden.

'Why wouldn't he accept you? You are mates, you are destined to be together,' Kaiden asked confused.

'Because of what has been done to him. He has been hurt so badly by powerful wolves that I am worried that he won't accept an Alpha as a mate,' I admitted.

'It may be hard but with time and help from our family and friends, your mate will get better and will come to accept you,' Kaiden said with a soft smile and I returned the smile. 'Wait a moment, if he is your mate, he could be mine as well,' Kaiden added after a few minutes of silence. I was slightly confused by what he said, until I remembered something that I had read when I was younger.

'Twins, especially identical twins, have been known to be mated to the same person,' I said to Kaiden, who nodded his head.

'Exactly, but we won't know for sure until I meet him,' Kaiden responded, 'Can you tell me about him?'

'I don't know much but what I do know is that he is absolutely beautiful. He is Asian with black hair and medium brown eyes. I think he is around a metre sixty in height. His hands are so soft to touch,' I said softly as I recalled what my mate looked like, deliberately trying not to recall seeing him covered in blood. I turned to see Kaiden looking at me with a big smile. 'What?' I asked my brother, confused as to why he was looking at me like he was.

'He seems like he is absolutely perfect,' Kaiden responded.

'He sure is perfect,' I replied happily. I was starting to feel tired so I laid my head down on Kaiden's shoulder and closed my eyes. I felt Kaiden wrap an arm around me just as I drifted off to sleep. Sometime later I was woken up by a knock on the door, so I sat up straight and stretched to wake myself up.

'Come in,' Kaiden called out. A moment later Jaden poked his head into the room.

'Sorry for the interruption Alphas but Doctor Veracruz is outside and asking to speak with the both of you,' Jaden replied.

'Let her in Jaden,' Kaiden said after a quick glance at me. Jaden nodded and then opened the door fully, allowing Doctor Veracruz to walk in, followed closely by Jaden and Rowan. Doctor Veracruz was dressed in hospital scrubs, over which she wore a white doctor's coat.

'How is the boy I brought in Doctor?' I asked as Kaiden and I stood up and approached Doctor Veracruz, Jaden, and Rowan.

'I'm sorry to say Alphas but the boy is in bad shape. He has so many injuries and both internal and external. He has bones which have been broken numerous times and almost all of them have healed incorrectly. He also has numerous bruises across his body. Our main concern at the moment is all the internal bleeding that he had. During surgery we dealt with it as best we could but it will still be some time before he heels fully,' When Doctor Veracruz told us, what was wrong with my mate I growled, causing her, Jaden and Rowan to back up and bare their necks in submission.

Easy Kyro, I don't like hearing what she said either but we need to remain calm, Kaiden linked me while sending calming energy through our brotherly bond. I did my best to do as Kaiden had said but it was hard to calm down.

'My apologies Doctor Veracruz, Jaden, Rowan,' I said with a slight bow towards them.

'No need to apologise Alpha. I too was angry when I saw the condition the young boy was in,' Doctor Veracruz said as the three of them nodded at me.

'Where is the young boy now Doctor?' Kaiden asked the Doctor.

'He is in a recovery room near in the surgical ward for the moment. He is currently asleep right now but would you like me to take you to see him now?' Doctor Veracruz asked.

'Yes, please,' I said before turning to face Jaden and Rowan, 'The two of you may return to the pack house now,' I told Jaden and Rowan. After leaving the waiting room, Kaiden and I followed Doctor Veracruz towards the surgical ward, while Jaden and Rowan left the pack hospital. As we walked through the hospital Kaiden and I talked over our private mind link. **Everything will be ok Kyro. We will do everything we can for the boy,** Kaiden said calmly. **Thank you for being understanding Kaiden,** I replied.

Of course, Kyro. I would never judge you. When the boy wakes up the three of us will talk. The Moon Goddess gave him to you and possibly me as well, for a reason. I believe everything will work itself out in time, Kaiden always made me feel accepted no matter what was happening. We stopped the mind link just as we arrived outside a room where I could sense my mate was located.

'Well, here we are, the young boy is just through these doors. I ask that you don't try and wake him up as he will do so in his own time,' Doctor Veracruz stated.

'Thank you Doctor,' Kaiden said and after a quick nod to the both of us, Doctor Veracruz left Kaiden and I alone outside the room that held my new mate.

CHAPTER 5: KAIDEN'S POV

KYRO AND I waited outside the room that Doctor Veracruz had indicated the young boy was in. I was very nervous about going into the room as I wasn't sure what would happen once we walked through the door.

Listen Kaiden, it doesn't matter if the boy is our mate or not. He is mated to Kyro and as such we will support our brother and his mate in whatever way we can, Storm said with a quick huff. Despite his words I knew he was also worried about what would happen.

'Are you ready to go in?' I heard Kyro ask from beside me.

'I am, I'm just a little nervous,' I said as I ran a hand through my hair.

'I know how you feel. I am worried about what will happen if we are both mated to the boy. I know it's not unheard of for twins to be mated to the same person, but I don't want it to affect our bond,' Kyro replied. I saw Kyro chew his bottom lip and rub his hands together, his nerves getting to him a bit.

'Let's go on in,' I said, putting a comforting hand on his shoulder. Kyro nodded and opened the door before moving aside to allow me to enter first. As soon as I walked into the room I was hit by the most amazing scent of cinnamon and hot chocolate. I quickly sniffed and soon realised that the scent was coming from the boy laying on the bed. I released a soft, possessive growl as I said, 'Mine,' I heard a soft gasp and turned to see Kyro looking at me with wide eyes.

'He is your mate too,' Kyro said, a little shocked. We looked at each other and stood silent for several minutes.

'How about we sit with our mate? Us just being near him might help him heal and it might help us feel better being near him as well,' I said to Kyro. After he nodded, the two of us made our way towards the bed that our mate lay sleeping on and we sat down on chairs on either side of the bed. For a couple of hours Kyro and I sat with our mate, neither of us saying anything, we were simply enjoying being together. Eventually we heard a light knock on the door and when I called for the person to enter, the door opened and in walked Doctor Veracruz.

'Hello Alphas. I'm here to examine the young boy,' she said, so my brother and I moved out of the way so she could do her exam.

I can't wait until we know his actual name. I don't like calling him young boy or the boy, I told Kyro.

Me either Kaiden. When he wakes up, we can ask him what his name is. I turned my head slightly and gave Kyro a smile, before turning back to watch Doctor Veracruz examine our mate.

'How is he Doctor?' I asked when I saw that she was finished her exam.

'His healing factor is extremely low so it is going to take some time before he is ok,' She replied.

'Why is his healing factor low?' I asked Doctor Veracruz.

'He is severely malnourished and underweight,' Replied Doctor Veracruz, 'I have given him some medication that will hopefully help boost his healing factor,'

'We can only hope it helps him,' I said, I didn't like that he was malnourished and underweight but I was happy that Doctor Veracruz had given him something that would help him heal. 'Thank you and your team Doctor,' Kyro added with a small smile.

'No need to thank me Alphas. I am a Doctor and I will always try to help those who need it,' Doctor Veracruz said as she smiled at us. 'He is going to be unconscious for a few more hours. Why don't you return to the pack house? I'm sure there are things that you need to do. I will have someone stay with him at all times and will let you know if something happens,' she added on. I heard Kyro growl in his head; neither of us liked the idea of leaving our new mate for any reason.

Doc said that he won't be awake for a while so we can go to the pack house and then come back here before he wakes up. Shadow said to me, Kyro, and Storm through our mind link.

I don't want to leave him any more than you do. However, we should prob-

ably go and have a shower and also get something to eat. We have been here for some time and neither of us has eaten anything since breakfast this morning.

Kyro didn't respond via the mind link, instead he responded aloud.

'Ok Doctor. But if anything happens, no matter how big or how small, I want you to contact us immediately,'

'I will Alpha,' Doctor Veracruz said.

After we left the hospital, Kyro and I headed straight to our rooms on the top floor of the pack house. Once at our rooms, we separated and went to our rooms to shower and change. As I was finishing getting dressed there was a knock on my door.

'Are you decent son? I don't want to see any more than I have to,' I heard my mother call out from the other side of the door.

'I'm dressed mother,' I replied with a chuckle, 'But I don't know what you are worried about, it's not like you haven't seen me without clothes before, after all we are werewolves,'

'I know as werewolves being naked around each other is an occupational hazard. But seeing as we are inside a house means that clothes are expected young man,' My mother replied as she opened the door and walked into the room.

'That's true mother. What brings you here?' I ask her.

'We are having dinner together with your father, brothers, Azalea, Jaden, Daniel, Susan, Sakura, Rowan and Tansy,' She replied. Azalea was mated to my younger brother Kingsley; she was a Trainee Doctor at our pack. Daniel was the Beta for my father and Susan was the Beta's Mate, they were the parents of Jaden and Sakura. Tansy was mated to Rowan and as such was the current Gamma's Mate.

'I knocked on your brother's door but he didn't respond, so I guess he is still in his shower. So, I want you to tell him when he is dressed to be in the Alpha dining room in half an hour,' My mother responded.

'He sure does take long showers,' I replied and my mother laughed.

'That he does,' My mother replied.

'I'll make sure to let Kyro know about dinner when he is out of the shower,' I told her. My mother nodded, gave me a kiss on the forehead and then left my room.

After she left, I made my way to Kyro's room and opened his door. As I walked inside and saw Kyro finishing getting dressed.

'Hey brother,' he said turning around to face me.

I relayed mum's message to Kyro. He nodded and gave his hair a quick dry with his towel. When he was finished, Kyro and I headed straight to the Alpha dining room. The pack house had several dining rooms, such as the Alpha dining room which was located on the Alpha floor. There was also the Beta and Gamma dining rooms which were located on the Beta and Gamma floor which was a level down from the Alpha floor. There were also several other dining rooms on the ground floor of the pack house, these were where the other members of the pack would have their meals. No one was allowed on the Alpha, Beta or Gamma floors of the pack house without permission, unless they were the Alpha, Beta, Gamma or their mates, children or other specific family members. When we got to the Alpha dining room, we were greeted by everyone that our mother had said would be joining us for dinner.

'Hello everyone,' I said as Kyro and I took our seats at the table, Kyro sat on my right next to Jaden, while my mother sat to my left. As we ate dinner, which consisted of roast chicken and roast vegetables, we all talked about what had been going on with each other. No one mentioned the young boy which had been brought to the hospital and for that Kyro and I were thankful. After dinner we said goodbye to Jaden, Daniel, Susan, Sakura, Rowan and Tansy.

'Can we talk with you two in private please?' my mother asked after the others had left.

'Of course,' Kyro answered.

'You three boys clean the dining table and do the dishes while we talk with your brothers,' My mother told my three younger brothers,

'Azalea you just sit and relax,' she said to Azalea who nodded in response. After leaving our brothers to clean up and Azalea to relax, Kyro and I followed our parents to our private office. Once inside the office, I closed the door and then the four of us sat down on the couches to the side of the room. There was a tense atmosphere in the room as Kyro and I waited quietly for our parents to tell us why they wished to speak with us. 'How have you boys been lately?' Our mother asked, breaking the silence.

'We have been fine mother. Busy with Alpha work but otherwise fine,' I replied for the both of us. Our parents exchanged a quick look and then turned back to us.

'What is going on at the pack hospital? We heard that someone was brought in and that Doctor Veracruz had to operate on them,' Our father said, looking at us with a hint of concern in his eyes. Kyro and I both froze at our father's question.

Neither of us were sure how to bring up the fact that firstly the boy was mated to the both of us and secondly that we were gay. Kyro and I had known for a long time that we were both gay, but we had never discussed it with anyone else. We were worried how others would look at us and what they would think about us. I heard someone clear their throat and looked up to see my parents looking at Kyro and I expectantly.

'Kyro and Jaden had gone to pick up Kaito, Kode and Sakura from school but they ran into some trouble and found a wolf that was badly hurt,' I started explaining, 'They brought him to our pack hospital where Doctor Veracruz and the medical staff have been taking care of him,' A thoughtful look crossed both of our parents faces when I finished speaking.

'He is mated to the both of you, isn't he?' my mother asked softly.

'He is mother. As soon as his scent hit our noses, we knew he was,' I replied. My mother smiled before saying,

'I'm so glad the two of you have finally found your mate. Hopefully now you will both be able to express yourselves more in public,' Kyro and I nodded before we realised what our mother had said. We looked at her with shocked expressions, we didn't realise she already knew. Our parents burst out laughing when they saw the looks on our faces.

'Don't look so shocked boys. We knew about the both of you being gay for a long time,' Our father said to us once he and our mother stopped laughing.

'Why didn't you say anything? Are you ashamed of us being gay?' I asked both of them as Kyro and I stood up. I could tell we were both feeling scared and a part of us was telling us to run.

I don't want them to be ashamed of us. I want mum and dad to love us, Storm said before whimpering. I heard a soft whimper come through the mind link from Kyro and realised that it had been Shadow who had whimpered after hearing Storm's words. Kyro and I were worried about how our parents would react and we had to resist the urge we had to run from the room. I grabbed my brother's hand, sometimes were just needed contact with each other to calm us down. Our parents got up and brought Kyro and I into a warm hug.

'Of course, we are not ashamed of you two. You are our sons and we love you both very much. We always have and always will. We just want you to be happy and now that you have found your mate, you two can be even happier,' Kyro and I burst into tears after hearing our mother's loving words.

'Your mother is right. No matter what happens your mother and I will never stop loving you two. You two have a long road ahead of you in regards to your mate and we will be here every step of the way to help you both and your mate,' Our father added kindly. Once we had calmed down, Kyro and I felt happier than we have in a long time because our parents finally knew about us being gay and they fully accepted it.

'Why don't you two go and get some rest? You both look exhausted,' Our mother said to us. Kyro and I simply nodded before the four of us left the office. While our parents went to go and check on our brothers, Kyro and I went straight to our rooms. After getting changed, I climbed into bed and fell asleep almost instantly.

CHAPTER 6: LEVI'S POV

BEEP, BEEP, BEEP, beep. What the hell is that sound? I groaned as I tried and failed to open my eyes. I struggled again and again to try and open my eyes, wanting to find the source of the annoying and incessant beeping sound. After trying for several minutes, I finally pried open my eyes. I noticed that I was in a sterile, white room and that I was on the softest bed I'd ever laid on. I decided to take a look around the room. My eyes eventually settled on some kind of monitoring type of machine, the source of the incessant beeping sound.

Where the hell are we Alpin? I asked my wolf, confused

I think we are in a hospital, I was a little shocked when I heard Alpin's response to my question.

How the hell did we get here? The last thing that I can remember is Jake and his goons beating us up. Someone must have brought us to the hospital. I sniffed, something didn't seem right to me and then it suddenly hit me. ***Oh, my Goddess. We are in a pack hospital. There are lots of wolves nearby. We need to get out of here before we are chucked in their prison. We should also get home as soon as possible otherwise we will be in so much trouble.*** I was scared we were technically trespassing on another pack's territory which could mean an automatic death sentence.

I agree, but first we need to unhook all these tubes and cords that are attached to us. What the hell are they doing in us any way?

After finally struggling and eventually succeeding to do as Alpin said, I carefully slipped out the door to my room. After taking a quick look around I took off down one of the hallways I saw. I snuck as quietly as I could through the hallways of the pack hospital, stopping and hiding when I saw someone approaching, and once the people passed, I continued on my way. I did not know which pack's hospital I was in and I wanted to get out of here before I found out; some packs didn't react well to trespassers. I was almost near what I thought was the exit to the pack hospital; I could smell fresh air just outside the double doors. Before I could exit the hospital, I smelt the most delicious scents. One was a combination of forest and fire and the other was a combination of apple and fresh rain.

We have to find these scents now. Come on, we must find them. The scents were driving Alpin crazy and I felt him take control from me. He followed the scents and we soon ended up in a relatively empty hallway, where I saw two identical gentlemen talking to a lady that I assumed was a doctor due to her wearing a white doctor's lab coat. *We should listen to what they are saying,* Alpin suggested and so using our wolf hearing, we tried our best to hear what the three people were talking about.

'How is the young boy doing Doctor?' One of the gentlemen asked the lady.

'He is improving slowly but he still has a long way to go before I would say he is ok,' The doctor replied.

'When do you expect him to wake up?' The other gentleman asked.

'I expect him to wake up sometime soon. Most likely within the next half an hour,' The doctor stated. The three people continued to discuss this boy.

They're talking about us Alpin. We need to go before they find out we are already awake. Alpin refused to budge causing me to growl slightly in my head.

Mates, they are our mates, Levi, I heard Alpin yip in my head.

What? They are our mates? Which ones? I asked Alpin, confused as I was always told I would never have a mate.

The two gentlemen are our mates, Alpin replied with a slight purr. I took a step backwards. *No, no, no that can't happen. If they knew what has been done to us, they wouldn't want us as their mates. They would see us as nothing more than used goods. We have to get out of here before they notice we are awake. I don't want them rejecting us for something that was out of our control.* Alpin started whimpering and I used his momentary distraction to regain control. I then returned to what I had thought was the exit to the pack hospital and made my way outside. Once outside I was surprised by what I saw, a wide-open space surrounded by trees.

It's so beautiful, Alpin said in awe. He was right, this area was definitely beautiful. No matter how beautiful the area was, I still had to get out of here before I was caught. I took off into the nearby forest and ran as fast as I could, which wasn't that fast given the condition I was in. The forest I ran through was full of colour and life. I noticed several foxes and other wild wolves nearby and did my best to stay clear of them.

Oh no. Someone is following us. We need to get out of here quickly, I told Alpin after sensing several wolves chasing me.

Let me have control Levi. I can shift and get us away from here. I relinquished control to Alpin; he then shifted and used everything we had left to get us away from the wolves and out of the unfamiliar pack's territory. Just before we crossed the border of the territory, we heard a couple of very loud howls. I could sense the power behind the growls and it scared me. I could also sense the pain within the growls and I couldn't help the whimper that escaped from me.

Oh Goddess no. I don't like that sound at all, I cried out to Alpin. Alpin did his best to ignore the howls. He didn't like the sound of the howls either as it made him sad to hear the pain in them. Despite this feeling we had after hearing the howls, we continued running until we finally made our way to school. Once we looked around to make sure nobody was around, we shifted into our human form and grabbed clothes we had hidden near the school in case of emergencies. We then made our way into the school and headed to my locker and grabbed my books for the first couple of lessons, as school had started for the day. As I made my way to my first class, I was thankful that most people didn't notice me on normal days, so they didn't notice that I was late. Throughout the day I thankfully managed to successfully avoid Jake and his group of friends. I knew however that this would not last when I eventually got back to the pack house. I knew that once I got back to the pack house that I was in for one hell of a beating. When my last class for the day ended, I slowly made my way to my locker, returned my books and grabbed what I would need for homework that night. I then slowly made my way back to the pack house. I dreaded the moment when I would finally arrive there.

As soon as I walked through the doors to the pack house I was grabbed by the back of the neck by a pair of strong hands and dragged down the stairs to my room in the basement. Once we were halfway down the stairs, I was roughly thrown the rest of the way to the bottom, landing hard on my stomach. I heard multiple heavy footsteps following me down the steps and I scrambled to get away from them.

'Where the hell have you been you stupid fucking cunt?' Alpha Redmond growled as he picked me up from the ground and punched me hard in the stomach, 'And why the hell do you smell like another fucking pack? You betray us to another pack? You tell them what we have been doing? Answer me you stupid, filthy prick,' He punched me several more times and kicked me in the stomach.

'I-I-I didn't say an-any-th-thing to th-them. I-I didn't kn-know where I-I was. I j-just woke u-up th-there,' I whimpered as he kicked me again.

'Lies. All of it fucking lies,' Alpha Redmond said before his eyes glazed over. 'Boys have fun with this lying piece of crap. I have some things I must go deal with,' Alpha Redmond then turned and walked up the stairs and closed the door to the basement when he was through the door. Now I was alone with eight of our pack's strongest and most fierce warriors. The looks on the warrior's faces made me whimper in fear and I tried to make myself appear as small as possible.

I'm so sorry Alpin. You don't deserve this, I said just as one of the warriors grabbed both my arms and another warrior grabbed both of my legs. The two of them held me down while the rest of the warriors kicked and punched me.

'I think we should have some other type of fun with him now. What do you guys think?' One of the warriors growled after about an hour of beating me. The rest of the warriors all growled their agreement and then started to strip me until I was left naked and whimpering in front of them.

'P-please don't d-do this. P-please l-l-leave me alone,' I cried out, 'Please don't t-t-touch me,'

'Aww hear that, boys? The little omega is begging us,' a warrior said while laughing.

'Mmmm I love it when he begs. It gets me all riled up,' another warrior said grabbing my face in one of his rough hands.

'Well since he's begging we should have our fun,' a different warrior added. This caused all the warriors to growl and then flip me onto my stomach. I tried to pull away but it was no use and I felt one of them force their way inside of me. I whimpered at the pain of the warrior inside me and started to cry. My crying only caused them to laugh and keep going. The warriors each took turns forcing themselves into me. At one stage, one of the warriors pulled my head up, while another forced my mouth open. One of the other warriors them put himself in my mouth and forced me to suck him. I hated this so much but I was too weak to fight them. They then started beating me again as they again took turns forcing themselves inside of me. Once they were all satisfied, they left me bloody and bruised on the basement floor, laughing about the fun they had as they made their way upstairs. I got dressed as best I could and decided to go to sleep. As I started to fall asleep, I heard the door open and someone come down the stairs. I whimpered as the person got to the bottom of the stairs, I couldn't take any more abuse right now.

'Get up you piece of shit. Did you forget you need to make dinner for the pack?' I shakily stood up and made my way past Joshua, another one of our pack's warriors. He pushed me causing me to fall and he laughed. 'Get up moron. Alpha expects dinner to be ready in an hour,' he said heading up the stairs. I made my way up the stairs as best I could and went to the kitchen. I made dinner for the pack which consisted of various different meats, vegetables, pasta and rice. I brought all the food into the dining room and then went and grabbed the drinks. After I was finished, I returned to my room, I didn't want to be around when the pack members came into the dining room.

What are we going to do Alpin? I don't think I can take this much longer, I said as I sat on my bed, whimpering because of the pain I was in.

I don't know Levi. I really don't, Alpin replied, then suddenly added, *maybe we could go to our mates. Maybe they could help us.*

We can't go back there. They won't want us when they learn what happened to us, I said causing Alpin to whimper.

Maybe they will want us, despite what has happened to us. Alpin tried to sound hopeful but I knew that he didn't truly believe what he said. I laid down and cried myself to sleep that night, dreaming of a time when this pain would finally be over.

CHAPTER 7: KYRO'S POV

WHEN I WOKE up the next morning, I felt happier than I had in a long time. After getting out of bed, I went to the bathroom to relieve myself and then had a quick shower. When I was finished in the shower, I wrapped a towel around myself and then walked out of the bathroom and into my walk-in wardrobe, and got dressed. Once dressed, I went to the kitchen where I grabbed out the ingredients for choc chip pancakes. I cooked up two large plates worth of pancakes and then started making two cups of coffee. By the time I had finished plating up the pancakes and had poured the coffee, Kaiden came into the kitchen.

'I made some choc chip pancakes and coffee for breakfast,' I told him. 'Did you want anything else to eat or drink?'

'No just the choc chip pancakes and coffee will be fine. I want to get to the pack hospital as soon as possible,' he replied.

'Same here. Well, let's eat then,' I said with a chuckle. The two of us quickly ate our breakfast. Once we were finished, we rushed downstairs and out the front door of the pack house. Once we were outside, we headed straight to the pack hospital. Kaiden and I have waited so many years to find our mate and now that we finally had, we wanted to be near him as much as possible.

As soon as we had stepped through the front doors of the pack hospital, we found Doctor Veracruz waiting for us.

'Alphas, I assume that the two of you are here about the boy that was brought in yesterday,' she said while smiling softly at the both of us.

'Your assumption is correct Doctor,' Kaiden replied with a smile.

'Well then if you would follow me, I will take you to the boy's room,' Doctor Veracruz said, before turning to escort us to the boy's room.

How do you think our mate is doing Kaiden? I couldn't keep the worry out of my voice when I spoke to Kaiden via our private mind link.

I'm not sure but I hope that he is ok. I could hear that Kaiden was as worried as I was, we both just wanted him to be okay. As we were making our way down the hallway Doctor Veracruz was stopped by one of the pack medics who asked to speak with her.

'Excuse me for a moment Alphas,' she said as she stepped away to speak with the pack medic. 'Is everything ok Doctor?' I asked her when she turned to face us.

'I just received the results of the blood tests that I had ordered on the boy this morning,' she replied, concern written all over her face.

'Is he ok?' Kaiden asked.

'He is improving slowly but he still has a long way to go before I would say he is ok,' Doctor Veracruz replied.

'When do you expect him to wake up?' I asked her.

'Soon. Most likely within the next half an hour,' Doctor Veracruz replied.

'What's wrong then doctor? You seem worried about something,' I asked. Despite giving us what seemed to be good news, I could still sense that something about the blood test results was still worrying her.

'The boy's blood test results show that he still has traces of wolfsbane and silver in his system. I'm hoping that it will be completely gone from his system by tomorrow,' She replied. Silver and wolfsbane were poisonous to us wolves, in high enough dosages it could kill us.

Goddess, I hope that the doctor is right. I don't like that he has silver and wolfsbane in him. I'm going to kill anyone who had a hand in hurting him, Shadow said with a growl.

Easy Shadow. For now, we focus on our mate. We will deal with those that hurt our mate in time, I told Shadow in a calming voice.

I hope our mate will be ok, Shadow said with a whine.

I hope he will be ok too Shadow. I don't know what Kaiden, Storm, you or I would do if we lost him now, I admitted to him.

'I will take you to the room where the young boy is now,' Doctor Veracruz then turned and escorted us to the young boy's room. 'I will go inside first and give him a quick exam. He will probably still be asleep, but once I've done my exam, I will call the two of you inside,' Doctor Veracruz stated once we got to the room.

I don't want to let her go in there with our mate alone, Kaiden said, I could smell the tang of fear on him.

I don't want her to either but she would never hurt him, I told Kaiden.

'Can't we come in with you Doctor?' I asked Doctor Veracruz with slight confusion.

'Normally I would say yes but I would like to examine under his bandages and I usually don't do that when non-medical personnel are in the room,' she responded before adding, 'I don't mean any disrespect Alphas. I just want to respect the boy's right to privacy,'

'Of course, you are right Doctor,' I replied. So, despite our feelings, we let Doctor Veracruz go into the room alone. It wasn't even a second later that we heard the doctor yell from the room, Kaiden and I rushed inside. I felt my heart break. Our mate was not in the room, he was gone. I heard Kaiden whimper at the sight, knowing he too was in pain. I let out a howl and a few seconds later Kaiden followed suit.

I want everyone on the lookout for the wolf that was brought in yesterday. When you find him, let Alpha Kaiden and I know immediately. Escort the young wolf back to the pack hospital straight away. No one is to hurt the boy.

Several 'yes alphas' sounded over the mind link and then Kaiden and I left the hospital to search for our missing mate. We tried to find our mate's scent and when we did, we followed it.

Alphas, I think I found the boy you are referring to; the patrol group are tracking him. He is almost at the border of the pack territory. One of our patrol wolves linked us as we started to follow the trail.

Do you want us to continue following him? The wolf asked

Yes, keep following him, I replied. Kaiden and I then sniffed out the patrol wolves' scents and headed straight for them since they were already on our mate's trail.

Alphas, he has crossed the border, what do you want us to do? Another patrol wolf asked moments later.

He is no longer in our territory and we can't follow him onto neutral territory, I said to Kaiden on a private link. There were many laws regarding what could and could not be done when on the neutral territory. These laws were put in place to protect not only werewolves but other supernatural creatures from exposing our existence to humans. Kaiden and I wanted to find our mate but at the same time we couldn't risk the exposure of our kind.

We can send a couple of warriors to follow his scent, Kaiden suggested and I agreed.

Rajesh, Lincoln, follow the boy's trail. See if you can find where he is going and report back to us, I told a couple of patrol wolves. The wolves we addressed nodded and then took off to follow the scent trail. After calling for two new patrol wolves to take over the spots left by Rajesh and Lincoln; Kaiden and I returned to the pack house. Once at our office, we sat down behind our desks and let out a sigh.

'Why would he leave?' I asked as I leaned back and closed my eyes.

'Maybe he was scared. I mean look at the condition he was in when you brought him here,' Kaiden replied. 'He must be being abused by his pack, so waking up in a strange pack's hospital would have probably caused him to think the worst,' I sighed, knowing that Kaiden was most likely right.

'I can't just sit here and do nothing,' I said as I stood up, knocking my chair back. I released a growl as I paced back and forth behind my desk.

'Why don't we get some paperwork done while we wait,' Kaiden suggested. I nodded and after grabbing my chair, I sat down and grabbed a file off my desk. After working on paperwork for an hour we got a phone call from an unknown number.

'Hello this is Kyro. To whom am I speaking?' I said when I answered the phone.

'Alpha Kyro this is Rajesh, I borrowed a phone to call you,' the person on the other end of the phone said. 'Lincoln and I have tracked the young boy to the school that your younger brothers attend. From what we can tell he has gone inside the school grounds. Unfortunately, because of all the scents of the students and staff mixing together, we are having trouble locating exactly where in the school he is,' Warrior Rajesh stated.

'Thank you for the update, Rajesh. You and Lincoln can return to the pack grounds now,' I told him.

'Are you sure Alpha? We could go into the school and locate him,' Rajesh replied.

'No. The school is in the neutral territory, if we went after him there it could start a war, especially since he is not a member of our pack,' Kaiden replied as he moved to sit beside me. 'Of course, Alpha. Heading back now,' Rajesh replied before hanging up the phone.

'Since we don't know what pack he comes from but we do know that he goes to that school, why don't we have a couple of our members who are students there, look for him tomorrow? It wouldn't be breaking any laws and if anyone asked, we could say that we were just checking up on him,' Kaiden suggested. He had a point. We had asked Kaito, Kode, and Sakura last night if they knew which pack the boy was from but they admitted they didn't really know him that well, so they couldn't say which pack he was from.

'Who should we send in? We should definitely send those with warrior training and probably a trainee medic,' I said to Kaiden. He got a thoughtful expression on his face.

'I think Cedric Yi and Marcus Grey, they are two of the best fighters in their age group. So, if it comes to it, they will be able to protect our mate,' Kaiden replied several minutes later.

'True, we should also send Payton Hollister; like Cedric and Marcus, he is a good fighter,' I stated.

'Mmhmm. Which trainee medic should we send? We don't have many trainee medics that are high school aged,' Kaiden asked.

'Tristan Pentecost has been training with Doctor Veracruz for the last few months. Our mate is still hurt and Tristan can give medical aid, at least until we get our mate back to the pack,' I suggested.

'That's a good idea. Let's call them here and let them know about what we want them to do,' Kaiden responded, 'If you want to let them know to come here in about half an hour, I'll see if I can get a picture from the security system to show them, that way they know who to be on the lookout for,' I nodded and while Kaiden went to check the security system for a photo of our mate, I contacted the four pack members we had chosen to look for our mate at the school. **Cedric Yi, Marcus Grey, Payton Hollister and Tristan Pentecost, report to the Alpha's office on the top floor of the pack house in half an hour,** I commanded over the mind link. After the four pack members acknowledged the order, I sat back and closed my eyes for a moment.

'Here is a photo of our mate,' Kaiden said as he handed me a photo of our mate laying on a hospital bed. He must have pulled it from the security cameras. I smiled at the photo of my mate. Our mate may not be in the best condition but he was still beautiful.

Half an hour later, Kaiden and I sat behind my desk, waiting for the four pack members to show up. Soon there was a knock on the door and at my invitation the four pack members walked into the office.

CHAPTER 8: KAIDEN'S POV

I COULDN'T BELIEVE that our mate was gone. We had only just found him and now he was missing. When we learned that he was missing from the hospital, it felt like my heart was going to break into a million pieces. But when Rajesh called and said that he and Lincoln had tracked the boy to the same school Kyro had first found him at, I felt a spark of hope. Hope that we would find our mate at the school tomorrow. So, while Kyro contacted Cedric, Marcus, Payton and Tristan, I moved back over to my desk. Once I was sitting behind my desk, I opened up my laptop and logged in. I went into the security files, putting in the username and password when asked, and found the best photo of my mate that I could. It was one of him lying unconscious on the bed in the hospital. Once I printed off six copies of the photo, I made my way over to sit beside Kyro behind his desk.

'Here is a photo of our mate,' I said to Kyro as I sat down beside him. I watched as a smile crossed my brother's face as he looked at the photo that I had handed to him. The two of us sat back in our chairs and waited for the four wolves we had selected to search for our mate at the school, to arrive at our office. Half an hour later there was a knock on the door and after Kyro called for them to enter, the four wolves we had selected walked into our office. 'Please sit down,' I told the wolves, directing them to the chairs in front of Kyro's desk. There was silence for a moment while Kyro and I gathered our thoughts before Kyro broke the silence.

'We have asked you all to be here because there is something important that we need your help with,' Cedric, Marcus, Tristan, and Payton all sat up straighter when Kyro said we needed their help.

'Whatever you need Alphas, we are here for you,' Cedric said, while the others nodded in agreement.

'As you may have heard, the boy that Alpha Kyro brought into the pack hospital yesterday has disappeared from the pack hospital,' I said.

'We did hear about that Alpha,' Cedric said, while the other guys again nodded in agreement. 'Tomorrow we would like the four of you to be on the lookout for him at school. We don't know what pack he is from but we know he goes to the same school,' I told them.

'What do you want us to do when we find him Alphas?' Tristan asked.

'We want you to notify us as soon as you find him. We also want you three to protect him when you do,' I said pointing to Cedric, Marcus, and Payton.

'What about me Alphas? What would you like me to do?' Tristan asked.

'The boy was in a bad condition when he was here and Doctor Veracruz was worried about him when he disappeared. So, I would like you to care for him until we can get him back here to the pack hospital. When you leave here, I want you to go to Doctor Veracruz, so she can give you a better idea of what is wrong with him. That way you will have a better idea how to help him when you find him,' Kyro said to Tristan, the other three guys listening intently as well.

'Once you find him, don't let him out of your sight for any reason. Do not let him leave the school and do not let anyone take him. He is to remain with at least one of you at all times,' The four guys nodded as I finished. After handing them each a photo of the boy, they left the room to go speak with Doctor Veracruz. Speaking of which, I needed to warn her that they were on their way to her. **Doctor Veracruz can you hear me?**

Yes Alpha, Doctor Veracruz replied immediately.

Cedric Yi, Marcus Grey, Payton Hollister and Tristan Pentecost are on their way to you now. Alpha Kyro and I have asked them to look out for the boy who left the hospital, at the school tomorrow. We have sent them to you so that you can give them an overview of his condition so that way they can care for him until we get him back here. I told her.

Of course, Alpha. I will get some stuff together for Tristan, in case the boy needs treatment before he gets back here, she said politely.

Thank you Doctor. I cut off the mind link and looked over to Kyro.

'I hope that they find him at the school tomorrow. I want him back here with us where we can keep him safe,' I said to Kyro. He moved from where he was sitting behind his desk and walked over to me.

'Let's go to the couch,' Kyro said to me. I stood up and then the two of us moved over to the couch at the side of our office. 'We know he goes to the school. So, tomorrow when Cedric, Payton, Marcus, and Tristan search for him there, they will find him. When they do find him, we will bring him home and once we have him here, we will show him a good life and make sure that he is happy,' he said to me calmly.

'We will definitely make sure that he is safe and happy,' I replied. I was starting to get tired so I laid my head on my brother's shoulder and closed my eyes. I heard Kyro start to sing quietly and I soon drifted off to sleep.

Sometime later we were woken up by a camera flash and a soft giggle. I was pretty sure that it was my mother who was in the office as she and my father were the only ones who would enter the Alpha office without invitation.

'Hello mother,' I said sleepily as Kyro and I sat up, rubbing the sleep from our eyes. 'Get a nice photo of us?' I asked in an amused tone.

'Of course. I got a photo of my two oldest boys cuddled up together on the couch. I can't wait to show it to your mate one day, along with all the other photos I got of you two,' She replied with a smirk.

'Oh Goddess. That is going to be one hell of an embarrassing day,' Kyro said while shaking his head.

'I assume you didn't come in here to simply take a photo of us. So, what brings you here dear mother?' I asked.

'I came to get you boys for dinner. The food is all cooked, the drinks are ready, the dining room is set and almost all the pack members are gathered. We tried to link you boys to find out where you were but you didn't respond, so I came to get you in person,' Our mother replied

'Let's go eat,' Kyro said happily before getting up and quickly heading out the office door. Mum and I watched him go, wondering how long it would take him to realise we weren't following him. It didn't take him long as he came back a minute later. 'What's wrong? You guys coming or not?' he asked as he poked his head inside the door. Our mother and I just chuckled at him and then the three of us headed to the dining room on the ground floor of the pack house. When we got to the dining room almost the entire pack was present and waiting for our arrival. Those members who were not present were either on duty or eating at their own homes. Eating at the pack house wasn't mandatory unless specifically ordered. Once Kyro and our mother had taken their seats, I addressed the pack.

'It is good to see everyone gathered here tonight. I would like to thank the chefs and cooks that made this lovely meal. Everyone, tuck in,' As soon as I finished speaking, I sat down and everyone started eating. I talked quietly to my family and friends, while we ate, enjoying the food and conversation. After dinner, several pack members remained behind to clear the tables, others returned to their homes or rooms, while the rest stayed at the pack house to talk. Kyro and I excused ourselves, saying that there was something that we had to do. We returned to our office on the top floor and sat down behind Kyro's desk.

'I'll send a quick text to Alpha Caldwell. See if he's up to having the meeting we were supposed to have yesterday, now instead,' I said to Kyro.

'Ok. I'll set up the computer and screen, so that we can be ready to go if he says yes,' Kyro replied. I took out my phone and dialled Alpha Caldwell's number.

'Alpha Kaiden. What can I do for you tonight?' Alpha Caldwell asked when he answered the phone, his tone respectful.

'Alpha Lucas, my brother and I were wanting to know if you would be up to having the meeting that we were supposed to have yesterday, now,' I replied.

'Sure, it's no problem. Just give me twenty minutes to set stuff up here and get my Beta and Gamma to join me,' Alpha Lucas replied.

'Of course. See you in twenty,' I replied. Once he had hung up, I made my way back over to my seat beside Kyro.

'He said it was alright to have the meeting now. Just asked us to give him twenty minutes to set up everything and for his Beta and Gamma to join him,' I told Kyro as I sat down.

'Cool, we should call Jaden and Rowan up as well,' Kyro responded.

Jaden, Rowan, we need the two of you in our office right away. We are having the meeting with Alpha Lucas Caldwell and his Beta and Gamma in twenty minutes, I said to Jaden and Rowan over mind link. Jaden and Rowan confirmed they heard me and a couple of minutes later they walked into the office.

'Hey guys, grab a seat,' Kyro said to our friends. Jaden and Rowan did as they were instructed; Jaden sat to the right of Kyro and Rowan sat to my left. Once we were settled, Kyro clicked the link that would connect us to Alpha Caldwell and we then waited for Alpha Lucas to respond. It took a couple of minutes for Alpha Caldwell, his Beta and his Gamma to appear on the screen in front of us.

'Alpha Kyro, Alpha Kaiden, it's a pleasure to see you again. I'm sorry it couldn't happen in person,' Alpha Caldwell said.

'No need to apologise Alpha Caldwell. Though we have not been through the experience personally, we understand the desire to be near your mate as she gets closer to giving birth,' Kyro responded. 'Speaking of which, how is Luna Sophie doing?' he added a moment later. 'She's doing well thank you. Our pack doctor said she will give birth anytime in the next few days,' Alpha Caldwell replied.

'That's good to hear. We hope everything goes well and that mum and pup are safe,' I said happily. The birth of a new pup was a happy occasion and this pup would be the first for Alpha Caldwell and his mate and as such the pup, whether it was a boy or girl, was the future Alpha of the Amber Sky Pack.

'Thank you. You remember my brothers Beta Samson and Gamma Theo?' Alpha Caldwell asked as he pointed to the two men sitting either side of him.

'Of course. It's a pleasure to see the two of you again. You remember Beta Jaden and Gamma Rowan,' Kyro responded pointing to Jaden and Rowan in turn.

'Of course. It's a pleasure to see the two of you,' Alpha Caldwell replied.

'My brother and I would like to apologise for not calling you yesterday as we had arranged. Something came up that took our attention,' I said.

'All good. We completely understand that sometimes other things come up that take priority,' Beta Samson responded.

'Ok, now for the reason for this meeting,' Kyro started. 'The treaty between our two packs is up for revision. It was last signed by the former Alphas of both our packs ten years ago,' Everyone nodded at my words. 'That is correct. I am happy to sign the treaty between our packs,' Alpha Caldwell said.

'So are we. Are there any changes that you wish to make to the treaty?' Kyro asked.

'Only one. When our father signed the treaty with your father ten years ago, he dropped the business relationship between the companies our families run,' Alpha Caldwell stated. I nodded thoughtfully, my father ran a major construction company, while Alpha Caldwell's father had run a timber company. Our two packs had previously had a long running business relationship before it was ended by Alpha Caldwell's dad for reasons our father had not revealed to us.

I think we should open the business relationship again. It was good for both of our companies, Kyro said to me.

I agree. However, the business is under dad's control so we should ask him first, I responded. 'Alpha Caldwell my brother and I are both for reinstating the business relationship between our two companies but we have to ask our dad first as the company is under his control,' I said to Alpha Caldwell.

'Of course. If you let me know when you find out and we can get to signing the deal,' Alpha Caldwell responded.

'Give me a moment, I will mind link our father and ask him,' I said and Alpha Caldwell nodded. **Dad can you hear me?** I called out to my father.

Of course, son. What's up? Our father replied.

Kyro, Jaden, Rowan, and I are just talking with Alpha Caldwell of the Amber Sky Pack about the treaty between our packs. Alpha Caldwell is happy to sign the treaty but has one change he would like to make, I said to my father.

What is it son? The pack is in your and your brother's control now, any decision regarding it is up to the two of you, my father replied.

Alpha Caldwell would like to reinstate the business relationship between our two companies. Seeing as the company is under your control, we thought we should ask you, I told him.

Of course, I am all for it. Let him know I am happy to talk to him any time to discuss it further, our father replied.

Will do. Talk later dad, I replied before ending the link.

'Alpha Caldwell, our father said he is all for the business relationship. He also said he is happy to talk to you any time to discuss it further,' I informed Alpha Caldwell.

'Sounds good. Well then, I will sign the treaty here and then send it to you. I will also send your father a message regarding the business relationship later on,' Alpha Caldwell responded. 'We will sign it on our end and send it back to you,' Kyro replied. After that, the meeting ended, we said goodbye and ended the video call. After ending the call, Jaden and Rowan said goodbye and left the office to do some paperwork of their own. 'Why don't we go back to our suite? Just relax for a bit, it has been a long day,' Kyro suggested.

'Sounds like a good idea,' I replied. The two of us got up, left out office and returned to our suite. When we got there, we decided to watch a movie before having something to eat and going to bed. The next morning, after a quick shower and something to eat, Kyro and I made our way to our office for a meeting with Cedric, Marcus, Tristan and Payton. Once we made sure they remembered what they had to do, the four of them left the office and headed off to school.

CHAPTER 9: LEVI'S POV

WHEN I WOKE up the morning after I had returned to my pack, I felt absolutely horrible. I was in so much pain from the beating and the rape, I could barely move.

I am disgusting. How could anyone ever love me? I thought while trying my best not to cry.

You aren't disgusting Levi. You are a wonderful person. The people who have hurt you are the ones that are disgusting, Alpin said, making me realise that I had said my previous statements over our private mind link.

I don't know Alpin. Look at me, I am covered in bruises and scars and I am absolutely fat. There is no way anyone could ever love someone who looks like me, I responded.

That's not true Levi. We are wonderful and we will find love with our mates. I groaned when Alpin mentioned our mates. Mates were created by the Moon Goddess and were designed specifically for us and were meant to love us no matter what. Unfortunately, I'd been told many times that my mate would never love me and that they would reject me as soon as they found me.

We should go get breakfast done before someone comes down here to get us, Alpin said tiredly. I agreed as I didn't think I could take another beating right now. So, despite the pain I was in, I got up from my bed and went upstairs to make breakfast for the pack like usual. After I had finished making breakfast and putting it on the tables, I grabbed a bowl of water and rushed back to my room in the basement.

I grabbed the cleanest rag I could find and using the water I had grabbed from the kitchen, I quickly washed myself off as best I could. After getting dressed I grabbed my school bag and headed off to school. I was hoping that today would not be as horrible as the last couple of days had been. When I arrived at school, I went straight to my locker and grabbed the stuff for my first couple of lessons. I then did my usual routine of going to an empty classroom to wait for the school day to start. When the first bell rang, I went to my first class and headed to my seat at the back of the room. As I waited for the teacher to arrive, I drew little doodles in my book. After a few seconds, I could feel someone staring at me. When I looked up, I saw Jake looking at me with daggers in his eyes. I whimpered slightly and looked down, fearing what would happen to me when class was finished. When class started, I tried and failed to focus, which resulted in me getting in trouble several times for not paying attention. Whenever I got in trouble, Jake and his friends would laugh at me. When class finished, I left the room as quickly as possible and made my way to my next class. I managed to avoid running into Jake and his group of friends, as I made my way to class for which I was grateful. Unfortunately, Jake and his friends had the same class as me again, so I was distracted throughout the lesson. My mind would wander to thoughts of what Jake and his friends would do to me once they got me alone.

'Mr Chang, can you tell me the answer?' I heard the teacher ask me, which broke me out of my thoughts.

'I-I'm sorry. I-I d-don't know w-what the question w-was,' I said, causing the entire class to laugh.

'Well, if you paid attention, you would know I asked you what element has an atomic number of 98 on the periodic table?' The teacher asked with a sneer, causing the class to laugh again. 'I-I don't kn-know sir,' I replied looking down at my desk. The teacher scoffed at that and looked at the rest of the class.

'Can anyone tell Mr Chang here what element has the atomic number of 98 on the periodic table?' Several students put their hands up at that.

'Mr Sutherland, can you please tell Mr Chang the answer,' The teacher said while pointing to Jake.

'The answer is Californium sir,' Jake replied before adding, 'Californium has the atomic number of 98 on the periodic table,'

'That is correct Mr Sutherland,' The teacher said looking at Jake, he then turned to face me shaking his head in disappointment before resuming the lesson. Jake looked at me with a smirk on his face, obviously enjoying that I was getting in trouble. After that I did my best to pay attention for the rest of class. Thankfully the teacher didn't call on me to answer again. When the end of class bell rang, I left the classroom and headed straight to my locker. As I put my things from my first two lessons into my locker, I felt tears start forming in my eyes.

I feel so stupid Alpin. I couldn't give the teacher an answer when he asked for one and Jake could, I said as tears fell down my face.

You aren't stupid Levi. It's not your fault that you didn't know the answer and Jake did. Jake has time to study and learn his school work. You don't have the time with everything the pack expects you to do for them. If it isn't pack work taking up your time, it's the abuse they put you through, Alpin replied, trying his best to comfort me.

Let's go find somewhere to sit while we wait for our next class, I said and we went to find an empty classroom where we could avoid Jake and his friends. Unfortunately, this didn't work as I felt myself get grabbed from behind. I was dragged into a nearby empty classroom and thrown roughly to the floor. When I turned around, I saw Jake, Howard, Mick and three of the friends from our pack. I heard a click and realised that Howard had just locked the door to the classroom. I tried to move backwards to get away from them but my back hit a table, stopping me. The six of them then moved forward, Howard grabbed me and threw me so I was now on the ground in the middle of the group. The six of them all growled at me, causing me to whimper in fear, something which made them laugh.

'So, mutt, seems like someone needs to pay for what happened the other day,' Jake growled at me, causing me to shrink back from him. Unfortunately, Howard stopped me as he stood right behind me.

'I-I'm s-s-sorry. I d-didn't know an-anyone was going t-to do anything,' I whispered. Jake harrumphed and kicked me in the stomach.

'I don't care if you didn't know. Because of you an Alpha from another pack threatened and attacked me,' He growled again and then signalled the others to start beating me. They all started kicking, hitting, and punching me wherever they could. This went on for fifteen minutes. I know that people say that trauma can sometimes alter a person's perception of time but for me it's different. I've never counted time as I was being hurt but for some reason, I've almost always been able to know exactly how much time has passed. This doesn't just apply to when I'm being hurt but it also happens at other times. For example, when I'm cooking, I always seem to know how long something has been in the oven for.

'Man, that was so much fun. Don't ya think guys?' said Mick.

'Hell yeah, it was,' Howard replied.

'You know, I think this fucking faggot needs to be taught a different lesson today. One that will make sure he remembers who his betters are,' Jake said with a sneer.

'Definitely. After all we are in school and we are at school to learn things,' Howard added. Their laugh scared me a lot and I was worried about what they were going to do next.

Oh, Goddess. Alpin what are they going to do to me? I said, worry in my voice.

I don't know Levi. I really don't know. I'm sorry that I can't stop them from hurting us, Alpin said, pain filling his voice.

It's not your fault Alpin, I said just as Jake and his friends started ripping my clothes off, before flipping me onto my stomach.

'Me first,' Jake growled out before I felt him force his way inside of me. I whimpered at the pain and they laughed at me. 'You like that you faggot?' Jake asked as he raped me. My only response to his question was a whimper. The others then took a turn at raping me, again asking if I liked what they were doing to me.

'P-please s-stop. I d-don't want this. P-please,' I cried out.

'Mmm we like it when you beg faggot,' Jake stated. The group then continued to take turns raping me, while I just cried at the pain and humiliation. When Jake went to take another go at me, I heard the door burst open and four people made their way into the room.

'What the fucking hell do you sons of a bitches think you are doing?' One of the newcomers growled out angrily. The newcomer didn't wait for a response and instead they rushed at Jake, grabbed him and punched him very hard in the face. The punch caused Jake to stumble backwards and before Jake and his friends could react two of the other newcomers joined their friend in attacking Jake and his friends. While his friends dealt with Jake and his friends, the fourth newcomer knelt down beside me.

Who are they? Why would they attack Jake and the others? I asked Alpin.

I don't know but I'm glad they are here, Alpin replied groggily. He had pulled back into my mind before the rape had started. Alpin does his best to ease my pain when I'm being physically assaulted but when I'm being raped, Alpin can't take the pain and retreats into my mind. The guy who knelt down beside me, took his jacket off and used it to cover my naked body as best he could. I then saw him give my body a quick look over. When I felt him touch me, I whimpered in pain and tried to move away from him.

'Easy there little one, please don't move. I don't want you to hurt yourself any further,' The unfamiliar guy said to me, looking at me in the eyes. Normally wolves liked to maintain eye contact when talking to each other, but I couldn't keep looking at him after what had just been done to me. So, despite the soft look on his face, I quickly looked away.

'My name is Tristan Pentecost. I am a student at this school and also a trainee doctor. I promise that I don't want to hurt you; I just want to see what injuries those assholes caused you,' The guy said in a gentle voice. I was glad he didn't try to force me to look at him.

Let him help us Levi. We don't have the strength to fight him off. Also, I sense that he is telling the truth, Alpin said, I could tell that he truly trusted Tristan. After I settled down, Tristan examined my body for injuries. Tristan did his best to keep my body covered by his coat while he examined me and for that I was thankful. All of a sudden there was a crash which drew my attention to my right, Tristan however didn't react to the sound. When I looked for the source of the crash, I saw that Jake was lying unconscious in a pile of glass. The glass cabinet behind him was smashed in, Jake must have been thrown into it. A few moments later, the rest of Jakes group were also lying unconscious on the ground.

'Marcus, Payton, stand guard around Tristan and the boy. Be ready in case any of these sons of bitches wake up,' One of the guys growled out and several minutes later the three other newcomers were standing guard around me and Tristan.

'How is the boy doing Tristan?' I heard one of the guys ask.

'Not good Cedric,' Tristan replied, he said something else but I was unable to make out exactly what he said as I started to drift off. As I slipped unconscious, I felt someone carefully wrap something around me. A moment later I felt myself being lifted up and carried out of the room. We weren't even out of the room before my vision faded to black.

CHAPTER 10: CEDRIC'S POV

'GOOD MORNING SON. Have a seat, I'm almost finished making breakfast,' Mum said without turning from what she was doing. Some people have asked why we didn't help mum with the cooking. We tell them that mum doesn't like anyone in her kitchen. Especially after an incident when I was ten. My dad, brothers and I were in the kitchen trying to make mum a special breakfast for her birthday. It did not end well. There was flour, chocolate, egg, butter and other stuff everywhere and we were all covered in it as well. As we laughed, we didn't realise that mum had walked in and seen us. To say she was mad would be an understatement. After she made us clean the kitchen top to bottom, she said that if any one of us went in the kitchen again and made anywhere close to the same mess, she would kick our butts. 'Here you go everyone,' My mum said as she placed five plates of food on the dining table, breaking me out of my thoughts.

'Thanks, my dear,' My father said while patting mum on the bottom, causing her to squeal. 'Eww dad. Trying to eat breakfast here,' My younger brother Corvin said with a groan.

'Yeah dad. I don't want to waste mum's cooking when I throw it up,' My other brother Carson said.

'Hey, she's my mate. I can do what I want,' My dad said smirking.

'Yeah, as long as mum says you can,' I said with a chuckle causing dad to glare at me. When mum saw him glaring, she flicked him on the ear and he mumbled an apology. My brothers and I all laughed at them and then we all tucked into the delicious breakfast in front of us.

'I have to go; I'll see you guys when I get home from school,' I said after I had finished eating. I stood up from the table and took my dishes to the kitchen and placed them in the sink.

'It's a bit early son. You still have over an hour until school starts,' My mum said in a questioning tone.

'I have to meet with the Alphas this morning,' I replied.

'Ok, are you still able to take your brothers to school?' Dad asked. No one asked why I had to speak with the Alphas. They knew that if I could, I would have told them about why I was speaking with the Alphas.

'I can still take them. I'll drive us over to the pack house and they can wait around until the meeting is over. After it finishes, I'll drive us to school,' I replied and my parents nodded at my response.

'Ok boys, go and get your stuff for school,' My mum said to me and my brothers. After grabbing our stuff and saying goodbye to our parents, my brothers and I went to the garage and got into my car. I drove us all to the pack house. My family didn't live in the pack house as my parents wanted to raise us in a home of their own. As I pulled up to the pack house, I saw Marcus, Tristan, and Payton getting out of Tristan's car.

'Hey guys,' I called out to them as my brothers and I got out of my car.

'Hey Cedric. How you this morning?' Payton responded as we approached.

'I'm good,' I replied.

'We'll wait here for you while you have your meeting,' My brother Carson said as he and Corvin walked off. Payton, Tristan, Marcus and I went into the pack house and up to the Alphas office. Once at the office, Marcus knocked on the door and a few minutes later Alpha Kyro called for us to enter. When we walked into the office, we saw the Alphas sitting on the couch to the side of the room.

'Alpha Kyro, Alpha Kaiden,' Payton, Tristan, Marcus and I all said as the office door closed behind us.

'Take a seat, gentlemen,' Alpha Kaiden told us. We all sat down on the available couches and waited for the Alphas to speak.

'Thank you for coming. You four all remember what we want for you to do today?' Alpha Kaiden asked.

'We do Alpha,' Marcus replied as the rest of us nodded, 'We are to look for the boy that got away from the pack hospital yesterday. Once we find him, we are to notify both of you immediately. Until you get to the school, we are not to let him out of our sight and we are to protect him if needed,'

'That's correct. I trust Doctor Veracruz informed you about the boy's condition,' Alpha Kyro said. 'She did Alpha,' I answered.

'Good. Now you all have the photo we gave to you yesterday, so when you find the boy let us know,' Alpha Kyro stated. Alpha Kaiden then dismissed us and after leaving the office, we headed downstairs. When we got outside, I saw Carson and Corvin wrestling with each other. 'Come on you two, we need to head to school now,' I said to my brothers as I pulled them apart.

'See you guys when we get to school,' Marcus said. My brothers and I then got into my car while Payton, Tristan, and Marcus got into Tristan's car. Tristan's car drove behind mine as we drove through the pack lands and then to school. As soon as we got to school, Carson and Corvin went off to find their friends, while Payton, Marcus, Tristan and I went and sat in our usual spot at the base of an oak tree near one of the outdoor courtyards. When we sat down, I leaned back against the oak tree and recalled the meeting with Doctor Veracruz yesterday.

I felt someone shaking me and as I opened my eyes, I realised that I had fallen asleep.

'Come on sunshine the first bell just rang,' Marcus said while chuckling. We all got up, headed into school and after grabbing our things from our lockers we went to our classes. Tristan and I had maths together, while Marcus and Payton went to science together. During the first two lessons of the day, I kept an eye out for the boy but unfortunately, I had no luck in finding him. During the first break, I headed to the cafeteria to catch up with the others and see if they had any luck. 'Did you guys have any luck?' I asked as we grabbed our food and then headed to our spot outside. They all shook their heads, I figured as much anyway, as no one had used their mind link during our day.

'No, we didn't have any luck and I'm guessing you didn't either,' Marcus replied.

'Ok, well we will keep looking and hopefully we will find him,' I said as we ate our lunch. All of a sudden, I started feeling off, it felt as if something bad was about to happen.

'I'll be right back,' I said standing up.

'You ok?' Payton asked.

'I'm fine. I just feel a bit anxious, so I'm going to go for a walk,' I replied. Once I got rid of my rubbish and put my tray back, I decided to go for a walk around the school.

Cedric, I think the boy over there is the one the Alphas told us to look out for, My wolf Cooper said to me. I looked to where he was referring and saw a young boy similar to the one in the photo the Alphas had given me. He was standing near the lockers in the building opposite the one I was currently in. I observed him for a few seconds to make sure I got the right wolf, as I did, I observed several other wolves approach the boy and start dragging him away. I took a quick look around and saw Payton, Marcus, and Tristan walking around the room.

Guys, head to the lockers at the side entrance to the art building. I think I saw the boy we were looking for being attacked. They others all confirmed they had heard me, as I raced to where I had last seen the boy. 'Some guys dragged the boy this way,' I said to the others before leading them in the direction I saw the boy being dragged, ignoring the bell for the next class when it went off. We soon heard whimpers coming from a nearby classroom and after realising the door was locked, Marcus and I broke it open. The others and I were all angry by what we saw when we got into the classroom. There were five guys holding a naked boy down; the boy was beaten and bleeding quite badly. 'What the fucking hell do you sons of bitches think you are doing?' I asked while growling. Without waiting for a response, I launched myself at a sixth guy who was about to rape the naked boy. I grabbed the asshole by the throat and punched him in the face hard, causing him to stumble backwards. Payton and Marcus then joined me in taking care of the other assholes while Tristan helped the injured boy. After throwing the lead asshole into a cabinet, he fell unconscious to the ground and moments later the rest of his friends were also unconscious.

'Marcus, Payton, stand guard around Tristan and the boy. Be ready in case any of these assholes wake up,' I growled, before Marcus, Payton and I moved to surround Tristan and the boy. 'How is the boy doing Tristan?' I asked while keeping an eye of the unconscious assholes.

'Not good Cedric,' Tristan replied, 'He is barely conscious; we need to get him to the nurse's office and contact the Alphas immediately,' Tristan added, concern filling his voice. I looked around the room for something that I could cover the boy with as his own clothes were destroyed. I then grabbed a sheet that was laying on a bench and gently wrapped it around the boy. I then picked the boy up and carried him out of the room, Marcus, Payton and Tristan following behind me. When I noticed the boy falling unconscious, I quickened my pace. I was thankful that class had already started as it meant that the hallways were empty as we made our way to the nurse's office. For the boy's sake, I didn't want anyone seeing him in this condition. Upon entering the nurse's office, I heard a gasp and saw our school nurse come rushing over to us.

'Oh, my Goddess, Levi. What happened to you? Get him on the table over there now,' the nurse said pointing to one of the beds in the room.

'Payton, Marcus, Tristan, stand guard outside. Let no one but our Alphas inside,' I told the guys, who then left to do as I said. While the school nurse checked Levi for injuries I moved to the side of the room and called our Alphas.

'What is it Cedric? Have you found the boy yet?' Alpha Kyro asked when he answered the phone.

'Yes, Alpha we found him,' I replied before going on to explain the situation, 'The boy has been attacked again. I am currently in the nurse's office with him. Marcus, Tristan and Payton are standing guard outside,' I heard two loud growls when I finished speaking and I almost cowered from them. An Alpha could project their Alpha voice through a phone just as easily as they could in person.

'We are on the way. Do not let him out of your sight,' Alpha Kyro ordered before hanging up the phone.

'I need you to go and wait outside with your friends,' The school nurse said.

'I'm sorry but I can't do that. I am under orders from my Alphas to keep the boy in my sights at all times,' I replied in a serious tone to show her I was not going to budge.

'In that case I will not ask you to go against your Alphas, but I do ask that you at least give me room to work,' The school nurse asked. As I watched the school nurse work, I couldn't help but wince every time the boy whimpered. I had to close my eyes and focus on my breathing to stop myself from going after the assholes who had hurt the boy. A loud growl brought me out of my mind a moment before someone mind linked me.

Cedric, I can smell the guys who attacked the boy coming closer. What do you want us to do? Marcus asked me.

Do whatever you have to do in order to keep them out of this room. Our Alphas are on their way now. Hopefully they will be here before those assholes try anything, I replied. Marcus cut off the link but I knew he would do as I said and I knew that the other two would do so as well. Sometime later I heard yelling from unfamiliar voices, followed by Marcus replying by telling the newcomers to leave before he ripped them apart. I smirked at what Marcus had said and had to guess that the newcomers were the same assholes who had hurt the boy. Several moments later, I heard two loud, angry growls and knew immediately that they came from my Alphas. Goddess, I hoped those assholes were smart enough to realise they should leave, otherwise they would most likely be dead by the time the alphas were done with them.

CHAPTER 11: KYRO'S POV

I WAS CURRENTLY at one of our pack's training fields with several pack warriors. We were conducting the day's training session, with today's focus being on fighting in our wolf form. I was currently fighting against Rodger, one of our pack's best warriors. He stalked around me while I stood still and silently watching him. Unlike some wolves who rushed their moves during a fight, Rodger was a patient wolf, who liked to think first and then attack. All wolves in our pack were trained in this way, to think first and then act. When Rodger thought he saw an opening he launched himself at me, unfortunately despite being a good fighter, he wasn't a match for me and I easily dodged his attack and then turned and pinned him down by placing both my front paws on his shoulder and putting my mouth around his throat.

Nice try Rodger, I said with a wolfish smirk. He let out a soft bark that sounded like a laugh and I let him up.

Good job boss, Rodger said in a joking tone.

Round two mate, I said while shaking my head at him. He nodded his head and we started circling each other once again. This time I didn't wait for Rodger to attack, I launched myself at him and he rolled out of the way. We launched ourselves at each other again, snapping our jaws at each other. Rodger got me a couple of times before I managed to pin him down again. **Got you.** I said with a laugh.

Let's go, I'm getting hungry, Rodger said. I was hungry to, so I motioned with my head towards where our clothes were sitting. We both headed over to our clothes and shifted into our human forms. Neither of us were bothered by each other's naked form, as ending up naked in front of someone was a daily hazard for werewolves. As we got dressed Kaiden made his way over to us, he was training against Rodger's older brother Rick, who was walking beside Kaiden. Once we were all dressed, we went and stood in front of the other warriors who had been training in the same field.

'Nice going everyone. Keep up the good work,' Kaiden said addressing the warriors. 'Hope you all have a great day,'

'Yes Alpha,' The warriors said together. Rick, Rodger, Kaiden, and I made our way back to the pack house, while everyone else went off to do their own thing.

'I am starving. Let's go see what they have in the kitchen,' Rodger said as we entered the pack house. We headed to the ground floor kitchen to raid the fridges. While Kaiden and I looked for something to drink, Rodger and Rick looked for something to eat.

'We have pizza,' Rodger called out happily. Turning around I saw Rodger holding a couple of pizza boxes above his head while he did a happy dance. I looked at Kaiden and then Rick before all three of us burst out laughing at Rodger's antics. Rodger pouted and sat down on a stool at the kitchen island bench, this only caused the rest of us to laugh even more. While Kaiden and I grabbed some glasses and juice, Rick sat down beside his brother. After we poured drinks for everyone, Kaiden and I sat down with the brothers. 'Mmm nothing is better than pizza. Even if it's cold pizza,' Rodger said while smiling and taking another bite of the pizza he had found. 'Let me be the judge of that,' Rick said as he shoved his brother and took the slice of pizza from him as he fell to the floor.

'Hey,' Rodger exclaimed as he got up off the floor, looking at Kaiden and I as if asking for help. Kaiden and I just shook our heads and smirked at him.

'Hmmm, your right brother this is good pizza,' Rick said with a smirk. Rodger harrumphed and gave his brother a dirty look, while muttering curses under his breath. Everyone just laughed at him and continued eating the pizza. 'What should we do now guys?' Rick asked after we had finished eating the pizza.

'Wanna go play some video games?' Rodger replied, 'If you guys don't have paperwork you need to do?'

'Unfortunately, we do have paperwork that we must get done,' I replied with a sigh.

'Anything we can help with?' Rick asked.

'We just got to read through some reports from other packs,' Kaiden replied,

'We also have to go over pack member details to make sure they're up to date,' Jaden and Rowen would normally have helped look over the pack member details but they are currently out on patrol. 'We can go over the pack member details for you while you read the reports if you'd like,' Rick suggested.

'That sounds good. Let's head up to the office,' I said and we all stood up and headed to our office on the top floor. Once inside I headed over to one of the filing cabinets at the side of the room, grabbed some files and then handed them over to Rick and Rodger.

'Here are some of the pack member files. If you can check the details and make sure they are current and up to date,' I told them. Rick and Rodger headed over to the coffee table and sat down, quickly getting to work on the paperwork.

'Let's get these reports over and done with. Hopefully, we will get through them quickly,' I said to Kaiden as we sat down behind our desks.

'I'm getting hungry again. Does anyone want anything to eat?' Rodger said an hour later.

'I could do with a bite to eat,' Rick replied. His stomach grumbled causing us all to laugh. It was as if his stomach was trying to prove his words.

'I'm not hungry right now,' Kaiden and I said at the same time.

'Ok. We will go get something to eat and we will be back,' Rick said as he and his brother stood up and left the room. Sometime later my phone rang out, so I put down the report I was reading and picked it up.

'What is it, Cedric? Have you found the boy yet?' I asked.

'Yes, Alpha we found him,' Cedric responded before adding, 'The boy has been attacked again. I am currently in the nurse's office with him. Marcus, Tristan and Payton are standing guard outside,' Hearing what had happened, Kaiden and I growled out loudly, accidently releasing our Alpha voice at the same time.

'We are on the way. Do not let him out of your sight,' I ordered before hanging up and slamming the phone down on the desk. 'We need to get to the school right now,' I growled as I stood up. Kaiden and I raced out of the office and down the stairs. Rick and Rodger were coming up the stairs but when they saw us, they stopped. When we passed them, they turned and followed us, not bothering to ask what was going on, instead following Kaiden and I silently to the garage. When we got to my car I hopped into the driver's seat, Kaiden hopped in the front beside me and Rick and Rodger hopped in the back. I didn't bother waiting for the others to put on their seat belts before I hit the gas and sped out the garage and through the pack lands.

I hope he is ok. I am going to kill whoever hurt my mate. Shadow was seething with anger. I could feel him trying to take control, which would not be good, especially since I'm driving. ***Easy there, Shadow. We will get to our mate and we will take care of him.***

He is right brother. Storm did his best to calm Shadow down, though I could feel that he too was just as angry.

They're right Shadow, we will get him back and we will take care of him, Kaiden told him softly.

'Is it alright if I ask what is going on?' Rodger asked hesitantly.

Kaiden, can you answer? I don't trust myself to speak right now, I said with a quick glance at my brother.

'While they were at school today, we had Cedric, Marcus, Payton, and Tristan look for the young boy that Kyro brought into the hospital the other day. Cedric called and said that the boy had been attacked again and was currently in the nurse's office,' Kaiden said with a slight growl. Rick and Rodger growled.

'Did Cedric say who attacked him?' Rick growled out; his eyes flashed quickly meaning his wolf was angry. Rick and Rodger had almost lost a cousin of theirs to bullies, so they have a very strong dislike for bullies.

'No, he didn't,' I replied slowly. Before we could say anything further, we had arrived at the school. I was driving very fast and managed to get to the school in just under fifteen minutes. We all got out of the car and using our enhanced senses we tracked our way to where Cedric and the others were. When we got in sight of Marcus, Payton and Tristan, we saw they were guarding a set of doors that we assumed was the nurse's office. I noticed several boys approach the nurse's office that Marcus, Payton, and Cedric were guarding, but before I could do anything Marcus growled at the assholes.

'If you do not leave now, I will rip you mother fuckers apart,' Marcus said, causing me to smile slightly. The assholes showed no intention of leaving so Kaiden and I growled loudly at them, making sure to add our Alpha voices to our growls. The assholes stopped short and turned to look at Kaiden, Rick, Rodger and I. When they turned to face us, I realised that they were the same assholes who had attacked my mate the first day I had seen him. Realising this caused me to become even more enraged than I already was.

'I guess that you didn't take my words seriously the other day,' I said as I stalked towards them. I could see each of the assholes shiver in response to the threatening tone. It only took them a few seconds to make the smart decision to leave the area.

I was about to hunt them down and kill them but I was stopped by a hand on my shoulder.

Kyro, I want to chase them down and kill them just as much as you do but we can't. Our priority right now is to see our mate. We can deal with those assholes at a later time, Kaiden said softly through our private mind link.

You're right brother, I said as I turned to look at Kaiden. We turned to face Rodger and the others who stood silent, as Kaiden and I talked.

'Rick, Rodger, I want you two to stay here with Marcus, Payton and Cedric. Keep guard and if the sons of bitches come back, I want you to kick their fucking asses. Don't kill them, just hurt them,' I ordered.

'Yes Alpha,' Rick responded. I took a deep breath before Kaiden and I walked through the doors and into the room that our mate was in. When we did, both of us were visibly shaken when we saw the condition our mate was in. When I saw an unfamiliar wolf with their hands on our mate, I lost control and launched myself at them. I didn't care that it was a she-wolf, I just cared that her hands were on my mate. Before I could get my hands on her, I felt myself being grabbed and pulled away. I was pulled into a hard chest and then two strong arms then wrapped themselves around me. I knew instantly that it was Kaiden who was holding me, he was the only one in the room who had a chance of restraining me.

Kyro, I need you to calm down. The she-wolf isn't hurting our mate, she's helping him. If she had tried to hurt him in any way whatsoever, Cedric would have stopped her. However, seeing as he hasn't, the she-wolf mustn't have tried to do anything bad, he said over mind link, while sending calming energy through our bond.

CHAPTER 12: KAIDEN'S POV

WHEN I WALKED into the room with Kyro to see our mate, I stopped short as I did not expect to see what was in front of me, our mate in such a horrible condition. The sight of my mate laying on the bed covered in bandages caused my heart to constrict and I heard Storm whimper in my head. I took a moment to catch my breath and as I did, I noticed Kyro lunge towards the she-wolf that appeared to be helping our mate. It took a lot of self-control on my part not to help him, instead Cedric and I got to Kyro before he reached the she-wolf. I pulled Kyro to my chest and then wrapped my arms around him tightly. I then talked to him over our private mind link, as I didn't want the others in the room to hear what I said to him.

Kyro, I need you to calm down. The she-wolf isn't hurting our mate, she's helping him. If she had tried to hurt him in any way whatsoever, Cedric would have stopped her. However, seeing as he hasn't, the she-wolf mustn't have tried to do anything bad. I sent calming energy to Kyro through our bond and several minutes later he calmed down enough that I felt that it was safe to release him from my hold.

Thank you for helping Kaiden, he said while looking at me and nodding.

Anytime brother. Anytime you need me I will be there, I told him. After taking several deep breaths I turned to face the she-wolf standing beside our mate.

'My apologies ma'am. When we entered, I saw the injured boy and thought you were trying to hurt him,' Kyro said with a slight bow of the head. Some Alphas would see even the slight action of nodding to someone they saw as an inferior, as belittling themselves. Kyro and I however, were raised to never be afraid to apologise to someone even if they were ranked below us.

'There is no need for apologies sir. I can understand the need to protect someone when they are hurt,' The she-wolf said, showing no signs of anger towards Kyro's reaction upon first seeing her. 'My name is Diomika Lang. I'm the school nurse. And before either of you ask about my lack of a pack bond, I am a lone wolf and not a rogue,' she said giving a slight bow of her head in return. Kyro, Cedric and I all twitched slightly when Miss Lang mentioned rogues. As pack wolves we have all had run ins with rogues in the past and most of them were not good experiences.

She seems uncomfortable around us, doesn't she? Storm said to Kyro, Shadow and I.

It is understandable Storm. Most rogues and lone wolves are uncomfortable around an Alpha and there are currently two in the room, Kyro replied.

'Hello Miss Lang, I am Alpha Kaiden de Luca and this is my twin brother Alpha Kyro de Luca. We are the joint Alphas of the Crimson Rose Pack. And we are aware of your status as a lone wolf and not rogue,' I said as I gave a slight nod of my head to Miss Lang in an attempt to diffuse some of the tension I could feel in the room.

'Alphas please, just call me Diomika,' Miss Lang, or should I say, Diomika, told us. 'May I ask how you knew I was a lone wolf without my telling you that I was?' she added with a hint of inquisitiveness in her voice.

'Well as you already guessed we could detect the lack of a pack bond. However, as I guess you have never learned, with training you can learn to tell the difference between a lone wolf and a rogue,' I said while Diomika nodded thoughtfully at my words, 'Now may I please ask what exactly is wrong with the young boy?'

'Levi,' Diomika said quickly causing Kyro, Cedric and I to become somewhat confused. 'Levi?' Kyro asked her in a questioning tone.

'The young boy, his name is Levi,' Diomika replied politely.

Levi. Storm said as he curled up and purred.

It is perfect don't you think? I said to Kyro.

It is, a perfect name for a perfect guy, he replied.

It is absolutely perfect. Shadow added. Both Storm and Shadow purred, causing Kyro and I to chuckle in our heads at their antics.

'I will give you some privacy to talk with Miss Lang about Levi,' Cedric said before giving a slight bow and then leaving the room. Diomika took a few deep breaths before she approached Kyro and I.

'Levi is in a very bad way Alpha Kyro, Alpha Kaiden. He has numerous broken bones including several ribs, internal bleeding and his umm…' Diomika took several deep breaths. I could see that whatever else she had to tell us was bad and it caused my anxiety to spike.

What isn't she saying? Oh goddess, what else is wrong with him? Goddess, please let him be ok, Kyro said through the mind link, his voice heavily laced with concern.

I don't know brother; we won't know until she tells us what else is wrong, I replied over mind link.

'Please continue Miss Lang, I mean Diomika,' I told her, trying to keep the edge out of my voice.

'His backside area is severely bruised and there is some bleeding from his…. from his anus. He needs more care than I am able to give him here at the school. But I don't want to call his pack's Alpha, from what I know about the man and the pack, it isn't a good place to be, especially for Levi. So, I don't particularly want to send Levi back there,' While talking to us, Diomika would pause several times. It was clear that she was very uncomfortable when she spoke about Levi's injuries. When Diomika said that Levi was bleeding from his anus I saw red and growled, closely followed by Kyro.

I will kill those sons of a bitches for touching our mate. Those bastards are so fucking dead, Shadow snarled over the mind link.

We will torture them first and then tear them apart piece by piece, Storm snarled out in response. Diomika whimpered as she knelt down in front of us and bared her neck in submission. It took a couple of moments for Kyro and I to regain control from our wolves and calm them enough that they wouldn't force a shift.

'On behalf of my brother, myself and our wolves, I would like to apologise for scaring you and forcing you to submit,' I said as I knelt down in front of Diomika and offered a hand to her. Diomika took my hand and I helped her to stand up.

'Thank you for your apology Alphas but it was not necessary. I understand your anger at hearing about Levi's injuries as I too am angry about what has happened to him,' Diomika replied before giving us a soft smile.

She is a very kind wolf, Kyro said softly over the mind link.

That she is, that she is, I replied.

I wonder what pack our mate belongs to, Kyro said as his brows furrowed thoughtfully.

I do as well. From the way she reacted when she mentioned it, I do not think

it is a good pack, I replied. I could sense from the way she had spoken that Diomika truly did not wish to call my mate's pack.

'I do not know what I am going to do. I am obligated to call his pack Alpha, even though I know he will not care. He will probably blame Levi for wasting his time,' Diomika said in a sad voice as she moved to stand beside Levi's bed, taking his hand in hers as she looked at him softly.

There is no way in hell that our mate is going back to his pack, Kyro said resolutely. I looked at him and nodded before turning back to face Diomika.

'My brother and I can solve that issue for you. He will come back to our pack with us. We will have our pack doctors and medics take care of him. We had treated him at our pack a couple of days ago after we found him being attacked here at school. We were going to talk with him but he ran away and we only found him again today,' Diomika let out an audible sigh of relief and she closed her eyes in silent prayer at my words.

'Thank you, so, so much for that. I don't want to see him go back to that Goddess forsaken place,' Diomika replied.

'There is no need to thank us. We only wish to see him happy and taken care of,' Kyro replied.

'Of course. If you would give me a moment, I will get him ready to move. I would normally move him using a stretcher but we do not have the time right now. We need to get him back to your pack hospital as soon as possible,' Diomika said before asking, 'Would one of you be able to carry the boy carefully to your car?' She looked between Kyro and I.

'I can carry him Diomika,' I replied.

'Ok, I will get him ready,' Diomika said and she moved to get Levi ready to move.

Guys get in here now, I called to the guys outside over our mind link.

Yes Alpha, they all replied over the mind link. Rick, Rodger, Cedric, Marcus, Payton, and Tristan came back into the room and all of them gasped when they saw Levi's condition, even Cedric, Marcus, Payton, and Tristan who had seen him when he was attacked. I cleared my throat to gain their attention and they all looked at me, though I could see the pain in their eyes. 'We will be bringing the young boy Levi back to the pack hospital for treatment. Cedric, Marcus, Payton, and Tristan, the four of you will remain at school to finish the school day. Rick and Rodger, the two of you will be returning with us to the pack,' I told them. There were a series of 'Yes Alphas' from all of them before they waited for further instructions.

'Diomika, I would like you to come to our pack house this afternoon after school has finished. There are some things that I would like to discuss with you in private,' Kyro said, addressing Diomika, who had a worried expression on her face.

'Is it safe for me to go there, Alphas?' Diomika asked.

'Of course. I will ensure that the patrol wolves are aware that you are coming,' Kyro responded. 'If you would like Alphas; I could escort her to the pack after school finishes this afternoon,' Cedric said while looking at Kyro and I.

'That is alright with us as long as it is ok with Diomika,' I responded.

'It is ok with me,' She responded.

'Ok, the four of you may now go back to class,' Kyro said to Cedric, Marcus, Payton, and Tristan, who nodded and then turned and left the room, returning to their classes.

'Levi is ready to go, so if you would like to pick him up, you can take him to your car,' Diomika said. I picked him up.

'Rick, you take the lead, Rodger you follow behind us,' Kyro said. We then left the nurse's office and headed to our car in our parking lot. Once we got to the car, Kyro hopped into the car and then Rick helped me to hand Levi to Kyro. I then hopped in beside him, carefully placing Levi's legs on my lap.

'We will see you this afternoon Diomika,' I said as the car door was closed. Diomika nodded and then left, while Rick got in the driver's seat and Rodger in the front passenger seat. While Rick drove, I had Rodger call Doctor Veracruz and inform her that we were bringing in the boy from a few days ago and that he would need immediate attention. Upon arrival at the pack hospital, Levi was taken by Doctor Veracruz and several other of the pack's medical personnel straight into surgery. Rick and Rodger returned to the pack house, while Kyro and I headed to the waiting room.

'What are we going to do Kaiden? How do we help our mate?' I looked at Kyro when he spoke and I could see the fear in his eyes. We sat down on the chairs and I wrapped my arms around my brother. 'I don't know Kyro. I honestly don't know. The only thing I do know, however, is that whatever we decide to do, we will decide together. We are a team. We'll work together to figure this out. We also have our family and friends who will help us if we ask them to,' Kyro nodded and I felt him slowly drifting off to sleep. I soon joined him, the stress of the last few days catching up with me. As I drifted off, I could hear someone come into the room and drape a blanket over Kyro and I, then leave the room. Soon the only thing I saw was blackness.

CHAPTER 13: KYRO'S POV

IT HAD BEEN almost four days since we brought our mate Levi back to our pack hospital. After my breakdown at the hospital the other day, Kaiden had done his best to make sure I was kept as relaxed as possible. I had tried multiple times to get him to relax with me but he always refused saying he would take care of our Alpha duties. I wanted to help but Kaiden refused, saying that Jaden and Rowan could help him. I had tried getting my mum to talk with Kaiden and get him to relax but he had told her that he was alright. Sometimes my brother and I being as stubborn as we were could be a pain. So, instead of doing what I normally would be for the last few days, I have done nothing but watch movies, read books and listen to music. Thanks to my spending entire days relaxing, I slept relatively well at night, something I haven't done in a while. Every morning after breakfast, Kaiden and I would visit the hospital where our mate lay unconscious. We prayed to the Moon Goddess that our mate would wake up soon. By our mate's side in the pack hospital, was where Kaiden and I currently were. We were sitting either side of our mate's bed talking about what we hoped our lives together would be like.

'I hope to have a family with you one day,' I said to my unconscious mate as I held one of his small hands in my bigger hands.

'I can't wait to have a family with you to. I can't wait to see our pups running around the house,' Kaiden said to Levi. I had to chuckle at Kaiden's words, having pups of our own with our respective mates was something Kaiden and I had always wanted. We had always imagined that we would have separate mates, so how we would work around us having the same mate was something we would have to discuss.

'I think he will look absolutely amazing round with our pups. Not that he doesn't look amazing now, just the thought of him being pregnant with our pups makes me happy,' I said to Kaiden, while keeping an eye on our mate.

'He is quite beautiful,' Kaiden said with a smile. I looked at Kaiden and saw that his eyes were filled with so much love that my heart swelled with happiness. Even though it was morning, Kaiden soon laid his head down on the bed beside our mate and fell asleep. While he slept, I thought back to the day we brought our mate to our pack hospital for the second time.

~ Flashback ~

Urgh where the hell am I? I thought to myself. When our mate had finally come out of surgery, Kaiden and I had taken a seat on either side of his bed. We spent several hours sitting beside our mate, silently praying to the Moon Goddess that he would wake up soon. Eventually the stress of the day's events caught up to us and Kaiden and I fell asleep beside our mate. When I opened my eyes again and took a look around, I noticed that Kaiden was still asleep on the other side of our mate's bed. I then turned to look at Levi's face, and I could feel my anger rising once again.

I don't like seeing him like this Shadow. I will kill every last son of a bitch that hurt him, I said with a growl.

We will tear them apart, Shadow said in agreement. When a hand touched my shoulder, I realised that when I growled, I had done so out loud.

'It's ok brother. He will be ok,' I turned to face Kaiden as he spoke. He had moved from his seat and was now kneeling down beside me, with a hand on my shoulder.

'I know that you are hurting because of what has happened to our mate because I am as well. But right now, we need to remain calm,' Kaiden said in a calming voice.

'I'm sorry brother, I forgot you would be hurting as well,' I said as I gave Kaiden's hand a squeeze.

'We must have faith that our mate will be ok. He will wake and he will need us to be strong for him. There will be a time when we get to rip apart the bastards who did this to him, but not right now. Right now, we need to stay here and help our mate get through this,' Kaiden said before letting go of my shoulder and moving back to his seat on the other side of the bed. I glanced at the clock on the wall behind Kaiden and saw that it was almost two in the afternoon.

'We should go and freshen up. It's almost two and we have a meeting with Miss Lang this afternoon,' I said to Kaiden.

'Of course,' Kaiden replied softly. After we each gave out mate a kiss on the forehead, we left the pack hospital and headed to the Alpha floor of the pack house. When we got to the Alpha floor, Kaiden and I split up and went to our own bedrooms. When I got to my room, I headed straight to my bathroom, wanting to wash up before I did anything else. I had already decided that a bath would be best for my tight muscles. After I was finished in the bathroom, I smelled food cooking so I put on my shoes and went to the kitchen to investigate. When I got to the kitchen, I saw Kaiden standing over the stove cooking something. He was wearing a pair of dark blue track pants; his shirt was hanging over a chair and his shoes were on the floor near the entrance.

'What you cooking bro?' I asked as I approached my brother.

'I'm cooking French toast. I thought we could do with something to eat before we went to our office. And seeing as we are a little stressed, I didn't think a big meal would be a good idea, so I went with this,' Kaiden responded.

'Mmm your French toast is good,' I replied. It's true, Kaiden made the best French toast I have ever eaten. He added cinnamon to it, which I found gave it a nice kick.

'Go sit down, it should be ready in a sec,' Kaiden told me. I did as he said and a few minutes later Kaiden placed two plates with French toast on it, on the table and then turned to grab some drinks. We ate our food in silence and when we were finished, I grabbed our dishes and put them in the dishwasher with the dishes from this morning and last night.

'We still have some time before Miss Lang is due to arrive, did you want to get some paperwork done?' I asked after I finished turning on the dishwasher.

'Not particularly, but I suppose we should get it done,' Kaiden replied with slight sarcasm. I chuckled at my brother and waited as he put his shirt and shoes on. The two of us then headed to our office.

'Let's get as much of this paperwork done before Miss Lang gets here,' I said as we sat down behind our desks. After working on paperwork for a while I felt someone trying to mind link me and by the look on Kaiden's face, someone was trying to mind link him as well. I opened the mind link and heard Marcus speak to Kaiden and I.

Alphas, Cedric and I have Miss Lang with us and we are about to cross the pack border, Marcus told us.

Thank you, Marcus. We will meet you out the front of the pack house. Kaiden responded. **Patrol wolves, Cedric Yi and Marcus Grey are about to cross the pack border. They have a lone wolf with them. Do not attack the lone wolf. They are here at our request,** I said in a mind link to the patrol wolves currently patrolling the border of our pack territory. I waited for the patrol wolves to acknowledge the order before I cut the mind link.

'We should head downstairs now,' Kaiden said when I looked at him. I nodded and then the two of us headed downstairs and waited outside for Marcus and Cedric to arrive with Miss Lang. We didn't have to wait long as we soon saw a couple of cars drive up and stop at the front of the pack house. Once the cars had stopped, Cedric, Marcus, and Miss Lang got out of one, while Tristan and Payton got out of the other car. The five of them approached us and stopped a few steps in front of us.

'Miss Lang, as mentioned when we met earlier today, I am Alpha Kyro de Luca and this is Alpha Kaiden de Luca. Welcome to the Crimson Rose Pack,' I said as I held my hand out to Miss Lang. I noticed that when she shook my hand and then Kaiden's hand, Miss Lang seemed quite nervous.

Considering that she is a lone wolf standing in front of two strong Alphas, in the middle of those Alphas' pack, it is understandable that she would be nervous, Shadow commented, to which I had to agree.

'Hello Alpha Kyro, Alpha Kaiden. Thank you for inviting me to your pack,' Miss Lang said after shaking Kaiden's hand.

'Cedric, Marcus, Payton, Tristan, thank you for escorting Miss Lang here. You may return to your normal activities now. Miss Lang, if you will please follow my brother and I, we will go to our office so we can talk in private,' Kaiden said to those in front of us. Once the four guys left, Kaiden and I escorted Miss Lang through the pack house and up to our office. When we got there, instead of sitting at the desk we sat on the couches to the side of the room. We sat in silence for several minutes before Kaiden decided to start the conversation. 'Would you like something to eat or drink Miss Lang?' he asked.

'No but thank you for asking Alpha, and as I said at the school, please call me Diomika,' Miss Lang replied with a soft smile.

'Of course, Diomika. And please just call us Kyro and Kaiden,' I said before asking what was on my mind. 'Can you please tell us how you know Levi?'

'Of course. I started working at the school about six months ago. It was my second week at the school when Levi came into the nurse's office for the first time. He came into my office badly beaten and was bleeding from multiple areas,' Diomika paused her story and after seeing her lick her lips to moisten them, I stood up and grabbed three glasses and a jug of water from the mini fridge in our office. I returned to the couches, poured three glasses of water, handed one to Miss Lang and my brother and keeping the last one for myself. 'I treated Levi's injuries as best I could with what I had on me. I always carried items that aided shifters in healing, just in case I needed them, so I used them on Levi. I noticed his poorly healed injuries and tried to get him to open up about them, but he wouldn't, no matter how many times I asked him to. I saw him almost every day from then on and overtime he slowly opened up about what was happening to him,' Again Diomika paused, taking another sip of her drink. I could see tears in her eyes when she mentioned Levi opening up to her. I could only imagine what he told her but I knew it was bad. 'I promised him that I would never tell anyone what he told me, so if you wish to know, you will have to ask him. I wanted to help Levi more but I didn't know how to. I'm a lone wolf and I didn't know anyone who could help me get him away from his pack. So, I am very grateful to the both of you for what you are doing for him,' Diomika said with a soft smile. I could see that she was genuine.

'Of course. We only wish we knew about him sooner so we could have got to him before he was hurt so badly,' Kaiden said sadly.

'What's Levi's last name?' I asked. I realised that though Levi has been at the pack for a few days now, we didn't know what his last name was. Kaiden and I could have tried to find out by asking the school but that would likely alert Levi's old pack that Levi was with us. Diomika would likely know Levi's last name, so asking her was the better option.

'Chang,' Diomika replied.

'Levi Chang,' I said, liking the sound of my mate's name.

Kyro, I have an idea, Kaiden said through mind link.

What is it Kaiden? I asked.

I think we should invite her to join the pack. She is probably the only person Levi trusts and I feel she will be a good fit for the pack, Kaiden replied.

That is a good idea. She could stay at the pack house or we could organise a house for her. She can even work at the pack hospital if she liked, I responded. Once we came to an agreement, we decided to ask Miss Lang what she thought. 'Diomika, my brother and I would like to invite you to join our pack. If you would like to, we can show you to a room in the pack house that will be yours and if you would prefer, we can arrange for one of our empty houses for you to have,' I told Diomika and I saw the smile on her face grow.

'I would love to join this pack Alpha Kyro and Alpha Kaiden,' Diomika replied. I was a little surprised she had accepted so quickly but then I realised that the reason she did so was most likely Levi. She obviously cared for him a lot, so it made sense for her to want to be close to him. We decided that we would leave the details about Diomika joining the pack for another time and instead we showed Diomika to a guest room. After showing Diomika to her room, Kaiden and I went to visit our mate in the hospital.

~ End of Flashback ~

CHAPTER 14: LEVI'S POV

FOR THE SECOND time in I don't know how many days, I woke up in a clean white room. By the familiar smell it was the same one I had woken up in after my previous beating at school.

Oh, my Goddess, Alpin, we are back here again. We need to leave and get back to our pack before the Alpha finds out we are here. He is going to torture us or might even kill us when we get back there, I said, my voice filled with worry.

I don't know if we should leave Levi, Alpin responded.

What do you mean Alpin? Alpha Redmond will kill us for being in another pack's territory, I answered.

I think we should stay Levi, at least for now. They haven't done anything to hurt us here, only help from what I can feel. And as you said, Alpha Redmond will beat us or even kill us when we get back to our pack. We should stay here, at least until we heal. Alpin said tiredly. *What? Alpin are you crazy? We are in another pack's territory; we are going to be in so much trouble from the Alpha of this pack,* I said worriedly.

I don't think we will Levi. This is the second time that we have woken up here and the only thing that seems to have been done to us is surgery. If they wanted to hurt us, I honestly don't think they would have treated our injuries first. We would have been thrown straight into their prison. Besides we saw our mates here the other day, perhaps we can talk to them and they can help us. They could talk to the Alpha and ask them not to hurt us, Alpin suggested. I didn't respond to Alpin this time. Instead, I thought about what he had said. He had a fair point but I was scared and didn't know what to do. I knew he was right about this pack having not hurt us, but I was worried about how long that would last. Eventually all the thinking made me tired, so I went back to sleep. I closed my eyes and let my mind drift off to the first peaceful sleep that I had experienced in a very long time.

When I next woke up, I quickly sensed that I was no longer alone in the room. A quick look around, revealed two people sitting either side of my bed. They had their hands folded in front of them on the bed and their heads were resting on their hands. While they were still fast asleep, I took a closer look at them. I quickly realised that they were the same two people that Alpin had identified the other day as our mates. As I continued to stare at them, I noticed they were identical, making me guess that they must be twins.

They are quite handsome. I can't wait to get to know them, Alpin said happily before letting out a soft purr. I had to agree that the two guys were handsome, they had nicely tanned skin and jet-black hair which was a bit messy. Despite how handsome I found them to be, I was worried as I didn't think that they would want me if they knew what has been done to me.

We need to leave Alpin. Once they find out what has been done to us, they will not want us anymore, I said. I could feel tears forming in the corner of my eyes. I didn't want to leave my mates, but at the same time I felt that they would be better off without me.

No, we are not leaving, not this time Levi. I think we should stay this time and give our mates a chance to accept us for who we are. As I said earlier, they have not done a thing to hurt us, Alpin spoke softly but I could hear the hope he had in his voice.

Ok, I will do as you say and stay for now. I hadn't realised that while talking to Alpin, I had moved slightly. I only realised that I had done so when I noticed my two mates start to stir. The two of them sat up and started rubbing the sleep from their eyes. Both of my mates looked at me and several seconds later, they gasped when they saw I was awake.

'Oh, my Goddess, you're awake,' The man to my left said quickly. My two mates stood up and hugged me, causing me to whimper in pain. 'Oh, I'm so, so sorry. We didn't mean to hurt you. My name is Kyro and this is my twin brother, Kaiden,' The man who had spoken said, as he introduced himself and the other guy, smiling as he did so. The man identified as Kaiden gently grabbed my hand.

'We learnt your name was Levi but we do not know which pack you come from. Could you tell us what pack you come from?' Kaiden asked, causing my fear to spike.

'M-m-my pack. I-I have to g-get back to m-my p-pack before I g-get in t-trouble,' I said fearfully. I was very nervous and I quickly got up from the bed. Unfortunately, when I tried to stand up, I fell. Thankfully before I hit the ground, a pair of strong arms caught me and placed me back onto the bed.

'Are you ok?' Kyro asked me after I had settled back onto the bed.

'Y-yes. I-I am o-ok,' I replied in a small whisper.

'Please don't try to get up again anytime soon. At least not until we have a doctor come and examine you,' Kyro added, a sad look in his eyes. He then got a glazed look in his eyes. Because of this, I knew that he was currently mind linking someone. That glazed over look was the same one the members of my pack got when they were mind linking.

'Our senior pack doctor is coming here in about fifteen minutes to give you an exam,' Kyro told me after he finished mind linking whoever he was talking to.

'Would you like to lie back down and rest until the doctor gets here, or would you like to talk for a bit?' Kaiden asked. I noticed that when my mates spoke to me they did so in a soft, gentle voice.

I think we should lay down for a while Levi. I want to get to know our handsome mates but I am really tired right now, Alpin said, I could hear the tiredness in his voice when he spoke. 'I-I'd like t-to rest,' I told Kyro and Kaiden.

'Ok. Do you mind if we stay here while you rest or would you like us to leave?' Kyro asked. I could see pain in his eyes when he asked if I wanted them to leave and that made me feel sad. ***Let them stay Levi. I feel better when they are near us.***

'Y-you can st-stay,' I stuttered out. After Kyro and Kaiden helped me to get comfortable on the bed, I closed my eyes and drifted off to sleep.

I'm not sure how much time had passed when I felt someone gently shaking my shoulder. I was startled by the sudden contact and sat up quickly. The movement made me dizzy and my vision blurred.

'Are you ok Levi?' I heard someone ask me. As my vision cleared, I realised it must have been Kaiden who had asked if I was ok. Thankfully the Goddess gave us wolves a heightened sense of smell, otherwise I might not have been able to tell the twins apart.

'I'm o-ok. J-just start-tled when some-someone touched me,' I replied.

'I'm so sorry. I didn't mean to startle you,' Kyro said to me. 'I was just wanting to wake you up and let you know the doctor is just outside. They are waiting to come in and examine you,' I could feel my panic rise. Should I trust the doctor? Alpha Redmond once had one of our pack doctors help him torture me by injecting me with various drugs. Remembering what had been done to me caused my fear to rise and I started panicking even more. When my breathing quickened, Kyro and Kaiden each grabbed one of my hands. 'Easy there Levi. You are safe here,' Kyro said softly.

'Just take nice even breaths,' Kaiden said and after I had calmed down, he asked. 'Can you tell us what is wrong? Are you scared about seeing a doctor? Do you feel unsafe? Whatever it is we will do our best to help you,' Both of my mates waited patiently for me to talk and for that I was very grateful.

'W-will th-the doctor h-hurt m-me?' I asked as I looked between the two of them, fear clearly in my voice.

'No, definitely not. The doctor will not harm you. She is a very kind and caring person. She will help make sure that you get better. She is the one who operated on your injuries,' Kaiden replied gently.

If she was the one who fixed our injuries, I think we should trust her. I don't think our mates would let her near us if she was going to hurt us, Alpin commented.

Are you sure about that Alpin? I want to trust them but I am scared, I replied.

I know you are scared Levi because I am too. But I think we need to trust our mates, Alpin said.

Ok Alpin, I said once I finished speaking to Alpin.

'I w-will speak wi-with the doctor,' I told my mates. I tasted a little blood in my mouth and realised that I had bit my lip as I stuttered out my response.

'Ok. I'll let her in,' Kaiden said as he stood up and went to the door. After the door was opened two women walked into the room. One of the women I recognised as Diomika, who was the nurse at my school, while the other women I did not recognise. The woman I did not recognise had medium brown hair and was slightly tanned. She was wearing black pants and a light blue shirt, over which she wore a white doctor's coat.

'Levi, you probably recognise Miss Lang from your school,' Kyro said as he smiled softly at me.

'The other lady here is Doctor Cora Veracruz. She is our pack's Senior Doctor. She and her team were the ones that operated on you the first time you were brought here and then again the second time you were brought here,' he said, explaining who the unknown woman was. 'Doctor Veracruz this is Levi,' he said finishing the introductions.

'Hello Levi. It is a pleasure to see you awake. Do you mind if I give you a check-up to see how you are going since the operation?' Doctor Veracruz asked me politely.

'I-its o-ok,' I told her without looking at her.

'Ok. Levi if you could sit up as best you can. Everyone else please stand to the side of the room,' Doctor Veracruz said, her authority as the senior pack doctor seeping into her voice. While I sat up, Kyro and Kaiden joined Diomika at the side of the room. Doctor Veracruz then came and checked the stitches I hadn't realised I had. She then checked my other injuries and then my vitals. She worked quickly but carefully, her skills as a doctor showing through. 'Your healing is slow but you are going in the right direction,' Doctor Veracruz said after she had finished. 'I am going to go and organise some further testing for you. I want to get a clearer picture of how you are healing on the inside,' she added.

'T-tests?' I asked worried.

'Yes. I would like to do some x-rays and a CT scan. I'd also like to do some blood tests,' she said in answer to my question. Doctor Veracruz smiled at me and after giving Kyro and Kaiden a small nod, she left the room. I looked over to Diomika and wandered what she was doing here, I was worried about her. It was one thing for a wolf from one pack being on another pack's territory without an invitation but it was another thing entirely for a lone wolf to enter a pack's territory.

'Diomika, wh-why are you h-here?' I asked, unable to keep the worry out of my voice.

'Hey Levi. It is a long story but I am here at the invitation of the two Alphas,' Diomika said in response, looking between Kyro and Kaiden when she mentioned Alphas.

'The t-two Al-Alphas?' I said, looking between Kyro and Kaiden, my fear rising as I did.

Alpin, they are the Alphas. Our mates are the Alphas. N-n-no, I c-can't do this. I can't do this. I-I'm not w-worthy of b-being an Al-Alpha's mate. Seeing me panic, Diomika moved and stood beside my bed.

'Levi, you need to remain calm. Take a deep breath, in and out,' Diomika instructed. I did my best to do as she said but I was unable to calm down and I felt myself drift off and lose consciousness.

CHAPTER 15: KAIDEN POV

SEEING OUR MATE pass out caused the fear in Kyro and I to rise.

'Doctor Veracruz we need you in here now,' I said as soon as my mate passed out. No matter where in the hospital she was, she would hear us thanks to her advanced hearing.

'Alphas please stand back and let me help him,' Diomika said to Kyro and I when we tried approaching our mate. Kyro and I went to argue with her, both of us wanting to protect our mate from further harm, but we were stopped when Doctor Veracruz came rushing back into the room.

'Alphas, I need the both of you to leave the room, right now,' Doctor Veracruz said to us in a tone that indicated there was no arguing with her. Normally an Alpha would never take orders from someone of a lower rank, but in this case, when it was a doctor giving orders for the benefit of their patient, an Alpha would do as they were asked. So, despite wanting to remain in the room with our mate, Kyro and I left.

'Let's wait over there,' Kyro said after we had closed the door to our mate's room. Tension surrounded both Kyro and I as we made our way over to the seats outside our mate's room. 'Goddess I hate this feeling. It fell as though my chest is about to explode,' I said as I leaned forward and clutched my chest. I took several deep breaths to relax myself as I didn't want to accidently shift in the middle of the pack hospital. Kyro placed an arm around me and gently rubbed my shoulder, helping me to calm down.

'Kaiden can I tell you something?' Kyro asked softly.

'Of course,' I replied as I turned to face him. I could feel the nervous energy coming from Kyro and it felt strange, Kyro rarely, if ever, got nervous.

'I feel like our mate's panic attack was our fault. I mean he was ok with us until he was told we were Alphas,' Kyro said.

What if our mate doesn't want us because we are Alphas? My wolf Storm asked in our heads. *Mate will reject us. I don't want mate to reject us. I want mate safe and happy. I want him in our arms.* Kyro's wolf Shadow said with a whimper.

He won't reject us. When he is ready, we will talk with him and help him feel comfortable and safe with us, I told the wolves.

Kaiden is right. We will help make him feel safe with us and over time our mate will feel better about being around two Alphas, Kyro added. Once the two wolves had calmed down, they curled up and retreated to the back of our minds.

'From how he reacted, his injuries and from what Miss Lang told us, I don't think our mate has the best of experiences with Alphas. But hopefully with time we can gain his trust and live happily together,' I said to Kyro after our wolves had retreated, they were likely trying to figure out how to get our mate to trust and accept us. Kyro and I laid back against the wall and closed our eyes, slowly drifting off to sleep. I don't know how much time passed before we heard a door nearby open and then shut again. The sound woke Kyro and I up and we were standing up in a flash. Doctor Veracruz flinched slightly at the speed of our movement but recovered quickly.

'Doctor Veracruz, how is he?' I asked when Doctor Veracruz came to a stop in front of Kyro and I.

'Alphas, your mate has woken up and has calmed down. Miss Lang and I thought it would be best if she talks with Levi before the two of you go back in. We believe he will be less likely to have a panic attack in your presence, if they talk first,' Doctor Veracruz explained and I nodded.

Wait, she called him our mate. How did she know he was our mate? I asked Kyro over mind link.

I don't know, he replied. Before either of us could ask how she knew Levi was our mate, Doctor Veracruz, having seen our puzzled looks, answered our unasked question.

'The way the both of you are around the boy, told me that you are mates. I haven't told anyone and I won't do so without your consent,'

'Thank you, Cora,' I said, using Doctor Veracruz's first name instead of her last name and title. 'No need to thank me Kaiden,' She responded. I smiled. It was rare for people other than our family and friends to address Kyro and I by anything other than our Alpha title. It was also rare for Kyro and I to address someone by their first name if they held a specific role in our pack like doctor or warrior. It was a sign of respect among wolves to address someone by their title. We usually only addressed someone by their first name if they didn't hold a specific role within a pack. Other than that, our family and friends were the only ones we addressed by their first names or nicknames.

'Could you tell us about our mate's condition?' Kyro asked Doctor Veracruz.

'Of course,' She replied and after giving us a rundown of our mate's condition, she excused herself.

'I would like to stay here and wait for our mate to be ready to talk to us but I think it might be best if we leave. Our mate can probably sense that we are still close by and it might be difficult for him to remain calm,' Kyro said.

'That's true. Did you want to grab something to eat while our mate talks with Miss Lang?' I asked in response. 'Sounds like a good idea. I am pretty hungry. We should find Doctor Veracruz on the way and see if we are allowed to bring any food and drink for Levi. He will likely be hungry as well,' Kyro replied.

'Good idea,' I responded. Kyro and I then went to find Doctor Veracruz, it took a couple of minutes but we eventually found her in her office near the front of the hospital.

'What can I do for you Alphas?' she asked after we knocked on her office door.

'We were going to go back to the pack house and get something to eat. Give our mate some time alone to talk with Miss Lang,' Kyro started explaining, 'After we had eaten, we thought we would bring our mate something to eat. We were unsure of what we could bring him, so we thought we would ask you,' he added.

'That's actually a good idea. I would suggest only simple foods and drinks for now. Probably some porridge and a cup of tea,' Doctor Veracruz replied.

'Ok. Thank you, Doctor,' I responded. Kyro and I then left Doctor Veracruz's office and headed to the pack house. When we got there, we headed straight to the kitchen on the Alpha floor.

'What did you want to eat Kaiden?' Kyro asked once we arrived at the kitchen.

'Some bacon, eggs and toast would be good,' I replied before adding, 'I'll make the food if you want to make something to drink,' Kyro nodded and then we each went and grabbed what we needed to make our meal. As I cooked the food, I smelled coffee brewing. Kyro must have decided to make coffee for us, probably a good idea as we were both tired. Once everything was ready, we sat down to eat our meal.

'Mmmm I love bacon. It is the best food ever,' Kyro said, he had a blissful look on his face as he took another bite of the bacon. My brother and I absolutely love bacon. We would eat it for breakfast, lunch and dinner if we could. 'I wonder if our mate likes bacon,' I thought aloud and I watched Kyro give a small smile as he thought about what I said.

'I will get started on the porridge for our mate while you finish eating your food,' Kyro said after he had finished eating. I hummed in agreement and continued eating as he stood up and took his dishes to the sink. When I was done eating, I put my dishes in the sink with Kyro's and then made a thermos of tea. After we had everything ready for our mate's breakfast, we placed it on a tray and then covered it with a lid. We then headed downstairs, out the front door and towards the pack hospital.

When we got to our mate's room, we could hear our mate and Diomika talking softly.

'Let's sit down and wait for them to finish talking,' I said to Kyro. Kyro nodded and we headed to some seat and waited patiently for our mate and Diomika to finish speaking. Five minutes later the door to our mate's room opened and Diomika walked out.

'Alphas,' Diomika said when she saw us. She gave a small bow of her head once she was standing in front us.

'How is he Diomika?' I asked her.

'He is as well as can be expected. He is a little startled by the fact that his mates are the Alphas of a pack. But I talked to him and told him about how you both took care of him when he was brought here. I also told him about how you treated me when I came here,' Diomika explained. She took several deep breaths before she continued to tell us about our mate.

'Before you ask, he told me a bit about why he panicked but I promised him I wouldn't say anything. I did however convince him to talk to you but I suggest letting him come to you. Do not try and force him to talk about anything if he doesn't want to, otherwise it could trigger another panic attack,' After Diomika finished talking we headed over to the door to our mate's room. Diomika knocked softly on the door before opening it and walking in with Kyro and I following behind. 'Levi, your mates are here to talk with you,' she said in a soft voice after the door closed behind us. Levi was sitting up in bed with a blanket covering his lap, he had a worried look on his face and I could see he was having difficulty looking at Kyro and I in the eyes.

'Hello Levi,' Kyro and I said at the same time.

'H-hell-lo Alphas,' Our little mate stuttered out.

'Levi, do you mind if I wait outside while you talk with your mates or did you want me to stay in here with you while you talked?' Diomika asked softly.

'Y-you can w-wait outside. I w-will b-be ok,' Levi replied. Diomika gave him a soft smile before she turned and left the room, quietly closing the door behind her.

'We thought that you might be hungry and thirsty so we brought you something to eat and drink. It's not much just some porridge and tea,' I said as we slowly approached our mate's bed. Kyro grabbed a bedside table from the side of the room and brought it closer to the bed. I then placed the tray with Levi's meal on the table and then Kyro and I moved back, giving our mate room. We didn't want him to feel as if we were smothering him. Kyro and I took a seat at the side of the room and waited quietly as Levi slowly at his food and drank his drink. From the way he sniffed the porridge and tea, I could tell that he had either never had them before or that he had, but not often. The other more concerning thought that crossed my mind was that what little food and drink he had been given in his life, had been poisoned. This thought almost caused me to growl out loud, but I was able to stop myself before I did. I didn't want to scare Levi any more than he already was.

Chapter 16: Levi's POV

GODDESS, THIS PORRIDGE is good. I wonder who made it, Alpin said happily, he loved the porridge and so did I. The tea they had brought was also lovely and was just the right temperature. There was also something in it that I couldn't identify, but it gave it a nice taste. When I had finished off the last of the porridge and tea, I leaned back, closed my eyes and sighed. I heard a slight purr which caused me to sit up. It didn't take me long for me to realise it had been my mates that had purred. I blushed at this and looked down at my hands, unsure of how to react to my mates purring and what to do now that I had finished.

'Is it alright if we come and sit beside your bed?' one of my mates asked. After I nodded my consent, my mates moved closer to my bed. While one of my mates moved the table out of the way, my other mate grabbed a chair for both of them, placing one on either side of the bed. 'We wanted to introduce ourselves again, in case you don't remember our names. My name is Kyro and this is my twin brother Kaiden,' The one to my left said as they both sat down. The one who had spoken had a nice voice and smelled amazing, he smelled like forest and fire.

'I'd like to start by saying that you have nothing to fear from either of us. We want nothing more than for you to be safe and happy with us. I know it might take some time for you to trust us and to open up to us but we are willing to wait however long you need for you to feel safe and comfortable enough to do so,' This time it was Kaiden who had spoken, like his brother he had a nice voice and smelled incredible. But his scent was different, he smelled like apples and fresh rain.

'Th-thank you for w-what y-y-you have d-done f-for m-me,' I said and my mates smiled and blushed. 'Wh-what h-happens now? D-do I h-have to l-leave or…,'

I didn't even finish my questions as both of my mates suddenly spoke up saying, 'No!' I flinched at their reaction and the volume at which they spoke.

'Sorry, we are so sorry. We didn't mean to scare you. It's just the thought of you leaving again scares us. We don't want to lose you,' Kyro said, quickly apologising for the reaction of him and his brother. I could see that they were both having trouble stopping themselves from touching me in an effort to comfort me and Alpin whined seeing that.

I want them to touch me but I also don't. Does that make me a bad wolf? Alpin asked before whimpering.

No Alpin, it doesn't make you a bad wolf. I feel the same way you do. Alpin whined again but made no further comment.

'S-s-so wh-what happens now?' I repeated my question from before again, this time not making any mention of me leaving my mates.

'Well Doctor Veracruz will most likely want to give you a check over and run some more tests before clearing you to leave the pack hospital. After you are able to leave the hospital, we will take you to the pack house. There you will have a room, clothes, bathroom, food…' Kaiden rambled a bit, before taking a breath and continuing. 'Well, you'll have anything you need and want really,' Kaiden said. He smiled shyly, realising that he rambled a bit.

'Wh-what room w-will I st-stay in?' I said as soon as the question popped into my head. Even though they were being kind to me right now, I was still a little worried that they were going to be like my old pack and make me sleep in the basement.

'You will have a bedroom on the top floor of the pack house. It's the Alpha floor and besides Kyro and I, only our parents, younger brothers and our sister in-law have rooms on that floor. Kyro and I are at one end, while our family live at the other,' Kaiden explained.

'The bedroom has its own bathroom and a walk-in closet. Normally as the mate of the Alpha or Alphas as this case is, you would stay in the same room as us. However, we thought that considering everything you had been through that you might want your own room,' Kaiden finished. When I heard Kaiden's answer, I felt a slight twinge of guilt about the fact that I was basically stopping my mates from being able to sleep in the same room as me.

'S-sorry,' I whimpered.

'What for?' Kyro asked.

'Th-that we w-won't stay in th-the s-same r-room,' I said in a whisper. My mates were wonderful wolves, I could see that now. They didn't deserve to have a broken mate like me. 'You have nothing to apologise for Levi. My brother and I both understand that you have had a rough past and that it will take some time for you to heal. We want you to know that we will both be with you every step of the way,' Kaiden said with a smile. This time both my mates grabbed one of my hands and I felt sparks shooting up my arms and through my body.

'A-are y-you sure? I m-mean y-you deserve b-better th-than me,' I said before breaking down and crying.

'Hey. Don't say that. You are a wonderful wolf, that has unfortunately had a very bad life. You may feel broken right now but it won't always be this way. It takes time to heal from trauma like you have experienced. We won't abandon you, especially not when we have just found you,' Kyro said softly.

'Do you mind if we call Doctor Veracruz in to give you a check over now?' Kaiden asked after giving me some time to gather myself. I nodded and then waited as Kyro mind linked Doctor Veracruz.

CHAPTER 17: KYRO'S POV

A COUPLE OF minutes after I had finished mind linking Doctor Veracruz, there was a knock on the door.

'Come in,' Kaiden called to the person outside. When the door opened, I was not surprised to see Doctor Veracruz walk in as I had smelled her as she had approached the room.

'Hello Alphas, Levi,' Doctor Veracruz said with a smile.

'Hello Doctor,' I replied as she approached Levi's bed and stopped when she got to the end of it.

'Levi the Alphas have asked me to give you a check over. Is that ok with you?' Doctor Veracruz asked Levi directly.

'I-It's ok D-doctor,' Levi stuttered out.

'Ok. Alphas could you please move to the side of the room while I complete my exam,' Doctor Veracruz said to Kaiden and I. While Doctor Veracruz did her checks Kaiden and I stood to the side of the room and watched silently.

'I promise that I will be as gentle as I can while I examine you, Levi. I apologise in advance if I cause you any pain. If you do experience any pain, just let me know,' Doctor Veracruz said kindly to Levi. As the exam was conducted, I noticed that every so often Levi would wince and I struggled to stop myself from attacking Doctor Veracruz.

It's ok Kyro. Doctor Veracruz would never hurt our mate, Kaiden said before giving my shoulder a gentle squeeze.

He's right Kyro, Doctor Veracruz is an amazing and gentle wolf that wouldn't hurt our mate, Shadow said, agreeing with Kaiden and Kaiden's wolf also agreed with them.

I agree with him, brother. Soon the three of us will be together and we will be happy, Kaiden said in agreement. I calmed down and waited patiently for Doctor Veracruz to finish. After she was finished her exam, I noticed Levi had fallen asleep.

'Alphas, can we talk outside please?' Doctor Veracruz asked when she was finished. My brother and I nodded and then followed Doctor Veracruz outside.

'How is he doctor?' I asked as soon as we were outside the room. The fact that Doctor Veracruz didn't wish to discuss Levi's condition in front of Levi caused me to worry.

'His condition is very poor Alphas. He has quite a few injuries and broken bones, some of which are going to have to be rebroken as they haven't healed correctly. He is not healing very well due to a very low healing factor which is the result of a long history of beatings and poor nutrition. We will need to put him on a special diet to help boost his healing factor,' Doctor Veracruz told us after which she took several deep breaths. It took me a moment to realise that Doctor Veracruz had said she wanted to break my mate's bones again. The thought of Levi having to go through the pain of having his bones rebroken was horrible.

No, no I don't want to hurt him, Shadow whimpered as he curled up.

'Will he have to be conscious when you rebreak his bones or will he be unconscious?' I asked. I was hoping that Doctor Veracruz would say Levi would be unconscious before anything was done. I didn't want my little mate to suffer any more than he already had and I knew Kaiden didn't either.

'I will place Levi into a coma before we do anything to him. That way he won't feel any pain while we rebreak and realign his bones. I would also suggest he stay in the coma for at least two weeks with a possibility of extending it further. We would do this so his body can heal without added stress. While he was in the coma, we would he ensure that he got the nutrients his body needs and we would also administer medications that will help with the healing process,' Doctor Veracruz replied. Two weeks, she wants to put my mate into a coma for two weeks. Goddess, what do we do? Two weeks without seeing his beautiful eyes or hearing his beautiful voice. I felt my panic rise, so I turned and put my hands against the wall while I tried to slow my breathing.

'Can you give us some privacy for a moment please Cora?' Kaiden asked Doctor Veracruz. Doctor Veracruz nodded and then left Kaiden and I alone so we could speak in private.

'What do we do Kaiden? I understand that this is being done to help him, but two weeks, two weeks of him just lying unconscious and us not being able to do anything about it,' I said as I turned around and sank to the floor, where I put my head in my hands and sighed. Kaiden sat beside me, wrapped an arm around me and gave my arm a squeeze.

'I think we should do it but first we should speak with Levi. He should have a choice in what is done to him,' Kaiden said gently. He was right both about the coma and asking Levi what he wanted. Kaiden helped me to stand and then we went back into our mate's room. We waited for three hours before Levi started stirring. He looked startled when he woke up but after taking a quick look around, he calmed down.

'Hey Levi. How are you feeling?' I asked once he had calmed down.

'S-sore,' Levi stuttered out, keeping his eyes down.

'That is understandable given your condition,' I told him gently.

Doctor, can you come to Levi's room please. He is awake and we would like for you to explain your suggestion to him, I said to Doctor Veracruz.

On my way Alpha, she replied.

'Umm, Levi. D-doctor Veracruz is umm, sh-she is on her w-way back here. Sh-she wanted to, to umm d-discuss with you,' I managed to eventually stutter out. I saw of flash of fear and concern make its way across Levi's face.

'Y-you're ki-kicking me out of y-your p-pack aren't you? I'm t-to m-much trouble f-for y-you to d-deal with,' Levi said before breaking down and crying. This time Kaiden and I did not hesitate to grab his hands and comfort him.

'No. We are definitely not going to kick you out. You are our mate, which means this pack is now your home and that we will take care of you,' I told Levi, trying to make sure my voice conveyed I meant exactly what I said. Just after I finished talking, Doctor Veracruz walked into the room.

'Hello Alphas, Levi,' she said as she approached Levi's bed.

'We told Levi that there is something that you wished to discuss with him,' Kaiden told the doctor and she nodded.

'Ok. Levi, as I'm sure you are aware, your condition isn't the best. This has impacted on your body's ability to properly heal, especially in regards to your bones, which almost all of which have healed incorrectly. I suggested to your mates, that your bones get rebroken and then reset so that they can be healed correctly,' Doctor Veracruz explained to Levi, who instantly recoiled in response.

'Y-you w-want to b-break my b-bones? You w-want t-to hurt m-me?' he said with tears in his eyes. I moved to sit directly beside my mate on his bed, after which I gently placed a hand on his face, while Kaiden stayed sitting where he was.

'I don't want to hurt you Levi. But unfortunately, I feel that this is what is needed. I also suggest that we put you in a coma for at least a couple of weeks so your body can heal without any added stress,' Doctor Veracruz told him as calmly as she could. 'I would also administer various nutrients and medications while you were in the coma to aid in the healing process and for your general health.' Doctor Veracruz added.

'Kaiden and I don't want you to go through any more pain. But we do agree that this needs to be done. However, before anything was decided, we wanted to get your opinion,' I said. I stayed holding Levi as I gave him time to process everything he had been told. While Levi thought about everything, Kaiden and I sat patiently and rubbed Levi's hands to help comfort and support him.

I love the feel of his hand in mine, Kaiden said to me.

As do I. His hands are so soft, I replied.

I am so happy that he has let us hold his hands, especially after how he reacted to the news of us being Alphas, Kaiden said and I had to agree with that. When Levi had the panic attack after being told my brother and I were Alphas, I was worried that we might never be able to touch or even be this close to my mate. So being able to hold Levi's hand and being able to touch his face made me very happy. I could feel that both Storm and Shadow were happy about being this close to their mate.

Same but I still think it will take time for him to be truly comfortable with us. But we will give him as much time as he needs, I said and Kaiden nodded at my words. Eventually we were brought out of our conversation by our mate's beautiful, soft voice.

'S-s-so in th-the c-coma, it w-wouldn't h-hurt when they b-break m-my b-bones? And th-the coma w-would help m-me h-heal b-better?' Levi managed to stutter out.

'You would not be hurt when we rebreak and reset your bones. You would be unconscious and I would administer medications to make sure you felt nothing,' Doctor Veracruz explained. Levi looked down and from the slight twitches of his face, I guessed he was talking to his wolf.

I can't wait to know the name of his wolf, Shadow said to Kaiden and I and we both smiled in agreement.

'I-if y-you both think th-this is best and s-so does th-the doctor, th-then I w-will do it,' Levi said before nodding.

'Levi are you sure this is what you want?' Doctor Veracruz said while looking directly at Levi. 'I-I am sc-scared of d-doing it b-but you all s-said i-it was the b-best course, so I w-will d-do it,' Levi said in response.

'Ok. I will go and organise everything that will be needed. I will come back this afternoon to put you into the coma,' Doctor Veracruz said with a soft smile.

'C-can Diomika be here wh-when you do i-it?' Levi asked, a hopeful look on his face.

'Of course, she can. Would you like the Alphas to be here as well or would you like them to wait outside?' Doctor Veracruz asked.

I want to be there when he is put into a coma, Kaiden said to me. I looked at him and I could see the sadness in his eyes. I wanted to be in the room with Levi as well but I knew that it was Levi's decision and I would go with whatever he decided to do. 'I w-would like th-them to b-be here to,' Levi said and Kaiden and I both relaxed.

'Ok. I will be back soon,' Doctor Veracruz said before leaving. A couple of minutes later Diomika came into the room and I noticed Levi relax in her presence.

I can't wait until he is that comfortable with us, Shadow said over mind link.

I can't wait for it either, I replied.

'Doctor Veracruz told me you wanted me here when you were placed into your coma,' I heard Diomika say as I left the mind link.

'Y-yes. I w-was hoping y-you would b-be h-here while th-they d-did it. K-Kyro and K-Kaiden to,' Levi told her.

'I will be here for you no matter what Levi and I know that your mates will as well,' Diomika told him and smiled at her. Goddess I was so glad Levi had her in his life, she was such an amazing person. That afternoon Doctor Veracruz came into the room with a couple of others to place Levi into a coma. When they were done, they took Levi to the operating room where they would be rebreaking and resetting his bones. While Levi was in the operating theatre, Kaiden and I went and sat in a waiting room close by the surgical room.

Chapter 18: Diomika's POV

AFTER LEVI HAD been placed into the coma, I went with Doctor Veracruz and her team to the operating theatre. It was hard being in the operating room while Levi's bones were rebroken but I wanted to be there for my little brother. Once Levi's bones had been rebroken and reset, Doctor Veracruz and I brought Levi back to his room. Once Levi was settled in the room, Doctor Veracruz did a quick exam to make sure nothing had shifted when we moved Levi from the operating theatre to his room, then she excused herself to go and inform the Alphas about the surgery. While she went to inform the Alphas, I sat and watched Levi for a while. Since the first time I met him, I knew he was in pain and I always did my best to ease that pain. Unfortunately, being a lone wolf meant there was only so much I could do for him. I didn't have the benefit of having friends who could help me to protect Levi. I definitely didn't have the benefits that came with being a pack wolf, that is I didn't have an entire pack that would help me to protect Levi. That's one of the reasons I am so grateful towards Alpha Kyro and Alpha Kaiden. They are doing everything they can to help Levi get better and it makes me very happy. Some might say that they are only helping Levi because he is their mate, but I get the sense that even if Levi wasn't their mate, then they would still do everything they could to help him. Alpha Kyro and Alpha Kaiden are wonderful, kind and amazing Alphas, and I am very happy that they are Levi's mates.

I'm so glad that Levi has them in his life now. Hopefully he won't be in any-more pain, my wolf Opal said to me.

Me too. I am glad that he has somewhere he will be safe and happy. We've only known him for a few months but I am very protective of him, I replied.

He is our little brother and no one will mess with our little brother ever again, Opal added, quickly followed by a growl. I chuckled slightly at that, I definitely agreed that I would not let anyone hurt my little brother again. I spent some more time talking with Opal about the things we hoped would happen now that Levi was somewhere safe and now that we had a place to call home. After sitting with Levi for about an hour there was a knock on the door and Alphas Kyro and Kaiden came into the room.

'Alphas,' I said as I stood up and bowed to them.

'Did Doctor Veracruz tell you about the surgery?' I asked the Alphas as they approached the bed.

'She did. She said everything went as planned, that all his bones had all been rebroken and reset correctly. She also said that although his healing factor is low at the moment, his bones appear to be healing as they should be. Doctor Veracruz said that once the healing factor is at a healthier level, it shouldn't take long for them to fully heal,' Kyro explained.

'Doctor Veracruz hopes he will be healed from within a week to two weeks. But it will still be some time before they are stronger,' Kaiden added. I could see the relief in Kyro's and Kaiden's faces when they told me what Doctor Veracruz had told them but their expressions quickly returned to ones of concern.

'Thank you for everything that you have done for Levi, Diomika,' Kyro said kindly.

'There is no need to thank me Alphas. I would do anything to make sure that Levi was safe. I am really glad that he has the both of you. And I know that in time he will be very happy,' I said with a smiled,

'I will leave you now so you can be alone with your mate,' I added.

'Where will you be going?' Kaiden asked as I moved towards the door.

'I will go to my room at the pack house. Tomorrow I will be going back to work and then when school is over, I will go to my apartment to get my things,' I replied.

'We can have some pack members help you with that if you would like,' Kaiden said.

'That would be good, thank you. Would it be possible for them to bring a larger vehicle to help move things? I only have a small car,' I replied.

'Of course. Marcus has a pickup truck so I will ask him to help move your things. I can also have Payton, Cedric, and Tristan help as well,' Kyro told me, 'I will mind link Marcus and the others later and let them know about helping you move. I will have them meet you at your office tomorrow once school is finished,' he added a moment later.

'Thank you, Alphas,' I said before bowing and leaving the room. After I had left Levi's room, I headed out of the pack hospital and headed to my room at the pack house. As I made my way through the pack grounds and then through the pack house, I got a few strange stares from several members of the pack. I didn't worry about the stares or about the pack members doing anything as the Alphas assured me that I was safe here and that they had informed people that there was a lone wolf currently staying in the pack. They had also informed the pack that I was going to become a full member of the pack in the future.

I decided to go for a shower as soon as I got to my room and wash away the stress of the day. I haven't left the pack since Levi was brought in, so I was glad that the Alphas had organised several sets of clothes for me when I first came to the pack. After I had my shower and got changed, I wondered if I should go find the pack kitchen and get something to eat and drink. I hadn't eaten at the pack house yet; I had taken all my meals at the pack hospital's cafeteria.

Let's go to the ground floor, there's got to be a kitchen down there, Opal said. Deciding she was right, I went to the door and opened it up. When I stepped out, I smacked into something hard and fell on my backside.

'Oh, my Goddess. I am so sorry. Please let me help you up,' I heard a voice say as a hand appeared in front of me. I took the hand and when I was standing, I saw a gentleman who appeared to be around the same age as the Alphas. I could feel power coming from the man and it made me wonder who he was.

'My apologies for knocking you over. I am Beta Jaden McCallister but you can call me Jaden,' The man said as he extended his hand to me.

'I am Diomika Lang, I'm a nurse at a school in the neutral territory,' I said as I shook Jaden's hand.

'It's a pleasure to meet you Miss Lang. The Alphas told me you would be joining our pack in the future, so I thought I would come and introduce myself. Also, I thought I would come and see if you were hungry and if you were, I would like to invite you to join me and several others for dinner,' Jaden said politely.

'Actually, I was about to go and search for the kitchen as I was starting to feel hungry,' I replied.

'Well then. if you follow me, I will show you to a dining room upstairs where we can have dinner,' Jaden said with a smile. I followed Jaden as he led the way down the hall, to the stairs and then to the next floor. 'Welcome to the Beta and Gamma floor. The dining room is just this way,' Jaden said when we got to the next floor. We made our way through a beautifully decorated hallway, passing several rooms before coming to a stop in the dining room. In the room there were two gentlemen sitting at the table talking to each other. 'Hey dad, hey Rowan,' Jaden said as we approached them. 'Everyone this is Miss Diomika Lang, she will be joining us for dinner this evening. Miss Lang, this is my father Former Beta Daniel McCallister and my friend, Gamma Rowan Matheson,' Jaden added.

'Miss Lang it is a pleasure to meet you,' Mr McCallister said while extending his hand.

'The pleasure is mine Mr McCallister. Please, call me Diomika,' I said as I shook his hand and then Gamma Rowan's hand.

'Diomika, please call me Rowan,' Gamma Rowan said with a smile.

'Where's everyone else?' Jaden asked his father.

'Your mother, sister, and Tansy are in the kitchen. We were going to help but your mother kicked us out and told us to set the table and then wait for them to finish cooking,' Jaden's dad said with a laugh.

'Ok. I will go and introduce Diomika,' Jaden said before leading me from the dining room and into the nearby kitchen. In the kitchen I saw a middle-aged woman standing in front of the stove while a young girl who looked around 13 or 14 and a young woman around 20 or so dished up several plates of food. 'Hello everyone, this is Diomika Lang. Diomika this is my mother Susan the Former Beta's Mate, my sister Sakura and Gamma's Mate Tansy Baker,' Jaden said, indicating that the woman at the stove was his mother, while the young girl was his sister and the young woman was Tansy. 'Hello Diomika. Will you be joining us for dinner?' Jaden's mother asked politely.

'I will be joining you if that is ok,' I replied.

'It is more than ok. The more the merrier,' Jaden's mother replied. 'Jaden go join your father and Rowan. Diomika why don't you stay here with us girls,' Jaden looked like he was about to protest but a sharp look from his mother cause him to raise his hands in surrender and then leave the room. As soon as Jaden left the room, his mother asked me if I would like to help cut up some bread and I said I would. Once I finished cutting up the bread, I helped Sakura with making some fresh orange juice and fresh apple juice to have with dinner. Once everything was ready and plated up, us girls brought everything out into the dining room and placed it on the dining table. As we ate, I got to know everyone a bit and I also told them about myself. I was surprised at how kind and accepting they were towards me. Some wolves weren't very accepting towards lone wolves like myself, there were some who had even been openly hostile towards me. After dinner was finished, I said goodbye to everyone and then returned to my room. I went to sleep straight away as I wanted to get as much sleep before tomorrow as I could as I knew it was going to be a long day.

The next morning, I was woken up early by a knock on my door. I got out of bed and after stretching, I went and opened the door. Once the door was opened, I saw Marcus Grey standing there with a bag in his hand.

'Good morning Miss Lang. I was asked to give you this bag. It has a change of clothes in it for you,' Marcus said as he handed the bag over.

'Thank you, Mr Grey,' I said as I accepted the bag from him.

'The Alphas spoke with Cedric, Payton, Tristan, and I yesterday and informed us you would be needing assistance in moving your things from your home. They told us that we were to meet you at your office after school has finished to assist you,' Marcus informed me.

'Thank you and thank the others for me,' I responded.

'No need to thank us Miss Lang. Will you be needing a lift to school this morning?' Marcus asked.

'I will need one,' I answered.

'No problem, Miss Lang. I will meet you out the front of the pack house in an hour,' Marcus told me before turning and leaving. Once Marcus had left, I closed the door and went to the bathroom to have a shower. After I finished my shower and getting changed, I gathered up my few belongings and headed downstairs to get something to eat before meeting Marcus out the front of the pack house, he was standing with Tristan. I drove to school with Marcus and Tristan, and once we arrived, I said goodbye to them and headed to my office. I spent the school day treating the various students and staff who were hurt. I also completed some paperwork that had accumulated while I had been away. There was roughly twenty minutes left of the school day when I heard my office door slam open. When I turned around there were five male students standing in front of me. From the way they were standing I could tell they weren't here for a good reason. The auras coming from three of them told me that they were the children of high-ranking wolves.

I don't trust them. Opal said, fear in her voice.

'Can I help you gentlemen with something?' I asked politely, keeping the fear out of my voice when I spoke.

'You can tell us where the little mutt is,' The lead male said. I knew instantly that the wolf was talking about Levi but I didn't let him know that.

'Little Mutt? I don't know who you are talking about. If you aren't here for treatment, I will have to ask you to leave the room,' I answered. Before I could do anything, the lead male rushed at me, grabbed me by the throat, smacked me against the wall and held me there.

'Where the fuck is the little bastard Levi? I know he has come to you before and I know you know where he is. So, you had better tell me where he is before I beat it out of you,' He growled and then punched me in the gut.

'I w-will never t-tell you wh-where h-he is,' I stuttered out as my vision started to blur.

'Let her go,' I heard someone growl out. The boy holding me dropped me to the ground to face the newcomer.

'This doesn't concern you,' The boy holding me said angrily.

'She is with us, so this concerns us. So, I suggest you leave now or did you want a repeat of the last time we met?' The voice growled back. After I took several deep breaths, my vision started coming back and I saw Marcus, Cedric, Payton, and Tristan standing in the doorway. The boy who had held me growled again before he and his friends left the room.

'Miss Lang, are you ok?' Cedric asked as he helped me to stand.

'I am thanks to you four,' I replied, looking between Cedric, Marcus, Payton, and Tristan. 'Anytime Miss Lang. Would you like to go back to the pack and get checked by the doctors?' Marcus asked. I could feel the anger coming from him and the others and it made me feel happy to be part of a pack who were so kind and helpful.

'No. We can go to my place and get my things first. I'll go see a doctor when we back to the pack,' I replied. The four guys nodded and waited as I gathered my things from the office. Once I had my stuff we headed out of the office and to the parking lot.

'We will follow behind you in our cars,' Marcus said before the boys split up between Marcus' and Cedric's cars. I got into my car, which had been left at the school several days ago, and drove out of the parking lot. I led the way to my apartment building and pulled up out the front. 'We brought some boxes to put your belongings into,' Payton said after we all got out of our cars and gathered in front of the building.

'Thank you for that,' I replied. The five of us then grabbed the boxes from Marcus' car and then I led the guys up to my apartment. After directing the guys to pack certain things, I went into my room and packed my personal belongings. After we had finished packing everything, we took the boxes downstairs and split them between Cedric's and my cars. Once the boxes were packed into the two cars, we grabbed my two bookshelves, coffee table and glass cabinet and put them carefully into Marcus' car. My bed and a couple of other cupboards would stay at the apartment, I would purchase some new ones later. After making sure I had everything I was going to take with me, we got into our cars and headed back to the pack. Once we got to the pack house, the guys and several other pack members helped to get my things up to my room and once everything was there, I was left to unpack. Marcus, Payton, Cedric and Tristan offered to help with unpacking but I had told them that I would be alright on my own. As the Alphas had offered me a home of my own, I didn't unpack the majority of my things, instead I just unpacked the things I would be needing more often. Once I had unpacked the necessities, I headed over to the pack hospital to get checked.

'Hello Miss Lang. What brings you here?' A young woman asked me. 'Hello Tansy. I was wanting to see one of the doctors here?' I replied. Tansy went to reply but she stopped and I noticed her checking me over.

'Oh, my Goddess. What happened to your neck?' Tansy asked as she came up to me and gently placed a hand on my neck and checked it. 'Let's get you into one of the rooms and get this checked out,' Tansy said before guiding me towards a nearby room.

'Could you tell me what happened?' she asked as soon as I was sitting on the bed in the room. 'Some students came into my nurse's office at the school and one of them grabbed me by the neck and held me against a wall. Thankfully Marcus, Payton, Cedric, and Tristan came and stopped them in time,' I told Tansy. A moment later, the door to the room opened and an older man walked into the room.

'Who do we have here, Tansy?' the man said as he closed the door and walked over to where I was sitting.

'Doctor this is Nurse Diomika Lang. Diomika this is Doctor Caerwyn Llewellyn,' Tansy replied.

'Nurse Lang, it's a pleasure to meet you,' the man said as he held his hand out to me. 'By the marks on your neck I'm guessing someone grabbed you and held you for a few minutes,' he added after we had shaken hands.

'Yes, I was,' I replied.

'Do you mind if I take a look?' Doctor Llewellyn asked politely and I nodded. Doctor Llewellyn gently checked my neck and a few moments later, he stepped back. 'From what I can see, it looks as though there isn't any permanent damage. But I would like to do a scan, just to make sure,' Doctor Llewellyn told me.

'Of course,' I replied. After I got the scan done, Doctor Llewellyn told me that his guess about no permanent damage was correct and he also told me that the bruising on my neck should be gone in a couple of hours. Once I had finished at the pack hospital, I returned to my room at the pack house and put away some of my things. That evening I had dinner with Beta Jaden, Gamma Rowan, and their families. After dinner I was called into the Alpha's office as Alphas Kyro and Kaiden wished to speak with me in private. They told me they had been informed about the attack and asked how I was doing. I told them that I had been seen to by Tansy and Doctor Llewellyn at the pack hospital and after a scan, I had been given the all clear. Alphas Kyro and Kaiden were glad to hear that I was alright and then they offered me work in the pack hospital again, this time I accepted the offer. The next morning, I met with Doctor Veracruz, who had been told about me coming to work at the pack hospital. We organised my work schedule and once I was finished at the pack hospital, I went to school. I told them that I had a new job offer and then handed in my two weeks' notice. After that was all done, I returned back to the pack, where I decided to spend some time sitting with Levi. Though he was unconscious, I felt comfortable just being near him.

Chapter 19: Kaiden's POV

IT HAD BEEN almost two weeks since Levi was placed into a medically induced coma and I had been finding it difficult to concentrate on my Alpha duties. As it was, I was currently in my office with Kyro, Jaden, and Rowan, trying to go over some pack paperwork. I did my best to focus on the paperwork but unfortunately, I kept finding my mind drift off to think about Levi. 'The guard schedule for the next two weeks has been set and I have a list of supplies that are needed for the pack hospital, nursery, and a list from Miss Gardner of some things she needs for the little ones in her care,' Rowan said, breaking me from my thoughts. He handed me the three supply lists and handed Kyro the guard schedule. I glanced over the three lists I had been handed before turning and addressing my Beta.

'Jaden how is training going?' I asked.

'It's going quite well. There are a group of fourteen youths that have started the warrior training. Ten of the youths wish to become warriors, while the other four do not. These other four wish to perform other roles when they are old enough. But they wish to do the warrior training so they can defend the pack if needed,' Jaden responded. Kyro and I both nodded at the information Jaden told us. All members in our pack were trained to fight but the more intensive warrior training was usually undertaken by those who were to become pack warriors. We didn't usually stop pack members from undertaking the warrior training if they wanted to, unless there were circumstances that might impact their safety, like pregnancy.

'Thank you, guys. We really appreciate everything you have done for us these last couple of weeks,' Kyro said and I nodded in agreement to his words.

'There is no need to thank us. You are our friends and it is our pleasure to help however we can,' Jaden replied. I am so glad that my brother and I are good friends with our Beta and Gamma. And in the last couple of weeks Jaden and Rowan have helped us a lot and for that Kyro and I were very glad.

'How is your mate doing?' Rowan asked. So far, the only ones who knew about Kyro and I being mated to Levi were our parents, Doctor Veracruz, Diomika Lang, Jaden, and Rowan. Everyone else in our pack thought Levi was just an injured wolf that had been brought into our pack for help with his injuries. We hadn't told the pack who he really was as we wanted to wait until he was awake and had time to get used to the pack first.

'He is doing better. Doctor Veracruz said that his bones are all healing correctly and that his other injuries are healing thanks to the nutrients and medications that he has been receiving while in the coma. She says that she will be waking Levi up tomorrow morning,' I said before letting out a sigh. Kyro and I were looking forward to our mate being woken up.

'That's good to hear. Rowan and I will continue to keep an eye on the pack for you tomorrow and for however long you need after that. That way you can be there when your mate wakes up,' Jaden told us.

'Thank you guys. Now, I don't know about you guys but I am starving. Let us go and get something to eat,' Kyro said with a slightly tired smile. We all decided to have something to eat up on the Alpha floor, as we didn't wish to be disturbed. When we entered the kitchen, we found my mother already preparing some food. She already had several bowls filled with different salads sitting on the bench.

'Hey boys, have a seat. I have already cut up some salads to have on tacos and I'm almost done with the mince,' My mother said, smiling at the four of us while continuing to prepare the mince. When she was almost done, she set us guys to work. 'Kyro, Kaiden you two go and set the table. Jaden take the salads and the tacos and put them on the table. Rowan grab some glasses and the drinks out of the fridge and take them to the table,' she said to us. Though we were the Alphas, Beta and Gamma of the pack, none of us argued with my mother. We knew better than that. Just as we were finishing our tasks several people walked into the dining room and took their seats around the table. The group included: my father, my brothers Kingsley, Kaito and Kode, Kingsley's mate Azalea, Jaden's parents and sister, Rowan's mate Tansy, Tansy's brother Benson and Tansy's and Benson's father.

'Hey boys,' My father said to Kyro and I as we sat some dinner ware on the table. 'Hey dad,' Kyro replied.

'How's the food going?' Kode asked, an eager look on his face.

'It's going good little bro,' I said with a chuckle before Kyro and I walked back into the kitchen. 'Is there anything else that needs to be done mum?' I asked my mum.

'No, just finished the mince so everything is done,' She replied. After the mince had been placed into a bowl, mum, Kyro, Jaden, Rowan, and I went out into the dining room. I placed the bowl of mince onto the table and then took my seat beside Kyro. During dinner we passed the food around, each taking a bit of everything we wished.

'Mmm this looks absolutely marvellous, thank you my love,' My father said as he looked at my mother lovingly. He took another bite of his taco and smiled at his mate again.

'Thank you my dear. I am glad that you like it,' My mother said as she blushed at my father's comment and then kissed his cheek.

'Eww,' Whined my youngest brother Kode, causing everyone to laugh.

'That was cute,' Jaden's little sister Sakura said with a blush.

'It's so not cute,' Kode whined again.

'Aww just wait until you find your mate son. You'll change your mind,' My father said with a smirk. Kode just shook his head in response before tucking into his meal.

'How is the young boy in the hospital doing?' My mother asked as we ate, looking at Kyro and I.

'He is doing better. Doctor Veracruz will be waking him up tomorrow,' Kyro said.

'I am glad to hear that. I can't wait to meet the boy and welcome him into the family,' My mother said, giving Kyro and I a soft smile.

'What do you mean, welcome him into the family?' Kaito asked, unaware of Levi being mated to Kyro and I. 'Your brother's have decided to welcome the boy into the pack when he is ready. And this pack is family,' Our mother responded, to which Kaito nodded. As I thought about Levi, I felt a wave of sadness wash over Kyro and I.

What's wrong, my sons? Our mum asked Kyro and I over mind link.

Just worried about our mate mum, Kyro responded.

Your mate will be ok. I have faith that he will wake up and then you three

will live a wonderful life filled with love, Mum told us before adding in a very happy voice. **Hopefully, that love leads to grandbabies one day.** Kyro and I blushed at her words.

It's a bit early to be thinking about pups, mum. We have only just found him and after everything we suspect he has been through it will be a while before he is ready for pups, Kyro told her.

I know that it will be a while before you three are ready for pups. I'm just making sure that you know I am expecting grandbabies from you, she said in her motherly tone. Kyro and I chuckled at my mother's words, causing everyone else to look at us like we were crazy. 'You guys ok?' Jaden asked us.

'We are fine. We just remembered something funny,' I responded with a quick look at my mother, who just smirked at me. After dinner, everyone headed into the lounge room and sat down. Some of us sat on chairs and the rest of us sat on the floor. We sat in silence for a while, during which time I noticed that Rowan and Tansy were giving each other strange looks.

'You two ok over there?' I asked them.

'Huh?' Rowan and Tansy both responded.

'You two seemed a little distracted and I wondered what was up,' I answered. Rowan looked at his mate, who bit her lip and nodded at him.

'We have something to tell everyone,' Rowan announced in a nervous voice.

'What is it son?' my father asked Rowan. Rowan had lost his parents, who were the former Gamma pair, when he was sixteen. He had then become the new Gamma, a role which he had been trained for, though not expecting to take over until he was eighteen. He had struggled at first with balancing his school work, Gamma duties and raising his younger sister Azalea, but my parents had helped him a lot. My parents looked at Rowan as another son and he at them like parents.

'Tansy and I are expecting our first pup,' Rowan said with a proud smile. Everyone was quiet as the news registered with everyone.

'You too?' Kingsley said breaking the silence. His response caused everyone to look at him and Azalea.

'What do you mean, 'you too'?' Our father asked Kingsley, who just gulped and looked at Azalea. Azalea sighed and looked from Kingsley to everyone else.

'We found out this morning that we are expecting our first pup,' Azalea announced.

'Yay!' Tansy squealed out before giving Azalea a hug. The room erupted into cheers for the two expecting couples. It took several minutes before the room had calmed down and we talked about the upcoming additions to the family.

'I'm going to be a grandma,' my mother said, taking both Azalea and Tansy into a hug. 'You girls need anything you tell me, ok? Any questions, just ask,' She told the girls before turning to face Rowan and Kingsley. 'You two better take good care of your mates. If you don't, I will kick both your butts,' Mum said in a stern tone and shooting a serious look at Kingsley and Rowan. Kingsley and Rowan nodded and assured her they would take the best care of their mates.

'I am so happy for you my dear,' Tansy's father said as he hugged his daughter, before turning and hugging Rowan.

'Do you guys have any ideas for names?' Sakura asked.

'Not yet. It's a bit early,' Azalea replied. At that point the ladies all went off to discuss baby things while us guys stayed where we were.

'You two boys are going to have your hands full but you will have our support,' My father said to Kingsley and Rowan.

'Thank you dad,' Kingsley said in response. After a while the ladies returned, saying that they wanted to go shopping. So, the ladies, my father, Kingsley, Rowan, and Tansy's father left to go shopping. While the rest of the guys went on their separate ways, Kyro and I decided to go and spend some time with our mate at the pack hospital. Kyro and I had made sure to spend as much time as we could with our mate every day. Sometimes we would sit quietly while at other times we would talk about the future that we hoped to have together one day. Both of us wanted to have several pups with our beautiful mate. However, the thing we both wanted the most was to make our mate happy and to make sure he knew we loved him. I couldn't wait until Levi woke up tomorrow and we could begin the rest of our lives together, making many happy memories.

CHAPTER 20: KYRO'S POV

GODDESS, I WAS so tired. Kaiden and I had both gone to bed early in an effort to make sure we were well rested for tomorrow but no matter how hard I tried I couldn't get to sleep. Thoughts of Levi filled my mind, I couldn't stop thinking about him being woken up tomorrow. I could sense that Kaiden was also still awake, his excitement and worry flowing through our twin bond. As I laid there thinking about my mate and my brother, I heard my bedroom door open and close. A moment later I felt my bed dip and I turned to see my brother lying there.

'What're you thinking about brother?' Kaiden asked as we laid on my comfortable bed.

'I could feel your excitement and also your worry,' I told him.

'I was just thinking about when we would finally have our beautiful mate in our arms,' Kaiden said and I smiled.

'I can't wait until he is here with us as well. I know that it will take time for him to be comfortable in our arms but it will be well worth the wait,' I said softly. 'I can't wait to formally introduce him to our friends and family. I'm sure they will help us make him feel safe and welcomed,' I added. I am so glad for our wonderful family and friends. I'm especially grateful for Jaden and Rowan. As I lay beside my brother, I recalled Jaden's and Rowan's reactions to finding out Kaiden and I were both mated to Levi.

~ Flashback ~

After Levi had been put into a coma and taken to the operating theatre where his bones were to be rebroken and reset, Kaiden and I went Levi's room on the opposite side of the hospital from the surgical ward. Despite the distance, Kaiden and I could still hear our mate's bones being broken. It was as if it were our bones that were being rebroken. Sometimes the enhanced senses that came with being a werewolf had their downsides. Right now, having enhanced hearing, meant we heard every snap which signified another bone had been rebroken. Kaiden and I both flinched and then struggled ourselves from rushing to our mate's aid. We didn't want to hurt Doctor Veracruz and her team, they were just helping Levi but he was hurting and it was hard to not rip those hurting him apart. Soon our self-restraint ended and when we heard another bone being broken, we both leapt from our seats and rushed towards the door. Just before we reached the door, it opened and Jaden and Rowan walked in. Seeing our tense postures and murderous looks, Jaden quickly turned and locked the door, not that it would stop Kaiden and I if we wanted to get out. Rowan then mind linked the pack and ordered them to stay away from the pack hospital unless it was absolutely necessary. When they were done, Jaden and Rowan carefully approached Kaiden and I and then led us back to our seats and sat us back down. Jaden and Rowan were careful to not do anything to set us off any further than we already were.

'Guys what's wrong?' Rowan had asked, keeping his voice gentle. Kaiden and I say nothing for several minutes, both of us still very tense and angry. Instead, we spent several minutes focusing on steadying our breathing.

'They're breaking his bones. We can hear it; we can feel them breaking,' Kaiden said when we had calmed down slightly.

'They are hurting our mate; we just want to rush in there and rip them apart but we can't because they are helping him,' I added sadly. I could see the confusion in Jaden's and Rowan's faces as they processed what was said.

'Your mate?' Jaden asked in a slightly confused voice.

'Before I say anything, I ask that you please don't judge us harshly,' I said to Jaden and Rowan. 'We would never judge you,' Jaden and Rowan said before nodding. Kaiden grabbed my hand and gave it a gentle squeeze, giving me the strength to tell our friends the truth.

'Levi is our mate. I found out the day we found him at the school and Kaiden found out later on at the hospital. We didn't say anything to anyone as we were worried about what people would think,' I paused for a moment and looked down before I continued talking. 'Kaiden and I have known we were gay from a very young age. We don't care what people think about us being gay, if people had a problem with it then they could go fuck themselves. Our sexuality is just something we wished to keep private. When we found out we were mated to the same person, we were worried. We love Levi and are happy that he is our mate, we are just worried what people would think about two Alphas being mated to the same person,' I could feel the tears in the corner of my eyes as I finished talking and when I looked at Kaiden I saw he had tears in his eyes too. When I turned to face Jaden and Rowan, I saw them exchanging looks with each other.

'We are so glad that you have finally told us about being gay, we've always known that you were. We are happy that you two have found Levi and when he wakes up, we hope that you have a wonderful life filled with love and happiness,' Jaden said kindly. The truth in Jaden's words caused Kaiden and I to break down.

'Hey, easy there,' Jaden said as he and Rowan brought Kaiden and I into a group hug and held us while we cried.

'Whatever you two need, we will be there for you,' Rowan had told Kaiden and I.

~ End of Flashback ~

I felt myself being pulled from the memory by Kaiden shaking my shoulder.
'You ok? You blanked out a bit,' Kaiden asked.
'Sorry, just thinking about the day Jaden and Rowan found out about us being gay and us both being mated to Levi,' I replied. A smiled crossed Kyro's face and I guessed he thought back to that day as well.
'I am so glad that we have such kind and understanding friends,' Kaiden said.
'Me too,' I said before I yawned.
'We should try to sleep now,' Kaiden said with a chuckle.
'Goodnight brother,' I said before closing my eyes and going to sleep.
'Goodnight,' Kaiden replied as I drifted off.

Wake up, come on sleepy head. Wake the bloody hell up. I sat up quickly clutching my head. Shadow decided to wake me up by yelling in my head, which was not the most pleasant feeling in the world.

Ok, ok I'm up. Will you please shut up? I said to my crazy wolf.

I just wanted to make sure we woke up and got to the pack hospital before they woke our mate up, Shadow said with a whine.

They won't wake our mate up until Kaiden and I are there, I replied before turning to wake up Kaiden.

'Kaiden, it's time to wake up,' I said as I gently shook my brother.

'Good morning,' Kaiden replied as he sat up and rubbed the sleep from his eyes.

'Good morning,' I responded.

'You ok? Your face is a little scrunched up,' Kaiden asked.

'Just a little headache. Shadow decided to wake me up by yelling,' I replied while rubbing my forehead.

Hey, I tried waking you up nicely but you didn't respond. Shadow said with a slight huff.

'We should go and have a shower and then have breakfast before we go over to the hospital,' Kaiden said. After we had both done as Kaiden suggested, we left the pack house and headed straight to the hospital. When we got to our mate's room, we saw Doctor Veracruz and Diomika giving Levi an exam.

'How is he doing?' I asked as Kaiden and I walked into the room.

'He is doing well considering. However, he is still underweight, but that will be dealt with when he wakes up. He is also going to have some serious mental health issues from the years of abuse that he suffered. He is going to need you two to help him get through everything,' Doctor Veracruz replied and I saw sadness in her eyes.

'We will be there for him no matter what. We will make sure he has everything he needs to live a wonderful life,' I replied sincerely and without hesitation. Doctor Veracruz and Diomika smiled and nodded at my words.

'I have spoken with Felix about arranging some counselling for Levi. When he is ready, Levi can decide if he wants to talk to Felix or his sister Aurora,' Doctor Veracruz told Kaiden and I. Felix and Aurora were both highly trained psychologists that have helped pack members through the different issues and concerns they may have. I knew that Levi would be safe with either one of them.

Have you noticed that when Cora mentioned Felix, Diomika blushed? I could hear the amusement in Kaiden's voice when he asked about Diomika blushing.

I did notice that actually. I was also amused by Diomika's reaction, though she has only been here for a couple of weeks, she has become important to us because of what she has done for Levi and what she has done to help other pack members. My brother and I chuckled lightly. 'So, Diomika I'm guessing that you've met Doctor Felix Blackwell,' Kaiden asked. Diomika looked away from Kaiden and I but we could still see her blushing deeply.

'Y-yes I have,' Diomika stuttered out, 'H-he is my mate,' My eyes widened in surprise when Diomika mentioned Felix was her mate.

'I am very happy to hear that,' I said and I was, Felix was a wonderful guy and I'm glad that he had finally met his mate.

'Thank you Alpha Kyro,' Diomika said with a smile, before turning and continuing with her exams.

'When do you think you will start waking Levi up?' I asked Doctor Veracruz and Diomika. I was hoping that it was soon as I wanted to see my mate's beautiful eyes.

'I'm hoping to start waking him up in an hour or so. I just want to finish my exam and get the blood test results back before I do,' Doctor Veracruz responded without looking up from the exam she was doing.

'Thank you, both of you, for everything that you have done for our mate,' Kaiden said. We were both very grateful for everything that Doctor Veracruz and Diomika have done for Levi. They had done so much for him over the last couple of weeks, they were very dedicated to ensuring that he would be alright when he woke up.

'Of course, Alpha. It is an honour to help the Luna however we can,' Doctor Veracruz replied. Kaiden and I both smiled when Doctor Veracruz called Levi, Luna. It was something Kaiden and I had yet to discuss, but I knew we were both worried about how the pack would react to a male Luna. It was nice to hear Doctor Veracruz react without malice, instead she seemed to have love and care in her voice when she called Levi, Luna, and I was grateful for that. Doctor Veracruz and Diomika continued their exams and then said goodbye, so they could go and get the results from the other tests they had done. While they did this, Kaiden and I took a seat on either side of Levi's bed and waited until it was time for our mate to be woken up.

CHAPTER 21: KAIDEN'S POV

TEN MINUTES LATER, Doctor Veracruz came in and told Kyro and I that they would be waking Levi up from his coma soon.

I am so happy that we will soon have him with us, Shadow said with a purr.

Mmm, I can't wait to show him the love he deserves, Storm said in agreement. I had to agree with Storm and Shadow, the fact that Levi would soon be awake made me very happy. Kyro and I couldn't wait to show him that we love him and will always protect him. The look on Kyro's face said that he also agreed with our wolves.

'It will be good to see his eyes again. He has such beautiful brown eyes,' I said to my brother who was sitting on the opposite side of Levi's bed.

'They are beautiful indeed,' Kyro replied softly before smiling. I could see that there was something else on Kyro's mind.

'What is wrong Kyro? I can sense something is on your mind,' I said as I reached over to grab one of his hands. My other held onto one of Levi's small hands.

'There is something but it's not the time nor the place for this particular discussion,' Kyro replied and I nodded. I knew that when the time was right, my brother would tell me what he was thinking about. I heard the door opening and saw Doctor Veracruz and Diomika walk into the room.

'Alphas, we are ready to wake your mate,' Doctor Veracruz said to us as Kyro and I stood up from our seats. 'Alphas, if you could please stand to the side of the room while we wake your mate up,' Doctor Veracruz added. Kyro and I nodded and after a quick look at our mate, we moved to the side of the room and watched Doctor Veracruz and Diomika work. 'Ok, we have done everything we need to do, now it is up to him,' Doctor Veracruz said as she and Diomika finished their work.

'How long will it take for him to wake, Doctor?' I asked the two women.

'It varies from person to person. However, I would say it will be anywhere from about an hour to hopefully no more than six hours,' Doctor Veracruz replied in a soft but confident voice, 'We will leave now so that you two can be alone with your mate. I ask that once he does wake up, you contact me immediately so that I can give him an exam. If he hasn't woken up in four hours, I will automatically come back to check him,' Doctor Veracruz added. Once they were finished, Doctor Veracruz and Diomika left the room. Kyro and I then moved to sit back down beside our mate's bed and waited patiently for him to wake up.

'I can't wait to bring you home. I really hope that you enjoy living with us. I think our family will love you very much,' I said to my unconscious mate.

'We will do anything to make sure you are happy my dear mate,' Kyro said to Levi.

I wonder what his wolf looks like. I bet he is absolutely gorgeous, Shadow said to us.

Mmm I wonder what colour fur he has, Storm added shortly afterwards.

No matter what colour fur his wolf has, he will be beautiful, Kyro replied over the mind link. *It will be a fun time, all three of us running through the pack lands in our wolf forms. We can even show him our special place,* I said. There was a special area in the pack grounds that Kyro and I found when we were younger and we continued to go there from time to time in order to relax and unwind.

I think that would be wonderful. We could maybe have a picnic or maybe camp for a couple of days. That way the three of us can get to know each other better, Kyro said in response to my suggestion. Kyro and I then sat in silence, both of us holding one of our mate's hands. Almost two hours after Doctor Veracruz and Diomika had started the process, Levi stirred, causing Kyro and I to become hopeful that he would wake up sometime soon. Our wish was granted twenty minutes after Levi had first started to stir. With a groan, Levi started rubbing his eyes and looking around groggily. After a few minutes Levi's eyes eventually settled on Kyro, before looking over at me.

'Hello beautiful,' I said as I smiled at him and he blushed in response. His blush was the cutest thing I had ever seen.

'How are you feeling little one?' Kyro asked. Levi turned to face Kyro and then answered my brother's question.

'I-I f-feel a little t-tired,' Levi said quietly. That was understandable considering everything that our poor mate had been through.

'Are you in any pain at all? Any at all?' I asked. Levi moved and when he did, he winced, answering my question.

'A l-little bit. M-my stomach is a l-little sore and m-my l-leg as well. B-but it's not as b-bad as I-I've had b-before,' Levi said in his soft voice.

'I will link Doctor Veracruz so she can come and have a look. She can give you something for the pain,' Kyro said as he gave Levi's hand a small squeeze. Five minutes later Doctor Veracruz walked into the room.

'Hello Levi, it is good to see you awake. Kyro told me that your stomach and leg were a little sore. Is it ok if I take a look at them?' Doctor Veracruz asked gently. Levi nodded and then Kyro and I moved out of the way, while Doctor Veracruz gave Levi an exam. 'You are ok considering everything that you have been through. Your body is going through changes from everything that has been done to help you get better. It's just now that you are awake, you are feeling the effects of it. I can give you some medication that will help with the pain. Hopefully in a few days the pain will subside,' Doctor Veracruz said to Levi when she was finished her exam. 'I have some medication for pain here,' Doctor Veracruz said as she grabbed a small vial and a syringe from her pocket. When Levi saw what Doctor Veracruz was holding, he got a look of fear across his face. 'Easy there Levi. I don't wish to hurt you with this syringe, I promise. It won't be put directly into you; I will inject the medication into your IV,' Doctor Veracruz said, quickly moving to calm Levi. 'That's it, just breathe in and out,' Once Levi had calmed down, Doctor Veracruz injected the pain medication into Levi's IV. 'It might take a moment for the medication to start working but that is normal,' Doctor Veracruz told Levi.

'How long will I stay in hospital?' Levi asked Doctor Veracruz.

'I want to keep you here for another night for observations and further tests. But after that you should be able to be released sometime tomorrow afternoon,' She replied before I felt someone mind linking Kyro and I.

I would also like to have him talk to either Felix or Aurora sometime tomorrow if possible. If you could talk to him about that and let me know who he decides to talk to, Doctor Veracruz said to Kyro and I over mind link.

Of course, Doctor. We will talk to him about it in a moment, I said to her.

'I will organise the tests for tomorrow. Don't hesitate to call me if you need anything,' Doctor Veracruz said before leaving the room. After she was gone, Kyro and I took our seats beside Levi's bed once more.

'Levi, there is something that Doctor Veracruz wanted us to talk to you about,' Kyro said to Levi, who became scared and I felt my heart constrict at the sight of his fear.

'There is nothing that you need to worry about my love. Doctor Veracruz wanted to see if you would talk with one of our two pack psychologists tomorrow,' I told Levi in a calm voice.

'W-w-what would th-they do t-to me?' asked Levi, his voice quivering. Kyro and I grabbed his hands and I was surprised but happy, when Levi didn't flinch at our touch.

'They would talk with you and help you to work through everything that has happened to you. Neither of them would force you to speak about anything but they will try and find ways to make you feel more comfortable about opening up to them. We have two psychologists here; they are siblings called Aurora and Felix Blackwell. You are free to speak with whichever one you would like,' I explained. Levi laid back on his bed and closed his eyes and for a moment I thought he had gone to sleep. It wasn't until I saw his face twitching, that I realised he was talking to his inner wolf. Eventually Levi sat back up and looked at Kyro and I.

'I-I will t-talk with th-them,' He said hesitantly.

'Which one would you like to speak with? Aurora and Felix are both very good at their job and are very kind and understanding. You would be safe with either one,' Kyro said but I was sure we both had a fair idea who he would choose to talk with.

'C-could I sp-speak with Auro-rora please?' Levi asked us.

'Of course. I will go and let Doctor Veracruz know that you wish to speak with Aurora,' I said. I understood why Levi would choose Aurora, given everything that he has gone through at the hands of males, he would most likely be uncomfortable around an unfamiliar male. After giving Levi's hand a squeeze, I stood up and went to find Doctor Veracruz. Since I was already going to leave the room to get us something to eat, I had decided I would go speak with Doctor Veracruz in person, instead of mind linking her. I found her in her office typing away on her computer. When I walked into the office, she stopped what she had been doing.

'Alpha, what can I do for you?' she asked as I took a seat in front of her desk.

'Levi has decided to speak with Aurora,' I told Doctor Veracruz.

'I will let her know when I see her later on,' Doctor Veracruz replied.

'As he will hopefully be released tomorrow afternoon, I wanted to ask about meal plans and other things that Kyro and I will need to arrange or know before Levi's release,' I said to Doctor Veracruz.

'Of course. I have one of the other Doctors working on a meal plan for Levi and later today I am going to prepare a list of dos and don'ts for him,' she replied, 'I will have a detailed meal plan, fitness plan and also the list of dos and don'ts ready for you before your mate is released tomorrow. Aurora will most likely have some things for you guys as well,' she added.

'Thank you Doctor,' I said. After nodding to Doctor Veracruz before standing and leaving her office. I then returned to Levi's room where I saw my brother sitting on the bed and holding Levi. The two of them were fast asleep and the sight was so cute that I decided to take a photo. After taking the photo I went and sat down beside the bed and just watched my brother and our mate.

CHAPTER 22: LEVI'S POV

I THINK WE should talk to the lady. After everything we have suffered because of guys, I don't think we would be comfortable with the guy, Alpin said and I quickly agreed.

'C-could I sp-speak with Auro-rora please?' I asked us. I didn't tell them why I chose her instead of her brother but I hoped they would understand my choice and realise that I wouldn't be comfortable around the man.

'Of course. I will go and let Doctor Veracruz know that you wish to speak with Aurora,' Kaiden said before standing up, giving my hand a squeeze.

He has nice hands, I thought to myself. Kaiden gave me a soft smile before he left the room. After he left, I laid back down on my bed with Kyro sitting patiently beside me. I found the silence nice but at the same time it made me nervous. I didn't know what else to do so I started to fidget.

Talk to our mate Levi. Ask him what happens now, Alpin told me.

I don't know if I want to know though, I said in a worried tone.

We need to know Levi. We will be worried until we find out what is going to happen to us, so ask him please. No matter what he says, I will be there for you, Alpin replied. I took several deep breaths trying to work up the courage to speak.

'So wh-what happens n-now?' I asked after I had eventually worked up the courage. I think he had already told me but my memory was a little fuzzy at the moment.

'Well once you are well enough to do so, which is hopefully tomorrow, you will move into the pack house. You will have a room on the Alpha floor,' Kyro replied calmly, I could see a smile playing at his lips.

'The A-Alpha f-floor?' I asked, confused. Why would they have me stay on the Alpha floor. *Maybe they want me closer so I can serve them whenever they need me to,* I said with a whimper.

I don't think that is why Levi. Ask our mate why we are staying there, Alpin said.

'Wh-what would I d-do th-there? Wh-what will m-my duties there be? W-will I sleep on th-the floor?' I asked, scared of what Kyro's response will be. Kyro got a surprised look on his face when he heard my questions and he got a slight edge to his voice when he spoke.

'You will most definitely not be sleeping on the floor. You will have your own room next to Kaiden's and my rooms. You will have a bed, a closet and well anything else you might need. And as for your duties, for now the only things you need to do is rest up, heal and get used to being here. When you are comfortable and ready then we can talk about the duties you will have as the Luna of this pack,' Kyro said before taking several deep breaths before speaking again, 'I'm sorry if I scared you with how I spoke. I was just upset that you would think I would let you sleep on the floor,' I looked down at my hands, ashamed that I had made my mate feel upset because I thought badly of him for a moment. 'I-I'm sorry,' I said to Kyro.

'There is nothing you need to be sorry for. Even though I don't know exactly what you have been through, I understand that you have been through a lot and as such it will take time to get used to Kaiden and I,' Kyro responded. We sat quietly for a moment, before I remembered something that Kyro said just before.

Luna? Oh, my Goddess, Alpin. We are mated to two Alphas which means we will be the Luna; we can't be a Luna. We aren't worthy of being a Luna, we are weak and powerless just like our pack Alpha says, I said to my wolf and I felt tears start to form in my eyes. Seeing me start to panic, Kyro moved to sit on the bed beside me and gently took both my hands in his own.

'Levi, look at me. What is wrong?' Kyro asked me his brow furrowed in concern. 'It is about being the Luna of this pack?' I nodded in response to his questions, not quite trusting myself to speak right now. 'You have nothing to worry about in regards to being Luna. You will not be alone in this; my brother and I are your mates and we will be there for you. And as I said, you won't start any of your Luna duties until you are ready to. Also, I am sure if we ask her, my mother will help teach you about the role of a Luna,' Kyro said happily. Kyro's voice was filled with love and sincerity and when I looked into his eyes, I felt a strange feeling build up within me.

This feeling is strange. I think I am feeling happy with him, I admitted to Alpin.

I feel the same way Levi. I feel happy with both of our mates, Alpin said to me.

'Th-thank you K-Kyro,' I saw Kyro's face light up when I said his name and I blushed. 'Wh-what would my duties as L-Luna be exactly?' I asked glancing back up at Kyro.

'Well, the Luna is the maternal figure of the pack. Some of your duties will be looking after the pack's pups, talking with expectant mothers and being in the delivery room when pups are born. You will also help Kaiden and I with our duties and if needed, you will help calm us down if we became angry. You will be our voice of reason, so to speak. There are other duties a Luna has but my mother is the better one to teach you about what you will be doing. But as I've said, you won't need to worry about any of the Luna duties until you are ready,' Kyro replied, as he talked, Kyro rubbed my hands and it felt wonderful.

'B-but who w-will do th-them if I d-don't?' I asked him. I didn't want this pack to suffer as a result of me being unready to perform the duties as the Luna.

'My mother has been continuing the duties of a Luna until my brother and I found our mate. I am sure that she will be ok with continuing to do so until you are ready to take over from her,' Kyro replied gently.

'O-ok. I-I'm sorry th-that I a-am such a b-bother. I hope the p-pack d-doesn't suffer b-because I'm n-not ready,' I said, dropping my gaze from Kyro to my trembling hands. I could feel the tears dampen my cheeks and I shook while I cried. Kyro wrapped his arms around me and brought me into a hug.

'You are not a bother; you are my mate. I would do anything for you and so would Kaiden. The fact that you are worried about this pack suffering because you aren't ready to take over, tells me you will be a wonderful Luna one day. You are able to think about the needs of this pack and not yourself, just as a Luna should,' Kyro told me and I felt myself cry harder. 'You must be quite tired. Why don't you lay back down and go to sleep?' Kyro said before moving and sitting back on his chair beside my bed. I whimpered when I lost contact with him and he quickly moved back to the bed and wrapped his arms around me.

'P-please d-don't leave m-me,' I said in a soft voice, followed by a whimper.

'I will never leave you my Little Wolf. Go to sleep Little Wolf, I promise that

I will be here when you wake up,' Kyro said before he started humming. I didn't recognise the tune, but it was beautiful and I soon felt myself starting to drift off to sleep. Just before I lost consciousness, I heard the door open and someone enter the room. From the scent, I was able to tell that the person was Kaiden. Soon after Kaiden came into the room, I drifted off to sleep.

CHAPTER 23: LEVI'S POV

IT WAS THE day that I would hopefully be leaving the hospital and moving into the pack house. What if I mess up and my mates don't want me anymore?

Stop thinking like that. We need to give our mates a chance, Alpin said. He had been trying to convince me all morning to give our mates the benefit of the doubt. Alpin has pointed out several times that our mates have done nothing bad to us and so I agreed to do as Alpin said. When I woke up that morning, I was still wrapped in Kyro's arms. It had made me happy to know that Kyro had kept his word and didn't leave me alone. I looked to the side of my bed and I saw my other mate Kaiden asleep in a chair. Kaiden stayed beside me, despite being in an uncomfortable chair. I was sad at the thought of my mate being uncomfortable, but I was also happy that he had stayed. Kyro and Kaiden started stirring, when they woke up, Kaiden got up from the chair and started to stretch. I could feel Kyro shifting under me, so I moved to allow him to get up from the bed. I then waited as both of my mates stretched out the kinks in their bodies.

'Good morning my Little Wolf,' Kyro said after he and his brother finished stretching.

'G-good m-morning,' I said with a blush.

'Are you hungry?' Kaiden asked and my stomach answered for me by growling loudly, which caused my mates to chuckle. 'We will go get some breakfast for the three of us. Are you ok with being here alone for a moment or would you like one of us to stay with you?' Kyro asked kindly.

'I w-will b-be fine on m-my own,' I replied. Kyro and Kaiden each gave me a kiss on the cheek, causing me to blush crimson. My mates then left the room and I took the time alone to speak with Alpin.

What do you truly think about everything that has happened Alpin? I asked my wolf.

I am actually happy that we have found our mates. I thought that if we ever found our mate that they would reject us like our pack said they would. So, when we met Kyro and Kaiden, I was surprised by how kind they have been to us. They don't know about everything that has happened to us but they have been understanding and respectful, Alpin responded. He had a good point; our mates have been good to us and they were very patient. Not once had they raised their voices at me or tried to hit me in any way. Instead, they also speak in kind voices, gently rub my hands and even give me hugs. As I sat there thinking about everything, the door to my room opened and Kyro and Kaiden walked in, both were carrying trays of food and drink.

'We brought some oats and tea for you,' Kyro said as he laid the tray he was carrying on a bedside table and brought it over to my bed.

'What about the two of you? Have you got something to eat for yourselves?' I asked.

'We do have something for ourselves,' Kaiden replied. 'We thought it would be nice to eat together. Also, we didn't want you to feel awkward having us sitting and watching while you ate alone,' Kaiden added as he placed the tray he was carrying onto another bedside table and brought it over to the bed.

'Th-thank you,' I said before giving my mates a soft smile. While the three of us ate our breakfast in a comfortable silence, I noticed my mates would glance at me every couple of seconds. 'S-so what h-happens now?' I asked after I had finished my breakfast.

'Well firstly Doctor Veracruz is going to do a final exam before she hopefully clears you to leave the hospital. After that Doctor Aurora Blackwell will come and talk with you. That is as long as you are still ok with talking to her?' Kaiden replied, while Kyro finished his breakfast. 'I-its ok. Wh-what time w-will Doctor Veracruz b-be coming?' I asked. My mates didn't need to answer as there was a knock on the door and at Kaiden's invitation, the door opened and Doctor Veracruz walked into the room.

'Good morning Levi, Alphas. I see you have eaten something this morning Levi. How was it?' Doctor Veracruz asked with a smile.

'I-it was qu-quite good,' I told her. Alpin and I were both starting to feel more comfortable in her presence and we were definitely starting to like her.

'That's good to hear, I wish my mate was as good a cook as your two mates,' Doctor Veracruz replied and it took me a moment to realise what she had meant.

'Y-you made the b-breakfast?' I asked after turning to face my mates. Kyro and Kaiden both blushed and nodded in response to my question. When they said they were going to get breakfast, I thought it meant that someone else would be making it and they would just be bringing it back. I didn't think that they had meant that they would be the ones who would make the breakfast.

'We did and we are happy that you liked it,' Kaiden said. Kyro and Kaiden then moved the bedside tables over to the side of the room and then stood out of the way while Doctor Veracruz completed her exam.

'Good news. You are well enough to leave today,' Doctor Veracruz said once she was done. 'I have a few forms here that I would like you to take with you when you go. They are a list of foods and drinks that you can and cannot have and also a fitness plan that I would like you to follow. I would like you to stick with these for at least the next couple of weeks, at which point I would like you to come back so I can do a follow up exam and make any necessary alterations to the plans. I will also do a couple of exams before the two weeks is up to make sure everything is progressing as it should be,' Doctor Veracruz said as she handed me a small pile of papers. I looked at the paperwork I was handed and I started getting confused. There was so much information on them that I didn't understand and I started to panic.

'It's ok Levi. Kyro and I will go over both of these with you later on so that we can all know what to do in order to help you get better,' Kaiden said before gently grabbing the papers from me and giving my hand a squeeze. There was a knock on the door and Doctor Veracruz went to answer it.

'Levi this is Doctor Aurora Blackwell. Aurora this is Levi,' Doctor Veracruz said, introducing the woman who just came into the room to me. I took a moment to have a look at the woman who had just come into the room. She had funny looking hair, it was an orangey-red colour at the top, followed by blue and then at the bottom her hair was green. She had tattoos on her chest and arms and wore black pants and a black short sleeved shirt that had a picture of a swan on it.

'Sh-she doesn't l-look l-like a d-d-doctor,' I thought to myself. Everyone started laughing and I realised that I had said my last thought out loud. I had just insulted someone which made me scared, so I brought my legs up to my chest and whimpered. 'I-I'm s-so s-sorry Doctor,' I said before waiting for the inevitable punch to come. To my surprise it didn't happen, instead Doctor Blackwell quickly moved to my side, taking my hands into hers

'There is nothing you need to apologise for Levi. I understand that I may not look like a traditional doctor but I promise that I am one. I find that by being myself, my patients generally feel more comfortable around me and it helps them to open up,' Doctor Blackwell explained. What Doctor Blackwell said made sense and it helped me to relax.

'Now if it's ok, I would like to talk to you for a bit. I would like to speak to you in private without the Alphas present. However, they can wait outside just in case you feel you need them,' Doctor Blackwell told me.

'O-ok,' I replied. With that my mates and Doctor Veracruz left me alone in the room with Doctor Blackwell. Once they had left, Doctor Blackwell took a seat beside my bed in the chair previously occupied by Kyro.

'First off, I don't want you to call me Doctor or Doctor Blackwell or Doctor Aurora or anything else like those. I would like you to simply call me Aurora or Rory, whichever you prefer. Ok?' Aurora said to me.

'O-of course, A-Aurora,' I replied.

'Good, now today we aren't going to get into too much. Today I would just like to get to know you a little bit. then I will talk a little bit about what our future sessions together will be like and then we will set up a schedule for those future sessions. Does that sound alright to you?' Aurora explained. I found myself relaxing while Aurora spoke, to me her personality seemed quite similar to Diomika's.

'I-it sounds o-ok,' I said after realising that Aurora was waiting for me to respond.

'Ok. Well to start with, could you tell me a little about yourself? You can tell me whatever you feel comfortable with sharing,' Aurora said kindly.

'L-like what?' I asked, unsure of what she wanted to know. I wasn't used to people trying to get to know me. Most people I knew didn't care about me.

'Whatever you want to share. Your name, age, likes and dislikes, hobbies, things like that,' Aurora replied. 'If you would like, I can go first,' she added politely.

'Y-yes p-please,' I said; I was actually quite interested in knowing about her.

'Well, my full name is Aurora Miriam Blackwell and I'm 31yrs old. I am a brown wolf and my wolf's name is Lily,' Aurora said and I felt myself smile.

Lily is a beautiful name. I wonder if she would let us see her wolf one day,

Alpin said and I agreed. 'I like to help people and when I'm not doing my work here as a psychologist, you can usually find me either with my mate or at the pack nursery playing with the pups. My favourite colour is purple and my least favourite colour is white as I find it too plain. I also love to watch movies; my favourite movie would have to be Independence Day 1,' Aurora said before she stopped and let me take in everything she had shared.

I could really see us liking her. I wonder if we could be friends one day, Alpin said.

I'm not sure if she would. She probably has friends and probably wouldn't want to be friends with someone like me, I said in response, but Alpin didn't agree.

I think she would like to be friends with us, Alpin told me.

'Are you ok Levi? You spaced out a bit,' Aurora asked me kindly.

'I-I'm ok. J-just talking t-to my w-wolf,' I told her.

'Do you mind if I ask what you talked about?' Aurora asked, 'You don't have to say if you don't wish to,' I bit my lip; I wasn't sure if I should tell her until Alpin encouraged me to do so.

Tell her Levi. I think we can trust her. I feel she's like Diomika, he said.

'W-we both l-liked your w-wolf's n-name and w-wonder if m-maybe we could s-see her one day. We also th-thought you w-would b-be a g-good friend,' I stuttered out. I then waited for her to say that she wouldn't show us her wolf and that she didn't want to be my friend. I braced myself for the shut-down I knew was coming, so was quite surprised by Aurora's response.

'I would love to show you Lily one day. Perhaps once you are better, we might be able to go on a run in our wolf forms together. And as for being friends, after getting to know each other better we can decide on that,' Aurora said and I smiled, while Alpin yipped happily in my head. After a few minutes of silence, I decided to open up to her a bit.

'M-my name is L-Levi Chang and I'm seventeen. I l-like to cook and l-like learning n-new things. M-my favourite colours are b-blue and g-green. My w-wolf's name is…' I started explaining before Alpin stopped me from telling Aurora his name.

No don't tell her. I want our mates to know my name first, Alpin said.

'S-sorry. My w-wolf wants our m-mates to kn-know his n-name first,' I told Aurora.

'That is ok. I completely understand that. If you would like we can talk about our future sessions now,' Aurora said and I nodded. 'Ok, so in our next session we will start off with getting to know each other a bit more. We will talk about any issues you might be experiencing and then in later sessions we will work through those issues. We will do this in several different ways such as simply talking them out, writing them down and even painting out our feelings. If at any time you feel that something isn't working for you, you can tell me and we will try something else. Also, if you need to talk at a time outside of our scheduled sessions you can come to me and we can talk. The only time I won't be able to talk is if I'm with another patient, if that happens, I'll try to talk with you as soon as I finish or if it's an emergency I'll try and see if another of the pack psychologist can talk to you or have them talk to my patient and I'll talk to you,' Aurora took a couple of breaths before she continued to speak, 'As for the scheduling of the future sessions, I would like to see you at least twice a week to start off with. Now these sessions can be either in my office in the pack hospital or they can be at the pack house if that is more comfortable for you. Do you have a preference as the what days you would like to talk and where you would like to talk?' Aurora explained. I thought about what Aurora had said and eventually decided upon when and where I would like to talk.

'C-could we t-talk M-Mondays and Th-Thursdays? And c-could we t-talk in my r-room at th-the pack h-house?' I asked. I felt that if we were in my room at the pack house, I would be more comfortable and I would feel safer.

'Of course. Let me have a quick check to see what times I have free,' Aurora had a quick look at the diary she had on her before looking back at me. 'Does 9am on Mondays and Thursdays at your room at the pack house sound good to you?' Aurora asked.

'Y-yes it d-does,' I replied.

'Well, I will put it into my diary,' She replied. After talking for a few minutes, Aurora stood up and let Kyro and Kaiden back into the room. Then after saying goodbye and promising to see me next Monday at 9am, Aurora left the room.

CHAPTER 24: KYRO'S POV

WHEN KAIDEN AND I had brought food back for Levi, we were both a little upset that we couldn't give him something better than oats. We hoped that it wouldn't be long until Levi could have normal food. Though upset about the food we gave our mate, we were happy that he liked it. When Doctor Veracruz mentioned her mate's cooking, I couldn't help but chuckle. Her mate was definitely not known for his cooking skills; at least not good ones. But he more than made up for his poor cooking skills with his fighting skills. Her mate was Roy Mikhaelson, one of our pack's best warriors. He had saved my life and Kaiden's life on more than one occasion. At least Doctor Veracruz can cook, otherwise the two of them might have been in trouble.

We can cook better though, Kaiden commented as we watched patiently as Doctor Veracruz examined Levi.

What she going to say? I hope she says that he can leave today. I really don't like seeing him in here, Shadow stated, a slight trace of worry in his voice.

He will be ok. He will be ok; he has the best medical team looking after him and he has been improving every day, I told my wolf. I was nervous but I tried my best to keep that from my wolf. Kaiden was also nervous, I could feel his nerves coming from him through our bond. I reached over and grabbed my brother's hand in order to provide comfort to him and myself. **Thank you brother,** Kyro said and I smiled in response. We then turned back to our mate just as Doctor Veracruz had finished her exam. After she had finished her exam and explained her plan for Levi, and Kaiden and I assured Levi, we'd help him through his treatment, there was another knock on the door. Doctor Veracruz walked over and let Doctor Blackwell into the room.

'Levi this is Doctor Aurora Blackwell. Aurora this is Levi,' Doctor Veracruz said, introducing Doctor Blackwell and Levi to each other once the door had closed behind them. I watched as Levi looked Aurora up and down before saying,

'Sh-she doesn't l-look l-like a d-d-doctor,' Everyone laughed at Levi's comment, and then I noticed the look on Levi's face. From his expression, I guessed Levi hadn't realised that he had spoken out loud. When his expression changed to one of fear, I knew he had realised he had done so. When Levi brought his legs up to his chest and whimpered, I felt my heart constrict and heard Shadow whine in my head. 'I-I'm s-so s-sorry Doctor,' Levi stuttered out. By the way he reacted after apologising, I guessed that he was waiting for someone to punish him for insulting Doctor Blackwell. Kaiden and I went to comfort our mate but before we took a step forward, Doctor Blackwell moved to Levi's side and took his hands into hers. Normally a wolf would not like seeing someone else touching their mate but I knew that I had nothing to fear from Doctor Blackwell, she was just trying to comfort my mate.

'There is nothing you need to apologise for Levi. I understand that I may not look like a traditional doctor but I promise that I am one. I find that by being myself, my patients generally feel more comfortable around me and it helps them to open up,' Doctor Blackwell told Levi.

That's true. I remember when I talked to her the first time. I was nervous but when I saw her, I relaxed a fair bit and was able to open up to her, I said to Kaiden.

Same here. I always found it harder to talk to the other pack psychologists that we have had but with her it was much easier, Kaiden responded.

'Now if it's ok, I would like to talk to you for a bit. I would like to speak to you in private without the Alphas present. However, they can wait outside just in case you need them,' Doctor Blackwell said to Levi. I then watched as Levi thought carefully before he responded.

'O-ok,' Levi told Doctor Blackwell. With that Kaiden, Doctor Veracruz and I left Doctor Blackwell and Levi in the room alone. Once outside, Doctor Veracruz excused herself saying that she had other patients that she needed to check on. Kaiden and I decided that we wanted to stay close to our mate's room, so we found some chairs and sat down. We made sure to dampen our hearing so that we did not hear what Levi and Doctor Blackwell talked about. Levi had the right to his own privacy and we did not wish to interfere with that. We would wait until he was ready to open up to us on his own.

Jaden can you bring some clothes to the hospital for me please, I said to Jaden over mind link. I didn't think that Levi would want to keep wearing the same clothes, so some clean clothes to leave the hospital in would probably be a good idea.

Of course, Kyro. Are they for the new Luna? Jaden responded quickly.

Yes, they are for Levi, I replied, before quickly adding, **Ask Kode for a change of his clothes. He is probably the closest in size to Levi.**

Of course. I will be at the hospital soon, Jaden responded before breaking the mind link. Twenty minutes later Jaden showed up outside of Levi's hospital room carrying a bag. 'Hey guys. I spoke to Kode and asked him for some clothes for Levi. I told him that the clothes were for the wolf that you had rescued. Kode wasn't sure what Levi would like so he put a couple of different outfits into the bag. He also put a pair of socks and shoes in there as well,' Jaden said as he handed me the bag.

'Thank you Jaden,' Kaiden said to our friend.

'So, I'm guessing that since you asked for some clothes for him, Doctor Veracruz has said that Luna Levi could leave the hospital today,' Jaden said with a smile.

'Levi has been cleared to leave today,' I responded. 'Just remember until Kaiden and I say so, no one is to refer to Levi as the Luna,'

'Of course,' Jaden replied, 'I am very happy to hear that Levi is leaving the hospital and I know the others who are aware of Levi will be as well,' After saying goodbye, Jaden turned and left the hospital. Once he had left, Kaiden and I sat down, waiting for Levi and Doctor Blackwell to finish talking.

CHAPTER 25: LEVI'S POV

ONCE WE HAD finished talking Aurora stood up and let Kyro and Kaiden back into the room. 'Well I shall say goodbye to you all now. And Levi, I will see you next Monday at 9,' Aurora said with a smile before turning and leaving the room.

'How was your meeting Levi? Did everything go ok?' Kyro asked. I would never tire of hearing his or Kaiden's beautiful voices.

'Y-yes it w-was ok,' I replied, my mates smiling in response.

'What days will you be meeting with Aurora?' Kaiden asked. I bit my lip, unsure if I was allowed to tell them. I wasn't sure if Aurora wanted me to tell the Alphas about what we discussed. I didn't have experience with psychologists and didn't know how they worked. 'We were just wanting to know what days and times you were meeting with Aurora so we can schedule our work around your appointments. We want to be there for you, not in the appointments themselves but nearby just in case you need us,' Kyro explained. Hearing this caused me to relax, it was nice knowing that my mates wanted to be there to support me.

'N-nine am on Mo-Mondays and Th-Thursdays. A-Aurora said w-we could m-meet in m-my room at th-the p-pack house,' I told them.

'Sounds good, we will make a note in our schedules so we don't forget,' Kyro told me. I then looked at the bag that Kyro was holding and wondered what was in it. Kyro must have noticed that I was looking at the bag because he approached and placed the bag on the bed. 'We had our Beta get some clothes for you to change into. We figured you wouldn't want to wear the same clothes all the time. The clothes belong to one of our younger brothers who is roughly the same size as you, so hopefully the clothes will fit,' Kyro said, explaining the presence of the bag.

'Wh-where do I g-get ch-change?' I asked.

'There is a bathroom just over there that you can change in,' Kaiden said as he pointed to a door I hadn't noticed before now. I sat up and then put my legs over the side of the bed, wincing slightly from the pain I felt. I then went to stand but unfortunately my legs were strong enough to hold me up, so I fell down. I was expecting to hit the floor, but thankfully Kyro had fast reflexes and caught me before I did.

'Are you ok?' he asked as he helped me to sit back on the bed. 'Would you like us to help you get to the bathroom?' he added, to which I responded with a nod. Kyro and Kaiden then helped me to stand again and then walked me into the bathroom. Kyro said after he and his brother helped me to sit down on a chair in the bathroom, setting the bag down on the sink next to it. I nodded and then my two mates left the bathroom, closed the bathroom door and waited for me in my hospital room. I opened the bag that was sitting on the sink and noticed there were a lot of nice clean clothes in it. On top of the clothes were a nice pair of black and green sneakers and a pair of white socks.

Wow these are some really nice clothes, Alpin commented.

Yeah, our mates' brother is really lucky to have such nice clothes, I replied as I took the shoes and socks out of the bag and placed them on the sink. I then had a quick look at the clothes in the bag and chose my favourite set. The clothes I had chosen were a pair of black boxers, a pair of dark grey tracksuits and a light green shirt. After taking the clothes I was wearing off and putting them in a pile beside the bag, I carefully got dressed in the outfit I had chosen.

I feel weird Alpin. These clothes are too nice, I said to Alpin.

I know Levi but let's not worry about it ok. Let's enjoy actually having something nice to wear for the first time, Alpin said in response.

I'll try but it still feels weird, I said as I brushed my shirt and pants with my hands as if there was dirt on them. *They are really nice and feel quite comfortable,* I said and Alpin chuckled. Goddess, it was a weird sound to hear, neither of us has had much of a reason to laugh in our life.

Let's get our mates in here before they start to worry about us, Alpin said. I then did as he said and called out for our mates. The two of them came into the bathroom quickly and when they saw me their jaws dropped and they both looked shocked.

'I-is something wr-wrong? D-do I l-look bad?' I asked with a whimper. I felt upset at the thought that I had displeased my mates.

'No,' Kyro said quickly before adding, 'Nothing is wrong. You just look very beautiful and it took us by surprise,' Alpin purred when he heard the Kyro and Kaiden thought we looked beautiful.

Mates think we are beautiful, Alpin said before purring.

'Wh-what h-happens now?' I asked as Kyro helped me walk back to my bed. While Kyro helped me, Kaiden grabbed the clothes I had worn in the hospital and placed them in a laundry basket before grabbing the bag with the other clothes and following Kyro and I out of the bathroom.

'Well now that Doctor Veracruz has cleared you and you have spoken with Aurora, we will be leaving the hospital and head to the pack house. Once there, we will show you the room that will be your bedroom,' Kyro replied.

Finally, we get to leave this room, Alpin said, neither of us minded being here as it was for our benefit. But I honestly don't think anyone liked being confined to one room for too long. 'Seeing as you are still a little wobbly on your feet, would you like us to help you walk or would you like one of us to carry you to the pack house?' Kyro asked me. I loved the fact that my mates were always asking for my opinion on things that concerned me before they did anything.

'C-carry m-me?' I stuttered out before blushing at the thought of being so close to one of my mates. 'Yes, we thought that it might be less stressful on your body but if you don't want to be carried than that's alright. We could probably find a wheelchair around here if you'd rather…' Kaiden replied, chewing his lip.

Let one of them carry us Levi. We don't have the strength to walk to far right now. Beside it will be nice to be in their arms, encouraged Alpin. He loved the idea of being close to our mates and I couldn't deny that I to liked the idea.

'I-it's ok. Th-thank you for off-fering to c-carrying m-me,' I said before Kyro gently picked me up. The three of us then left the room and headed out of the pack hospital. Once outside we headed in what I guessed was the direction of the pack house.

It is quite beautiful here, there is so much colour. And the air, it doesn't smell like pain, misery, and death. It is so fresh and smells like happiness and enjoyment, Alpin noted as we made our way through the pack. Being in a place that smelled like the complete opposite of our old pack was a wonderful experience. As we walked through the pack I took in the sights, we passed several buildings, I could tell some of them were homes for pack members while others I was unsure of their use. As we walked, I also took note of the trees and other plants that I saw along the way. There was so much green and brown, not dreary greens and browns but rather vibrant and happy greens and browns. There were also so many other colours in the other plants that I saw. All this colour was making me feel emotions I never thought I would feel.

I also took note of the smells I could detect as we walked through the pack grounds. I lifted my head a few times to get a better smell of scents that piqued my interest. If my mates noticed me doing this, they didn't say anything instead they kept walking with smiles on their faces.

It's rather quiet isn't it Levi? You would think that there would be pups running around the place and pack members going about their daily lives. Alpin noted. It was strange that as we walked, we hadn't seen a single other person.

'Wh-why is there n-no one around?' I said taking another look around, trying to see if there was anyone I missed.

'We asked everyone to stay away, we thought you would feel more comfortable. We figured it would be best to wait a few days before we introduced you to any of the pack members,' Kaiden said.

'Th-thank you for th-that,' I said and my mates smiled. I was very thankful that my mates were kind enough to think how I would feel. As the three of us continued on our way to the pack house in a comfortable silence, I made sure to take in all the sights, sounds, and scents that I could.

Our mates are so thoughtful, Alpin said with a happy purr.

They are very… I started, in response to Alpin's statement. I didn't finish because we had stopped and in front of us was the biggest house I had ever seen. As I looked at it, I realised that it would be more accurate to call it a mansion rather than a house. 'How m-many people l-live h-here?' I asked, turning my body so I could look at Kyro and Kaiden.

'About half the pack live here. Pack members that have families, live in houses of their own which are spread around the pack grounds,' Kaiden replied before adding, 'Would you like to see inside?' I nodded and smiled, I really wanted to see inside the beautiful pack house. Kaiden smiled and then stepped forward to open the front door. He allowed Kyro and I to go through first before following us in and closing the door behind him. 'This is the main foyer. Here we usually meet with visitors to our pack,' Kyro said as I took in the view. The foyer was lightly but beautifully decorated and I liked what I saw.

'I-its b-beautiful,' I said.

'Thank you. On the ground floor of the pack house there are kitchens, dining rooms, games rooms, lounge rooms, entertainment rooms, libraries and several other rooms which have other uses. We also have Alpha, Beta and Gamma offices on this floor. However, there are more private offices for us, our Beta and our Gamma on the higher levels,' Kaiden explained, pointing out various rooms as we walked through the pack house. We eventually came to a stop in front of a set of doors and I wondered what they led to.

'Y-you have an el-elevator in y-your h-house?' I said questioningly to my mates who chuckled in response.

'We do. Because of the number of floors, it made sense to have a couple of elevators put in. They make it easier to move between each of the floors,' Kaiden explained.

'H-how m-many floors are th-there?' I asked as Kaiden pressed a button. Kaiden was standing in front of the keypad so I was not able to make out the number of floors listed on it.

'Well there is the ground floor, then there are two floors with rooms for pack members, then the Beta and Gamma floor and lastly the top floor is the Alpha floor. So, five floors,' Kyro replied.

'Five floors above ground that is,' Kaiden added, causing me to look at him with a confused expression.

What does he mean by that? Does he mean there are floors underground? I asked Alpin. He didn't answer as he was just as confused as me.

'There are a couple of floors underground. Some under this house and some under several other buildings throughout the pack grounds. We will explain later where they are and what they are used for,' Kyro said when he saw my confusion.

Wow, I can't wait to explore this place. I think we could have a lot of fun, Alpin said to me and I silently chuckled. Just after I finished talking to Alpin, the elevator came to a stop and the doors opened. We stepped out into a small, open foyer like area. On the wall directly opposite the elevator, there were a couple of chairs situated on either side of a small table with a small painting hanging above it. On the wall to the right as you stepped out of the elevator, hung a couple of larger sized paintings, one was a painting of mountains and trees and the other was a painting of several wolves. On the wall to the left as you stepped out of the elevator there was a bookcase filled with books and various trinkets. There was also a staircase beside the elevator and I guessed they led to the lower floors. The area reminded me of the foyer downstairs, in that it too was beautifully decorated. I could only look in wonder at the beauty of this place.

'Welcome to the Alpha floor,' Kaiden said with a slight bow and a sweep of his hand.

CHAPTER 26: KAIDEN'S POV

WHEN WE STEPPED out of the elevators at the Alpha floor, I noticed Levi's eyes open wide and his mouth dropped. Seeing his expression made me happy and I hoped that it was an indication that he would like living here.

'Welcome to the Alpha floor,' I said to him as I bowed slightly and gave a sweep of my hand. I looked at Levi, waiting for him to say something, I saw Kyro smirk at my theatrics.

'It's v-very pretty,' Levi said once he took everything in.

'I'm glad you like it,' Kyro said to him with a smile.

'Would you like us to show you around more or would you like us to show you your room so you can rest?' I asked.

'C-could I l-look around?' Levi asked and I nodded. 'C-could I walk p-please?' he asked while chewing his lip.

Goddess, he has beautiful lips, Storm said to me, Kyro and Shadow.

Mmm, goddess I can't wait to kiss him, Kyro replied. I shook my head, trying not to think about my mate and brother kissing. I heard a chuckle and turned to see Kyro had a big smile on his face, while Levi looked confused.

'D-did I s-say something wr-wrong?' Levi asked.

'No Little Wolf. My brother is just being weird,' Kyro responded and I shook my head at him. 'If you would like to walk you can, but if at any time you need to stop just let us know, ok?' Kyro said as he gently set Levi on his feet. Kyro held onto

Levi's arm the entire time so he wouldn't fall. After putting the bag I was carrying down on a table, I gently grabbed onto Levi's other arm. The three of us then headed down one of the hallways before coming to a stop in our lounge room.

'This is our lounge room. We usually spend time with our family and friends here when we can. We sometimes play games or watch movies,' I said as Levi looked around, 'That is us with our parents and younger brothers. We were seventeen at the time and we went for a picnic at the secluded lake,' I added when I saw Levi looking at the photo above the television. 'I-it l-looks nice th-there,' Levi said.

'If you would like, we can take you there one day,' Kyro told him and he smiled.

'I w-would like th-that,' Levi replied happily.

'Let's continue our tour, shall we?' I said and we headed out of the lounge room. The next room we looked at was the library, followed by the games room, entertainment room and then our office.

Goddess, he is so cute. I love how his eyes light up as he takes everything in, Storm commented as we walked through our suite on the Alpha floor and showed Levi around.

I love it too. It saddens me that this sort of place is such a shock to our mate. However, I am glad that we get to show him a good life, Kyro said to us.

Yeah. It is good to know that he appears to be at least a bit happy being here, I said to Kyro and our wolves. As we continued our tour, Levi would ask questions about each area and Kyro and I would happily answer them. Levi seemed worried at times, probably concerned he would ask something that would offend us. But Kyro and I were quick to assure him that he could ask us anything he wanted and we would do our best to answer him. The next room we came to a stop in was the kitchen.

'This is our kitchen and it's one of our favourite places,' Kyro said to Levi. I could see Levi was going to say something but his stomach chose that moment to make itself heard. I chuckled as his stomach rumbled and so did Kyro. 'Let's get you to a chair and then Kaiden and I will make us all something to eat,' Kyro said with a smile.

'Do you like cauliflower and broccoli soup?' I asked as Kyro and I helped Levi to a chair at the island bench.

'I've n-never tr-tried it b-before,' Levi admitted.

'Well then, we will make it now for you and you can try it,' I replied. Kyro and I then grabbed everything that we would need to make the soup, before getting to work making it. Once we had finished preparing and cooking the soup, we filled three bowls with it and placed them on the island bench.

'Would you like a cup of tea or would you like something else to drink?' I asked Levi.

'C-could I g-get some w-water p-please?' Levi asked.

'Of course,' I replied. I grabbed a glass of water for Levi, Kyro and myself and then joined them at the island bench. The three of us then started eating the soup Kyro and I had made. As we ate, I watched Levi; I was pleased to see the happy expression he had on his face as he ate. **It seems that he likes the soup,** I said to Kyro.

Yep. We will definitely make it for him again, Kyro replied.

'Do you like the soup?' I asked Levi, even though I knew from his facial expressions that he did.

'I d-do. It i-is v-very y-yummy,' he replied as he took another drink. Several minutes later everyone had finished eating, so I took our dishes to the sink.

'Would you like to go sit in the lounge room for a bit?' Kyro asked as I sat back down. Levi nodded, so we all stood up and headed back to the lounge room. Once there, Kyro and I made sure Levi was comfortable on a seat before we sat down on a couple of chairs opposite him. 'How are you feeling about everything Levi?' I asked my mate.

'I d-don't know ex-exactly,' Levi admitted in a worried tone. My heart constricted when I saw the pain that he was in.

'Whatever you are feeling you can tell us. We will never judge you,' I told Levi, trying my best to comfort him. I saw Levi look between Kyro and I, a thoughtful expression on his face. I went to say something but was stopped by Kyro.

Give him a moment to think. He has had a lot happen to him in the last few weeks, Kyro told me and I nodded. We all sat quietly for several minutes before Levi broke the silence with his soft voice.

'I-I am h-happy that I f-found you t-two…' Levi started and I heard both Shadow and Storm howl with joy in mine and Kyro's heads. 'But…' Levi continued, causing my heart to drop. **But. But what? What is wrong? Does he not like us? Does he want to leave?** I said as my anxiety levels rose, causing Storm to try and take control.

Storm calm down. Do not take control. Let our mate tell us what he is feeling, Kyro said, trying to comfort my wolf. While this happened, Levi looked at both Kyro and I with fear in his eyes.

'What is it Levi? No matter what you tell us, I promise that neither of us will hurt you,' Kyro said to our mate.

'I-I'm scared th-that you w-will reject m-me,' Levi admitted with tears in the corner of our eyes, 'I h-have b-been told all m-my life th-that if I e-ever found m-my mate, they would r-reject me. So, I-I'm scared y-you will b-both reject m-me. Especially wh-when you kn-know what's b-been done t-to m-me,' I felt my heart break. What had been done to him his whole life that he's so scared we would reject him because of it? Unable to sit on the couch and see and feel the fear and pain pouring off of him, I got up and moved to kneel in front of Levi and took his hands in mine. Kyro joined me soon after, placing a hand gently on Levi's knee.

'No matter what has happened to you Levi, you are mine and Kyro's mate. I love you for who you are. What has been done to you is not your fault. And when you feel ready to tell us everything, Kyro and I will be here for you with open arms. You have been through a lot but no matter what we will always be there for you,' I poured as much love and affection into my words as I could, hoping Levi would feel the truth in my words.

'Little Wolf. What my brother has said is true. No matter what you tell us, we will always love you for you. Since we first met, you have been a strong wolf. Despite everything that has happened you are still here and we are very proud of you,' Kyro told our mate.

'Y-you love m-me?' Levi stuttered out; confusion written all over his face. Kyro and I blushed at Levi's question, both shocked that we had told him we loved him so soon after meeting him. 'W-we do. I know it is soon but we both love you very much and we would do anything to make sure you are safe and happy,' I admitted to Levi with a smile.

I love him too, please tell him that, Storm said to me.

Me too. I love him too, let him know. We love him and his wolf. tell him, tell him, Shadow urged me, both he and Storm were yipping in mine and Kyro's head.

'Our wolves want us to tell you that they love you as well,' Kyro told Levi who smiled and blushed.

'Wh-what are th-their n-names?' Levi asked us, curiosity written on his face.

He wants to know our names. OMG, he wants to know our names, Storm said with a giggle.

Did you seriously just say OMG. What are you, a teenage girl? I questioned my wolf.

Shut up. Was Storm's only response before he cut the link. Kyro gave me a slight shove, breaking me out of my thoughts.

'Sorry. My wolf was being an idiot,' I told Kyro and Levi.

__Hey I'm not an idiot,__ Storm said. I ignored my wolf's comment and just smiled.

'My wolf is called Shadow and Kaiden's wolf is called Storm,' Kyro told Levi, 'Can we know your wolf's name?' he added. Levi bit his lip and appeared to be talking with his wolf.

'H-his n-name is Alpin,' Levi told us with a blush and looked down.

'That's a beautiful name. We look forward to meeting him in person one day,' I said.

__I bet his wolf is just as beautiful as he is,__ Storm said.

__I agree. I wonder what colour his wolf is,__ Kyro responded.

__That's a good question.__ There are five different types of wolves: grey wolves, red wolves, brown wolves, black wolves and white wolves. There was a pretty much even spread of grey, red, brown, and black wolves in the world. White wolves however are extremely rare. I was thinking that Levi was most likely a grey wolf or red wolf. As an Omega, Levi's wolf would be smaller than most, but once Kyro and I marked Levi and he in turn marked us, Levi's wolf would become the size of a Luna wolf.

CHAPTER 27: LEVI'S POV

HOW CAN THEY** love me? **Just look at me, I'm ugly, I said to Alpin. My mind started racing. Meanwhile, Alpin rambled.

They are so kind and wonderful and amazing and… then my wolf started purring. I didn't understand how anyone, let alone my mates, could ever love me. After being used and abused for pretty much my entire life, I honestly didn't believe I deserved to be loved. ***Stop that right now Levi,*** Alpin growled in a rare show of anger. ***You deserve love just as much as anyone else does,*** he continued, a hint of anger still in his voice.

You remember what Alpha said to us. We are disgusting and we don't deserve love, I replied. Alpha Redmond had told us that so many times and at first, I didn't believe him but after years and years of being told the same thing, I gave in and started believing everything my pack had told me, no matter how much I wanted not to. I wanted to believe my mates could and did love us but it was just very hard to do.

Alpha has probably lied to us about so much, including this. We deserve to be happy with our mates. I want to try to be happy with them, Alpin whimpered.

I'm sorry Alpin. I don't want to upset you, but after everything I just don't know what to believe anymore, I admitted to him and he whimpered again.

Both of my mates looked at me with love in their eyes and I knew that they both meant it when they said that they loved me. One day I hoped to be able to tell them that I loved them to. 'We hope that you will like it here in the pack. I know you may be scared but we really do want you to be happy,' Kyro told me as he and his brother returned to their seats. It would be nice to be happy for a change and I think that being here in this pack with my mates would be the perfect place to be happy.

I just realised something Levi, Alpin said.

What's that Alpin? I asked.

We don't know what pack this is. We have been here for a while but we don't even know what this pack's name is, Alpin said. He was right, we have been here for over two weeks and we didn't even know what the pack was called.

Oh Goddess. For all we know this could be a bad pack. They may like to bring people in, trick them into thinking they are good and then turn around and hurt them, I said before looking between my mates. They didn't seem like bad people. No, they are good people. I want to trust them.

Ask them Levi, Alpin said.

Ask them what? I asked, not understanding what Alpin wanted me to ask.

Ask them where we are, Alpin said in a slightly sarcastic voice. Wait, Alpin spoke sarcastically? He has never spoken sarcastically before.

Shut up. Just ask our mates where we are. Alpin said with a huff. Shaking my head, I looked at my mates and did as Alpin had asked.

'Wh-what pack is th-this?' I asked my mates.

'Oh, my Goddess. I am so sorry. We totally forgot to tell you where you are. We meant to when you first came but with everything that happened it slipped our minds,' Kyro said nervously. He added, 'right, I should actually say which pack this is. We are the Alphas of the Crimson Rose Pack,' Kyro said before chuckling nervously and rubbing the back of his neck.

Oh, my Goddess. Did he seriously just say the Crimson Rose Pack? This is the Crimson Rose Pack. The second largest pack in the world, I said to myself. I have heard of the Crimson Rose Pack several times before. My pack's Alpha had spoken of them before, he never had anything nice to say about them though. He had said that they were evil and that they enjoyed hurting people. I felt scared and looked between my two mates. I couldn't see them being bad people or seeing them hurting others without just cause.

Levi, I don't think we can believe Alpha Redmond. He has hurt us more than anyone else; he beat us, raped us and as I said before he as probably lied to us about so many things. We can't trust anything he has ever told us. Our mates on the other hand, they have been kind, caring, and understanding towards us. They are patient and gentle. For crying out loud they have told us they love us. Something our Alpha said would never happen, Alpin said. He has never said so much in one go before and it shocked me slightly. I could feel myself wanting to start crying again. Alpin was right, there was so much our Alpha had lied about. I didn't know what to believe anymore. *Believe in our mates Levi,* Alpin said gently and I decided that I would do so. I decided to take the chance and trust my mates, after all they have never lied to me yet.

'Would it be alright if we ask which pack you came from?' Kaiden asked. Oh, Goddess. I felt my fear spike, my heart start racing and I struggled to breathe. I was scared to tell my mates where I came from.

'M-m-my pack w-will come af-after me. Th-they will h-hurt me. Or w-worse th-they will h-hurt you. I-I c-can't st-stay here,' I said, feeling the urge to flee the pack. Before I could move however, Kyro and Kaiden came to kneel either side of me, each taking one of my hands into theirs.

'Levi please listen to me. I'm not going to lie; you pack is probably going to come after you,' Kyro said making me realise that I had said my previous words out loud. 'But I promise that if they come after you, Kaiden and I will do everything in our power to protect you. You are our mate and you are the Luna of this pack. We love you and promise to always be there for you. Our pack is strong, it's the second strongest pack in the world. If your pack wants to get to you, they will have to go through us and our pack warriors first and that won't be easy,' Kyro said in a soft and gentle voice, his words making me feel better.

'Now I know you are scared to tell us which pack you are from but we need to know which pack it is so we can better protect you,' Kaiden said once Kyro had finished talking.

I don't want our mates to get hurt because of us. If they got hurt it would be our fault, I whimpered.

Please tell our mates Levi. They can't protect us or themselves if they don't know who is after us, Alpin said in a surprisingly calm voice. I took several deep breaths before I felt that I could talk again.

'I-I am f-from the R-red M-Moon P-pack,' I said and the room became deathly silent until Kyro and Kaiden both let out thundering growls. Their faces went from calm to very angry, their eyes turned gold showing their wolves had taken over and then they clenched their jaws, bared their teeth and snarled loudly. Kyro and Kaiden stood up and moved away from me, or I should say Shadow and Storm moved away from me, as they were the ones in control.

'Those sons of bitches hurt our mate. I am going to rip those fucking bastards into fucking shreds,' Shadow snarled. The anger in his voice scared me and I shrunk as far back in the chair as I could, before bringing my legs up to my chest and hugging them.

'Fucking oath those arseholes are dying, slowly and painfully. I'm not letting them arseholes touch our mate again. He is ours and we will kill anyone who tries to hurt him,' Storm snarled out in agreement. If it wasn't for what they were saying, I would be worried that they were going to hurt me. Though their words made me think they wouldn't hurt me right now, I was still scared of the suffocating anger that was coming off of them.

I'm scared, Alpin. What do I do? I don't know what to do? I said. I started whimpering, though I didn't exactly what I should do right now, I knew that I needed to get out of this room as the anger was suffocating me. I looked around, trying to find somewhere, anywhere to go. Seeing an exit, I bolted out of my seat and headed for it, hearing my mates turn towards me as I did. Storm and Shadow both called out to me but I ignored them and instead focused on trying to find somewhere safe to hide until they calmed down. I eventually found myself in front of the bedroom area. I opened the first set of doors my hands landed on and went straight inside, shutting the door behind me. I took a quick look around the room, it had a black and grey colour scheme. There was a giant bed with a small bedside cupboard situated either side. On the wall directly in front of the bed was a large flat screen tv and hanging from the ceiling was a beautiful chandelier. I was about to admire the room more but I heard footsteps coming closer, so I ran to one of the sets of doors on the other side of the room. When I opened the door, I saw that it was filled with a lot of clothes. *Wow this closet is huge. There are so many clothes in here,* I said to Alpin. I took a quick sniff and quickly realised that the scent in the room was familiar. The room smelled of forest and fire. *Oh, my Goddess. This is Kyro's closet,* I said once I realised why the scent smelled familiar.

It smells so nice in here, Alpin said happily. I went to say something else but my head started to hurt and I suddenly felt tired. Looking around I saw a couch and decided that it would be a good place to take a nap while my mates calmed down. Before laying down on the couch, I took one of the jackets that was hanging up and put it on, taking a sniff as I did, it smelled like Kyro. I then laid down on the couch, quickly falling asleep once the events of the day caught up to me.

CHAPTER 28: KYRO'S POV

'I-I AM F-FROM the R-red M-Moon P-pack,' Levi told us nervously. All of a sudden, the room became very quiet.

Did he just say that he was from the Red Moon Pack? I asked Kaiden, my anger rising.

He did. He said the Red Moon Pack, Kaiden replied, I could hear the anger seeping into his voice. We have both heard of the Red Moon Pack and none of it was good. I looked at Kaiden, he was just as angry as I was to learn about where our mate had come from and after a moment neither of us could keep the anger in and we each released a loud thundering growl. I could feel Shadow fighting to take over and I struggled to rein him in.

Shadow stop. We don't want to scare our mate, I told him but he didn't listen, instead he kept trying to take over.

I am going to kill those fuckers. I'm going to rip them apart and burn their fucking bodies, he said angrily. Eventually I felt myself lose control to my wolf and I slipped to the back of my mind, while Shadow came forward. From the look on Kaiden's face, he too lost control to his wolf.

Shadow's POV:

I am going to kill those fuckers. I'm going to rip them apart and burn their fucking bodies, I said angrily to Kyro before I took control from him. Storm also took control from Kaiden and he turned to look at me. Storm and I snarled before standing up and moving away from our mate. We loved our mate and neither of us wanted to accidently hurt him while we were angry. 'Those sons of bitches hurt our mate. I am going to rip those fucking bastards into fucking shreds,' I snarled out.

'Fucking oath those arseholes are dying, slowly and painfully. I'm not letting them arseholes touch our mate again. He is ours and we will kill anyone who tries to hurt him,' Storm snarled in agreement. I heard a whimper and turned to see my mate sitting on his chair with his legs pulled up to his chest with his arms wrapped around them. He is scared. Why is he scared? I was confused. We loved our mate and would never hurt him so why was he scared right now. Then it hit me. He could probably feel the anger radiating off of Storm and I. I went to try and comfort my mate but he surprised Storm and I by bolting from the room. 'Levi come back,' Storm and I called out together.

Where is mate going? Storm asked.

I don't know, I replied. *Let's follow him. We have to make sure he is ok,* I added. The two of us headed off in the direction our mate went, before we stopping when we heard the elevator ding. Who the hell was coming up here right now? Kyro and Kaiden had told everyone to stay away for a while, so it was strange for someone to be coming here right now. Despite the strong urge to go after our mate, Storm and I headed towards the elevator. When we got there, we saw our parents waiting for us. Our dad had a concerned expression on his face, while our mother wore an annoyed expression on her face and had her arms folded across her chest.

Uh oh. I say to Storm when I see our mother's expression, it was never good when our mother wore that expression.

Uh oh? Seriously, that's all you have to say? Our mother looks annoyed with us and all you can say is uh oh, Storm responded.

'Hey mum, dad. What brings you here?' I asked as calmly as I could, still upset after what my mate had told me.

'Don't you 'hey' me mister,' Mum responded. Oh crap, we are definitely in deep shit.

'What are you boys doing out? What happened with Kyro and Kaiden?' Dad asked as they approached us.

'We were talking to our mate…' Storm started saying before being cut off by our mum.

'Your mate? Where is he?' she asked while looking around.

'Uh, we're not quite sure,' I replied before hurrying to explain further when I saw our parent's concerned expressions. 'We were talking to our mate as I said, when we asked what pack he was from. When he told us, we may have gotten a bit angry and he ran off,'

'You got angry at your mate? Are you insane?' mum asked angrily.

'We didn't get angry at him. We got angry at what he told us and then we took over,' Storm replied. My mum went to step towards us, but our dad stopped her.

'What did he tell you sons?' dad asked calmly. 'He told us which pack he came from,' I replied.

'What pack does he come from?' Our dad asked. I didn't know if I should tell our parents what pack Levi had come from. I was scared of how they would react to the news. 'What pack son?' mum asked as she took one of my hands and one of Storm's hands into her own.

'Red Moon Pack,' I whispered after feeling the calming energy she sent through our bond.

'What was that?' Dad asked. Even with their advanced hearing our parents had trouble hearing what I said.

'He is from the Red Moon Pack,' I repeated. My mum stiffened, while my dad growled lowly at the news about where Levi came from. I could feel my dad getting angrier by the second, thankfully before he did anything, my mum quickly turned and hugged him in order to calm him down.

'We will discuss this matter later. For now, you two need to go to your mate and speak with him. You probably scared him when you growled earlier,' our mum said after she turned to face him.

'Your mother is right. Talk with your mate, explain why you reacted like you did. Do not lie or keep anything from him, you need to be completely truthful. And no matter what happens, do not get angry like you did again. It won't help him open up to you,' our dad told us. 'Actually, it's probably best if Kyro and Kaiden talk with him. So, before you go and find your mate, let them back in control,' he added a moment later. After saying goodbye our parents headed towards their own suite on the Alpha floor. Storm and I stood still for a couple of minutes trying to calm down. Once we were calm enough, Storm and I let Kyro and Kaiden back in control.

Kyro's POV:

I felt Shadow slowly fade to the back of my mind, allowing me back in control. Goddess I hate when that happens.

Sorry Kyro, Shadow whimpered.

It's ok Shadow. We just need to try and not lose control of our anger again, especially in front of our mate, I told my wolf, before turning to face Kaiden. He had a painful look on his face and tears in the corner of his eyes.

'You ok?' I asked my brother gently.

'No, not really,' Kaiden replied with a shake of his head, 'We scared him Kyro. We told him we would be there for him and that we would protect him but instead we scared him,' he added a moment later. I pulled Kaiden into a hug and we just stood there for several minutes, trying to work up the courage to go and speak to Levi.

'We should go and find Levi now,' I said as I stepped back from Kaiden.

'Hopefully, we can get him to talk with us,' Kaiden said, a hint of sadness in his voice. 'I wonder where he hid from us,' Kaiden said as we walked through our suite.

I think I smell him; he seems to be near the bedrooms, Shadow told me. I took a deep breath in, trying to track Levi's scent.

'Wait I think I know where he is,' I said as I followed the scent of my mate, finally coming to a stop in front of my bedroom doors.

'Why would he come here after we scared him?' Kaiden asked, confusion evident in his voice.

'Our scents,' I replied.

'What?' Kaiden asked as he turned to face me.

'He followed our scents, probably unconsciously and they led him to our rooms,' I explained. 'Yeah, that makes sense,' Kaiden replied. Kaiden and I then stood there for a couple of minutes looking at the handles of my bedroom door. I knew we were both worried about what would happen once we went inside and saw our mate. 'I don't know if I can do this,' Kaiden mumbled. 'I don't know if I can either. We scared him and he probably doesn't want to see us again,' I replied honestly. I was ashamed of how I reacted when I learned which pack Levi came from and I didn't know how I was ever going to make it up to my mate.

It wasn't your fault guys. You aren't to blame for what happened, Storm said sadly to Kaiden and I.

Storm's right. You guys aren't to blame. It is our fault, Storm's and mine. We are the ones who took control and scared him. We are to blame for what happened, Shadow added. I looked at Kaiden and then with shaky hands I opened the doors to my bedroom. As soon as we stepped into the room, I closed the doors behind us. When I looked around my room, I couldn't see my mate anywhere. Kaiden tapped my shoulder and when I looked at him, he pointed towards my walk-in closet.

'His scent appears to be coming from your closet,' Kaiden said before walking towards it. I walked over as well and then opened the doors of my closet. Once we walked inside, I saw Levi laying on a small couch to the side. I smiled when I noticed that he had one of my jackets wrapped around him as he slept.

'Oh, my Goddess. He looks so cute,' I said, taking in the view of my mate sleeping while wrapped in my jacket.

'Definitely. Maybe we should move him to a bed where he could be more comfortable,' Kaiden said and I had to agree. Though he looked comfortable, it wouldn't be good for Levi to sleep on the couch for to long.

'I'll go and make room for Levi on my bed, while you get him ready to move,' I said to Kaiden. 'Ok,' Kaiden replied as I left my closet and walked into my bedroom. I quickly grabbed the clothes I had laying on my bed and went and put them in my laundry basket in my personal bathroom. I then grabbed the book I had been reading and placed it back on my bedside cupboard.

You should pull the covers back and fix the pillows, Shadow suggested, a hint of nervousness in his voice.

I will, thank you for the suggestion, I replied. I didn't tell him I was already going to do that. He was already feeling guilty over how he reacted in front of our mate. I wasn't going to make him feel any worse than he already did. Following Shadow's suggestion, I pulled the covers on my bed back and then rearranged my pillows. When I was done, I called out to Kaiden and told him he could bring our mate out. A minute later Kaiden walked out with Levi in his arms. Kaiden gently placed Levi down and then I pulled the covers up and tucked him in. I smiled when I saw that Kaiden hadn't taken my jacket off Levi when he moved him.

'I like seeing him in our clothes,' Kaiden said when he saw what I was looking at.

'Me too,' I said with a smile.

'Should we stay until he wakes up or…' Kaiden asked, leaving his question open. I didn't like the thought of leaving Levi alone but I also worried about how he would react when he eventually woke up.

'We should stay but maybe keep some distance between us and him. He might feel safer when he wakes up if we aren't too close,' I responded. Kaiden nodded and then the two of us moved over to a couch at the side of my room. I don't know how long the two of us sat watching our mate sleep, but eventually the two of us started to drift off. The last thought I had before my eyes closed was 'I hope our mate will talk with us,'

CHAPTER 29: LEVI'S POV

WOW, THIS COUCH is so comfortable, I thought. As I snuggled further into the comfort, I started to think that it didn't feel like I was on the couch any more. I slowly opened my eyes and noticed that I was now on the bed I had seen when I came into this bedroom earlier.

It smells like Kyro, I said after taking a sniff of the sheet and pillows.

This bed is really comfortable and it smells very nice, Alpin responded happily. I sat up slowly and as I did, I noticed that I was still wearing Kyro's jacket that I had put on before I had gone to sleep.

I wonder how we got to the bed. Last thing I remember is falling asleep on the couch, I said slightly confused.

I don't know. Maybe mates moved us, Alpin suggested. Our mates, oh my Goddess. The last time I saw them, they were very angry and I had run away from them. Where are they now? I took another look around the room and saw my mates cuddled up together on a couch. *Aww, they look so cute. Look at them cuddled up together,* Alpin noted happily, I noticed a strange tone when he spoke but decided not to ask about it.

I don't remember seeing that couch when I came in here, I said.

We weren't exactly paying too much attention when we came in, Alpin responded. I'm not sure how much time passed before I noticed Kyro and Kaiden starting to wake up. At first, I was happy to see them but then I remembered what happened the last time I saw them. When my mates noticed that I was awake, they started to move towards the bed, causing me to flinch. I didn't like feeling scared of my mates but I couldn't help it after what had happened. Kyro's and Kaiden's faces fell when I flinched away and I felt ashamed of my reaction to them.

'I'm s-sorry,' I said with a whimper.

'No, you have nothing you need to apologise for. We are the ones that are sorry. Our actions yesterday scared you and for that we cannot apologise enough,' Kyro told me softly, his eyes and the eyes of his brother held sincerity and also something else, pain. A look passed between Kyro and Kaiden, that I couldn't decipher. As I tried to decipher the look, Kyro and Kaiden suddenly knelt near the end of the bed and then bared their necks to me.

What on earth are they doing? I asked Alpin, confused by Kyro's and Kaiden's actions.

I think they are submitting to us, Alpin replied, equally as confused as I was.

Why are they submitting to us? They are Alphas, we are just an Omega, I said. I am so confused right now. Alphas never submit to anyone. It was seen as a sign of weakness. So, an Alpha would never normally choose to submit to another, especially a weak Omega like me.

I don't understand either Levi, Alpin responded. *I don't like seeing them like that,* he added. I had to agree with him on that, it made me really uncomfortable seeing my mates submitting to me. When Kyro and Kaiden made no attempt to move from their position, I rushed off the bed and knelt down in front of them.

'P-please d-don't do th-this. You are Al-Alphas, you d-don't h-have to s-submmit to m-me. I'm n-nothing b-but a l-lowly, p-pathetic O-Omega,' I whimper out before hanging my head. My mates bring me into a hug and I start crying. While I cried, my mates held me, rubbed my back and sent calming energy through the mate bond we share. Several minutes later, we moved away from each other and my mates looked at me.

'You are not a lowly, pathetic Omega. Please never say that about yourself again. You are a strong, wonderful wolf who just happens to be an Omega,' Kyro said as he and Kaiden each took one of my hands.

'He is right Levi. In the short time we have known you, you have been very strong. Not many wolves would be able to go through what you did and survive,' Kaiden added. I couldn't look at either of them, I felt so weak and ashamed of myself.

'W-why would y-you submit t-to me?' I asked softly, knowing that they could still hear me. 'It pained us...' Kyro began, 'When we saw you flinch back from us before and we felt sad knowing we had made you scared of us. We wanted to show you that we meant you no harm. We wanted to show you that we would do anything and everything for you. At first, we couldn't think of anything, but then we realised there was something we could do. We decided to do something an Alpha would never do; we would submit to you. As our mate, you are our equal; it may not feel like it but you are,' Kyro had started to ramble slightly towards the end of his speech and once he was done, he took several deep breaths.

I love them, Levi. I know you may not be able to say it right now but I love them, Alpin admitted. I know I feel strongly about both my mates but he was right about me not being ready to say it yet.

'Why don't we move somewhere more comfortable so we can talk,' Kaiden suggested. I nodded and then Kyro helped me get up from the floor, before we all moved and sat on his bed. My mates made sure I was sitting comfortably against the bed head, propped up against pillows before moving to sit at the end of the bed.

'Firstly, I want to say that our reactions yesterday weren't because of you but rather they were about what you told us,' Kyro said and I could hear the truth in his voice.

'W-why d-did you react l-like y-you did?' I asked looking between both my mates. Both of my mates took deep breaths, exchanged looks and then turned back to face me.

'It is because of which pack you said you came from,' Kaiden told me.

'M-my p-pack?' I asked confused, why would they react that way they did just because I said my pack's name. I know my pack isn't the best but I didn't think my mates would have heard about it. *I am so confused right now Alpin.* I admitted to Alpin.

I am too Levi. It doesn't make any sense. Alpin replied. I looked between my mates, trying to figure out why they were so angry about where I came from.

'There are two main reasons we reacted like we did when you told us which pack you came from. Firstly, your pack has a reputation and I'm sure you know it is not a good one. Your old pack is known for being ruthless and for torturing and killing others for the most ridiculous of reasons,' Kaiden explained.

'Wh-what's the o-other r-reason?' I asked. Kaiden was right, I knew that my pack was horrible and that others would know at least some of what they did, but that didn't stop me from wanting to know the other reason.

'The second and most important reason is that you are our mate. As your mates, it is our duty to love and protect you,' Kyro said with a soft smile.

No matter how many times they say it, it makes very happy hearing them say they love us, Alpin told me and I could feel him smiling.

It does feel nice hearing them say it. They really are amazing and kind people. I feel bad that I flinched away from them, I said. I looked up at both my mates and gave them both a soft smile.

'I hope you can forgive us for how we reacted and I hope that you can give us another chance,' Kyro said as he and Kaiden looked at me with hope filled eyes. When I didn't respond straight away, they both looked down and let out soft whimpers.

Forgive them please, Levi. I don't blame them. Please, please forgive them, Alpin begged me. Without a second thought I threw myself towards my mates and put my arms around the both of them and they quickly wrapped theirs around me.

'I f-forgive y-you. B-both of y-you,' I whispered. I broke down and started crying and soon my mates did as well. It was strange to hear two Alphas crying.

'We probably have a lot more to talk about but I think we should leave it until another time. For now, I think we should go and get something to eat,' Kaiden said as we moved back from each other. When I looked up, I watched Kyro and Kaiden as Kyro and Kaiden wiped the tears from their eyes. Once he was done, Kyro reached over and gently wiped the tears from my eyes.

I think they might need a shower. They kind of smell, Alpin said with a chuckle. When I saw the quizzical looks on Kyro's and Kaiden's faces, I realised that I must have chuckled out loud. 'What is it?' Kaiden asked.

'A-Alpin said y-you m-might n-need a sh-shower, cause y-you sm-smell,' I replied, a little worried about how they would react. I had technically just insulted them and Alphas didn't usually react well to insults. To my surprise, Kyro and Kaiden burst out laughing.

'He has a point, we do smell,' Kyro said, before laughing again. 'Do you mind waiting a moment while Kaiden and I go and shower?' he added once he stopped laughing.

'I-it's ok,' I replied. 'C-can I l-look around p-please? I p-promise to st-stay on th-the Al-Alpha floor,' I asked. I wanted to have a better look around this floor and see what else there was to do.

'Of course you can,' Kaiden responded. After saying see you soon to Kyro, Kaiden and I left the room. We then headed towards Kaiden's room, once there Kaiden said goodbye and then headed into his room.

What should we do now Alpin? I asked Alpin as we stood outside of Kaiden's room.

Maybe look for the kitchen, we are hungry, Alpin replied and my stomach rumbled in agreement. Once I decided where I wanted to go, I headed off in what I hoped was the direction of the kitchen. When I got there, I stopped and smiled. The kitchen looked amazing. Even though I had seen the kitchen before, I hadn't taken a very good look around. This time I took a better look around. The kitchen had a black and white colour scheme. There was a good-sized island bench, shiny appliances, a nice looking stove and many other cool things.

Goddess, I would love to cook in here. It looks so nice, I said to Alpin. I wanted so badly to step into the kitchen but I wasn't sure if I was allowed to do so. I know that my mates said I was ok to look around, but I was still having trouble getting what my old pack drilled into me out of my head. In my old pack I had been told that I was only allowed to enter the kitchen if I was told to cook for someone. A sound to my right caused me to turn and when I did, I saw a woman entering the kitchen from another entry. The woman was Caucasian, looked about forty or so and had brownish-blonde hair.

She's very beautiful, Alpin said and I agreed.

'Can I help you with something little one?' the woman asked. I realised that I must have blanked out while staring at the woman. I quickly shook my head in response, unsure of how else I should respond. 'Are you hungry little one?' she asked.

'I-I am b-but I-I'm n-not s-sure if I-I'm allowed t-to eat,' I replied truthfully.

'What do you mean you aren't sure if you are allowed to eat?' the woman asked, looking quite shocked by my response.

'I-in m-my pack I c-could only eat wh-when g-given permission and th-that wasn't v-very off-t-ten,' I replied before hanging my head, ashamed of my old life.

'How could someone do that to another person? It is absolutely horrible,' she said before slowly approaching me and gently bringing me into a hug. I surprised myself when I didn't flinch at the sudden contact and I surprised myself even more when I actually hugged the woman back. After standing and hugging for a couple of minutes, the woman stepped back and looked at me gently.

'Well, in this pack, you can eat whenever you want to,' she said with a smile. 'Now come sit down while I make you something to eat,' she added, before leading me over to the island bench and had me sit down on one of the stools. As she was about to go and grab the things she would need, I realised that for the next few weeks I had a strict diet that I was to follow. 'U-um M-Miss,' I said quietly.

'What is it young one?' the woman asked politely after turning back to face me.

I like her Levi, Alpin said. ***It feels nice to be near her, she has this presence about her that I just can't explain,*** he added and I had to agree.

'D-doctor V-Veracruz p-put m-me on a d-diet,' I told her.

'I am aware of that. I am going to make some soup for you to have,' the woman replied. The woman's response made me think, who had told her about my diet and why did they do so? I shook my head, deciding to ask her later about who had told her. I then focused on watching the woman gather various ingredients from around the kitchen, before she started preparing the soup. As I watched her cook, I became captivated by her skill. After she had finished making the soup, the woman put some into two bowls, grabbed a couple of spoons and then came and sat down beside me. She placed one of the bowls in front of me and kept the other for herself. I took a sniff of the soup and had to admit that it smelled amazing. I then took a sip of the soup, after which I let out a happy sigh.

Oh, my Goddess, this soup is absolutely amazing. I wish I could cook like this, I said to Alpin who just hummed in agreement. I then continued eating the delicious soup, unable to contain the happy feelings I got from eating it. Once I was done eating, I went to thank the woman but I stopped when I realised, I didn't even know who she was.

'I-if you d-don't mind, c-can I kn-know who y-you are?' I asked the woman.

'Oh, my, I totally forgot to introduce myself. My name is Maevis,' The woman said as she held her hand out to me.

'N-nice to m-meet you M-Maevis. I-I'm Levi,' I said as I took her hand and shook it.

'It is a pleasure to meet you, Levi,' Maevis replied with a smile.

'C-could you t-teach me to c-cook?' I asked after the two of us were both finished eating. I looked down at my hands while I waited for Maevis' response. I was worried she would say no and I didn't want her to see my disappointment if she did.

'Of course, I can. Do you like cooking?' Maevis replied, causing me to look up at her with a big smile.

'Y-yes, j-just not wh-when I was f-forced to b-by my p-pack. I kn-know some b-basics,' I told her.

'Well then my dear Levi, I will gladly teach you. We can even make it a weekly thing if you would like,' Maevis said, which made me quite happy.

'R-really? Y-you would d-do th-that?' I asked and she nodded. I think I shocked her when I suddenly hugged her but she recovered quickly and returned the hug. As we broke apart, I suddenly smelled my mates close by. I quickly turned around just in time to see both of my mates walking into the kitchen and I blushed at the sight.

'Hello mother,' Kyro and Kaiden said at the same time.

'Is there any soup for us?' Kyro asked a moment later.

'Of course, there is. Sit down and I will get you boys some,' Maevis replied. Kyro and Kaiden then sat down on the opposite side of the island bench from me, while Maevis got up and grabbed them some soup.

They called her mother, Alpin noted in a slightly confused tone just after Maevis stood up. His comment made me look between both of my mates and Maevis.

CHAPTER 30: KAIDEN'S POV

AFTER I SHOWERED and dressed, I headed to Kyro's room. Once inside, I saw Kyro sitting on his bed.

'How're you feeling?' I asked as I sat down beside him.

'I'm a little nervous to be honest. I know Levi said that he forgives us but I am still worried that he is still going to be scared of us,' Kyro replied.

'I know, I am too. I don't know how exactly we are going to do it, but we need to focus on making Levi feel safe and comfortable around us,' I replied.

'I think we should go and find Levi; it's been about half an hour since I've seen him and I'm getting restless being away from him,' Kyro said and I quickly agreed. The two of us left the bedroom and when we heard sounds coming from the kitchen, we headed that way. Kyro and I both smiled at the sight we saw when we got to the kitchen. Levi was sitting at the island bench beside my mum, the two of them had empty bowls in front of them. As we walked into the kitchen, Levi turned around to face us with a blush on his face.

'Hello mother,' Kyro and I said at the same time.

'Is there any soup for us?' Kyro asked.

'Of course, there is. Sit down and I will get you boys some,' Mum told us. While mum hopped up and grabbed some soup, Kyro and I took a seat at the island bench. As we sat down, I looked over to Levi who was sitting opposite Kyro.

'What's wrong Levi?' I asked when I saw the confused expression on his face.

'Y-you called h-her mother,' Levi said as our mother placed a bowl of soup in front of Kyro and I.

'Yep, I am the mother of these two knuckle heads,' Mum said as she sat down beside Levi, taking in his shocked expression.

Hahaha, she called you two knuckle heads. Hahaha, Storm said to Kyro and I before laughing.

Hehe yeah, our mum is awesome, Shadow responded.

You two do realise that by calling us knuckle heads, she is also calling you two knuckle heads? I asked the both of them. They just ignored me and continued to laugh so I cut the link. 'Sorry,' I said after being brought out of my thoughts by a loud clap.

'Levi this is our mother and current Luna of the Crimson Rose Pack, Maevis de Luca. Mum this is Levi our mate,' Kyro said, formally introducing Levi and our mother.

'As I said before, it is an absolute pleasure to meet you Levi,' Mum said, holding her hand out to Levi.

'P-pleasure to m-meet you L-Luna de L-Luca,' Levi replied as he shook mum's hand.

'Please Levi, just call me Maevis or mum, whichever you find easier,' Mum replied.

'O-ok M-Maevis,' Levi said and mum smiled and gave him a hug.

Thank you sons, for introducing him to me. I knew who he was but I didn't want to say anything. I wanted you to be the ones to do so, Mum said to Kyro and I over mind link.

'Would the three of you like me to take Levi shopping tomorrow? I'm sure that Levi would like some clothes of his own and also some things for his bedroom,' Mum said as she looked between Levi, Kyro and I.

'M-my bedroom?' Levi asked; he spoke in a confused tone and he wore an equally confused expression. As soon as Levi asked about his bedroom, our mother turned to look at Kyro and I.

'You two haven't showed him his bedroom yet? Where did he sleep last night?' our mother asked, her tone held a hint of annoyance.

'We haven't shown him yet. After we had spoken yesterday, Kaiden and I went to find Levi so we could talk to him. We eventually found him asleep in my walk-in closet. We decided that he would be more comfortable on the bed so we brought him out and put him on my bed. Kaiden and I were tired so we sat down and we fell sleep,' Kyro told mum.

'Tell me you two didn't sleep in the same bed as your mate without his consent,' Mum said, her voice holding a hint of anger.

'No, we didn't,' I said hurriedly wanting to make sure mum knew we would never do as she said. 'We stayed in the same room as Levi but we slept on the couch,' I added. Mum took a few deep breaths to calm herself before nodding.

'Good, I knew I raised you boys to know better,' she responded. 'Now, about taking Levi shopping tomorrow?' I looked over at Levi and saw him looked down at his lap. I then felt a wave of nerves wash over me and from the way he shivered, I knew Kyro felt it to.

'I've n-never b-been shop-ping before,' Levi said and I barely held back my surprise.

Seriously, he has never been shopping before. Goddess, I am hating his old pack more and more, Storm said, his voice held an unusual hint of annoyance in it.

I hate his old pack too. If Levi goes shopping tomorrow, I wish we could go with him, I replied.

Me to but unfortunately, we have a meeting with Alpha Caldwell tomorrow, Kyro replied. I tried to think of a way Levi could go while still being protected at the same time. The shopping centre was in the human town of the neutral territory, which meant that it would be harder to protect him as anyone who went with him wouldn't be able to shift if something happened, they would be forced to remain in human form.

What if we send some of the more experienced warriors with him? They have a good chance of protecting him if something happens, Shadow suggested.

That's a really good idea Shadow, Kyro told his wolf.

Of course, it was. After all it was my idea, Shadow replied smugly. I shook my head and raised my eyebrows at Shadow's antics.

'If you would like to go shopping Levi, you are more than welcome to. We just ask that if you do that you take some of our pack warriors with you for protection. Kyro and I would go with you, however we have a meeting with Alpha Caldwell of the Amber Sky Pack that we must be present at,' I told Levi honestly. I wanted him to know that whatever he chose to do was entirely up to him. I also wanted him to know that Kyro and I would support him as best we can.

'I d-don't have any m-money to g-get stuff,' Levi said as he looked down, shame filling his eyes.

'Don't worry about that Levi, my sons will give you whatever money you need to buy stuff,' Mum said while looking at Kyro and I with a look that dared us to contradict her.

'O-ok. I th-think sh-shopping would b-be nice,' Levi replied.

'Awesome, if we leave at 9am and head straight into the city, we can get a few hours of shopping done,' Mum said before asking, 'Is that ok with everyone?'

'That sounds good,' Kyro replied, I saw him bite his lip and I wondered what else he was thinking about.

'Would you like to have dinner with our family Levi?' Kyro asked after a few minutes of silence.

'Y-your family?' Levi said questioningly. I saw fear in his eyes and my heart broke a little. 'You will be ok with them Levi. I promise that they will love you,' I replied as Kyro and I each reached over to grab one of our mate's hands.

'They are right my son. My husband and other sons will love you a lot,' Mum said, gently rubbing Levi's back.

'O-ok. I w-will meet th-them,' Levi stuttered out.

'Ok. I'll leave you three alone now and will see you at dinner. Don't worry about cooking anything, I will take care of everything. We will have dinner in the dining room in the other suite,' Mum told us before standing up, giving Levi a hug and leaving the kitchen.

'Would you like to see your room?' I asked Levi after mum left.

'Y-yes please,' he replied softly. Kyro and I then grabbed the dishes from the bench, put them into the dishwasher and turned it on.

'If you will follow us, we will show you your bedroom now,' Kyro said as we waited for Levi to hop off of his stool. The three of us then left the kitchen and headed towards the bedrooms. When we came to a stop just outside of Kyro's room, Levi looked at Kyro and I with a quizzical look.

'Wh-why are we h-here? I th-thought this w-was your r-room,' Levi said while looking at Kyro.

'This is my room and the room next to mine is Kaiden's,' Kyro replied, 'Your room is directly across from mine,' he added before he gently turned Levi around. Levi looked at the rooms to his door nervously. I gave Levi a smile before stepping forward and opening the doors to his room. I then held the doors open and allowed Levi to enter first, followed by Kyro and once they were inside, I went in. When I stepped inside, I saw Levi standing there with his eyes wide open and his jaw hanging open.

Aww he looks so cute like that, Shadow commented.

It is pretty nice seeing him look happy, Storm replied. Kyro and I smiled as we watched Levi walk around his new room. Judging by his facial expression, Levi likes his room.

'What do you think of your room?' Kyro asked when Levi turned back to face Kyro and I.

'I-it's beautiful,' Levi replied softly. Kyro smile and then moved towards a set of doors to the side of the room.

'Through these doors is your walk-in closet, there aren't any clothes in there yet but you will have plenty of room for the clothes you get at shopping tomorrow,' he said before moving to another set of doors. 'Through these doors is your bathroom. In there you have a shower, bath, a sink and a toilet. There is also a closet for bathroom supplies in there too,' Kyro and I then waited for as Levi took in everything Kyro had told him, his face changing several times.

'Th-thank you for ev-everything,' Levi eventually stuttered out, a slight blush on his cheeks. *Goddess, I want him so bad. That blush is a turn on,* Storm said. I had to take several deep breaths in order to calm my horny wolf and stop him from jumping Levi, as that would not be a good thing right now.

Goddess, he has a beautiful blush, doesn't he? Kyro said to me privately.

He sure does. Storm just told me and I quote: 'That blush is such a turn on', I told Kyro and I saw him struggle not to laugh.

Shadow just said something similar to me, Kyro chuckled.

What it's, true and he really is cute. But I can wait until he is feeling better and is ready to open up to us, Storm said. I agreed with him on that, I knew that Levi had been through a lot and it would take time for him to heal, but I hoped he knew that Kyro and I would wait as long as he needed. When Levi yawned, I realised that although we haven't done much today, in his condition Levi would be exhausted.

'Are you feeling tired Levi?' Kyro asked our mate.

'A-a l-little,' Levi admitted, after which he does a cute little yawn.

'How about you go for a rest before dinner tonight? While you sleep, Kyro and I go and get you some more clothes. That way you can have a change of clothes for dinner tonight,' I told Levi.

'Th-that sounds o-ok,' Levi replied. Kyro gave me a quick look before turning to face our beautiful mate.

'Is it ok if we give you a hug before we leave?' Kyro asked gently. After Levi nodded his consent, Kyro and I carefully approached him. We then brought him into a hug and we just stood there for several minutes.

'We will leave you to rest now. If you need either one of us just call out to us and we will come straight away,' I said as we stood back. After giving Levi a small bow, Kyro and I turned and left the room.

CHAPTER 31: LEVI'S POV

AFTER KYRO AND Kaiden had left the room, I decided to take a better look around my new bedroom. The first thing I did was look at the bedroom itself; when I had been told that I would have a room of my own, I didn't think that it would be anything like this. The room was coloured in varying shades of brown and grey, there was a large bed against one of the walls with a bedside table on either side. On the wall opposite the bed there was a flat screen tv with a couple of small paintings on either side.

Wow, it is beautiful in here. I can't believe that our mates gave us such a nice room, I said to Alpin.

Yeah. I really like the colour of the room, Alpin replied. He was just as amazed as I was by the room. *Let's have a look at the bathroom now,* Alpin suggested.

Sounds good, I replied as I walked towards the doors that led to my bathroom. When I walked inside, I was amazed by what I saw. It was light and open and was mostly white with some light brown tones throughout. *Wow, a walk-in shower and a large sized bath,* I noted while looking around.

I think they call that a spa bath actually. I remember hearing Luna Phillipa mention it back at our pack once, Alpin responded. I had a look inside the cupboard, it was currently empty but I could see that it could hold a lot of stuff. I then walked around the bathroom, gently running my hand over different things in the room. Everything was so clean and shiny, which was good to see. *Let's have a look at the closet,* Alpin said. I walked out of the bathroom and headed into the walk-in closet. The walk-in closet was huge, and I honestly didn't think that I would need all this space.

I don't think I will need all this space, I said to Alpin honestly. Alpin went to respond but I whatever he was going to say was cut off by me letting out a loud yawn.

Let's go get some sleep before dinner, Alpin suggested.

Ok, I replied before walking out of the walk-in closet and going to the bed. I took my shoes off, placed them beside the bed and pulled back the covers. I then hopped onto the bed, surprised by the softness I felt when I sat down. Shaking my head, I moved to the centre on the bed, pulled back the covers and snuggled into the soft pillows and blankets. Thanks to the bed being very comfortable, it didn't take long for me to start falling asleep and soon all I saw was blackness.

I don't know how long I was asleep for before I was woken up by the sound of knocking. I slowly opened my eyes, stretched gently and then got out of bed. I then headed over to the door and when I opened it, I saw Kyro standing there looking at me with a gentle smile.

'Hello Little Wolf. How are you feeling?' Kyro asked.

'I-I feel g-good,' I replied and I did, nothing like having a rest on a nice, comfortable bed.

'I'm glad to hear that,' Kyro said before showing me a bag he was holding. 'I have some clothes in here for you. There are a couple of different sets in there for you to choose from,' he added as he handed the bag over to me.

'Th-thank you,' I stuttered out, before looking down as I felt my cheeks heat up.

'You are very welcome. I will go now, so that you can get ready in private. There are a couple of bath products in the bag too; a wash cloth, shower gel, and towel. I will be back in about half an hour and then Kaiden and I will take you to dinner with our family,' Kyro told me. Once Kyro had left, I closed my door and headed into my bathroom. Once I was inside my bathroom, I headed straight to the vanity and placed the bag I had been given on it. When I opened the bag, the first thing I did was take the bath products out and walk over to the bath. I placed the towel on the rack near the bath and then placed the shower gel and wash cloth on the edge of the bath. I then turned the bath taps on and while it filled up, I went to choose a change of clothes to wear to dinner with my mates' family. After choosing a set of clothes and making sure the bath was warm enough, I hopped in and lay back in the water.

Oh, my Goddess. This feels so amazing. I wonder if I am allowed to have a bath every day, 'cause it feels very, very good. I feel so relaxed right now, I said to Alpin as I close my eyes and enjoy the feel of the water.

I totally agree with you. We have to ask our mates if we can have a bath every day, Alpin replied with a purr. For several minutes, I simply lay still and enjoyed the calming feeling the water had on me. Eventually I washed myself off and after getting out of the bath, I walked over to the mirror and had a look at myself. I was very thin; you could even see several of my bones sticking out. I also had numerous scars all over my body and I could see a few fading bruises. *I look horrible. How can our mates like us when we look like this?* I whimpered. Alpin's only response was a whimper before he went silent. I shook my head, trying to clear the negative thoughts from my mind. I wanted to try and be as positive as I could for this dinner, I wanted it to go well. I then unhooked the towel from my waist and start drying myself off. After drying off and getting dressed, I packed up the rest of the stuff I was given and put the bag into my walk-in wardrobe. Once I was finished, there was a knock on the door.

'Come in,' I call out softly. The door opened and in walked Kyro and Kaiden, both were dressed very nicely and I had to take a moment to appreciate how sexy they looked.

Hehe you think they are sexy. That's so cute, Alpin said before laughing at me.

Hey, I'm not the only one who thinks they are sexy, you do as well, I said but that didn't stop Alpin from laughing, so I just cut him off. I heard someone clear their throat and when I looked up, I saw Kyro and Kaiden were smiling. I quickly realised that they knew I had been checking them out but thankfully they didn't mention it.

'Hello Levi. How are you feeling?' Kaiden asked me.

'I-I am g-good,' I replied as I saw Kyro and Kaiden both look me up and down, causing me to blush.

'That's good to hear. How was your shower? Did you enjoy it?' Kyro asked.

'A-actually I h-had a bath. It w-was v-very good. I w-wish I c-could have one a-again,' I told them honestly.

'That's good and you can have a bath or shower whenever you want. They are yours to use,' Kyro said to me and I felt myself smile at my mates. I was happy to hear that I could have a bath whenever I wanted.

'Th-thank you,' I told my mates. Kyro went to say something but stopped as his and Kaiden's eyes glazed over. They must be mind linking with someone.

'Mum just linked us to ask where we are so we should get going,' Kaiden said after they came out of the mind link. The three of us then left my bedroom, as the door closed behind us, Kyro and Kaiden held out a hand for me and I took them. We walked through the Alpha floor and eventually passed the elevator.

'W-where are w-we going? I th-thought we w-were having d-dinner wi-with your family,' I asked stopping and looking between my mates.

'We are going to dinner with our family. There are a couple of suites of rooms on the Alpha floor. Kyro and I live in one of the suites and our parents and younger brothers live in another suite,' Kaiden explained as we continued walking. We soon entered another suite on the Alpha floor and continued walking until we came to a stop in a dining room.

'Kyro, Kaiden you guys finally got here,' a young boy said. The boy approached us quickly, causing me to pull away from Kyro and Kaiden as I was scared by the boy. The boy stopped moving when he saw me pull away and he got a confused look on his face.

'Did I do something wrong?' the boy asked me. I couldn't speak as my mind started racing from the fear I felt.

'Are you ok Little Wolf?' Kyro asked as he took a couple of steps closer to me and placed a hand on the side of my face.

'I-I'm ok, he j-just scared m-me a b-bit,' I replied honestly.

'It's ok. I promise you have nothing to fear from him,' Kyro said gently before taking my hand and leading me towards the young boy. When we stopped in front of the boy, several others approached us and stood beside the boy. 'Levi this is our father Former Alpha Denton de Luca and our brothers Kingsley, Kaito, and Kode,' Kaiden said, introducing the guys standing in front of us. 'Everyone this is our beautiful mate, Levi,' Kyro said once Kaiden had stopped talking.

Oh, my Goddess. He called us beautiful. He told them we are his mate, Alpin said happily. 'It is a pleasure to finally meet you in person Levi,' Former Alpha Denton said as he held his hand out to me.

'H-hello F-former Al-Alpha D-Denton,' I stuttered out while shaking his hand. Even though he was the Former Alpha, I could still feel the power radiating off of Denton de Luca.

'Please little one, just call me Denton,' Denton told me, a smile on his face.

'O-ok D-Denton,' I replied with a blush.

He seems quite nice, Alpin noted, to which I agreed. Even though we had just met him, Denton seemed to be nothing like the Alpha of my old pack. Even though he radiated power, Denton seemed kind and understanding, which was a nice change to what I had previously lived with. 'It is nice to meet you, Levi. I'm Kingsley, I am a pack warrior. If you ever need anything, just let me know and I will be happy to help,'

The guy standing next to Denton said, 'This is Kaito and Kode, they go to the same school as you did,' he added, introducing the other two boys. After shaking everyone's hands, a voice called out from the kitchen.

'Boys, is that Levi?' the voice said.

That sounds like, Maevis, Alpin said and I smiled, I really like Maevis. A moment later Maevis walked out of what I had to guess was the kitchen.

'Levi,' Maevis called out as she called out before rushing over to me and bringing me into a hug. 'It's so good to see you again, little one,' she added before taking a step back. There was a slight huff from beside me and I turned to see Kyro and Kaiden both standing there with stunned looks.

'Wow. Hi sons, how are you? It's good to see you again. How was your afternoon?' Kaiden said sarcastically. I would have been worried about his reaction but I noticed the laughter and amusement in his eyes. And realised he was kidding.

'Oh, shush. I see you two all the time. Levi on the other hand is new and he also happens to be a cute young man,' Maevis replied and I blushed hard.

'Now Kaito, Kode you two help me bring everything from the kitchen. Everyone else go and take a seat at the table,' she said, before turning and heading into the kitchen, followed by Kaito and Kode. Kyro and Kaiden directed me to a seat at the dining table, after I had sat down, Kyro and Kaiden sat down on either side of me. Denton sat at the head of the table and Kingsley sat directly opposite me. Maevis, Kaito, and Kode then walked out of the kitchen carrying several dishes. After they put the dishes on the table the three of them sat down; Maevis sat down beside her mate while Kode sat beside Kingsley and Kaito sat at the other end of the table. It took me a moment to notice the young woman who took a seat in between Maevis and Kingsley, when I did notice her, she smiled at me.

'Levi, this is my mate Azalea. Azalea this is Levi, Kyro's and Kaiden's mate,' Kingsley said when he noticed me looking at the young woman.

She is very pretty, I said to Alpin who hummed in agreement.

'It is a pleasure to meet you, Luna Levi. If you ever need anything, I am happy to help,' Azalea said politely, the truth showing in her eyes. I think I am going to like it here, Kyro's and Kaiden's family all seemed like very kind and loving people.

It took me a moment to realise Azalea had called me Luna and when I did realise, I felt myself panic.

'Easy there Levi, just take a deep breath. In and out. That's it,' Kyro said as he gently grabbed my hand and Kaiden rubbed my back.

'I'm so sorry. Did I say something wrong?' Azalea asked.

'N-no you d-didn't,' I told her. 'J-just surprised by y-you calling m-me Luna,' I added. Azalea became confused and then looked between my two mates, seemingly asking for an explanation. 'We told Levi that we would wait to begin his Luna duties until he was ready,' Kyro explained. 'Oh, my apologies Levi,' Azalea said.

'N-no problems,' I told her.

'We were hoping that you would be alright with continuing as Luna until he was ready to take over,' Kaiden said while looking at Maevis.

'Of course,' Maevis replied with a smile. After that we all started eating, a light conversation picking up as we ate. By the end of dinner, I felt quite comfortable around Kyro's and Kaiden's family. Before Kyro, Kaiden, and I headed back to our suite, Azalea asked if it was ok for her to join Maevis and I at shopping the next day and I quickly agreed. Kyro, Kaiden and I then said goodbye to everyone and returned to our suite. We stayed up and talked for a little while before deciding to go to bed.

CHAPTER 32: LEVI'S POV

GODDESS, THIS BED is amazing. I actually feel happy right now, I said to Alpin happily, when I woke the next morning.

I don't want to get up. I'm so comfortable right now, Alpin replied with a purr.

I don't want to either, but we promised to go shopping with Maevis today, I replied with a sigh. I slowly get out of bed, before going into my closet, choose a change of clothes for the day and then head into my bathroom to have a bath. ***Goddess I love this bath. I'm so glad our mates said we can have a bath whenever we want,*** I said enjoying the warm water on my still aching body. As soon as I finished, I got dressed and headed to the kitchen. When I got to the kitchen, I stopped short at the sight in front of me. Kyro was standing in front of the stove stirring a pot, while Kaiden was chopping up some food and then adding it to the pot in front of Kyro. But that was not what had stopped me. It was the fact that the two of them were only wearing a pair of boxers, the rest of them was uncovered.

Holy Moon Goddess, they are sexy. I am liking this sight very much. Mhmmm, Alpin said before letting out a long and happy purr.

Oh, Goddess. Alpin stop, I said before blushing and looking down. Alpin ignored me and continued to ogle our mates while purring. I was brought out of my thoughts by someone clearing their throat. I looked up and saw Kyro and Kaiden staring at me.

'Good morning my love. How are you feeling?' Kyro asked as he placed the pot on the island bench.

'I-I'm ok,' I replied. I kept glancing at my mates, finding it hard to not stare at them when they were shirtless, so I looked down at my shoes. When I glanced up again, I saw Kyro and Kaiden exchange a quick look.

'If it would make you more comfortable, we can go and get dressed,' Kaiden told me.

No, don't let them get dressed. I like what I see in front of me, Alpin purred.

'N-no it's o-ok. I d-don't mind,' I said smiling and I felt my face heat up. Kyro and Kaiden smiled at me and waved me over to the island bench and helped me to sit down.

'We made some soup for breakfast,' Kaiden said as Kyro dished up some soup between three bowls.

'I-it sm-smells nice,' I said honestly as the bowl was placed in front of me.

They smell nice. They look even nicer, Alpin said and I chose to ignore his comment. The three of us then ate our breakfast in a comfortable silence. The only time we talked is when I was asked if I wanted a drink or some more to eat. After we all had a second bowl of soup, Kyro and Kaiden put the dishes into the sink, before coming and sitting back down.

'Th-thank you for b-breakfast. It w-was v-very tasty,' I said as I smiled at my two handsome mates.

'We are glad to h…' Kyro started before his and Kaiden's eyes glazed over. They were silent for a moment before their eyes returned to normal and they looked straight at me. 'Sorry, our mum just linked us. She and Azalea will be on the way over here soon,' Kyro told me.

'We should get dressed before they get here,' Kaiden said with a laugh.

'That's probably a good idea,' Kyro replied. 'Do you mind waiting while we go and get dressed Levi?' he added.

'N-no. I-I'll go sit in th-the l-lounge room,' I replied.

'Sounds good, we will see you soon,' Kaiden said before we all stood up and headed out of the kitchen. While Kyro and Kaiden headed to their bedrooms, I headed to the lounge room.

I'm kind of nervous about going shopping, I said to Alpin as I sat down on the couch.

Me too but Maevis is a really nice person and I think this will be good for us.

I really love our mates and they have been amazing to us, so I really want to give them a chance, Alpin replied.

Yeah. I think I love them too. I'm just worried about telling them and then them turning around and hurting us, I told Alpin honestly.

I am worried about that too but we must try and be brave, Alpin responded before he retreated to the back of my mind. I laid my head back and closed my eyes; waiting for my mates to come back. A couple of minutes later, Kyro and Kaiden walked into the lounge room and sat down on another couch.

'Nothing like a quick shower to wake you up,' Kaiden said with a smile.

'I-I like baths m-more,' I told my mates.

'Baths are pretty good. It's nice to just lay in one and relax after a long day,' Kyro replied. There was a knock on the door to the suite, so Kyro, Kaiden and I headed out to answer it. 'Good morning mum, Azalea,' Kyro said as we opened the door and saw Maevis and Azalea standing there.

'Good morning sons,' Maevis said as she gave me a hug. She was probably one of only two people I felt comfortable hugging, the other being Diomika.

Four people actually. Don't forget out mates, it's nice hugging them as well, Alpin said, correcting me.

They definitely are nice to hug as well, I replied.

'How are you feeling this morning Levi?' Maevis asked as she stepped back from me.

'I-I'm good,' I replied.

'It is good to see you again Levi. Are you looking forward to today?' Azalea asked with a smile.

'I-I am a little nervous, b-but I am l-looking f-forward to shopping w-with you,' I told her truthfully.

'That's understandable. But Luna de Luca and I will be with you and will not let anything happen to you,' Azalea replied.

'Now, now Azalea. What have I told you about calling me Luna de Luca?' Maevis said to Azalea with a smile.

'Sorry mum,' Azalea replied. Maevis smiled at her before we all turned to look at Kyro and Kaiden.

'We've also arranged for several of our best pack warriors to come with you today as protection,' Kyro said as he placed a hand on the small of my back.

'Well let's head downstairs now. I'm sure the warriors are waiting for us,' Maevis said. The five of us turned and headed towards the elevator and once we were all inside, Kyro pressed the button for the ground floor. After exiting the elevator, the five of us headed outside where I saw nine people, eight males and one female, standing in front of three cars. As we walked towards them, the people all stood up straighter and bowed their heads to us.

'Alphas, Luna, Mr Levi, Miss Azalea,' The oldest of the guys said to us.

'Everyone thank you for being here,' Kaiden said as we came to a stop.

'No need to thank us Alpha. It is a pleasure to help however we can,' The guy who had spoken before said.

'Levi, let us introduce everyone,' Kyro said to me before turning and looking at those in front of us. 'These are the brothers Roy, Rick, and Rodger Mikhaelson,' Kyro said, introducing three guys who looked similar. One was the guy who had spoken before, that was Roy.

'This is Victoria Mikhaelson. She and Rick are mates. Next to her is Rajesh and then Lincoln,' Kyro added a moment later. I took a moment to look at the three people Kyro had just introduced. Victoria was a beautiful and strong looking woman; she was standing close to her mate Rick. Rajesh was a shorter looking Indian man who seemed to be about twenty-five or so and Lincoln was an African American guy who seemed to be about the same age as Rajesh. I then turned to look at the final three guys. They were definitely younger than the others, the three seemed to be around my age. They also seemed familiar to me, but I wasn't sure where I had seen them before. 'The last three guys are Marcus, Payton, and Cedric,' Kyro said, introducing the last three guys. Marcus was Caucasian and quite tall; Payton was Native American and also quite tall and Cedric was Asian and was shorter than the other two. I looked between all nine warriors, they all seemed like very capable warriors.

'Everyone you already know my mother and Azalea,' Kaiden said and the warriors all nodded.

'This is Levi. Levi was brought to the pack a couple of weeks ago. When he is ready, he will be joining the pack. For now, he is staying on the Alpha floor with Alpha Kaiden and I,' Kyro told the warriors, before adding, 'My mother and Azalea are taking him shopping today to get some things that he will need. The nine of you will be going with them as bodyguards,' Kyro turned to face me and took one of my hands into his own. 'Levi, you may or may not remember Marcus, Payton, and Cedric,' Kyro said, causing me to look between the three guys I thought were familiar. 'They attend the same school as you. They were the ones who rescued when you were hurt at the school a couple of weeks ago,' he added. My eyes widened, so that's why they were familiar.

'S-sorry I d-didn't fully rec-recognise you,' I said softly.

'It's ok. You were seriously hurt at the time we met, so it is understandable for you not to recognise us,' Cedric said.

'Marcus, Cedric and Payton, we would like the three of you to act as close bodyguards, meaning you three will stay close to Luna de Luca, Levi and Azalea. The rest of you will keep watch from a distance,' Kaiden explained to everyone.

'We will protect them with our lives Alpha,' Roy said. By the looks on everyone's faces they realised who or should I say, *what* I was to Kyro and Kaiden but if they thought it was unusual, they didn't say anything about it.

'Well now that everyone has been introduced, we should get going. Levi you will ride with Azalea and me in my car. The rest of you will split between the other two cars,' Maevis said.

'If I may suggest something Luna Maevis?' Rodger said while taking a step forward.

'Of course, Rodger,' Maevis replied.

'I would like to suggest that one of us ride in the car with the three of you,' Rodger suggested. 'That's actually a good idea,' Kaiden told him. 'As it was your suggestion Rodger, you can ride in the car with them,' he added. While everyone else moved to their cars, Kyro and Kaiden turned to face me.

'We hope you have a wonderful time while you are out today,' Kyro said to me.

'I w-will try,' I replied.

I'm going to miss them, Levi, Alpin whined softly.

'Al-Alpin and I w-will m-miss you,' I said quietly to Kyro and Kaiden. I could feel tears in the corner of my eyes when I looked at my mates.

'Hey come here,' Kyro said as he brought me into a hug, followed by Kaiden who wrapped his arms around us from behind me. 'We will miss you as well Little Wolf. But we will see you when you get back later,' Kyro said softly.

It feels so good being in both of our mates' arms, I said to Alpin.

I love it too. I never want to leave here, Alpin replied. I heard purring and it took me a moment to realise that I was the one who was purring.

'Aww, that's so cute,' Kyro and Kaiden say at the same time. I smiled as Kyro and Kaiden stepped back from me.

'Well, we better let you go before our mum comes over here and smacks us,' Kaiden said with a laugh. The three of us then walk over to the car where Maevis, Azalea and Rodger were waiting.

'Would you like to sit in the front or the back Levi?' Rodger asked me.

'C-could I s-sit in th-the front p-please?' I asked. I had never sat in the front seat of a car before; in fact, I had never been in a car at all.

'Of course, you can sit in the front,' Rodger replied. I turned to face my mates and after saying goodbye to them, I hopped into the front passenger seat of the car. Maevis then hopped into the driver's seat, while Rodger and Azalea hopped into the back of the car. Once everyone was buckled in, Maevis started the car and drove away from the pack house. One of the cars of warriors drove in front of us, while the other car with warriors drove behind us. After leaving the pack territory, we drove for about an hour before we eventually pulled into the car park of a large mall.

CHAPTER 33: KYRO'S POV

KAIDEN AND I stood and watched as our mate and the others drove away from the pack house. We continued watching until they were out of sight and once they were, we turned and headed straight to our office on the Alpha floor.

I miss him already, Shadow whined in my head.

Me too, I want him back with us, Storm agreed.

Easy, you two. He will be back later, I told Storm and Shadow who both whimpered and then retreated to the back of Kaiden's and my heads.

'I'll get the computer and screen set up,' I told Kaiden as I sat behind my desk. While I did that Kaiden gathered some files that we would need for the meeting with Alpha Caldwell.

'I sent Lucas a message and he said he would be online in ten minutes,' Kaiden said as he sat down beside me and placed the files he held onto the desk. I nodded and then linked Jaden and Rowan and told them to come to our office, as we were about to have the meeting with Alpha Caldwell. Ten minutes later Kaiden and I were sitting in front of the screen I had set up with Jaden on my right and Rowan on Kaiden's left. Moments later the screen lit up and the Alpha Lucas Caldwell and his Beta and Gamma appeared on the screen in front of us.

'Alpha Lucas, Beta Samson, Gamma Theo it is a pleasure to meet you again,' I said to the three men on the screen in front of me.

'It is a pleasure to see you to Alpha Kyro, Alpha Kaiden, Beta Jaden, Gamma

Rowan. Let's get this meeting underway,' Alpha Lucas replied. For the next couple of hours, the seven of us finalised the details of the treaty between our two packs and discussed doing a swap of our warriors. The warrior swap was proposed as a way for our packs to learn different techniques that we could use to protect ourselves. We also discussed any other issues we could think of. Just as we were about to end the meeting, we heard a knock coming from Alpha Lucas' end of the screen.

'Come in sweety,' Alpha Lucas called to the person that had knocked on his office door.

'Sorry to interrupt. I was coming to remind you that we are going to meet with the doctor in half an hour,' A woman said in a polite voice.

That must be Luna Sophie, Shadow said. A moment later Luna Sophie came into view on the screen and what we saw surprised Kaiden and I. ***Oh, my Goddess. Luna Sophie had her pup,*** Shadow said. The happiness in his voice was contagious and I couldn't help but smile. Looking either side of me, I could see that Kaiden, Jaden and Rowan were also pleased to see the little pup in Luna Sophie's arms. It didn't take long for the four of us to all say, 'Aww,' I watched as Luna Sophie handed the little pup in her arms over to Alpha Lucas, who blushed as he held his pup. Though the pup was wrapped in a little blanket, I could tell he was beautiful. He had pale skin like his mother, but his hair was like his dad's, brown.

'What a beautiful pup you have there, Alpha Lucas,' I said to the smiling Alpha. It was then that Luna Sophie realised that we were on the screen.

'Oh my. I'm so sorry to interrupt you Alphas, Beta, Gamma,' Luna Sophie said to Kaiden, Jaden, Rowan and I.

'No need to apologise Luna Sophie,' Kaiden replied. 'Who is the little angel in your mate's arms?' Jaden asked Luna Sophie, his voice filled with aww.

'Gentlemen, this is our son Future Alpha Liam Caldwell,' Luna Sophie said, introducing her son before adding, 'I gave birth to him a week ago,'

'Aww. On behalf of myself, my brother and the Crimson Rose Pack, I would like to say congratulations on the birth of your beautiful son,' I said to Alpha Lucas and Luna Sophie.

'Thank you Alpha Kyro. We ask that you don't reveal the news of our son's birth to anyone else just yet. We want to wait until Liam is at least a month old before we announce it to people outside of our pack,' Alpha Lucas said.

'Of course, we will not reveal anything until you say so,' Kaiden promised Alpha Lucas.

'Well, we will let you go so you can spend time with your family,' I said with a smile.

'We will let you know when we will be having a party to announce our son's birth,' Luna Sophie said kindly, before we all said goodbye and ended the video call.

'Their son is so beautiful,' Jaden said with a large smile.

'Yeah, he definitely is,' Kaiden replied.

'In a few months that will be you Rowan,' I said happily to my friend and Gamma.

'I am totally looking forward to my little pup getting here,' Rowan told us with a smile.

'We should go and have a quick bite to eat before training this afternoon,' I said. The three of us stood up, left the office and headed to the kitchen on the Alpha floor. Once we had eaten something, we went to our respective rooms and changed into our workout gear. The four of us then met up at the front of the pack house and then headed to the training field. For the next hour, Kaiden and I spent the next hour training the newest warriors of our pack.

'Ok everyone, one partner will shift into wolf form while the other will remain in human form. You will then spar with each other until one of you surrenders to the other,' Kaiden explained to the warriors in front of us.

'Yes Alpha,' the warriors responded before doing as he told them. The sparing went on for another hour before we call an end to training and all the warriors went on with their day. Jaden, Rowan, Kaiden and I went to our rooms, to shower and change before meeting back up in the lounge room of Kaiden's and my suite.

'What's everyone going to do now?' Jaden asked Kaiden, Rowan and I as we sat down on the couches.

'Tansy and I have an appointment with Doctor Veracruz to check how the pregnancy is going,' Rowan replied.

'I was going to go over to the pack day care and see how things are going there before checking how things are at the hospital,' Kaiden answered. One or both of us generally checked on the day care, pack hospital and other areas of the pack at least twice a week.

'What about you Kyro?' Jaden asked as he turned to face me.

'I was going to go and see Lauryn Gardner and the pups she's looking after,' I replied. It had been a while since either Kaiden or I had visited Lauryn, so I thought that I would do so today. 'I might join you Kyro. I love playing with those pups,' Jaden said with a smile.

'Sounds good. I'm sure the pups would love to see their crazy Beta,' Rowan said with a chuckle.

'Hey you're the one who's crazy. I'm the one who's awesome,' Jaden responded and we all laughed.

Come on, let's go see the pups. It's been too long since we last saw them, Shadow said with a huff.

Ok, ok we'll get going now, I told my wolf. My wolf had always had a soft spot for pups and longed for the day when he would have pups of his own to take care of. Jaden and I met back up at the front of the pack house before heading over to Lauryn's place. It took Jaden and I a couple of minutes to walk from the pack house to Lauryn's place and when we got there, I knocked on the door.

'Alpha Kyro, Beta Jaden what a pleasure to see you both here,' an older woman said as she opened the door.

'Now, now, Lauryn what have we asked you to call us?' I asked with a slight chuckle.

'My apologies Kyro, Jaden,' Lauryn replied with a smile. After inviting us inside, she showed us to the lounge room where six pups were playing with various toys.

'How have you been Lauryn?' Jaden asked after we sat down on a couch.

'I've been ok. Had some bad days but the little ones have helped me to focus and keep going,' Lauryn replied with a sad smile, no doubt thinking about the mate she had lost a few months ago.

'I'm glad the pups are helping you to keep going. If you ever need anything you can call on us,' I told her.

'Thank you Kyro,' Lauryn replied. I am glad that she had the pups to help her through her pain. Some wolves would slowly fade away and die when they lost their mate. The two of us turned to look at Jaden whose attention was on the pups that were playing on the floor in front of us. 'Go on now Jaden. We all know that you want to play with them,' Lauryn said. Jaden quickly moved to the floor to play with the pups. Lauryn and I watched Jaden play with the pups for several minutes before one of the pups started crying. Lauryn picked the pup up and gave him a cuddle, however, the little one didn't settle.

'Kyro, do you mind giving Gabriel a cuddle while I go make him a bottle? Actually, it's almost time for their afternoon feeds. Do you two mind putting them in their bouncers and seats while I make them all a bottle and food?' Lauryn asked.

'Of course, we don't mind at all,' I replied. Lauryn then handed me Gabriel, before going to her kitchen. As soon as he was in my arms Gabriel settled right down and Shadow purred in contentment.

'Jaden can you go and get their bouncers and booster seats from the closet, while I watch the pups,' I said to my Beta. Jaden nodded and then went and grabbed what I had asked him to. When he returned, we put the pups Olivia, Gabriel and Michelle into the bouncers and then put the pups Dean, Nate and Marley into the booster seats. We then spent a couple of minutes making funny faces at them while we waited for Lauryn.

'Could one of you give me a hand to bring the stuff out please?' Lauryn called from the kitchen. Jaden quickly stood up and went to help her and a moment later the two returned, each carrying a tray. The tray Lauryn held had three bottles of milk and three bowls of pureed food on it, while the tray that Jaden held had three bottles of juice and three bowls of fruit chunks on it. 'Ok for Nate, Marley and Dean, we have some juice and chunks of fruit. They will need to be watched to make sure they don't choke,' Lauryn said. 'Do you mind watching them Kyro?' she asked a moment later.

'No, I don't mind at all,' I replied as I took the tray that Lauryn was carrying from her.

'Ok, Jaden if you can give Michelle her food and bottle, I will give Oliva and Gabriel theirs,' Lauryn said as she turned to Jaden, who nodded at her. The two of them then moved in front of the pups they would be feeding, while I moved in front of the pups I was going to look after. 'Hello you little cuties. Are you guys hungry today?' I said happily to the three pups.

'Num nums,' all three pups said as they all made grabby hands.

'Well ok then. What have we got here today?' I said in a funny voice. 'Oh, we have three lovely bottles of juice to drink. And to eat we have some chunks of cucumber, chicken, tomato and cheese. What a yummy meal you have here, I'm a little jealous,' I added, causing the pups to smile and giggle.

Goddess they are so bloody cute, Shadow said happily.

I know what you mean, I replied. For the next twenty minutes I watched the pups eat, helping them when needed but other than that I just sat and watched, making sure they didn't choke. When they were finished, I helped clean them up, while Lauryn and Jaden did the same for the pups they were feeding. After the pups were all cleaned up, Jaden, Lauryn and I put the pups to bed and they fell asleep straight away. Lauryn, Jaden and I then took the dishes into the kitchen and when Lauryn to wash them, Jaden and I stopped her and said that we would do it. 'Thank you both for your help,' Lauryn said as she gave us a hug.

'You are very welcome,' I replied. 'We have to get going now but we will make sure to come again soon,' I added.

'Of course. I look forward to seeing you both again,' Lauryn replied, showing us out. Jaden and I headed to the pack house as soon as we left Lauryn's home. As we walked, I received a mind link from Roy saying that he and the others were almost back, so I picked up the pace. When Jaden and I arrived at the pack house, I saw Kaiden there waiting for us.

'Roy messaged you too?' Kaiden asked as Jaden and I came to a stop.

'Yeah,' I replied. A couple of minutes later, three cars drove up to the pack house and came to a stop. The warriors were the first to exit the lead and follow cars, before Rodger got out of the middle car. My mother and Azalea were the next to exit and then lastly, Levi got out of the car he was in. Kaiden and I moved straight to Levi, stopping just in front of him.

'Hello Little Wolf. How are you feeling? Did you have a good time?' I asked Levi, resisting the urge to take him in my arms. We would have to wait until we revealed who Levi was before we could be open with our affections in public.

'I h-had fun,' Levi said before yawning.

'We got a lot of stuff today. Most of it is in the cars. There are a couple of things that needed to be ordered in but we will get a call when the stuff arrives in store. When that happens, we will go and pick them up,' my mother said.

'Sounds good. Would you like something to…' Kaiden started to say before being cut off by a loud howl.

'Rogues. Mum, Azalea please take Levi and get to the safe room,' Kaiden ordered our mother and Azalea. 'Levi please go with them. We will be back soon. We love you and we will fight to get back to you,' I said to Levi, putting as much love into my voice as I could. The threat of rogues caused me to ignore my previous plan to restrict public displays of affection.

'P-please be s-safe. I d-don't want t-to lose y-you,' Levi said with a whimper. Kaiden and I gave Levi a quick hug before our mother grabbed his hand and then she and Azalea escorted Levi into the pack house. One of the entrances to the safe room was located within the pack house and I knew that mum and Azalea would get Levi there safely.

'Rodger, Lincoln, Rajesh and Rick, the four of you head to Lauryn's place and make sure she and the pups get to the safe room,' Kaiden ordered four of the warriors in front of us. Once the four warriors had left, Kaiden, the other warriors and I went to fight the rogues.

CHAPTER 34: LEVI'S POV

AS WE LEFT the territory, I felt my heart get heavy. I didn't want to be away from Kyro and Kaiden for very long. Maevis seemed to understand how I was feeling, as she kept talking to me about different things Kyro and Kaiden had done when they were younger. It was a good distraction and in about an hour, we arrived at the large mall. Maevis, Rodger, Azalea and I remained sitting in our car, while the warriors in the other two cars got out and waited in front of our car.

'You ok Levi?' Maevis asked from beside me. I turned to look at her, she had a soft smile on her face and I felt myself calm down.

'I-I'm a b-bit nervous,' I told her honestly.

'That is understandable. But I won't let anything happen to you and neither will Azalea or any of the warriors that are with us,' Maevis promised. I nodded and then the four of us got out of the car and headed to the where the warriors were waiting. 'Ok, now that we are here let's go over a couple of things before we head inside the mall. Marcus, Payton, and Cedric stay close to Levi, Azalea and myself. The rest of you spread out and keep an eye out on everything around us. If you see a possible threat, you let us know immediately,' Maevis instructed.

'Yes Luna,' the warriors all said, keeping their voices low so the nearby humans didn't hear them. After that, Maevis, Azalea, Payton, Cedric, Marcus, and I headed towards the entrance. The warriors held back and waited until we were some distance away before following us.

'I think the first place we should go is Sleepy Time Venture. It is a really nice store where we can find sheets, blankets and pillows. What do you think, Levi?' Maevis suggested as we walked.

'S-sounds g-good,' I replied.

'Wonderful, let's go then,' Maevis said before leading us through the mall.

'How have you been Levi?' Cedric asked me as we walked.

'I-I've b-been ok,' I replied softly.

'That's good. Are you healing, ok?' Payton asked. I bit my lip unsure how to answer the question. I wasn't used to receiving such expert medical care after being hurt, so I wasn't sure if I was healing ok or not.

'I'm sorry if I overstepped Levi,' Payton said softly.

'I-it's ok. I've n-never g-gotten such g-good care af-after being h-hurt b-before, so I-I'm not sure h-how to t-tell how w-well I'm h-healing,' I replied.

'Oh,' Payton responded before he looked at Marcus and Cedric.

'Well, you might be able tell by how your injuries feel. Do they still hurt a lot? Or do the injuries feel somewhat numb?' Marcus asked me.

'Umm th-they don't f-feel as b-bad as b-before. Th-they're k-kind of n-numb,' I replied.

'Are you able to move better than you have before or is your movement still restricted?' Payton asked.

'I c-can move b-better than I-I have in a w-while,' I replied.

'Sounds like your injuries are healing pretty good then. Thanks to our high healing factors our kind heal quickly. If we still feel pain and we can't move well after being hurt, it means we aren't healing properly. So, the fact that your injuries don't hurt as much and you can move better, means you are healing quite good,' Marcus explained. Maevis and Azalea walked quietly behind Marcus, Payton, Cedric and I as we walked. They remained silent as I talked to the guys and when I took a quick look behind me, they both smiled encouragingly at me. After walking for a couple of minutes, we came to a stop in front of a store that had a sign that read Sleepy Time Venture.

'Ok Levi, as I said here. we are going to have a look at some sheets, blankets, pillows and pillow cases,' Maevis explained to me, 'What colours do you like Levi?'

'U-um I'm n-not sure. I-I've n-never th-thought ab-about it b-before,' I told Maevis.

'Green and blue are a nice,' Payton suggested.

'Brown and black are also nice colours to have for sheets and blankets. But honestly any colour is pretty good for them,' Cedric added.

'If you had to choose one or two colours that you like more than any other, which would you choose?' Marcus asked me. I thought about what Payton and Cedric had said for a moment.

I like green Levi, like the forest and also blue like pictures of the ocean we have seen, Alpin said to me.

'W-we like g-green l-like the f-forest and b-blue like th-the ocean,' I told Maevis and the others. 'We?' Marcus asked before a look of understanding crossed his face. 'We as in you and your wolf like those colours?' he said.

'Y-yes we d-do,' I replied.

'If you don't mind me asking? What is your wolf's name?' Payton asked.

Tell them Levi, I'd like them to know my name, Alpin urged.

'H-his n-name is Alpin,' I told everyone and they smiled.

'My wolf's name is Topaz,' Maevis told me.

'Mine's Ruby,' Azalea said next with a smile.

'Mine's Ash, Payton's wolf is named Copper, and Marcus' wolf is named Zephyr,' Cedric added after her.

Please tell them I say hello, Alpin said.

'Alpin s-says h-hello,' I told everyone. They all smiled and then said hello to Alpin. Once they all said hello, we walking into the store and had a look at the items I would need for my bed. Sometime later I had four sets of sheets, one in blue, another in green and two in light brown. I also had four new pillows and eight pillow cases which matched the sets of sheets. Maevis had also gotten three blankets, one black, one forest green and the last was ocean blue.

'Ok now that we have some stuff for the bed, we should go and have a look at clothes,' Maevis said happily.

'Yay clothes,' Azalea said with a smile. There was a groan from Marcus, Cedric, and Payton and when I looked at them, I saw that they didn't seem excited about looking at clothes.

'W-what's wrong?' I asked them.

'We have been clothes shopping with Azalea a few times and it usually took several hours,' Marcus explained.

'Hey it wasn't that bad,' Azalea replied with a slight pout. I would have been worried if it wasn't for the humour I could see in her eyes. Marcus and the other went to say something else but they were cut off by Maevis.

'Now, now, children, no fighting,' Maevis said. The boys and Azalea all nodded and then we all turned and headed towards some other shops. All the things we had gotten from Sleepy Time Venture was in a trolley being pushed by Marcus. After walking for several minutes, we headed into a store called Fashion Essentials. As soon as we walked into the store my eyes went wide. The store had so many clothes to choose from.

Oh, my Goddess. Where on earth do we start? I asked Alpin. He didn't reply but I could feel that he was just as stumped as I was. I took a couple of steps forward, looking around as I moved.

'Are you ok Levi?' Maevis asked me kindly.

'Th-there's so m-much st-stuff. I d-don't kn-know w-where to st-start,' I responded, turning around to face Maevis and the others.

'That's ok. We are here to help you,' Maevis replied warmly.

'Azalea why don't you and Marcus go find some nightwear and cold weather clothes for Levi to try on. Payton, Cedric the two of you come with Levi and I to have a look at some shirts, pants, shorts and singlets,' she added.

'Ok,' Azalea replied before she and Marcus walked off. While Azalea and Marcus looked in one section of the store Maevis, Payton, Cedric and I headed to another. The first thing we look at were some shirts and singlets.

What shirts should we try Alpin? I asked my wolf as I walked around looking at shirts.

Maybe those shirts over there? They look kind of like the shirts our mates wear, Alpin replied. I walked over to where I could see some dress shirts and picked out a couple of ones that I thought Kyro and Kaiden would like. After grabbing several shirts, I went and grabbed a couple of singlets. As I grabbed a singlet, I noticed Maevis looking at me strangely.

Why is she looking at me like that? I asked Alpin but he didn't have a clue as to why Maevis was looking at us strangely. 'I-is some-something wrong?' I asked Maevis. I looked down at my feet and shuffled slightly as I waited for her reply.

'I was just wondering if you like the shirts that you picked out,' Maevis replied. I wasn't sure if I liked the shirts that I had chosen but I thought that Kyro and Kaiden would like them.

'I-I'm not s-sure, b-but I th-think K-Kyro and K-Kaiden will l-like th-them' I replied honestly, 'I w-want th-them to l-like me,' I added before looking down.

'Oh, my dear Levi,' Maevis said as she brought me into a hug. When she eventually stepped back, she had a sympathetic look on her face.

'My sons love you for you. It doesn't matter to them what you are wearing, so long as you like it and are comfortable. They just want you to be happy,' Maevis said and I could feel myself tear up.

'Th-thank you Maevis,' I said with a soft smile, before wiping away my tears.

'You're very welcome. Now let's put these back and get you some clothes that you actually like,' Maevis said. We did as she said and put most of the shirts I had selected back. We kept a couple that I did like. After choosing some new shirts and singlets, we moved on to look at some pants, shorts and underwear. At that point Azalea and Marcus joined back up with us. They had a good selection of sleepwear and cold weather clothes with them.

'Ok. I think we should go to the change rooms now and have you try on these clothes,' Maevis said to me and I nodded. The six of us headed over to the change room where Maevis had me try on all the clothes we had grabbed. She had me show her each outfit that I tried on and eventually we decided on which clothes we would get. After putting back the clothes we didn't like, we grabbed a couple more of the clothes that we did like. As we exited the store after paying for my new clothes, my stomach rumbled loudly.

'Sounds like you have a bear stuck in your belly,' Payton said with a laugh and I blushed. Everyone then laughed when Payton's own stomach grumbled as well.

'You have a beautiful laugh, Levi,' Azalea said.

'Th-thank you Az-Azalea,' I replied with a smile.

'Let's go get something to eat. We still have a few more things that we need to look at but I am pretty sure we are all hungry,' Maevis said. She quickly mind linked the warriors following us before we headed towards a different section of the mall.

'Ok, where does everyone want to eat? I was thinking either, Lily's Diner or Chiliad Brews,' Azalea asked as we got to the food court. After a quick vote we decided to go to Lily's Diner, a small friendly diner located on the far side of the food court. When we walked into the diner, I felt as though we had stepped into someone's dining room rather than a diner. The place had a very nice homey feeling to it and was nicely decorated. The walls were painted to look like a meadow, several paintings hung on the walls and there were several potted plants hanging from the ceiling.

I think this is just became one of my favourite places, Alpin said happily.

Yeah, where is your favourite place then? I asked him.

Where else? Our mates' arms of course, Alpin said. Alpin had a point, our mates' arms were my favourite place to be to. A gentle tap on my elbow brought me out of my thoughts and I turned to see the others looking at me.

'Let's go take a seat,' Maevis said. Our group moved to one of the larger tables in the diner and sat down. I sat in between Maevis and Azalea, while Payton, Marcus and Cedric sat across from us. After we were all seated, I noticed the other warriors walk in, split up and sit down at two different tables, one at the back of the diner and one near the entrance of the diner. I looked between them; I was confused about why they sat apart and not together.

'Are you ok Levi?' Azalea asked.

'Wh-why are th-they s-sitting apart?' I asked in a low voice before looking between the two groups of warriors again.

'It is for protection,' Cedric replied.

'Pr-protection?' I asked.

'The group of warriors at the back will watch for potential threats coming from the storage and kitchen areas, while the group of warriors at the front watches for potential threats coming from the entrance. While they do that, Marcus, Payton, and I will keep an eye on potential threats near us,' Cedric replied.

That makes sense, Alpin noted and I had to agree.

'Ok before the server gets here, let's decide what we will be having,' Maevis told us. We all looked over the menus, with Maevis helping me as I struggled with a few things on the menu. After the waiter took our order, we filled the time waiting for our meals with conversation. I didn't talk much, instead I listened as everyone else talked about their lives in their pack. The conversation, stopped when the waiter brought our food, but it picked up as soon as the waiter had left.

I'm kind of glad that none of them have asked where we are from, Alpin said, I could hear sadness in his voice as he spoke.

I feel the same way. I think I'd like to be friends with these guys one day, I admitted to Alpin.

Yeah, they are quite nice. I am surprised, I thought all warriors were bad and wanted to hurt people. But these guys are kind, understanding and accepting. I said softly before adding.

It makes me feel better about our mates. If their warriors are this kind, then they were likely to be as well, Alpin sighed when we met out mates.

Half an hour later everyone had finished our meals, so we paid and left the diner. After we left the diner, we went to several more shops to buy various other items. By the time we finished shopping I had clothes, sheets, blankets, pillows and pillow cases. I also had bathing items, books, CDs, DVDs, a watch and various other things. Maevis had also taken me to get a mobile phone and laptop, promising to teach me how to use them. We also put a computer desk and a couple of shelving units on order. We were told that we would be contacted when they were ready to be picked up. After we had finished shopping, we went to the cars and packed the things we had brought in the boots. We then hopped into the cars and headed back to the pack. When we got back, I was quite happy to see my two mates waiting for me out the front of the pack house. The warriors were the first ones to get out of the pack house, followed by Rodger, Maevis and then Azalea. I was the last one to get out of the car and I was immediately approached by my mates.

'Hello Little Wolf. How are you feeling? Did you have a good time?' Kyro asked me.

'I h-had fun,' I replied, quickly followed by a yawn.

'We got a lot of stuff today, most of it is in the cars. There are a couple of things that needed to be ordered in but we will get a call when the stuff arrives in store. When that happens, we will go and pick them up,' Maevis told Kyro and Kaiden.

'Sounds good. Would you like something to…' Kaiden started to say before he was cut off by a loud howl. When I saw everyone stiffen, I felt my fear rise, there was only one thing that I could think of that could cause that sort of reaction. 'Rogues. Mum, Azalea please take Levi and get to the safe room,' Kaiden ordered his mother and sister in-law.

'Levi please go with them. We will be back soon. We love you and we will fight to get back to you,' Kyro said with a smile, the love he had for me evident in his voice.

'P-please be s-safe. I d-don't want t-to lose y-you,' I said, unable to stop the whimper that followed. My mates quickly gave me a hug, before Maevis grabbed my hand and then she and Azalea escorted me into the pack house.

CHAPTER 35: KAIDEN'S POV

AS SOON AS Levi, Azalea and our mother had gone inside the pack house, Kyro, the warriors and I all shifted into our wolf forms and headed off towards the fighting. I felt stronger as I ran in my wolf form and I felt my senses heighten.

These bastards will regret messing with our pack, Storm growled out.

Damn right they will regret it, I replied. After a few minutes there was carnage right before our eyes. There was blood everywhere and there were also several rogues already dead on the ground. I could also see several of our pack's warriors were also on the ground. Thanks to the pack bond, I could tell that they were still alive. Unfortunately, I didn't know how long they would last.

Now's not the time to think about it. Let's deal with the rest of these rogue bastards, Storm growled out. Kyro and I then split up in order to deal with the rogues that had dared to come into our pack. I took down rogue after rogue; I tore and slashed at their throats, their legs and their backs. I did whatever I had to in order to neutralise the threat these bastards posed to my pack. I would not allow anyone to harm my pack and I definitely wasn't going to let them hurt Levi. *Oh, those fuckers have another thing coming if they think they can get anywhere near our precious mate,* Storm said as we tore out the throat of the rogue that we had pinned beneath us. As we went to move, another rogue jumped onto my back and went for my neck. The rogue is an idiot if he thinks he can take us on. I thought. I easily threw the rogue off and quickly turned to face him. I stood still as the rogue circled me, looking for an opening but not finding one. ***Put the bastard out of his misery,*** Storm said with a huff. I leapt at the rogue and pinned him to the ground easily. I then applied pressure to his throat and continued to do so until they were unconscious. When I looked back up, I saw one of my warriors being pinned down by a rogue. I quickly snarled as I leapt towards the rogue and knocked him off of the warrior. I quickly dispatched the rogue; when I turned back, I saw the warrior get back up and shake himself off. We quickly nodded to each other before we both resumed fighting the rogues. It took an hour for all rogues in the pack borders had been dealt with and by that time I was bleeding from multiple wounds. As I went to move to assist in rounding up the surviving rogues, I felt a sudden pain in my side which nearly brought me to my knees. There were only two things that could have done that, either my brother or my mate was hurt. Seeing as Levi was currently secure in the safe room, it had to be Kyro.

Kyro, where are you? I called out to my brother over mind link. When I got no response, I felt my fear spike, not much could stop him from responding. Since I wasn't able to get in contact with him, I tracked his scent. It took me a while to track his scent amongst all the blood but when I did, I followed it straight away. When I eventually found Kyro, I saw him standing face to face with a rogue. Behind Kyro, two of our warriors were lying unconscious in human form. I noticed that Kyro was struggling to stand and then I noticed that there was a large gash on Kyro's side that was bleeding badly.

That fucker hurt our brother, Storm snarled out and I felt him take partial control. We leapt towards the rogue standing in front of Kyro and tore into him. As I tore into him, I felt myself slowly losing control of my actions. Our brother had been harmed, so Storm and I wanted blood.

Storm, Kaiden, stay with me, Kyro called to me softly, bringing me back from the edge. I quickly turned around and when I saw Kyro fall to the ground, I rushed to his side. I nudged Kyro's neck and let out a soft whimper, I hated to see my brother hurt like this.

I need help near the northern border marker. Alpha Kyro and several warriors are down, I said to the pack warriors over mind link. It didn't take long for several warriors to come and help me temporarily patch up Kyro and the other wounded warriors. Before placing them on stretchers, and transporting them to the pack hospital. Despite wanting to go with my brother to the pack hospital, I stayed to help gather the other wounded pack warriors and bring them to the pack hospital. Once that was done, I gave orders for the surviving rogues to be taken to the pack hospital and for the deceased rogues bodies to be dealt with. After everything was taken care of, I headed straight to the pack hospital where I shifted into human form. I then quickly grabbed a pair of pants from a bag that was stashed near the entrance of the pack hospital. We had multiple bags of clothes stashed throughout the pack lands, for when pack members needed something to wear after shifting. As soon as I was dressed, I went into the hospital where I was met with my wounded pack members.

I hate seeing our pack members hurt, Storm whimpered.

I hate the feeling too. I wish I could say they won't be hurt or even killed but I can't. The only thing we can do is make sure we do our best to fight those that would dare harm our family, friends and pack members, I responded.

'Hey Victoria. How are you?' I asked as I saw Victoria sitting on a chair. She had several bandages on her and I could also see several bruises starting to form.

'I'm a little sore but overall ok Alpha,' Victoria replied.

'I'm glad you're not badly hurt,' I replied as I looked around, trying to find Kyro.

'He is in one of the rooms in the surgical ward Alpha,' Victoria said, the look on her face told me that she knew who I was looking for.

'Thank you, Victoria. I hope you heal soon,' I said to Victoria before turning and heading to the surgical ward. When I got there, I was met by Doctor Veracruz and Diomika Lang.

'Alpha, Warrior Victoria told me you were on your way,' Doctor Veracruz said to me as I came to a stop.

'How is my brother?' I asked, not bothering with formalities.

'He is alright Alpha. We have given him some blood and dressed his wounds. He may be a bit tired for a while but being an Alpha, he will be alright in a couple of hours,' Doctor Veracruz replied. I could feel a wave of relief wash over me when I heard that Kyro would be ok.

'You can go in and see him if you wish Alpha. He is just down the hall, room five,' Doctor Veracruz added. I quickly thanked Doctor Veracruz and Diomika before heading down the hall to Kyro's room. I didn't bother knocking on the door, I just walked in. I stopped short when I saw Kyro sitting on the bed covered in bandages.

'Oh, my Goddess,' I said as I moved to his side. 'How are you feeling brother?' I asked as I looked over his injuries.

'My side is a bit sore but my other injuries are feeling ok,' Kyro replied with a tired smile.

'Are you sure? Do you need m…' I started before I felt someone mind link Kyro and I.

Alphas I was wondering if you wanted us to open the safe room now and let everyone out, Jaden said to us.

Are all the bodies and blood cleaned up? I don't want pack members to have to see anything unnecessarily. Also are the surviving rogues locked up securely? Kyro asked.

All the bodies and blood have been cleaned up. There are still signs of the fight such as several broken trees, but other than that that there shouldn't be anything that the pack might see. As for the surviving rogues, they are all secured in the pack prison, Jaden replied.

Ok, open the safe rooms, I told Jaden.

Yes Alpha, Jaden said before cutting the mind link. Just as Kyro and I came out of the mind link, we felt someone else open up a mind link with us.

Boys what's going on? Are the rogues gone? Are you two alright? Our mother asked.

I'm ok mum, but Kyro is hurt. Doctor Veracruz said he should be alright soon, I responded.

Oh, thank the Moon Goddess. You boys had me worried. And not to mention, you had your mate worried. He felt you two get hurt and has been crying for the last twenty minutes, Our mother told us. Hearing that Levi had felt us get hurt and that he was crying made me feel horrible.

I'm so sorry mum. Where is Levi now? I asked.

Levi and I are headed to you now, Our mother replied before she cut the mind link. After we came out of the mind link, Kyro and I turned to look at each other.

'Our mate felt our pain,' I said sadly.

'I didn't think he would be feeling our pain already. We've only known each other for a short while. I didn't think the bond would be that far along,' Kyro said with tears in his eyes.

'Hey easy now. Neither of us realised he would feel our pain,' I told him as I hugged him. 'We will explain to him what had happened and we will make sure that he is alright,' I added softly. We sat there in silence for several minutes before there was a knock on the door. I stood up from the bed and went and opened the door. What I saw broke my heart, my mother had an arm wrapped around Levi who had tear stained, puffy cheeks.

'Oh, my Goddess. Levi' I said, my voice breaking as I did. I quickly brought

Levi into a hug and he started crying causing my heart to break even more. I looked up at my mum and then felt her mind link me.

Take him inside, he needs the both of you right now. I will instruct Doctor Veracruz to let no one into the room unless you and Kyro say so, My mother said with a soft smile before turning and walking away. I stepped back from the hug but kept an arm wrapped around Levi. I then led him into the room and closed the door behind us. As we approached the bed, Levi suddenly stopped and let out a whimper.

'Oh, my Little Wolf. I promise that I'm ok,' Kyro said softly. Then to Kyro's and my surprise, Levi rushed to the bed, hopped onto it and then hugged Kyro tightly.

'I felt you get hurt. I didn't like it; I don't like you getting hurt,' Levi whimpered as he started crying. It took me a moment to realise that when he had spoken, Levi did not stutter. If it weren't for the fact that he was crying right now, I would be smiling widely.

'He is ok Levi. Doctor Veracruz said that in a couple of hours he'll be back to normal,' I said as I gently rubbed Levi's back. Levi turned around to face me, the tears subsiding slightly.

'I'm sorry. You got hurt too, I forgot about that,' Levi said, again speaking without stuttering. 'Are you ok?' he asked.

'I'm ok Little One,' I replied. 'I got a few injuries but nothing too bad, I promise.' Levi surprised me again by pulling me into a hug. Despite my surprise I quickly wrapped my arms around him. A moment later Kyro wrapped his arms around the both of us and we stayed like that for quite a while. Sometime later, I heard a soft snore and when I looked down, I saw that Levi had fallen asleep. 'Oh, he is so beautiful when he is asleep,' I said softly in order not to wake him up.

'That he is. I'll shift over a bit so you can lay him down,' Kyro said before he moved over. He then rearranged the pillows on the bed and once he was done, I gently laid Levi down beside Kyro. As soon as his head hit the pillow, Levi turned and snuggled into Kyro's side.

'I wish the bed was bigger so you could lay down with us,' Kyro said with a smile. 'I'd like that but right now I'm happy seeing the two of you are safe,' I replied as I took a seat beside the bed that held my mate and brother.

CHAPTER 36: LEVI'S POV

AS SOON AS we were inside the pack house, Maevis and Azalea escorted me through the pack house before stopping at a large painting.

'W-why are w-we h-here?' I asked them. Maevis turned and gave me a soft smile before turning back and pressing a small flower on the panel beside the painting. A few seconds passed before the panel shifted and exposed a previously hidden keypad. Maevis then typed in a few numbers and stepped back. I was startled when there was a hissing sound and then the painting swung open.

Oh, my Goddess. A secret tunnel, Alpin said, surprised by the passageway that was now in front of us.

'Come on let's get inside,' Maevis said. Azalea went into the tunnel first, then I followed her. Maevis was the last to enter the passageway and she closed the painting behind her. For a moment we were in complete darkness and my fear rose. Before my panic got out of control a soft light come on, illuminating the passageway.

'You ok Levi?' Maevis asked from behind me.

'Y-yes,' I replied softly.

'Ok. Let's keep going, we'll be at the safe room soon,' Maevis said. Azalea then led the way through the passageway with Maevis and I following closely behind. We walked for another couple of minutes before coming to a stop at another set of doors. This door was guarded by four well-built men. I knew straight away that these four men were pack warriors.

'Luna Maevis, Miss Azalea,' one of the warriors said, addressing Maevis and Azalea. The four warriors turned to look at me and I could see from the looks that they were giving me, they were wondering who I was and what I was doing there. After all I was an unfamiliar wolf, that had entered a passageway that led to the pack's safe room. I shuffled under their gaze, extremely uncomfortable with the looks they were giving me.

'Levi is a future member of this pack,' Maevis said. Her voice had a slight edge to it which caused the warriors to straighten up and look towards her.

She used her Luna voice on them, Alpin noted.

Wow, was the only response I had; I was too surprised by how comfortable I felt when Maevis had used her Luna voice. When my old Luna used her Luna voice, I always felt uncomfortable and stressed.

'Of course, Luna,' one of the warriors said, breaking me from my thoughts. The warriors then gave Maevis a respectable nod before one turned and typed a code into the panel behind him. The warriors then moved aside when the door opened and allowed us to pass through. There was another passageway on the other side and we walked for a little while before we stepped onto a small balcony which had a set of stairs off to the side. I looked down and saw a large room with several people spread throughout it. I could also see several rooms off to the sides of the one before me.

'It's a lot to take in, isn't it?' Azalea said to me.

'Y-yes. I-I've never s-seen anything l-like th-this before,' I replied as I looked around.

'Well the area before us is a common area for people to interact while we wait to be let out. there are several bedrooms where people can sleep if they wish, there's also a large, fully stocked kitchen and a couple of dining rooms. We also have games rooms, lounge rooms and a small library to keep people occupied while we wait,' Maevis explained as we walked down a set of stairs and into the common area. People said hello to Maevis and Azalea as we passed them and they said hello in response.

There are so many people here. I knew the pack was big but I didn't realise it was this big. And there's so much to do in here. I have heard of packs having safe rooms for their people in case of emergencies, but I never thought it would be something like this, I told Alpin. I had never been in the safe room of my old pack before, I was always forced to stay in my basement room during attacks. So being in a safe room, especially one so big, was a shock for me.

'Let's go find somewhere to sit and wait,' Maevis said before leading Azalea and me to a room on the other side of the common area. Inside I saw three men and four women sitting on chairs, while several young pups played in front of them.

'Maevis, Azalea. You've made it safely,' an older woman said as soon as we entered the room. 'We have Lauryn. Is everyone alright in here?' Maevis responded.

'We are alright Luna,' a younger man replied. 'May I ask you the young man is Luna,' the young man asked as the adults all looked at me with curious expressions.

'Of course, you can Emmanuel,' Maevis replied. 'Everyone, this is Levi. Levi, this is Emmanuel, Lauryn, Carla, Sarah, Francesca, Maurice and Neil,' Maevis added, introducing the adults in the room.

'Hello Levi,' one of the men said as he held his hand out. 'I am Maurice. It is a pleasure to meet you,' Maurice added. I noted that Maurice was small like me and he had this playful energy about him.

'H-hello M-Maurice. I-it's a p-pleasure to m-meet you too,' I replied as I shook his hand. After saying hello to the other adults in the room, Maevis, Azalea and I went and sat down. While Maevis and I sat down with the older woman named Lauryn, Azalea went and sat with a couple of the pups. While Maevis and Lauryn talked to each other, I sat and watched the pups, finding myself relax as I did. I loved being around pups, they never judged and they always seemed to calm me down.

'Would you like to hold one of the pups Levi?' Lauryn asked.

'Y-yes please,' I replied. Lauryn stood up, went over to the pups and carefully picked one up. She then walked back over to Maevis and I and carefully handed the pup to me. 'This is Michelle. She is one of the orphans that I take care of,' she said as she helped me to adjust my position so it was more comfortable for me and the pup in my arms. *Aww she is so beautiful,* I said with a sigh.

She is gorgeous, Alpin replied.

I wonder why she's an orphan, I said sadly. There were a few reasons why a pup would be an orphan; they had been abandoned by their parent/s, the pup's parents had been killed or the pup had been kidnapped and they were unable to find their birth families. Any of those reasons were sad and I felt my heart break for the little one. 'Y-you said she is o-one of th-the orphans y-you care f-for? H-how many d-do you c-care for?' I asked Lauryn.

'I care for six orphans in my home. Over there is Nate and Marley they are both fourteen months old, with them is Dean who is eight months old. Then in the bouncers over there are the twins Olivia and Gabriel who are six months old,' Lauryn said, pointing to each of the pups as she introduced them. She then looked at the little one in my arms and smiled. 'Michelle there is also six months old,'

Lauryn added with a smile. I was surprised to hear that she cared for six very young pups and I wondered if she had help.

'D-do you h-have someone at h-home t-to help w-with them,' I asked her.

'No, I lost my mate a few months ago in an attack. It was only a short time afterwards that these little ones came into my care,' a sad look crossed Lauryn's face when she mentioned losing her mate.

Please tell her I am sorry about her mate, Alpin said.

'My w-wolf Alpin s-says to say w-we are s-sorry for y-your loss,' I told Lauryn.

'Thank you Levi and your wolf Alpin as well,' Lauryn replied. 'It's been hard losing my mate but these little ones have kept me going. And I have had help from Maevis, the Alphas, Beta Jaden, Gamma Rowan and several other pack mums. If I ever need anything for the little ones or if I need some help, I just have to ask,' she added. I was happy to hear that she has help with the pups.

Imagine seeing our mates playing with the pups. It would be so cute, Alpin said with a sigh. I smiled at the thought of our mates and pups, I wondered if I would ever have pups with my mates one day.

'How are you liking the pack so far?' Lauryn asked.

'I-it's pretty g-good here,' I replied. I spent quite a bit of time talking with Lauryn and the other mothers, when Michelle started to squirm. 'Wh-what's wrong? D-did I d-do something wr-wrong?' I asked in a panic. I looked between Maevis and Lauryn, unsure of what I did to upset the pup.

'It's ok. You've done nothing wrong. Michelle is probably getting hungry and that's why she is starting to get a bit fussy,' Lauryn told me and I nodded.

I'm glad it wasn't something we had done. I wouldn't want to do something which could hurt this pup, or really any pup for that matter, I said to Alpin.

Me neither, Alpin replied.

'Do you mind holding her for a bit longer while Lauryn and I get some bottles for Michelle and the other pups?' Maevis asked me.

'O-ok,' I replied. Maevis gave me a quick smile before she and Lauryn went over to a bench at the side of the room to prepare some bottles for the pups. Once they were done Maevis, Lauryn and the other mothers got the pups settled and gave them their bottles. Maevis and Lauryn then came back over to me, with Lauryn holding the bottle for Michelle. 'C-can I f-feed her?' I asked quietly.

'Of course. Let's get Michelle into a better position first,' Lauryn replied before helping me to adjust Michelle. Once Michelle was in a more comfortable position, Lauryn handed me her bottle and I fed the cute little pup. When Michelle finished her bottle, Lauryn showed me how to burp Michelle and when that was done, Michelle fell asleep almost straight away. I stood up with Michelle asleep in my arms and started humming softly.

'You have a beautiful voice, Levi,' Maurice said to me. My mouth dropped open slightly as I hadn't realised that I had started singing out loud.

'Can you sing something else?' Carla asked. I bit my lip; I wasn't sure if I should sing again but the kind looks that everyone in the room were giving me gave me the encouragement to do so. I sang several songs before I started to feel myself getting antsy. I tensed up as I felt an unfamiliar feeling passed through me. I then felt myself start to sway and my mind drifted off. 'Lauryn, take Michelle now,' I heard someone say. Shortly afterwards I felt someone take Michelle from my arms. I noticed someone gently grab my arm and lead me out of the room. The person then led me to another room, closing the door behind us. When I got inside, I felt a wave pain pass over me that brought me to my knees.

'Wh-what's happening t-to me?' I asked as I started crying from the pain.

'One or both of your mates are hurt,' a soft voice told me.

Mates are hurt. Our mates are hurt. No, no, no. That can't be. Mates can't be hurt, Alpin said with a whimper. The pain I was experiencing was high and it was hard to handle.

'No, no, no. They can't be hurt. Mates can't leave me,' I cried out. I felt someone pull me into a hug and gently hold me in their arms. The person whispered to me in a soothing voice, telling me that everything would be ok.

'Your mates are strong. They will be ok and you will be back with them soon,' the person said. The pain lasted for several minutes before I finally felt some relief.

Alpin, what's going on? I asked Alpin but he didn't answer. All I felt coming from him was pain and fear for our mates.

'Easy Levi. You will be ok and so will your mates,' the person said to me as I felt myself coming back to reality. I gently looked up and saw that it was Maevis who was holding me. 'Hey, there you are Little One,' Maevis said with a gentle smile. Though she had a smile on her face, there was still pain in her eyes. The pain of knowing her children we hurt and knowing there wasn't anything she could do about it right now.

'I w-want m-my mates. I w-want K-Kyro and K-Kaiden,' I whimpered.

'I know you do. I'll link them to find out where they are,' Maevis said softly. Maevis' eyes then glazed over as she mind link her sons. I waited as patiently as I could for Maevis to come out of the mind link and let me know where my mates were. 'Kyro and Kaiden are at the pack hospital. They've given orders to open the safe room, so we can go to them now,' Maevis said after she came out of the mind link. Maevis then helped me to stand and then we left the room we were in. Azalea met us at the door and then the three of us left the safe room together. Once outside of the pack house Maevis escorted me to the pack hospital, while Azalea went to go find her mate Kingsley. It took us a couple of minutes to get to the pack hospital and when we finally got inside, I was pained by what I saw. There were several pack members inside and they were all injured in some way or another.

Those bastards hurt our pack. They hurt our people, Alpin growled out. I was shocked to hear Alpin refer to the pack and its members as ours. But I guessed as the mate of the Alphas, this pack would be mine and I would its Luna.

'Doctor where are my sons?' Maevis asked an unfamiliar man.

'They are in room five of the surgical ward Luna,' The doctor replied and Maevis quickly led me away from the hospital foyer. Maevis knocked on the door to the room where my mates were and as I waited for someone to answer I felt my fear spike. What if they are badly hurt? What if they die? 'They will be ok Levi,' Maevis said as she wrapped an arm around me and I nodded. When I heard the door open, I looked up and saw Kaiden standing in front of me.

'Oh, my Goddess. Levi,' Kaiden said, his voice breaking as he did. Kaiden quickly pulled me into a hug and I broke down crying. Kaiden had most likely been hurt because of me and so was Kyro.

CHAPTER 37: KYRO'S POV

WAKING UP WITH Levi in my arms was the best feeling in the world. I hoped to wake up like this every morning for the rest of my life. The only change I would make is that we were in my bedroom and not the hospital.

'What's got you blushing so much?' I heard someone ask. I turn to see Kaiden looking at me with a big smile on his face.

'Just thinking about how perfect this moment right now is,' I replied.

'Yeah, would be better if we weren't in the hospital though,' Kaiden stated.

'I had the same thought,' I replied before I felt Levi shift in my arms. Kaiden and I looked at our mate and waited as he started waking up. Levi rubbed his eyes several times before slowly sitting up and taking a look around. When he saw that he was in my arms he blushed and shifted slightly, putting a bit of space between us. As we were on a hospital bed, Levi was unable to move too far.

I want him back in my arms, Shadow whined as soon as Levi had moved.

I know. I want him back too, I replied. Shadow whined again and then curled up in a ball. I then blocked him out, wanting to focus on my Little Wolf. 'How are you feeling Little Wolf?' I asked my mate.

'I-I'm ok,' Levi replied with a small yawn.

'We are glad to hear that,' Kaiden told him before adding, 'We would like to apologise for what you went through yesterday. Neither of us thought you would feel our pain, especially as much as you did,'

'We didn't realise the bond had progressed far enough for you to have felt our pain,' I added after Kaiden had finished.

'I-it's not ei-either of your f-faults,' Levi told us. 'B-but why d-did I f-feel it?' he then asked.

'Well, when a mate bond progresses to a certain point, mates can feel the other's emotions, read each other's thoughts and know when the other is in danger or hurt,' Kaiden told him as he sat down on the edge of the bed. 'As we said neither of us thought that the bond between the three of us had progressed that far yet,' he added apologetically.

'The only reason we can think of is that it is because we are Alpha. It's natural for a wolf to want to protect their mate but for an Alpha that desire is stronger. So, you being able to feel our pain and in turn us being able to feel yours allows us to protect each other better,' I explained to Levi.

'Th-that m-makes sense,' Levi replied. 'You a-are b-both ok now th-though?' he asked a moment later.

'We are alright. I was completely healed a few hours after the fight was over and so was Kaiden,' I told him.

'Th-that's good. Wh-what happens n-now?' Levi asked.

'Well first we call the doctors to see if Kyro is allowed to leave. After that, we will check in with our pack members who were wounded yesterday and see how they are. After that the three of us will go to the pack house. I'm sure we would all like a shower and a change of clothes,' Kaiden replied. 'Once we've showered and changed, we can get something to eat. Kaiden and I can then help you to put away everything you got at shopping yesterday,' I added after Kaiden finished talking.

'D-don't you want t-to rest? You w-were h-hurt,' Levi replied.

'We are fine. The sleep last night was all we needed to recuperate,' I told him.

'O-ok,' Levi replied, just as we heard a knock on the door.

'Come in,' Kaiden called out. The quietly opened up and then Diomika walked into the room. 'Hello Alphas, Levi,' Diomika said with a smile.

'Please Diomika. Just Kyro and Kaiden will do,' Kaiden told her. As Levi's adoptive sister, Kyro and I saw Diomika as our family to.

'My apologies Kyro, Kaiden,' Diomika replied.

'It's alright. What brings you here?' I asked Diomika.

'Doctor Veracruz asked me to come and give you an exam before discharging you. She said she would have come and examined you herself but something else came up,' Diomika replied. 'Of course,' I replied.

'Levi I am going to have to ask you to move for a moment so I can give Kyro an exam,' Diomika told Levi who pouted and whined slightly.

'It's ok. We will have plenty of time later to cuddle Little Wolf,' I said to my mate. Kaiden hopped off the bed and then helped Levi get off the bed. Kaiden then led Levi over to the couch at the side of the room. As soon as they had sat down, Levi immediately snuggled into Kaiden's side.

Aww that is so cute, I said to Kaiden over mind link.

It feels so good having him next to me, Kaiden replied with a purr.

I'm glad to see he is comfortable enough with us to snuggle up to us, I said happily. After what he had been through, I thought that it would take longer for Levi to be comfortable around Kaiden and I to get as close to us as he was.

'Well Kyro, I am happy to say that you have healed quite well and are cleared to leave the hospital,' Diomika said twenty minutes later, breaking me from my thoughts.

'Thank you Diomika,' I said with a smile.

'You're very welcome. I have to go do rounds on some other patients,' Diomika told us.

'Of course. Thank you for everything you have done to help the pack,' Kaiden said as he and Levi got up from the couch and made their way over to the bed.

'Of course, it's my pleasure to help however I can,' Diomika replied before turning and leaving the room.

'D-do we ch-check on our w-warriors now?' Levi asked.

'Yes. We'll go and check on them now,' I told him. I like how Levi referred to the pack warriors as ours; it made me quite happy to hear. I quickly got out of bed and then Kaiden, Levi and I left the hospital room. After checking on all the pack members the three of us went to the pack house. Once we were on the Alpha floor, Kaiden and I led Levi to his room and then we went to ours. After we had all shower and gotten changed, we met back up in the kitchen, where Kaiden and I made something to eat and drink for Levi and ourselves.

'Would you like to go put the stuff from shopping away now Levi?' I asked after we had all finished our meal.

'Y-yes but y-you two d-don't h-have to help just b-because you f-feel you have t-to?' Levi stuttered out.

'We aren't helping because we feel like we have to, we are helping because we want to,' Kaiden replied.

'Kaiden is right. Besides we love spending time with you. It makes us happy,' I added with a smile.

'It m-makes m-me happy t-too,' Levi replied with a blush.

We make our mate happy, Storm and Shadow said together before they started yipping happily.

'Well let's get going. Our mother had people help to bring everything you brought at shopping yesterday brought up and put into your room,' Kaiden said as the three of us walked into Levi's room. When we walked inside Levi's room, Kaiden and I were stunned by the number of bags that were piled on the bed and floor. When our mother had said they had brought a lot of stuff, we didn't think she meant this.

'I g-got to m-much d-didn't I?' Levi said as he looked at the floor. 'I w-will take it b-back. I am s-sorry for sp-spending t-too much,' he added. When I turned to look at him, I could see tears in the corner of his eyes. He really thought that we were mad at him for the amount of stuff he had gotten.

'Hey it's ok Little Wolf. You didn't get too much stuff at shopping we promise,' I promised Levi.

'Besides we know our mother and Azalea pretty well. It's pretty hard to say no to either one of them, especially when it comes to shopping. And I'm guessing that they made sure you got anything you needed and then just to be sure they made sure you got some other things as well,' Kaiden said, before we all laughed, even Levi.

Goddess he has a cute laugh, Shadow said. Shadow was right, Levi's laugh was soft and beautiful. Once we managed to stop laughing the three of us spent the next couple of hours putting everything away. By the time we were done, we were exhausted. We decided to spend the rest of the day relaxing and enjoying each other's company.

~ One week later ~

There had only been one rogue attack since the one a week ago. Thankfully our patrol wolves were able to take them down before anyone got hurt. During the week, Kaiden and I spent as much of our free time with Levi as we could. When Levi wasn't with us, he was with our mother who was teaching him about being a Luna. Levi had also spoken with Doctor Aurora Blackwell a couple of times. After Levi spoke with Doctor Blackwell; Kaiden and I made sure to be there for our mate as we had promised him we would be. Right now, our mother had taken Levi to the Alpha floor library to show him books about the roles and responsibilities that would one day be his. While Levi was with our mother; Kaiden and I were in the Alpha office with Jaden and Rowan going over some paperwork that needed to be done.

'Ok that's the patrol and training schedules done for the next two weeks. What's next?' I asked while stretching the kinks out of my body.

'Actually, I don't think there's much left to do. Rowan and I took care of the members forms and we also spoke with pack members about any complaints or suggestions that had. So, all in all I think we are done for the day,' Jaden replied.

'What would my brother and I do without you two?' Kaiden asked with a short laugh.

'Curl up in a ball and cry probably,' Rowan replied with a smirk.

'That or lose their minds,' Jaden added before the two burst out laughing.

'Very funny you guys. In all seriousness we are grateful for everything the two of you have done for us and for how you both stepped up while Kaiden and I spent time with Levi,' I said to Jaden and Rowan.

'It's a pleasure. How is your mate doing?' Rowan asked.

'He is doing quite well. Mum said that he is improving quite rapidly in his Luna studies. And Doctor Veracruz said that at the end of this week, he should be off the diet and can eat whatever he would like,' Kaiden told them and the two smiled.

'It might not seem like much to some people but Levi has stopped stuttering when he talks with the two of us and he also doesn't stutter with mum, dad, or Azalea anymore,' I added.

'That's good to hear. And it is a big deal that he's stopped stuttering. It means that he is feeling more comfortable and confident,' Jaden told us and I had to agree with him. Before I could say anything more the pack phone rang and I answered it.

'Alpha Kyro speaking,' I said as I put the phone on speaker.

'Alpha Kyro what a pleasure to finally speak with you,' a rough voice responded. I felt a chill go down my spine when the person had spoken and by the looks on their faces, so did Kaiden, Jaden and Rowan.

'To whom are we speaking?' Kaiden asked the person.

'Oh, where are my manners. I am Alpha Redmond Sutherland. I am the Alpha of the Red Moon Pack. I believe that you have something that belongs to me and I would like it back,' the person replied in a bored voice.

'What would that be Alpha? I'm pretty sure we don't have anything in our pack that belongs to you,' I replied, fighting to keep the anger in my voice. I knew exactly what Alpha Redmond was referring to but I wasn't about to say that.

'Oh, I believe you know *exactly* what I am talking about Alpha. I know that the little cunt Omega Levi is in your pack right now and I suggest you give him back. I have been quite bored since my plaything was taken from me,' Alpha Redmond said with a dangerous edge to his voice.

'I'm afraid that Levi isn't going anywhere. He is staying in our pack and he will soon be a full member of this pack,' Kaiden said to the pathetic Alpha on the other end of the phone. Kaiden, Jaden, Rowan, myself and our wolves were all angered by Alpha Redmond calling Levi his plaything and by calling him a little cunt Omega. Our wolves were fighting to take control so they could find Alpha Redmond and rip him apart. Thankfully they knew that that would only cause more problems than it would solve.

'Oh, you are going to want to hand him over Alpha. You don't want to mess with my pack. Besides, you don't want the trouble of dealing with that pathetic Omega,' Alpha Redmon said and I lost it.

'He is not a pathetic Omega; he is a kind and amazing wolf. Besides my brother and I are not going to hand our mate over to you. We will defend and protect him with all that we have,' I snarled out.

'Oh, your mate? That *is* wonderful news. It will make breaking him that much better now that he has found his mates,' Alpha Redmond said. 'I hope you are prepared to fight us because we will have him back and we will make him pay for the time he wasn't with us,' he added before he hung up. After he hung up, Kaiden and I lost our minds.

'He is not getting his hands on our mate,' Kaiden flipped his desk, letting a snarl out.

'I will kill him,' I punched the wall behind me, several times. 'Alphas I know you are angry but we must be calm. We need to think clearly if we are to protect our Luna from harm,' Jaden said, trying to calm us down.

'We will always stand by the both of you. And we will stand by our Luna and would give our lives to protect him,' Rowan added. Kaiden and I knew that they were right and we managed to calm down. I was so glad that we had two wonderful people as not only our pack's Beta and Gamma, but also as our best friends. Before we could thank them for standing by us, there was a knock on the door and our mother came in, followed by Levi.

'What on earth happened in here?' Our mother asked when she saw the mess Kaiden and I had caused.

'It's a long story but we got angry for a moment. Thankfully Jaden and Rowan were able to calm us down,' Kaiden told her. By the look on her face, our mother wanted to question us further but she chose not to.

'What brings the two of you here? Not that we aren't happy to see the both of you, especially our beautiful mate,' Kaiden said, causing Levi to blush and our mother to get a fake hurt look at us wanting to see Levi more than her. She gave us a quick smile before telling us the reason for her visit. 'I was talking with Levi and he decided that he wanted to show the two of you his wolf form. And before you ask, I already contacted Doctor Veracruz and she said it was ok for him to shift,' our mother replied.

'We would love to see your wolf, Levi,' Kaiden said to our mate with a smile.

'Ok then, the three of you go and spend time together. I will help Jaden and Rowan clean up this mess,' our mother said before shooing Kaiden, Levi, and I from the office. Once we were out of the office, Kaiden, Levi and I headed downstairs and out the front door. Kaiden and I decided to take Levi to our haven; it was a secluded part of the pack where only Kaiden and I were allowed. Now that we had found Levi, he was now the only other person allowed in the haven. When we arrived at the haven, Kaiden and I waited quietly as Levi took in the scene in front of us.

'Would you like us to turn around so you can undress in private?' Kaiden asked Levi.

'Y-yes please,' Levi stuttered out. Kaiden and I turned around so that Levi could undress and shift without us seeing him naked. Once we heard a soft bark, Kaiden and I turned around and were stunned by what we saw in front of us.

'Oh, my Goddess. You're a white wolf,' I said with awe in my voice.

CHAPTER 38: LEVI'S POV

I WAS SITTING in the Alpha floor library with Maevis. We had just discussed some of the duties I would have when I officially became the Luna of the Crimson Rose Pack. I was very worried when we had started discussing some of the things that I would have to do when I took over from Maevis as Luna. However, Kyro, Kaiden, Maevis, Beta Jaden, Gamma Rowan and their families have all promised to help me when I need it. It felt really good to be surrounded by such a kind and caring group of people. They have made me feel truly happy to be here.

'Do you recall the five different types of wolves Levi?' Maevis asked me. Maevis had decided a little while ago that we had done enough work on learning about Luna duties for the day, so now we were talking about the different types of wolves.

'There are red wolves, grey wolves, brown wolves, black wolves and white wolves,' I replied.

'That's correct. I am a grey wolf and my mate Denton is a black wolf. Both of your mates are black wolves and so are Beta Jaden and Gamma Rowan,' Maevis said. 'Not counting royal wolves; Alpha and Luna wolves are the biggest wolves followed by Betas. A Beta's mate and children are roughly the same size as Gammas and after them are a Gamma's mate and children,' she explained further.

'My wolf is the smallest size because I am an Omega?' I asked, not quite remembering if I was right.

'Yes, that is correct. But after you complete the mate bond with Kyro and

Kaiden, your wolf will get bigger. But you will probably still be a little smaller than Kyro's and Kaiden's wolves,' Maevis replied. 'Do you mind if I ask what colour Alpin is?' she asked a moment later.

Don't tell her, I want mates to see me first, Alpin said to me before I could say anything. 'Alpin and I want Kyro and Kaiden to know first,' I told Maevis politely.

'Of course, I completely understand,' Maevis told me. I loved the way Maevis talked. She had such a beautiful voice.

Can you ask if we are able to show our mates what we look like today? Alpin asked in a hopeful voice.

Are you sure you want to? I asked. I wanted to show my mates what Alpin looked like but I was quite nervous about it.

I'm sure. They have been so kind and wonderful to us and I think that it is time for them to see me, Alpin said truthfully.

'Alpin was wondering if we could show Kyro and Kaiden what he looks like today,' I said to Maevis and she smiled.

'I think they would love that very much. I will link Doctor Veracruz and see if its ok for you to shift,' Maevis replied. Her eyes glazed over for a moment and when they returned to normal, she had a smile on her face. 'She says that it is ok. So, let's go and find your mates and let them know,' Maevis said and I nodded quickly, a big smile on my face. The two of us put away all the books we had used and then headed to the Alpha office. When we opened the door to the office, I was stunned by what I saw. One of the desks was turned over and there were several holes in one of the walls. 'What on earth happened in here?' Maevis asked as we looked around the room.

'It's a long story but we got angry for a moment. Thankfully Jaden and Rowan were able to calm us down,' Kaiden responded before asking. 'What brings the two of you here? Not that we aren't happy to see the both of you, especially our beautiful mate,' I blushed at Kaiden's response. I quickly looked at Maevis and saw that she had a hurt look on her face. If it wasn't for the slight twitch at the corners of her mouth, I would think she was truly hurt.

'I was talking with Levi and he decided that he wanted to show the two of you his wolf form. And before you ask, I already contacted Doctor Veracruz and she said it was ok for him to shift,' Maevis told her sons.

'We would love to see your wolf Levi,' Kaiden said to me with a grin. When I looked at Kyro he also had a grin on his face.

'Ok then, the three of you go and spend time together. I will help Jaden and

Rowan clean up this mess,' Maevis said before shooing Kyro, Kaiden and I from the office. When we got outside, Kyro and Kaiden said that they would take me to a secluded part of the pack where I could shift without anybody seeing me. We walked quietly for several minutes before coming to a stop in a small clearing. I took a moment to admire the scenery in front of me. There was a waterfall in front of us and it led into a small sized lake with crystal clear water.

That water looks amazing. I want to go for a swim, Alpin said happily.

Me too. It's been a while since either of us had gone for a swim, I replied. I have only shifted into Alpin about six times in my life and on one of those occasions, I managed to sneak into the lake at my old pack and go for a swim. I quickly turned around and looked towards Kyro and Kaiden. I looked at them nervously, I wanted to show them what Alpin looked like but I was a little worried. I hadn't shifted in about a year and I was worried it would hurt.

'Would you like us to turn around so you can undress in private?' Kaiden asked me kindly.

'Y-yes please,' I stuttered out; I hadn't stuttered in a few days but right now I was nervous. Kyro and Kaiden turned around, giving me privacy to undress. Once I was undressed, I focused on my wolf form and eventually I felt my bones starting to break and reshape. I wanted to cry out from the pain, but I managed to stop myself from doing so. As soon as I had shifted into my wolf form, I felt stronger and safer. I quickly gave a soft bark so that Kyro and Kaiden knew that it was ok to turn around and when they did, they both got stunned looks on their faces.

'Oh, my Goddess. You're a white wolf,' Kaiden said with aww in his voice. I waited as Kyro and Kaiden looked me over, feeling proud of the looks they were giving me. A moment later, Kyro and Kaiden slowly approached me and I decided to sit back on my haunches. Once they were beside me, one on either side, they gently placed a hand on me. When they started to rub my fur, I purred.

Goddess that feels so good, I said happily as I purred again.

'Is it ok if we shift? Storm and Shadow would like to spend some time with Alpin,' Kaiden asked.

Yes, yes, yes. I want to see my mates, Alpin said with a yip. I nodded as best I could in wolf form and then Kyro and Kaiden stepped away from me. I looked down as they started to undress, only looking back up when I heard two soft barks. When I looked back up, I saw two big and beautiful black wolves standing in front of me.

Oh, my Goddess. Our mates are so big and strong. Mmm very nice indeed, Alpin said in a strange voice.

Oh, Goddess stop that Alpin, I whined lightly to him after he sent some not so clean images through our mind link.

Ok, ok. I'll try, Alpin responded.

I'll let you take control so you can spend some time with them now, I said to Alpin before pulling back and letting him take control.

About an hour later, Alpin pulled back and handed control back over to me. Once I was back in control, I realised that Kyro, Kaiden and I were all soaking wet.

I'm guessing you went for a swim in the lake, I said and Alpin yipped happily in response. I looked at Kyro and Kaiden and Kyro and Kaiden nodded towards their clothes and then to the trees. I guessed that they were telling me that they were going to behind the trees to shift and change. I quickly nodded to my mates and they grabbed their clothes and went behind the trees. Once they were out of sight, I shifted and got dressed.

'I'm dressed now,' I called out to Kyro and Kaiden so they knew it was ok to come back out. After walking out from behind the trees, Kyro and Kaiden walked towards me.

'Let's have a seat. Kaiden and I would like to tell you about what happened before you came to the office earlier,' Kyro said to me. The three of us moved to a dry patch of grass under a large tree and sat down.

'You don't have to tell me what happened in your office if you don't want to,' I told my mates. I wanted to know what had happened but I didn't want my mates to feel like they had to tell me.

'We want to tell you. We want to be completely open and honest with you. We don't want to hide anything from you,' Kaiden told me.

'Ok,' I replied with a smile.

'Now what we have to tell you is likely to upset you but we want to know that we will protect you,' Kyro informed me, a sad look on his face.

'I understand,' I told them. Kyro and Kaiden quickly looked each other before facing me again and taking several deep breaths.

'Alpha Redmond called us earlier,' Kyro stated with a slight edge to his voice.

No, no, no. He wants us back, I know it. He wants to take us from our mates. No, no, no, I whimpered to Alpin. I just found my mates; I didn't want to lose them.

'Hey, you will be ok. As Kyro said, we will protect you,' Kaiden said as he and Kyro each placed a hand on mine.

'Your old Alpha said he wanted to take you back but we told him that we would never give you back. You are our mate and we will love and protect you forever,' Kyro promised me.

'As for your old Alpha and old pack, Kaiden and I will look into ways of keeping them away from you. We aren't going to let them get their hands on you,' Kyro added.

'We will keep you informed of everything we find,' Kaiden promised me. 'Now, how about we enjoy this beautiful day behind us,' he added. The three of us sat quietly for a while and enjoyed the company and scenery.

I love them, please tell that Levi, Alpin said to me after several minutes of silence.

Are you sure Alpin? I said nervously.

I'm sure Levi and I know you love them too, Alpin replied. He was right, it's only been a few weeks since we first met my mates but I already loved them. In fact, I had been thinking about asking Kyro and Kaiden to mark me.

Ask them to Levi. Neither of us are ready for more right now but we are ready for marking our mates, Alpin encouraged. I took a deep breath before I got the courage to tell my mates how I felt about them.

'I know that you will protect me from my old Alpha,' I said to my mates, 'I l-love you. B-both of you,' I added with a blush. Kyro and Kaiden both smiled widely and they got tears in the corner of their eyes.

'We love you too Levi. We are so, so happy to hear that you love us as well,' Kaiden said before giving me a hug. After Kaiden moved back, Kyro moved forward and gave me a hug to.

'There was something that Alpin and I wanted to ask the both of you,' I said nervously.

'What is it? You can ask us anything,' Kyro promised.

'We would like the both of you to mark us as yours,' I told them and both their mouths dropped open.

'Are you sure about this Levi? We can wait as long as you want if you need us to,' Kaiden said, honesty evident in his voice. The fact that they were willing to wait for me to be ready only made me even more sure about my decision to have them mark me.

'I am sure. The two of you have been so wonderful to me and you have shown me so much love,' I said to the both of them.

'Do you know how the marking is done?' Kaiden asked and I shook my head.

'I don't know much. I just know it's something mates do and that it's done by biting each other on the neck,' I replied.

'You are right but there's a little more to it. There is a specific spot on the neck that mates bite during the marking. You nuzzle the neck of your mate until you find the special spot where you will bite down. You will know the spot by a feeling you get inside you. Once you find that spot, you bite down for several seconds. When you finish biting, you lick the bite mark in order to clean and close it. A few seconds later, the mate mark will appear on either the neck or on the shoulder,' Kyro explained.

'Would you like to mark us first or would you like us to mark you first?' Kaiden asked.

'I'm not sure,' I replied.

'I would suggest that you mark us first,' Kyro told me.

'Why?' I asked. I didn't mind that Kaiden suggested I mark them first; I just wondered the reason for it.

'Being marked can sometimes make you feel quite tired. For Kyro and I, the marking shouldn't tire us out too much. But for you it will quite likely tire you out and you will likely require a few hours of sleep afterwards,' Kyro explained.

'Ok,' I replied nervously.

'We'll walk you through this, ok?' Kaiden told me and I nodded, 'Ok, come over here and kneel in front of Kyro,' he added. I moved from where I was sitting and knelt down in front of Kyro as Kaiden had told me to. 'Ok, gently hold onto Kyro's shoulders and then nuzzle his neck until you find the sweet spot. You will know as soon as you find it,' Kaiden explained. I did as Kaiden said and a moment later I knew I had found the sweet spot when I suddenly felt sparks stronger than anything I had ever felt before. 'Good, now that you have found the right spot bite down gently. Hold the bite for a minute, yep like that,' Kaiden said softly. As soon as I bit down, I felt a stronger connection forming between Kyro and I. 'Ok, now remove your teeth and then clean and close the wound by licking it,' Kaiden said. After cleaning and sealing the bite, I sat back and looked at the bite. I admired the bite for a moment before looking at Kyro who had a big smile on his face. I was very happy and didn't want to move from where I was but I knew I needed to as I wanted to mark Kaiden as well.

'Kaiden's turn Little Wolf,' Kyro said to me. I nodded and then moved to sit in front of Kaiden. 'You ok?' Kaiden asked.

'Y-yes,' I replied with a smile.

'That's good. Now to mark Kaiden, you do the same to him as you did to me,' Kyro told me. I nodded and then proceeded to nuzzle Kaiden's neck to find the sweet spot. When I did, I bit down and waited for a moment like I had done with Kyro. I then pulled my teeth out and cleaned and closed the bite. I then sat back and looked between both of my mates; they each had big smiles on their faces and were purring softly.

'Thank you Little Wolf,' Kyro said happily.

'Are you ready for us to mark you? Or would you like to wait?' Kaiden asked.

'I want you to mark me now,' I replied confidently.

'Ok. I think it might be a good idea for Kaiden and I to mark you at the same time. I've read before that trying to mark someone who is already marked can sometimes cause serious problems. Even though we would be marking you straight after each other, you will still technically be marked when the second person goes to place their mark,' Kyro explained.

'When we mark you, it might hurt a little and you might feel a bit weird afterwards. It might feel as though you are floating,' Kaiden told me and I nodded.

'I understand,' I replied as I smiled at my two mates. Kyro and Kaiden nodded and moved so they were on either side of me. They both then started nuzzling my neck in order to find the sweet spots.

'Are you sure about this Levi?' Kyro asked his breath warm against my skin.

'I'm sure,' I whispered. I heard a soft purr before I felt a sharp sting on either side of my neck. I winced at the pain before feeling endorphins fill my body. Kaiden was right, it felt like I was floating right now. I then felt Kyro and Kaiden retract their teeth and start licking the bites they had made.

How do you feel Levi? Kaiden asked as he and Kyro moved back a bit.

I feel very happy right now. I love you both very much, I replied. Kyro and Kaiden exchanged a quick look before looking at me with big smiles on their faces. They were silent for a bit and I wondered what was wrong.

He didn't speak out loud, Alpin said. I was a little shocked to hear his voice as he had been quiet since telling me that he wanted our mates to mark us.

What do you mean? I asked my wolf, a little confused by his words.

When mate asked how we felt, he didn't speak out loud. He mind linked us, Alpin replied. Oh, my Goddess. Alpin was right. Kaiden had mind linked us and I had responded in the same manner. But how was that possible, I thought only those of the same pack could mind link each other.

'How's that possible?' I whispered softly.

'How's what possible?' Kyro asked.

'How did Kaiden mind link me? I thought we had to be from the same pack to mind link,' I replied.

'Yes, for the majority of wolves, you need to be from the same pack to mind link, but there is an exception. When mated wolves mark each other, they create their own special mind link. This means Kaiden and I can mind link you and you can mind link us in return. However, until you become a full member of the pack, you won't be able to mind link anyone else in the pack,' Kyro explained.

'Oh, that makes sense,' I replied. I felt a tingle on either side of my neck, reminding me I had just been marked by my mates and that I had marked them both in turn. 'When do the marks appear?' I asked. I had read a little about mate marks but I couldn't remember what it said about how long they take to appear after the marking process.

'It varies for everyone, but normally mate marks will appear within a couple of hours of the marking process being completed,' Kaiden replied.

'But for us, our marks are appearing right now,' Kyro said with a smile. I quickly looked at both my mates' necks and saw that the mate marks were indeed starting to appear. When they fully appeared, I took my time to admire them. Kyro's mate mark was a large tribal wolf howling at the moon, where the wolf's heart would be, there was a small wolf paw print. Kyro's mark was absolutely perfect. I turned to have a look at Kaiden's mate mark and was surprised by what I saw. His mate mark was a tribal wolf head, but that wasn't what surprised me. What surprised me is that unlike Kyro's mark which was a bold black colour; Kaiden's mark was a faded black. What also surprised me was that it seemed to be fading right in front of me. I quickly got up and ran to the water; I wanted to see what my mate marks looked like and to see if either was fading like Kaiden's was. I firstly checked the side which Kyro had marked; the mate mark was identical to the one I had seen on Kyro and was also a bold black colour. After seeing that Kyro's mate mark on me was ok, I checked the mate mark that Kaiden had done one me. I saw that the mate mark was identical to the one on Kaiden's neck and that it too was slowly fading.

'Why's it doing that? Why is it fading?' I whimpered as I fell to the ground. My mates rushed to me and helped me to sit up.

'I don't know Little Wolf. I've never heard of a mate mark fading like the ones you and Kaiden gave each other,' Kyro told me, a sad look in his eyes.

'Did I do something wrong? Is that why they are doing this?' I said as tears started flowing. 'No. I promise that you did nothing wrong ok,' Kaiden quickly assured me.

'As Kyro said, we don't know why this is happening but we will look into it. I promise we will find out what's going on,' he added. I went to respond but I felt a sudden wave of tiredness pass over me and I let out a yawn.

'You are exhausted. How about we go back to the pack house so we can get some rest. We can look into the fading mate marks after we've all had some rest,' Kyro suggested. I nodded and then Kyro and Kaiden helped me to stand. When I was standing, I swayed slightly and would have collapsed to the ground if Kyro hadn't of caught me first.

'Sleep Little Wolf. I'll carry you back to the pack house,' Kyro said softly. I nodded and the let out another yawn. Kyro gently picked me up and then the three of us headed back to the pack house. We had only walked for a couple of minutes before the events of the day caught up to me and I passed out in my mate's arms.

CHAPTER 39: KAIDEN'S POV

IT HAD BEEN almost a month since Kyro and I marked Levi and he in turn marked us. A couple of days after we had marked each other, the marks Levi and I had given each other had completely faded and we had lost the ability to mind link with each other. Though I was worried and upset by this, I was more concerned about Levi. He had taken it pretty hard and was worried that he had done something wrong. I promised him that he had done nothing wrong and that we would figure out what was going on together. We had decided not to try the marking again until we had figured out what had gone wrong the first time. Two weeks after we had done the marking, Kyro found a book in our library which gave a possible reason for the marking to have failed. The book stated that in the case of someone having two mates, the mate bond will be stronger with one of the mates than it will be with the other mate. The book also stated that when it came to marking each other, a marking might fail if the bond with one of the mates is not strong enough. I was upset at the thought that my bond with Levi was not strong enough to hold a marking and it took some time for me to accept it. Kyro was worried about how the news would affect both Levi and me, so we decided to speak with our parents before telling Levi the news. After some discussion, our parents promised to help us however they could but at the end of the day, there wasn't much they could do to interfere with a mate bond. Mum also told us to be open and honest with Levi, if we lied to him, it would only backfire on us.

So, one day, Kyro and I took Levi to our special spot and told him about what we had learned. Levi was scared that he was the reason for the weaker bond between him and I but I promised that it was not his fault. I told him that sometimes a mate bond just wasn't very strong and that it could happen between anyone. Kyro had also told Levi that we would try and strengthen the bond between us and that had helped make Levi feel better. Though I hoped to be able to strengthen the mate bond between Levi and I, I knew that it might not work and that our mate bond might fade completely one day. Aside from the mate bond issue that we were working around, Kyro and I were also dealing with the many threats which had come from Levi's old pack and also rogues which had attacked several times in the last month. Though we were unable to prove it; Kyro and I had a feeling that the rogues were being control by Alpha Redmond Sutherland, the Alpha from Levi's old pack. Besides the mate bond issue, the threats from Alpha Sutherland and the rogues, things had been good. Levi had started working alongside Kyro's and my mother when she was performing her Luna duties, so that he could have on the job training. As we hadn't fully introduced Levi to the pack yet, whenever we were asked about who he was and why he was here, we said that he was a wolf that had been rescued and brought to the pack to rehabilitate. We had also said that once he was ready, Levi would be officially joining the pack. And talking about Levi's official joining ceremony, it was taking place later today. And to say that Kyro and I were excited would be an understatement. Kyro and I had wanted to plan the whole ceremony ourselves but our mother had said that with the threats from Alpha Redmond and the rogues, we had enough to worry about and that she would handle the planning for the ceremony. She also said that she would have Diomika, Azalea, Tansy and several of the other pack women help with the planning.

There was excitement in the air, as there always was when a new member joined the pack. Before Diomika had joined a few weeks ago, the last joining ceremony had taken place several years ago. Most joining ceremonies were small affairs, but because Levi was the Future Luna of the pack, his ceremony was of a bit more importance than others were. Right now, Kyro and I were in our rooms getting dressed for the ceremony, while Levi was with our mother in her suite getting dressed. Our mother had said that Kyro and I weren't allowed to see Levi before the ceremony. Kyro and I told our mother that it was only a joining ceremony; we weren't doing the Luna ceremony or getting married but she was adamant that we weren't going to see Levi until he walked onto the stage. Oh, I forgot to mention that a week after we had marked each other, or attempted to in Levi's and my case, Levi had asked if he could sleep in the rooms with Kyro and I. Kyro and I happily agreed and so Levi alternated sleeping in Kyro's and my rooms. We had decided to turn Levi's old room into a studio/study for him and it took a couple of weeks to remodel to fit its new purpose. The only parts of his room that we didn't remodel were his wardrobe and bathroom, as Levi still preferred to bath and change in private. While I had been thinking about the last month, I hadn't realised Kyro had walked into the room until he called out to me from my bedroom.

'You dressed Kaiden?' he called out.

'Yeah,' I replied as I walked out of my wardrobe and saw Kyro sitting on my bed.

'Awesome. How you feeling about today?' Kyro asked nervously.

'I'm a bit nervous but I am ready for today,' I responded truthfully.

'Same here but let's get going. The sooner we move the quicker we can see our mate,' Kyro said with a big smile. I laughed and then raced my brother down the stairs. When we got to the foyer our father, Jaden, Jaden's dad and Rowan were waiting for us.

'Woah, slow down boys. You're acting like a couple of kids that have been let loose in a candy store,' our father said as he and the others laughed at us.

'Sorry we are just excited for today,' I replied.

'I know how you feel. When I formally introduced your mother to the pack, I was so nervous and excited that I could hardly stand still,' our dad told us.

'Do you have any advice for us?' Kyro asked. In addition to having Levi joining the pack today, Kyro and I were also informing the pack that Kyro and I were mated to Levi, which would also be our way of coming out, so we were nervous about that to.

'Just be honest with the pack. They love and respect the both of you,' our dad responded. 'Ok, we better get going now. Your mother has mind linked me several times asking where we were,' Dad added with a laugh. The five of us quickly headed to the back of the pack house and once outside we headed towards the pack's meeting hall.

Due to the size of our pack, we had to build a building specifically for events like the one today. When a new wolf joined the pack, we usually just had a few people attending like we did when Diomika joined, but because Levi was the Future Luna, almost every pack member would be in attendance. The only ones not attending were the patrol wolves on duty or those that couldn't attend for work or other reasons. When Kyro, myself and the others got to the pack hall, those in the room sat up straighter, stopped their conversations and watched as we walked to the stage at the front. Our dad, Jaden, his dad and Rowan went and sat down on their designated seats. While Jaden's dad and Rowan sat beside their mates; our dad went and sat beside Kingsley and Jaden went and sat beside his sister Sakura. Near our dad sat our other brothers and Azalea. Beside dad was a spare seat for our mum to sit on. Once everyone was sitting down, Kyro and I made our way to the front of the stage.

'Welcome everyone. Thank you for coming to today's joining ceremony,' I said in a loud, clear voice. The gathered pack members clapped and Kyro and I waited for it to die down before we continued. 'There are a couple of things that Alpha Kaiden and I would like to tell you all today. Firstly, you may have seen a young wolf walking around with either our mother, Kaiden or I, at some point in the last month and a bit,' Kyro said, followed by a mummering of yeses from the pack.

'Today we would like to formally introduce you to that wolf,' Kyro added once the murmuring died down. As soon as Kyro finished talking, Levi walked onto the stage with our mother. Levi was dressed in a nice pair of black dress pants and a light grey dress shirt with the sleeves rolled up. He also wore a pair of suspenders over the shirt and on his feet were a pair of black dress shoes.

Damn, he is hot, Shadow purred to Kyro and I. From the blush that suddenly appeared on Levi's face, Shadow had linked him too. Kyro and I watched as our mother walked Levi across the stage to us, and after giving Levi a quick hug, she went and sat down beside our father. Kyro and I each took one of Levi's hands and moved him so that he was now standing directly in between us.

'Everyone Alpha Kyro and I would like to introduce you to Levi Chang. Our mate and Future Luna of the Crimson Rose Pack,' I said in a proud voice. Levi flinched when the pack suddenly howled with joy at meeting their Future Luna. Though the pack loved my mother and respected her greatly as their Luna; they had been waiting to meet the new Luna ever since Kyro and I took over as Alphas. Kyro and I gently squeezed Levi's hands to provide comfort to him and then we waited for the pack to settle down. Once they had settled down, a few hands went up. Kyro pointed to one of them, silently telling them that they could stand and speak.

'It is a pleasure to meet the Future Luna of our pack. But I'm sure we are all wondering what this means; the two of you being mated to the same person that is. Are you also mated to each other or just the Future Luna?' an older pack member named Bill asked. He was once a warrior wolf but he had retired a few years ago and now spent his time helping out around the pack hospital. Kyro and I had expected this question and had already decided how would we respond when asked this question.

'Alpha Kaiden and I are only mated to Future Luna Levi, not each other. Alpha Kaiden and I share all aspects of the mate bond with Future Luna Levi, but with each other we share only our bond as twin brothers,' Kyro explained. We then waited silently as the pack processed the information that Kyro and I had told them. While we waited, we scanned the crowd and were proud to see the happy looks on almost everyone's faces. A couple of the women weren't happy, but those were women who had hoped that Kyro and I would choose them as our Lunas despite the many times we had turned them down.

'Are there any other questions?' I asked and hands went up again, so I pointed to one of the pack members.

'I don't have a question Alphas, Future Luna. I just wanted to say that I am happy to see that you have both found your mate and that if Future Luna Levi should need anything I and I believe the rest of the pack, will be happy to help however we can,' A younger woman named Nora said with a big smile.

'Thank you Nora,' I replied.

I mean it Alphas. If either of you or Future Luna Levi need anything, I'll be there, Nora said over mind link to Kyro and I, before sitting back down.

Thank you again Nora, Kyro replied. Nora and her mate Cleo were two of only a few of our pack members who were openly gay. They had experienced hostility from some fellow pack members when they came out but Kyro and I had been quick to put a stop to it.

'Now that we have introduced Levi, we will move onto making him an official member of the pack,' I said before turning to face Levi. Kyro moved to stand beside me facing Levi who looked nervous. 'Levi Chang you are here before us today because you wish to become a full member of the Crimson Rose Pack. Is that correct?' I asked Levi.

'Yes, it is,' Levi replied.

'You have been taught about what being a member of this pack entails. So, do you accept the responsibilities that come with being not only a member of this pack but also its Future Luna?' Kyro asked Levi.

'I do,' Levi responded, no hesitation in his voice at all.

I can't wait until a certain other day when he says I do, Storm purred out. I shook my head at his words, it was a little early to be thinking about that and right now we had to focus on Levi joining the pack.

'Do you accept that you may be required to give your life for this pack?' I asked.

'I do,' Levi said, once again there was no hesitation in his voice.

'Then Levi, please hold out your hand so that we can give you the pack bite,' Kyro said in a proud voice. Levi held out his right hand and Kyro gently took it. I could see the bite from his previous pack on his wrist, but it would disappear as soon as he was marked as a member of our pack. As Kyro brought Levi's hand towards his mouth, he smiled. Kyro then bit down on the inside of Levi's wrist; officially marking Levi as a member of our pack. Kyro then quickly licked the bite to clean and close it before stepping back, still holding Levi's hand. I instantly felt the connection form between us and our new pack member, and a moment later so did the rest of the pack. Kyro and I noticed Levi starting to sway as he connected with the entire pack, so we quickly grabbed a hold of his so he wouldn't fall.

'You are ok. Remember what we taught you about blocking out the links,' I whispered softly to Levi. Levi nodded and once he was ok, Kyro and I stepped back to address the pack once more. 'Everyone, please welcome the newest member of our family, Future Luna Levi Chang,' I said and everyone cheered. 'The official Luna Ceremony will take place in a month's time. Until then Alpha Kyro and I ask that everyone please assist Future Luna Levi if he needs it and please show him the respect that he deserves,' I added once the noise died down.

'We would now like to invite everyone to join us to celebrate Future Luna Levi joining our pack. So, if you could all make your way to the yard behind the pack house, there are food and drink waiting,' Kyro told everyone. Kyro, Levi and I waited for the gathered pack members to leave before making our way over to our family and friends who now stood at the side of the stage.

'Congratulations son,' our mother said as she gave Levi a hug. It made Kyro and I proud every time we heard our mother call Levi son. Levi had opened up to us about how he didn't know who his parents were or if he had any other family. He told us that his old pack had told him that he had been abandoned as a pup, but he wasn't sure if he believed them after all the other lies, they had told him. Kyro and I told our mate that even though he didn't know his birth family, he had a new family in Kyro and I. We also told him that our family were also his and that made Levi very happy. It was a few days after this conversation that Levi had stopped calling our parents by their first names and instead started calling them mum and dad. The first time Levi called them mum and dad; our parents cried. Levi had been worried that he had offended them but they were quick to assure him that they were quick to assure him that they were happy tears and that they were proud to have such a wonderful son. Our brothers were also quick to greet Levi as a brother and they often invited him to spend time with them.

'Oi! You boys coming, or what?' I heard someone call. I shook my head and saw that while Kyro and I had been standing there, everyone else had moved towards the door. Kyro and I quickly caught up with the others and then we all headed to the area where the party was being held. When we got there, Kyro and I walked around with Levi and introduced him to a few of the pack members. Eventually we came across Kyro's and my grandparents who were excited to meet Levi. Both our grandmas told Levi that if Kyro or I gave him any trouble, he was to tell them and they would deal with us. Our parents had chosen that moment to join us and when she heard what our grandmothers had said, our mother agreed.

'They're right Levi. If either of these boys give you any trouble, no matter how big or small, you come tell us. We will deal with them,' Mum said with a smile.

'Grandmas, Mamma,' Kyro and I whined at the same time.

'Don't grandma me young man. I don't care how old you boys get. I will happily put you both over my knee and smack your behinds,' Grandma said as she put her hands on her hips. Looking at her it was if she was daring us to challenge her. 'Same here boys,' Nanna said, copying Grandma's pose.

Ha ha. I love our Grandma and Nanna. Storm commented with a chuckle. Kyro and I looked to our grandpa and pop for help but they both shook their heads.

'You boys are on your own with this one,' Pop said and Grandpa nodded in agreement. Our Nanna and Grandpa were mated to each other, while Grandma was mated to Pop. Grandma and Pop were the Alpha and Luna of the pack before Kyro's and my parents. A small giggle broke me from my thoughts and Kyro and I turned to see Levi looking at us with a smile on his face.

'Levi, help us please?' Kyro begged theatrically.

'Nope, I'm with them,' Levi replied before giggling again. Kyro and I pouted which only served to make everyone laugh at us. Levi eventually took pity on us and gave Kyro and I a hug. After parting from the family, Kyro and I took Levi around to see a few more pack members. After spending a couple of hours talking to pack members, eating and drinking the delicious foods and drinks and simply enjoying the celebration. Soon it was time for the party to end and after thanking everyone for attending Levi, Kyro and I headed up to our suite on the Alpha floor. Once there we went to the lounge room to spend some time together.

'Is it alright if I go for a walk around outside?' Levi asked a couple of hours after we had returned to our suite. 'Of course, you are free to do as you wish Little Wolf,' Kyro replied.

'You two want to come with me?' Levi asked.

'We would love to but unfortunately we have some paperwork that we need to do. But don't let that stop you from enjoying your walk,' I replied with a smile.

'Ok,' Levi said. Kyro and I walked Levi downstairs and after Levi walked out of the pack house, Kyro and I went to our office on the Alpha floor to go over the paperwork that needed to be done.

CHAPTER 40: LEVI'S POV

AFTER I LEFT Kyro and Kaiden, I walked around the pack grounds taking in the various sights, sounds and smells. Over the past couple of months, I had gotten to know almost the entire pack territory. My favourite spot in the pack territory was the spot where I had first shown Kyro and Kaiden my wolf form. Thinking of that day, I decided to go to that spot for a while and let Alpin out for a swim. As I walked through the pack territory several pack members said hello, while others waved. It was nice to be in a pack filled with such kind and wonderful pack members. After walking for a few minutes, I sensed that I was no longer alone, so I stopped and looked around. At first, I couldn't see anything but then three females stepped out from behind a couple of trees and approached me. All three females were dressed in revealing clothing and wore a lot of makeup. I wasn't sure what they wanted but something about the way they looked at me as they approached instantly had me feeling defensive.

I don't like them, Levi, Alpin said as I felt him become on edge.

I feel the same Alpin, but we should give them a chance, I replied.

'Hello I'm Levi. Who are you?' I asked the females kindly.

'I'm Abigail and this is Ashley and Jessica,' The lead female replied as they came to a stop a few feet in front of me.

'It's a pleasure to meet you,' I replied, though it didn't currently feel like a pleasure. 'Is there something I can help you with?' I asked a moment later. The three of them smirked before Abigail responded to my question.

'Oh, there is something you can do for us,' Abigail said. The way she spoke cause Alpin's hackles to rise.

I don't think we are going to like what she says, Alpin said and I agreed.

'What is it that I can help you with?' I asked politely.

'You can stay the hell away from our Alphas and get the fuck out of our pack,' Ashley responded in an annoyed tone. *Oh, hell no. I am not leaving our mates,* Alpin replied with a snarl.

Of course, we aren't leaving them. They are our mates and we are staying with them. They make us happy and I'm sure we make them happy to, I told my angry wolf.

'I'm sorry but I can't do that. They are my mates and we belong together,' I told the girls. The three girls growled and took a step closer to me. It took a bit of effort for me not to step back in response to the girls' movement.

'You are not the Alphas' mate. You are just a weak, pathetic Omega. You aren't worthy of being an Alpha's mate, let alone the mate of two Alphas,' Abigail responded in an aggressive tone.

'It is not up to you to decide who is and isn't worthy of being an Alpha's mate. It is up to the Moon Goddess and she has put the Alphas and I together,' I told her as confidently as I could. Abigail snarled, grabbed the front of my shirt and shoved me to the ground.

'You are not the true mate of either of our Alphas. I don't know how you tricked them but I will make sure they know,' Abigail snarled. I went to stand back up but I was shoved back to the ground by the other two girls who then moved to stand either side of me. 'Are you going to leave the Alphas and this pack you pathetic Omega?' Ashley asked with a growl.

'No, they are my mates and this is my pack now,' I told her, trying very hard to not let my voice break. I tried to stand up again but was stopped by Ashley pushing me down again.

'They aren't your mates and this isn't your pack. I don't care what you may think but you don't belong here. No one wants you as the Luna of this pack. The Luna titles belongs to one of us, we are strong and most importantly we are female,' Abigail growled out. Abigail then went to hit me but a sudden snarl from close by caused Abigail, Ashley and Jessica to straighten up and look away from me. I too looked to where the snarl had come from and I saw a woman emerge from the trees a few metres away. As the woman came to a stop, I took note of how she looked. The woman was dressed in work out gear and from her build I guessed that she was a warrior.

'What the fucking hell do you three think you are doing to the Future Luna?' the woman asked in an even tone.

'It's none of your business and he isn't the Future Luna. He is just some pathetic Omega trying to weasel his way into the lives of those better than him,' Abigail replied. The unknown woman growled and then took several measured steps towards Abigail, Ashley and Jessica, who backed up several steps in response.

'He is the true mate of Alpha Kyro and Alpha Kaiden and as such he is our Future Luna. You will treat him with the respect that he deserves or so help me if the Alphas don't rip you to fucking shreds I will,' the woman growled out. 'Actually, I suggest you three leave right now or I might decide to rip you to fucking shreds for the hell of it. Though I haven't done my daily training yet and you girls don't pose much of a challenge for me, I'll still have fun beating the crap out of you,' the woman added with a smirk. Abigail, Ashley and Jessica looked as though they wanted to argue further but another growl from the woman caused them to turn tail and run. A couple of minutes after the girls had disappeared from sight, the unknown woman approached me. 'Future Luna Levi, are you ok?' the woman asked as she knelt down in front of me.

'I-I'm ok. Th-thank you for helping me,' I replied and the woman gave me a soft smile.

I like her, I wonder who she is, Alpin said.

I wonder that too, I responded.

'Can I know who you are?' I asked the woman.

'Of course, Future Luna. My name is Emerald Knox and I am the Head Warrior of the Crimson Rose Pack,' the woman replied.

Wow she's the Head Warrior. That's so awesome, Alpin said, awed by what Emerald had said.

'Why haven't I seen you before?' I asked Emerald. In the entire time I've been at the pack, not once had I seen Emerald.

'I've been at another pack for the last couple of months, helping to train their warriors,' Emerald replied.

'That sounds like fun,' I said and Emerald chuckled.

'It was at times but it was also a bit difficult. The pack had a lot of inexperienced warriors, which is why they had asked for our help to train them,' Emerald replied.

'Can I ask how you knew I was the Future Luna if you haven't been here for the last couple of months?' I asked.

'Of course. Though I haven't been here for the last couple of months, I've been kept up to date with everything going on. A few days ago, the Alphas sent me a photo of you and told me that you were their mate and the Future Luna of the pack,' Emerald explained. 'They weren't sure exactly when I would get back, but they wanted to make sure I knew who you were and what you looked like so I could look out for you when I did get back,' she explained further.

'Oh, that makes sense,' I replied. I loved the fact that my mates were looking out for me.

'Now, you have a couple of scratches on you. Would you like me to escort you to the pack hospital or to the Alphas?' Emerald asked as she helped me to stand.

'It's ok. I'm not hurt that bad,' I replied. 'Honestly, I just want to go somewhere I can think,' I added. Emerald looked at me thoughtfully for a moment before coming to a decision.

'I know I nice spot that you will probably like. There is a nice waterfall and lake there,' Emerald told me.

'I think I know the place you are talking about. Kyro and Kaiden took me there before. I mean Alpha Kyro and alpha Kaiden,' I said in response.

'You can call the Alphas by their first name Future Luna. You are their mate after all,' Emerald told me.

'Ok,' I said.

'Please call me Levi,' I added with a smile. Though I've only known her for a short while, I quite liked Emerald.

'Of course, Levi,' Emerald replied with a smile.

'Wait, I'm not sure if you can go to the haven. Kyro and Kaiden told me it was their secret spot,' I said to Emerald.

'I don't think they would mind,' Emerald replied. I nodded and then the two of us headed to the haven. It didn't take us long to get there and once we did, we sat down on some grass under the shade of a large tree. 'I should let you know that I have informed the Alphas of what happened. I apologise if you did not want me to do so, but I felt that I should,' Emerald said. I became worried about how Kyro and Kaiden would react to what Emerald told me and I started fidgeting.

'Are they angry with me?' I asked Emerald.

I hope they aren't angry. I don't want them to be angry with us, Alpin whined.

Me neither Alpin, I replied.

'No Levi, they aren't angry with you. They are angry with the three girls who dared to harm you and say those horrible things about to you,' Emerald responded. 'The Alphas were going to come and see how you were, but they were in the middle of a meeting. They were about to leave the meeting but Luna Maevis told them to give you some time alone, so they stayed at the meeting. They did tell me to tell you that if you need them just mind link them and they will come right away,' Emerald added and I smiled at her words. I was happy that Kyro and Kaiden were willing to drop what they were doing to come and make sure that I was alright. I was also happy that mum convinced them to stay in the meeting. I felt safe with Emerald and I didn't want my mates to miss a meeting if it could be avoided. 'The Alphas also wanted me to tell you that they will be speaking with the three wolves about they had done and that they would also like to speak with you about it to,' Emerald told me.

'Thank you for telling the Emerald. I don't know if I would have been able to,' I told Emerald honestly.

'No need to thank me Levi. It's a pleasure to help you however I can,' Emerald replied with a smile.

I wonder if she would teach us how to fight. As head warrior she must be strong and skilled, so having her teach us would be awesome, Alpin said to me.

It would be nice to be able to defend ourselves and the pack if something ever happened, I agreed.

Ask her then, Alpin urged.

'My wolf Alpin and I were wondering if you would be able to teach us how to fight,' I said to Emerald.

'It would be an honour to teach you. But and I don't mean any offence by this, why not ask the Alphas? They are better fighters than me and I'm sure they would be happy to teach you,' Emerald replied.

'They already have enough to worry about. I didn't want to bother them with this. I know you are probably busy with your duties as Head Warrior to but I thought you would have a little more free time than the Alphas,' I replied. 'I'm sorry if I offended you in any way,' I added. 'No offence taken Levi. You are right, as head warrior I am quite busy but compared to the Alphas I do have a bit more free time,' Emerald replied with a smile. 'And to answer your initial question I would be happy to teach you,' she added. After spending another hour or so talking and getting to know each other, we decided to head to the pack house as we were both starting to get hungry. Once we got to the pack house, we headed inside to the ground floor kitchen. 'Hmm what to eat?' Emerald asked no one in particular as we entered the kitchen.

'I think some ham and cucumber sandwiches would be nice,' I told her.

'That does sound good,' Emerald agreed. The two of us gathered the necessary ingredients and after making our sandwiches, I took them to the table. While I sat down with the sandwiches, Emerald grabbed us a couple of glasses of water and then she sat down beside me.

'Mmm yummy,' Emerald said as she took a bite of a sandwich.

'Definitely,' I agreed, polishing off my sandwich.

'What would you like to do now Levi?' Emerald asked after we had finished eating and placed our dishes into the sink.

'Do you want to watch a movie?' I asked.

'I like the sound of that. Did you want to watch one down here or one upstairs in your room?' Emerald replied.

'My room. That way we can lay down and watch the movie,' I responded. Emerald smiled and then they two of us headed to the elevator, taking it up to the Alpha floor. After getting off the elevator at the Alpha floor, we headed to the room Kyro's room.

'Are you ok?' I asked Emerald when I saw her stopped at the door to Kyro's room.

'This is Alpha Kyro's room, I'm not sure if I can go in there without his consent,' Emerald replied.

'Oh, I share this room with Kyro and I also sometimes share rooms with Kaiden,' I told her, 'I don't think Kyro would mind you coming in to watch a movie with me,' I added. Emerald nodded and then the two of us went inside and sat on the bed. 'What sort of movie do you want to watch? Mum took me shopping a couple of times and we brought a few movies I liked the look of,' I said to Emerald.

'Mum? Does your mother live here as well? What about your father?' Emerald asked with a hint of confusion in her voice.

'No, I don't actually know who my mother and father are,' I replied. 'Mum is what I call Kyro's and Kaiden's mother. I also call their father, dad,' I added and Emerald nodded in understanding.

'Nice. Do you have any Disney movies? I quite like Disney movies,' Emerald said.

'Yes, I have a few Disney movies. I've seen most of them since I got them though,' I answered. 'What ones haven't you seen yet?' Emerald asked.

'Umm there is Mulan one and two, Princess Diaries one and two and a couple of other movies,' I replied. 'How about we start with the Mulan movies?' Emerald suggested. I nodded and then went and put the first Mulan movie on. I then got comfortable on the bed and so did Emerald. The two of us enjoyed the movie and afterwards we decided to get some snacks before watching the second Mulan movie. Once we had grabbed some popcorn, chips and drinks from the kitchen, we returned to the bedroom and put the second Mulan movie on. About half way through the movie I started feeling tired and then I started drifting off. Knowing I would soon fall asleep, I moved up to the pillows and snuggled up under the blankets. A few minutes later all I saw was darkness.

CHAPTER 41: EMERALD'S POV

AFTER LEVI HAD fallen asleep, I decided to turn the movie off so it didn't wake him up. Once I had turned it off, I decided I should link the Alphas and see what they wanted me to do now that Levi was asleep.

Alpha Kyro, Alpha Kaiden. Future Luna Levi is asleep in Alpha Kyro's room. What would you like me to do? I asked the Alphas.

Could you stay there with him? A problem has come up that we need to deal with and we'd rather Levi not be alone right now, Alpha Kyro replied.

Of course, Alpha, I answered. After the Alphas cut the mind link, I turned my attention back to Levi.

There's something about him isn't there, Emerald? My wolf Cyan said to me.

There is, I'm not sure what it is but there is definitely something special about him. I feel very protective of him, not just because he is our Future Luna but also because of something else, I said to Cyan. Neither of us had felt this sort of feeling before, so we were confused.

Let's shift and lay down beside Levi, Cyan said.

Why shift? I asked Cyan. It would be easier for me to lay down on the bed in my human form than my wolf form.

I don't know. I just feel the need to shift and be near Levi right now, Cyan responded. I nodded to myself before standing up, undressing and shifting into my black wolf form. I then carefully got onto the bed carefully, making sure to not disturb Levi. I then curled up and quickly fell asleep.

When I woke up the next morning, I saw Alphas Kyro and Kaiden, Former Alpha Denton, Beta Jaden and Gamma Rowan looking at me with confusion written on their faces. I quickly turned to face Levi to see if something was wrong with him but I saw that he was still sleeping peacefully.

Could you please shift Emerald? There's something we need to talk about, Alpha Kaiden said to me over mind link. I nodded and then the guys turned around the give me privacy to shift and get dressed. 'You can turn around now,' I said after I finished getting dressed.

'We need to discuss what happened last night,' Alpha Kyro told me.

'What happened?' I asked concerned. What could have happened that both Alphas, the Former Alpha, the Beta and Gamma needed to talk with me. Could there have been an attack? Did something threaten the pack?

'When I came in last night to get you and Levi for dinner, you swiped at me in your sleep,' Gamma Rowan replied.

'What?' I asked. I don't remember anyone coming into the room and I certainly don't remember swiping at them.

'There is that matter and there is also the matter of the matching marks on yours and Levi's inner left wrist,' Former Alpha Denton added. I looked down at my inner left wrist and sure enough there was an unfamiliar mark there. The mark was small tribal wolf paw print with an arrow in the middle of it. The paw print was bold black in colour while the arrow was forest green.

Wow. It's so pretty, Cyan commented with a purr.

It definitely is, I agreed. Despite how beautiful or pretty I found the mark to be, I couldn't help but wonder how it got there. 'How did this get here?' I asked no one in particular.

'Rowan perhaps you should tell Emerald exactly what happened when you came in here last night,' Alpha Kyro said to Gamma Rowan who nodded before turning to face me.

Rowan's POV:

It was close to midnight and Kyro, Kaiden, Jaden and I had just finished a meeting we had been in since the joining ceremony ended. We were all very tired but we decided to get something to eat before we went to sleep. We headed to the kitchen on the Alpha floor and quickly decided to have noodles as it was the easiest thing to make at this time of night.

'Do you want me to check on Levi and Emerald while you guys make the noodles?' I asked the others.

'Yes please,' Kyro replied tiredly. I nodded and then turned and left the kitchen. I then headed to Kyro's room to check on Levi and Emerald. When I knocked on the door, I got no response so I opened the door and walked inside. Once inside, I saw Emerald was curled up asleep in her wolf form at the end of the bed with her head was facing towards the door. Levi on the other hand was snuggled under the blankets at the head of the bed. I decided to leave them be but as I turned to leave, I noticed a bowl sitting on the edge of the bed near Levi. I decided to move the bowl before leaving so it wouldn't be accidently knocked off the bed. However, when I was only a short distance from the bed, Emerald suddenly swiped at me. I was annoyed and surprised by this as she wouldn't normally try to attack me. Emerald remained fast asleep when she swiped at me, so I figured she must have been dreaming. However, when I went to move the bowl again, Emerald swiped at me and also added a soft growl. I made sure to keep looking at Emerald as I reached for the bowl, so I had seen that she again remained asleep the entire time.

'What the hell was that?' I asked myself quietly.

Hey guys, can you come in here for a moment? There's something you need to see, I called to Kyro, Kaiden and Jaden over mind link. A moment later, the three of them came into the room quietly.

'What's up?' Kyro asked after seeing that nothing was amiss.

'Watch this,' I replied before moving to grab the bowl again. This time, Emerald sat up on her haunches, swiped at me and growled a little louder than before. Though it wasn't loud enough to wake Levi up. After Emerald reacted, I stepped back from the bed and Emerald returned to her previous position.

'What the hell was that? She remained asleep when she reacted. I've never seen something like that before,' Jaden said, startled by Emerald's actions.

'I don't know. We should ask my parents about it in the morning. For now, we should leave them be,' Kaiden replied.

'Sounds good, let's go,' Kyro responded. The four of us then quietly left the room, with me closely the door behind us. After we left the room, we returned to the kitchen and had the noodles that we had made. When we had finished eating, we promised to meet up in the morning to discuss what had happened with Emerald and then we all went to bed.

Emerald's POV:

I couldn't believe what Rowan had just told me.

Cyan, do you have any clue about why we did that? I asked my wolf. Cyan didn't respond as she was just as confused as I was about what had happened. 'I'm so sorry for my actions Gamma Rowan. I promise that I did not mean to,' I said to Rowan before bowing my head in submission.

'You don't need to apologise. I know you didn't mean to do it Emerald,' Rowan replied with a smile.

'The boys told me this morning about what had happened. Unfortunately, I don't know why you did what you did but we might be able to find some information in the library,' Former Alpha Denton told me.

'Could it have something to do with Levi being a white wolf?' Kyro asked his father.

'It might,' Former Alpha Denton replied.

Wow Levi is a white wolf. That's amazing, Cyan said and I agreed. I had always wanted to see a white wolf.

'Emerald why don't you go have a shower, get changed and then have something to eat before meeting us in the Alpha floor library,' Former Alpha Denton said. I quickly looked at Levi. I didn't want to leave him for some reason but I knew he would be safe with his mates nearby, so after saying goodbye to everyone I left to do as Former Alpha Denton suggested. After I had finished showering and changing, I grabbed a quick bite to eat before heading to the Alpha floor library. There were a lot of important items and books in the Alpha floor library and no one was allowed in there without the express permission of the Alphas. When I went inside, I found Former Alpha Denton, Beta Jaden and Gamma Rowan already looking through some books.

'Former Alpha Denton, Beta Jaden, Gamma Rowan,' I said respectfully.

'Please Emerald. There's no need to be so formal, just use our first names,' Former Alpha Denton told me and I smiled.

'Of course, Denton. Where do you want me to start?' I replied politely.

'There are some books about the different bonds wolves experience over there that you can start with,' Denton replied while pointing to a section of the library behind me. I nodded and then went and grabbed several books from the section

Denton had suggested. I them brought the books over to a seat and sat down with them.

'I think I found something,' Jaden called out almost an hour later. Denton, Rowan and I moved over to where Jaden was sitting at a table and looked at the book he had found. 'It's specifically about white wolves,' Jaden said as Denton moved the book in front of him. Denton quietly read through the information for several minutes before nodding several times.

'This is it,' he said as he looked up at us. 'Listen to this,' he added before reading from the page opened in front of him. 'White wolves are some of the strongest and most powerful wolves in the world. White wolves are specifically chosen by the Moon Goddess and are said to be destined for great things. However, the Moon Goddess is said to have recognised that being destined for great things meant that these white wolves would be targets for those who wanted to harm others. Because of this the Moon Goddess created wolves who were tasked with protecting the white wolves. These wolves are known as Guardian wolves and were linked to a specific white wolf. Though rare, a white wolf and their guardian may be mated to each other. The bond between a white wolf and their guardian is similar to that of the bond between mates. They will have the protective instincts and special mind link like mates do but they won't have the sexual aspects of the mate bond. Unless of course the white wolf and their guardian are mates, in which case they will have the sexual aspects of the bond as well. Guardian wolves are highly protective of their charges and have been known to do things other wolves are unable to do, such as reacting to threats in their sleep. A white wolf and their guardian can be identified by a unique mark located on the inner left wrist of both wolves,' Denton explained. We all sat quietly, trying to take in all the information that he had told us.

'Wow, that explains why you reacted like you did and it also explains the marks on yours and Levi's wrists,' Rowan said and I nodded.

'We should tell Kyro, Kaiden, and Levi about what we found,' I said.

'Let's go to the Alphas' office. It will be easier to discuss this with them there,' Jaden said, 'I'll link Kyro and Kaiden to let them know,' he added. Denton nodded to Jaden before putting a marking the page and then closing and picking up the book. Once that was done, the four of us left the library and headed to the Alpha's office. When we went into the Alphas' office, we found Kyro, Kaiden and Levi already waiting for us on one of the couches.

'We told Levi about what had happened last night and about the mark on both your wrists,' Alpha Kyro said to me as Denton, Jaden, Rowan and I sat down on another couple of couches. 'They also said that you found out why this happened,' Levi said softly.

'We have, son,' Denton said to Levi as he placed the book that we had found down on the table in front of us. He then opened the book to the page he had marked and turned it so that Kyro, Kaiden and Levi could read it. as Kyro, Kaiden and Levi read through the page, the rest of us sat quietly and waited for them to finish reading.

'Wow. So, you are Levi's Guardian Wolf,' Kaiden said to me, a hint of admiration in his voice. 'It would appear so,' I replied.

'So, what happens now?' Levi asked. None of us responded, instead we just looked at each other. I don't think any of us knew quite what to do with the information we had discovered. 'Jaden, Rowan, let's leave Kyro, Kaiden, Levi and Emerald to discuss this between themselves,' Denton said as he stood up. 'If you four need anything let us know,' he added before he, Jaden and Rowan left the office.

'Firstly, how do the two of you feel about this?' Kyro asked Levi and I.

'I am good with it. When I had met Levi yesterday, I felt strangely protective if him. I mean I felt protective of him as my Future Luna but there was also this feeling that there was something more to it,' I explained, hoping they would understand what I meant.

'I felt very safe when I met Emerald yesterday. I haven't felt this safe with anyone other than the two of you,' Levi said to Kyro and Kaiden.

'We don't know much about the bond between white wolves and their guardian, so for now I think you should move into one of the spare rooms on the Alpha floor,' Kaiden said to me.

'He's right. We will have to read up more information about white wolves and Guardian wolves to better understand the bond the two of you now share. But for now, it's probably best if you two stick close together. That is when Kaiden and I aren't spending time with him,' Kyro said after Kaiden finished talking.

'What about my duties as Head Warrior? When I doing those, I won't be able to fully keep my eyes on Levi,' I asked.

'If you don't mind Levi, we will arrange for a warrior to be with you whenever one of us three can't be with you,' Kaiden said to Levi.

'I don't mind. I know the three of you will feel better if there was someone protecting me at all times,' Levi responded. 'And it would honestly make me feel better too,' he added.

'Ok well let's leave it there for now,' Kyro said and we all nodded.

'Would you like some help to pack up your room Emerald?' Levi asked.

'That would be nice,' I replied with a smile.

'Ok then. Kyro and I are going to do some more research on white wolves and Guardian wolves. If you two need help moving stuff just call us and we will come help,' Kaiden told Levi and I. The four of us then left the Alpha office, before Levi and I headed to my room and Kyro and Kaiden headed to the Alpha floor library. It took a few hours for Levi and I to completely pack up my room and when we were done, we contacted Kyro and Kaiden who came and helped move my things to my new room.

CHAPTER 42: LEVI'S POV

IT HAD BEEN a week since I learned that Emerald was my Guardian wolf. During that time, Kyro, Kaiden, Emerald and I had done a lot of research into the bond. During our research we had discovered some interesting information. For example, we learned that Guardian wolves gained strength and speed once they had connected with their white wolf charge. We also learned that a Guardian wolf's senses heightened even more than normal. Kyro thought that this might explain how a Guardian wolf could react to threats in their sleep. A couple of days after learning about our bond, Emerald had started teaching me how to fight. Emerald had said that would train me to fight in human form before teaching me how to fight in my wolf form. Kyro, Kaiden and several others had also given me some pointers in regards to fighting. Being part of a pack that was so kind and so willing to help its fellow pack members, felt really good. Today I had planned to take time off from research and just rest and relax at the pack house, but I had gotten a mind link from Diomika early this morning. She had told me she had the day off from the pack hospital and was wondering if I wanted to spend some time together. I said yes straight away as it had been some time since we had gotten the chance to hang out. I decided that today would also be a good time to introduce Emerald and Diomika to each other. With everything that's been happening in the last week, I hadn't gotten the chance to do so before this.

'Where are we going Levi?' Emerald asked as we walked through the pack.

'I want to introduce you to someone,' I replied.

'Ok,' Emerald said. She didn't ask me who it was that I was going to introduce her to and I figured that was because she was from this pack and would know pretty much all the pack members already. And as she had said when we first me, she was kept up to date with what happened in the pack during her absence, so she has probably already guessed who I was going to introduce her to. When we got to the home Diomika shared with her mate Felix, I took a moment to admire the home. It would be best to describe the home as a quaint little cottage. Out the front of the home were several small gardens filled with beautiful flowers and trees. Surrounding the home was a lovely white picket fence.

'Are you ok Levi?' Emerald asked from beside me.

'Yes. Just admiring the lovely cottage,' I replied. Emerald smiled and then the two of us walked up to the front door. I knocked on the door and then Emerald and I waited for someone to answer. We didn't have to wait long and when the door did open, Felix was standing in the doorway.

'Future Luna Levi, Head Warrior Knox, welcome to my home,' Felix said politely with a smile on his face.

'Felix, I've told you it's just Levi and I'm sure Emerald won't mind if you call her by her name,' I said to Felix.

'He's right, please just call me Emerald,' Emerald said in agreement with me.

'My apologies Levi, Emerald,' Felix said with a small chuckle. 'Come on in,' he added before stepping aside and letting Emerald and I inside.

'How have you been Felix?' I asked as we walked through the home. 'I've been pretty good. And the two of you?' Felix replied.

'I've been a little busy but overall, I've been ok,' I answered.

'Same here, there's been a bit to do and take in during the last week,' Emerald said after me. I went to say something but stopped when I heard someone call out to me.

'Lee-Lee,' I heard the person squeal out. I turned to see Diomika standing across the room from us with a big smile on her face.

'Dio,' I replied before running over to Diomika and giving her a hug.

'How have you been Little One?' Diomika asked as we broke from the hug.

'I've been good. Sorry I haven't come to see you in a while,' I replied. I felt bad that I haven't spent much time with Diomika since coming to the pack.

'It's alright. I understand that as Future Luna you have a lot to learn. Besides I've been quite busy with work at the pack hospital myself,' Diomika responded before giving me another hug. I heard someone clear their throat and I turned to see Emerald looking at Diomika with a slightly puzzled expression.

'Oh, I'm sorry. I haven't introduced you two yet,' I said as I grabbed Diomika's hand and walked her over to where her mate and Emerald were standing.

'Emerald this is my sister Diomika. Diomika this is Emerald, Head Warrior of the Crimson Rose Pack and also my Guardian wolf,' I said, introducing Emerald and Diomika to each other. 'It's a pleasure to meet you Diomika,' Emerald said as she held her hand out. 'I didn't realise that Levi had family here,' she added.

'It's a pleasure to meet you too,' Diomika replied as she shook Emerald's hand. 'Levi and I aren't biologically related but we consider each other family,' Diomika added as she gave me a smile.

'Blood doesn't make family. Love and respect do,' Emerald said with a soft smile.

'That's true,' Diomika agreed.

'What's a Guardian wolf? I've never heard the term before,' Felix asked, interrupting the conversation between Emerald and Diomika.

'Why don't we go sit down first and then Levi and I can explain what it is?' Emerald suggested.

'Of course, let's head to the kitchen. I just made some snacks,' Diomika said before leading the way to the kitchen. When we got to the kitchen, the four of us sat down at the dining table. The dining table was covered with different foods and drinks and my tummy rumbled at the sight.

'Mmm this looks really yummy,' I said as I grabbed one of the sandwiches.

Diomika is a good cook, Alpin commented.

'Thanks. I originally planned to only make a few things but I got a little carried away,' Diomika replied with a small laugh.

'I don't mind one bit,' Emerald said as she eyed the food. One thing I have noticed about Emerald is that she had a big appetite.

She sure does, she eats about the same as our mates. Yet none of them seem to put on much weight, Alpin said.

That is true, I replied, chuckling silently to myself.

'I don't mind either,' Felix agreed as he grabbed a slice of meatloaf. The four of us spent a little while enjoying the food and drink before I decided that it was time to explain the bond between Emerald and I.

'You two were wondering what a Guardian wolf is?' I asked Felix and Diomika who both nodded.

'We were,' Diomika replied for her and her mate.

'Well, the first thing you need to know is that I am a white wolf,' I said. Diomika's and Felix's eyes went wide at my words.

'A white wolf? Really?' Diomika asked, her voice filled with wonder. I had never told anyone about the colour of my wolf before my mates. I knew that white wolves were rare and I was always worried what my old Alpha would do if he found out.

'I am really a white wolf,' I said in response to Diomika's questions.

'I am guessing the fact that you are a white wolf has something to do with Emerald being your Guardian wolf,' Felix said. I wasn't surprised that Felix had figured out the connection. From the first time I met him, I had found him to be a quick thinker.

'It does. From what we have read, white wolves are apparently some of the strongest and most powerful wolves in the world. They are said to be chosen by the Moon Goddess for great things,' Emerald explained. 'The Moon Goddess recognised that this would mean the white wolves would become targets and as such they would need protecting. So, the Moon Goddess created special wolves called Guardian wolves whose duty it was to protect the white wolves. Each Guardian wolf is charged with protecting one white wolf,' Emerald explained further.

'How do you know who is a Guardian wolf?' Felix asked.

'You can tell a white wolf and their Guardian wolf by the unique marks they have on their inner left wrist,' I replied. Emerald and I held out our left wrists to show Felix and Diomika the mark that we shared.

'Wow. It's very pretty,' Diomika said as she looked at the mark.

'Did either of you gain any special abilities from the bond? Any superpowers so to speak?' Felix asked, an excited look on his face.

'Superpowers, ha ha. They are wolves, not superheroes,' Diomika said with a chuckle.

'I know, I know. I'm just curious,' Felix said before pouting.

'Aww. I know my love,' Diomika said before giving her mate a kiss on the cheek.

'We don't fully understand the bond between us. We only learned about it a week ago but we have been researching it as much as we can since then,' I said.

'If you want some help doing some research, I'm more than happy to help. I love to research stuff,' Felix offered. Felix was a bookworm; the first time I had met him was in the main pack library. However, if you looked at him you wouldn't think that Felix was a bookworm. He was tall, tanned, had several piercings and was covered in tattoos. He looked more like a biker than a bookworm. But as Felix told me just after we met, you can never judge a book by its cover. 'Thanks for the offer, Felix,' Emerald said in response to Felix's offer.

'You're more than welcome,' Felix replied. 'I've got to get going now as my shift at the hospital starts soon,' he added as he stood up.

'You have a good day at work my dear,' Diomika said as she stood up and gave her mate a hug.

'I will my love. You three have a good day too,' Felix replied before giving his mate a kiss and then leaving the kitchen.

I like Felix. He's a really good guy, Alpin said as Felix left the kitchen. After Felix had left, Diomika, Emerald and I grabbed some of the food and drink off the dining table and brought it to the lounge room. Once there, we had a look at the collection of movies on the shelf and chose one to watch. We then spent a couple of hours talking, eating and enjoying the movie. When Emerald and I left Diomika's place, we promised to spend some more time together soon. After we left, Emerald and I headed back to the pack house. Once there we headed straight up to the Alpha floor. I wanted to do some reading, so I went straight to my study, which was my old room. While I went to my study, Emerald said she would go to her room and do some paperwork. Since her room was right next to my study, we didn't worry about getting a warrior to come stay with me. Emerald however did say that if I needed her, I just had to call and she would be right there. After separating from Emerald and heading into my study, I went straight to my bookshelf and looked through the different books I had. In the time that I had been at the pack, I had gotten quite a few books. Once I had chosen a book, I went and sat down on one of my bean bags and started reading. After reading for about an hour I started feeling hungry, so I got up to grab something to eat. I put the book I had been reading back on the bookshelf and then went over to my mini fridge. Kyro and Kaiden had gotten me the mini fridge a few days ago and we had gotten some food and drinks to put in it. They said that this would save me from having to walk back and forth to the kitchen every time I got hungry. I had a quick look in the mini fridge before grabbing an apple and a bottle of water. I then took my stuff back to the bean back and sat down. As I ate the apple and drank the water, I thought back to the first time I had met Felix.

~ Flashback ~

I had just had a wonderful breakfast with Kyro and Kaiden in our private kitchen. My mates had made a big breakfast consisting of eggs, bacon, toast, fruit, juice and tea. At first, I had been worried that we weren't going to be able to finish it but I had forgotten about my mates' appetites. While I had one egg, a couple of slices of bacon, a slice of toast, a banana and a small juice; my mates finished off everything else. After breakfast, Kyro and Kaiden went to their office to deal with some of their Alpha duties and I went to my room and had a quick shower before getting changed. After I had changed, I went downstairs to meet Diomika. Diomika had asked me last night if I wanted to meet her mate and I had quickly agreed; I had been looking forward to meeting her mate. As I walked out of the elevator, I saw Diomika standing there waiting for me.

'Good morning, Lee-Lee,' Diomika said as I walked over to her.

'Good morning, Dio,' I replied as we hugged.

'How are you doing this morning?' Diomika asked after we broke the hug.

'I'm doing good,' I replied. 'How are you?'

'I'm also good,' Diomika answered.

'So, where we headed?' I asked as Diomika led the way through the pack house.

'The library,' Diomika replied. I nodded and the two of us walked to the library in silence. When we got to the library, I saw a few pack members sitting around the room. Some were reading, some were talking and others were just enjoying the quiet.

'Future Luna Levi,' Someone called out. I turned to see Nora and her mate Cleo sitting at a table playing a board game.

'Nora, Cleo. How are you two this morning?' I asked as Diomika and I walked over to the two women. 'We are doing alright. How are the two of you?' Cleo replied.

'We are doing pretty well,' I replied.

'Would you like to join in? There's always room for more,' Nora offered.

'We'd love to but we are here to see Felix,' Diomika replied, 'Maybe another time though,' she added. 'Sounds good,' Cora replied with a smile.

'Doctor Blackwell is at the back of the library,' Nora said.

'Thanks. I hope you enjoy the rest of your day,' I said to Nora and Cleo. The girls both smiled and then Diomika and I headed to where Nora said Felix was. When we next came to a stop, I saw a nicely dressed guy with his head stuck in a book. I looked at Diomika and she put a finger to her lip, signalling for me to be quiet.

That's my mate Felix, Diomika said. I smiled, nodded and then watched as Diomika walked up behind her mate. 'Guess who?' Diomika asked after placing her hands over Felix's eyes. 'Hmm it's either the most beautiful woman in the world or it is my mate,' Felix replied with a smile. Felix gently removed Diomika's hands from his eyes, stood up and then turned to face Diomika. 'Well, if it isn't my mate who just so happens to be the most beautiful woman in the world,' Felix said with a big smile. Felix took Diomika in his arms and then gave her a kiss on the cheek. Felix's actions caused Diomika to blush and then let out a soft giggle. 'How are you my dear?' Felix asked Diomika.

'I'm am good my love,' Diomika replied.

'I am glad to hear that,' Felix said, giving Diomika another kiss on the cheek. I blushed and looked away; giving the two mates some privacy.

'Oh, I'm so sorry,' A man's voice said causing me to look back up. 'I didn't mean to ignore you Future Luna Levi,' Felix said while still holding Diomika in his arms.

'It's ok. I understand that being around your mate can sometimes make you forget everything else,' I replied with a smile.

'Let me introduce myself. I am Felix Blackwell. I am one of the pack psychologists,' Felix said, introducing himself. 'Blackwell. Are you Aurora's brother?' I asked.

'I am,' Felix replied. I mentally face palmed myself, I can't believe I didn't realise the connection before this.

'It's a pleasure to meet you. Diomika has told me a lot about you,' I said and Felix smiled.

'Hopefully it's all good stuff,' Felix said with a chuckle.

'Mostly,' Diomika said and Felix feigned a hurt look. Diomika chuckled and then gave Felix a kiss, causing him to smile.

'Why don't we all take a seat,' Felix said. Diomika and I nodded and then the three of us sat down at the table. As I sat down, I had a look at the book that Felix had been reading. It was a book of poems from around the world.

Wouldn't have thought, he would be someone who read poetry, Alpin commented. He was right, Felix looked more likely to be someone who would read about bikes and cars, than to read poetry.

'Is everything ok Future Luna?' Felix asked when he saw me looking at the book.

'Yeah. I just wouldn't have picked you to be someone who read poetry,' I replied. 'I mean no offence by that,' I added quickly.

'None taken,' Felix replied. 'You can't always tell what someone is like just by looking at them. As the saying goes, you can't judge a book by its cover,' he added.

'That's a good saying,' I said with a smile. Felix, Diomika and I spent the next couple of hours talking and getting to know each other. By the end of it, I really liked Felix; he was so kind and respectful.

'It was a pleasure meeting you, Levi,' Felix said. After he had called me Future Luna several times, I had asked Felix to just call me Levi.

'It was a pleasure to meet you as well. I am glad that Diomika has such a wonderful mate,' I said with a smile. 'Just know that if you hurt her, I will come after you,' I added in a serious tone.

'I will never hurt Diomika. I promise you Future Luna,' Felix replied, using my title to show he was serious. I smiled and then after saying goodbye to Diomika and Felix, I left the library and returned to my study.

~ End of Flashback ~

CHAPTER 43: LEVI'S POV

IT HAD BEEN a month since I had become an official member of the Crimson Rose Pack. During that time, I hadn't had any more run ins with Abigail, Ashley and Jessica. Kyro and Kaiden had told me that they had spoken with the girls and told them that what they had done to me was considered treason and as such, they could be banished or executed for their actions. Kyro and Kaiden had warned the girls, telling them that if they did anything even remotely similar to me again, then Kyro and Kaiden wouldn't hesitate to banish or execute them. I was glad that Kyro and Kaiden hadn't banished or executed the girls. I knew that what the girls had done was serious but I didn't wish to see them hurt because of it. Kyro and Kaiden also told the girls that there wouldn't be a second warning. In addition to the girls not bothering me, we had also not received any more calls from my old pack and there also hadn't been any more rogue attacks. However, Kyro and Kaiden said they would remain on alert until the threats from my old pack and the rogues were dealt with. Though we would remain on alert for threats, Kyro and Kaiden said they wouldn't let it stop us from focusing on something more important, my Luna Ceremony. My Luna Ceremony was taking place at lunch time today and I was nervous and excited all at the same time. Right now, I was in my bathroom having a nice relaxing bubble bath.

I really love this bath. Alpin purred in contentment.

Me too. I replied with a sigh.

How do you feel about today, Levi? Alpin asked me.

I feel a bit nervous but I'm also happy, I admitted. *I am very grateful for all that mum has taught me about being a Luna and I feel ready to put it to use. I know that we have only been training with her for a few months but I am confident we will be ok with our mates, family and friends by our side,* I added. If you had asked me a few months ago how I felt about being the Luna, I would have told you that I was scared and that I would never be a good Luna. But now, after training with mum I felt much more confident that I could do it. And if I ever stumbled or needed help, I knew that my mates, family and friends would be there to help me. *We should get out of the bath before we look like prunes,* Alpin said, breaking me from my thoughts. I laughed before getting out of the bath and wrapping a towel around myself. After emptying the bath, I made my way to my walk-in closet. I still haven't gotten used to having such a large closet to myself and I don't know if I ever will. Once I walked into my walk-in closet, I sat down on a chair and looked at the suit that I would be wearing for the ceremony. Mum had taken me shopping with Emerald, Diomika, Azalea and Tansy a few days ago to find a suit for today and I really liked the one that I picked out. The suit was dark blue and consisted of dress pants, a vest, jacket and a tie. Under the vest I would wear a white dress shirt. I also got a new pair of shiny black dress shoes to wear. As I sat and looked at my suit, I thought about everything that has happened to me in the last few months. I had found my mates, I had gained a family, had a personal guardian assigned by the Moon Goddess herself, joined a new pack and I was set to become the new Luna of the Crimson Rose Pack. All in all, my life had gotten so much better and I wouldn't trade it for anything. I was distracted from my thoughts by someone knocking softly on the door.

'Come in,' I called out.

'Levi, where are you?' I heard Azalea call out from my study.

'I'm in the closet,' I replied. A moment later a heavily pregnant Azalea walked into the walk-in closet; well waddled would probably be a better description.

'How are you feeling Azalea?' I asked as I stood up and looked her over. She was wearing a light green dress and had her hair half up, half down. She honestly looked like an elven princess I had read about in a couple of my books.

'I am doing alright. The little one hasn't kicked too much today and I'm thankful for that. I can't wait for the little one to be born,' Azalea replied with a smiled. Azalea was due to give birth next month and so was Tansy. As I looked at Azalea, she got a surprised look on her face and then turned away. 'Umm Levi. Your towel has slipped,' Azalea said softly. When I looked down, I saw that my towel was sitting dangerously low on my hips.

'Oh, my Goddess. I'm so sorry,' I said to Azalea as I adjusted my towel.

'It's alright,' Azalea replied with a smile. 'Ok we have an hour to get you ready for your ceremony, so I want you to get your clothes on and when you are done, I'll come back in and make any final adjustments,' she added before smiling and then leaving the closet. After Azalea left the closet, I took my towel off and dried myself off as best I could. After I had dried myself off, I put my suit on being careful not to crinkle it as I did. I chose to leave the vest and jacket off for now and instead I would put them on before I headed out.

'You can come in Azalea,' I called out as I sat down and put my socks and shoes on. When I heard the door to the walk-in closet open, I looked up and saw Azalea walk in.

'Oh, my Goddess. You look so handsome Levi,' Azalea said with a big smile on her face.

'Thank you,' I replied. I couldn't help that blush that came over my face as Azalea looked at me. Azalea smiled as she directed me to a chair in front of a large mirror.

As she styled my hair, Azalea used gel and hair spray to keep it in place. By the time she was done with my hair, I was speechless.

'What do you think Levi?' Azalea asked as I stared at myself in the mirror.

Wow. She is good. We look so different from the old us, Alpin noted, awed by what we saw. He was right, we were looking better than ever thanks to the wonderful treatment we had received since coming to the pack.

'I love it. Thank you so much,' I said to her before getting up and giving Azalea a hug, making sure to not crinkle my suit.

'You are very welcome. Now let's get your vest and jacket on because it is time to head to the hall,' Azalea as she stepped back. After I put the vest and jacket on, Azalea helped to make sure that they were sitting right. 'Ok. Everything looks good, so let's get going,' Azalea said with a smile. After leaving the closet, the two of us made our way out of the study. We then went to the elevator and headed to the ground floor of the pack house. I was shocked by what I saw when we stepped out of the Elevator. Emerald was standing there looking like a supermodel. She had a black suite on and her hair was tied up in a bun with a braid on the left-hand side.

'Wow,' I said as my eyes went wide.

She looks awesome, I said to Alpin. It was weird to see Emerald wearing something so formal looking. She usually wore workout gear or casual clothes. Emerald chuckled before bowing her head to me.

'Hello Future Luna Levi,' Emerald said respectfully. 'Luna Maevis asked me to escort you to the meeting hall for the ceremony,' she added. I had to shake my head to clear the surprise from my mind before I could reply to Emerald.

'Thank you,' I replied. It not only felt weird see Emerald dressed so formally, it also felt weird to hear her being so formal towards me. However, considering the importance of today, I understood why she was.

'Let's head off, shall we?' Emerald said. I nodded and then Azalea and I followed Emerald as she led the way to the meeting hall. As we walked in silence, I noticed that there was no one around.

Everyone is probably at the hall already. And those that aren't are either on duty or unable to attend for other reasons, Alpin stated and I agreed. When Emerald, Azalea and I got to the meeting hall, we saw Tansy waiting outside for us.

'Future Luna Levi,' Tansy said with a big smile on her face.

'Hello Tansy,' I replied. 'How are you? Are you sure you should be out here and not sitting down already?' I was worried about both her and Azalea, seeing as both were due to give birth soon.

'I'm ok,' Tansy replied. 'Now, Luna Maevis has asked me to take you in through the back so no one sees you until you are called up to the stage,' she added. Emerald, Azalea and I followed Tansy as she led us to an entrance on the other side of the meeting hall. 'Ok Levi. Emerald, Azalea and I have to go and take our seats now. You are to wait here until Kyro and Kaiden call you to the stage, ok?' Tansy told me.

'Are you ok waiting here on your own or would you like me to stay with you?' Emerald asked. 'I will be ok,' I replied. Emerald nodded and then she, Azalea and Tansy left the room to go and take their seats on stage. I waited nervously in the back for several minutes before I finally heard Kyro call for me to come one stage. As I walked out of the room and onto the stage, I was almost deafened by the loud, joyous roars that came from the pack members gathered in the hall. As I walked onto the stage, I saw mum, dad, Jaden, Rowan and Tansy sitting at the back of the stage, while everyone else was sitting in the hall in front of the stage. As I walked across the stage, I noticed Kyro's and Kaiden's jaws drop open as they looked me over. Judging from their expressions, they liked what they saw. I also checked them out as I approached them. They were wearing identical black suits which made them look very handsome.

Damn our mates are the sexiest mofos in the world, Alpin said with a purr.

Firstly, yes, our mates are sexy. Secondly, 'mofos'? Where on earth did you learn that? I responded.

Rowan taught me it. He said it means mother fuckers, Alpin replied happily. I shook my head at my crazy wolf. Over the last couple of months, I had decided that I would let Alpin have full control of us. During those moments he had picked up some interesting language and behaviour, mostly from Rowan. I broke from my thoughts as I came to a stop in front of my mates, giving them a big smile as I did. Kyro and Kaiden each grabbed a hold of one of my hands, before they took turns kissing both of my cheeks.

'Ok everyone, quiet down,' Kyro called out as we turned to face the crowd in front of us. We had to wait a couple of minutes for the noise to quiet down. 'As we mentioned a few moments ago, we are here today to officially welcome the new Luna of the Crimson Rose Pack,' Kaiden said and then pack cheered again. 'To perform this ceremony, Alpha Kaiden and I will now ask Luna Maevis de Luca to come forward to perform the transfer of title to Future Luna Levi Chang,' Kyro said proudly as he turned to face Mum. 'Luna Maevis de Luca, please come forward,' he added. Mum got up from her chair and walked towards up, stopping just in front of me. After giving my hands a small squeeze, Kyro and Kaiden stepped back to give mum and I room.

'Future Luna Levi Chang you are here today to officially take over as the Luna of the Crimson Rose Pack,' Mum began. 'As the Luna of this pack you will have many duties that you will have to perform. Over the past couple of months, I have taught you as much as I can to prepare you for this role and I think you are ready,' she added proudly.

I love mum so much, Alpin said.

Me too. She is an amazing woman, I replied.

'Future Luna Levi Chang do you believe you are ready to take over as the Luna of the Crimson Rose Pack?' Mum asked me.

'I believe that I am ready to take over as Luna of the Crimson Rose Pack,' I replied confidently. 'Do you accept the responsibilities that come with being the Luna of the Crimson Rose Pack?' Mum asked.

'I accept the responsibilities that come with being the Luna of the Crimson Rose Pack,' I replied.

'Do you promise to stand by your mates' sides and support them in their duties as Alphas of the Crimson Rose Pack?' Mum asked next.

'I promise to stand by my mates' sides and support them in their duties as

Alphas of the Crimson Rose Pack,' I said. I noticed my mates smiling proudly as mum asked me the different questions.

'Do you promise to be there for your pack members in times of need, to support them in their endeavours and to listen to their issues and concerns?' Mum asked.

'I promise to do so,' I answered.

'Do you promise to help the pups of this pack become strong and confident wolves? Do you promise to take care of any pups that for whatever reason become orphans?' Mum asked next. 'I promise to help the pack's pups become strong and confident. I also promise to take care of any pups that may become orphans,' I promised. I noticed my voice changed slightly when I mentioned helping the pack pups. I had grown close to the pups of the pack and I felt very protective of them. Mum had explained that this was normal for a Luna.

'Then Future Luna Levi Chang, I am happy to hand over my title to you. No longer are you the Future Luna of this pack. You are now Luna Levi Chang of the Crimson Rose Pack,' Mum said proudly. I felt a wave of energy flow over me as the power of Luna transferred from mum to me. I staggered a bit from the weight of it but mum quickly grabbed a hold of my hands and made sure I didn't fall. Once the transfer was done, Kyro and Kaiden engulfed me in a hug. We stood there quietly for several minutes before breaking apart. Mum gave me a smile before turning and returning to her seat beside dad. Kyro, Kaiden and I then turned to face the pack members.

'Everyone Alpha Kaiden and I are proud to introduce to you, Luna Levi Chang of the Crimson Rose Pack,' Kyro said proudly. The pack cheered loudly, I could tell they were happy for us and this made me very happy too. I was so proud to be the Luna of such a kind and caring pack. 'Luna Levi Chang will now say a few words,' Kaiden said after the noise died down.

'Firstly, I would like to thank Former Luna Maevis de Luca for all the years she served as Luna of the Crimson Rose Pack. You did an amazing job and I hope that I can live up to the example that you set,' I said as I turned to face mum. 'Mum, I also want to thank you for everything you have done to help me since I came here,' I added and I saw mum smile as she wiped tears from her eyes. I bowed to mum before turning back to face the pack. 'Secondly, I want to thank the pack for being so kind and accepting of me. I hope to make you all proud as Luna and I want to promise again that I will always do my best for the pack,' I said confidently, before looking at Kyro and Kaiden. 'Kyro, Kaiden. I know we got off to a bit of a rough start and I want to thank you both for sticking by me and for helping me to get to this moment. I promise that I will stay by your sides and love you both will all my heart,' I said. Kyro and Kaiden engulfed me in another hug as the pack cheered at my words. Goddess I loved this feeling. Kyro and Kaiden stepped back and smiled at me before Kyro turned to address the pack. 'I would like to invite everyone to join us out the back of the pack house to celebrate the induction of our new Luna,' Kyro said. Once he finished speaking, everyone stood up, left the meeting hall and headed to the back of the pack house. Once there, we celebrated my becoming Luna of the pack. The area behind the pack house was decorated with balloons, streamers and fairy lights. As Kyro, Kaiden and I walked around the pack, various pack members came up to us and congratulated us. As we walked around, I took in all the smiling faces and I couldn't help the smile that crossed my face.

'I am so proud of you Levi,' Kaiden said as we stopped near the steps at the back pack house. 'Me too. I am so very happy that you are here with us,' Kyro said in agreement.

'I am happy too. Thank you for sticking by me through everything,' I replied. Feeling confident, I stood on my tippy toes and gave each of my mates a kiss on the lips. They both looked a little shocked but they quickly recovered and they each gave me a longer kiss on the lips.

'Aww,' I heard someone say. I turned to see Jaden and Rowan standing there looking at us with big smiles. I blushed and that just made Jaden and Rowan say aww again.

'How are you doing Luna?' Jaden asked me.

'I am doing great. I am feeling very happy,' I replied.

'That's good to hear,' Rowan replied.

'As the Beta of the pack, I want to promise you that Gamma Rowan and I will do everything in our power to help you,' Jaden said.

'Thank you. I am so glad that we have such an awesome Beta and Gamma,' I replied. 'I also glad to have such amazing Alpha mates,' I added. I suddenly caught a whiff of something that smelled amazing and sniffed the air. 'Bacon,' I squealed happily.

'Ha ha. You are definitely Kyro's and Kaiden's mate. They love bacon too,' Jaden said with a chuckle.

'True,' Kyro agreed. The five of us then decided to go and get some bacon before it disappeared. Afterwards Kyro, Kaiden and I went for another walk around the party. While did that Jaden went to speak with his parents and sister, and Rowan went to find his mate. About an hour later, I got up on the stage we had set up and asked everyone to quiet down. I was surprised at how quickly everyone did as I asked. ***Comes with being the Luna,*** Alpin commented.

'I would like to thank everyone for gathering here today. I am proud to stand before you as your Luna and I am looking forward to speaking with all of you at some point in the future,' I said to the pack gathered in front of me. 'Now I have something special for everyone here. Could you all please welcome the Crimson Roses to the stage,' I added. The Crimson Roses was the name given to a group I had formed about a month ago. The group consisted of both pups and adults from the pack. It was a group that would gather at least once a week to sing and play instruments. I had asked the group a couple of weeks ago if they would like to perform at my Luna Ceremony celebration and they had said yes. So, now here they were all gathered on stage, twelve pups and six adults, myself included ready to perform for the pack. 'We are would like to perform a few songs for you all. So, please sit back and enjoy, and if you feel like dancing, please do so,' I said before taking my position behind the piano. I had started learning the piano just after forming the group and had been told that I was quite good. Together the group performed a total of six songs as the pack clapped and danced along, enjoying the performance that we put on. The party went on well into the night, with pack members leaving to return home at different times. When Kyro, Kaiden and I had left the party at eleven o'clock, the party was still going strong. After leaving the party, the three of us went to the Alpha floor. Once there, we headed to Kyro's room and headed over to his bed.

'Goddess, thank you for today,' Kyro said as he sat down.

'Same here, Moon Goddess,' Kaiden said. I chuckled as I sat down in between my mates, finding their comments funny and cute at the same time.

'I don't know about you guys but I am exhausted,' Kyro said as he played with one of my hands.

'Me too,' I replied before letting out a yawn.

'How about we get changed and go to bed?' Kaiden said. I liked the sound of that, so I nodded in response.

'Why don't we just grab something from my closet to wear? Save you two from having to go and get something from your closets,' Kyro suggested.

'Sounds good,' Kaiden replied. The three of us headed into closet and grabbed some clothes to change into. I just grabbed one of Kyro's shirts to wear, it would be like a dress on me but at least it would cover everything it needed to. While Kyro went to change in the bathroom, Kaiden went and changed in the bedroom and I changed in the closet. When we were all changed, we went into the bedroom and laid on Kyro's bed. As I laid in-between my mates, I felt happy and soon all three of us drifted off to sleep.

CHAPTER 44: LEVI'S POV

IT HAD BEEN a month since I became the new Luna of the Crimson Rose Pack and though I had a few difficulties, I found I could handle my duties quite well. I helped Kyro and Kaiden with their duties, also spent time listening to complaints and issues from pack members and doing my best to resolve them and I also spent time helping out at the pack nursery and pack hospital. Today I was at the pack hospital with my mates, mum, dad, Kaito, Kode, Jaden, Daniel and Susan McCallister, Sakura, Mr Baker and Benson Baker. Benson Baker was Tansy's brother and Mr Baker is their father. We were all gathered at the pack hospital because Tansy and Azalea had gone into labour a few hours ago. While we all waited in the waiting area, Tansy and Azalea were in a nearby room with their mates and some of the pack's medical staff. While everyone else sat patiently, I paced back and forth nervously. As I heard a scream come from the room where Tansy and Azalea were, I felt my instincts kick in and tell me to go into the room and comfort the two she-wolves who were in pain. I struggled to not give in and do as my instincts told me.

'They are ok Levi. The doctors and midwives know what they are doing,' Mum said as she came over to me.

'I want to go in there and help them,' I told mum.

'I know how you feel Levi because I feel it to. It is a Luna's natural instinct to comfort pack members when they are hurting. However, right now we need to stay calm and wait for the doctors to tell us what they need,' Mum told me before guiding me over to my mates.

'Sit with us Little Wolf,' Kyro said as he gently grabbed my hand. I sat down in-between my two mates and then snuggled into Kyro's side. Kyro wrapped arm around my shoulders and Kaiden placed a hand on my leg. I was glad for the comfort my mates were providing right now.

Are you ok Levi? Kaiden asked me over mind link. I turned my head slightly so I could look at him and then I shook my head.

I'm a little scared. I admitted.

What are you scared of Little Wolf? Kyro asked softly.

I don't know why but I have this feeling that something is going to go wrong. I don't know if it is to do with the birth or if it's something else but I can't shake this bad feeling, I whimpered. Kyro and Kaiden exchanged a look before I felt the mind link expand to include several others.

Patrol wolves be on alert, we may have trouble coming. I want extra wolves on each shift until further notice, I heard Kyro command the patrol wolves over mind link.

Yes Alpha. I'll see it done. Emerald replied. She would have been here at the hospital with us but she wasn't able to be present as she was on patrol.

Alert us to anything that doesn't seem right, no matter how small or insignificant it might seem, Kaiden added.

Yes Alpha. Emerald replied.

'Is everything ok Alphas, Luna?' Jaden asked as Kyro, Kaiden and I came out of the mind link. As the three of us looked at Jaden, everyone else looked at us. 'Levi said that he felt that something was going to go wrong. He isn't sure what but he can't shake the feeling,' Kyro replied.

'We've ordered for extra wolves to join the patrols and for them to let us know if anything doesn't seem right,' Kaiden added.

'I will go join the patrols now. I'll keep you up to date if we find anything,' Jaden said as he stood up quickly. 'I'll go to,' Dad said as he stood up.

'No Denton. You stay here. I'll go with Jaden,' Daniel McCallister said as he stood up and put a hand on dad's shoulder.

'No, I should go and help,' Dad said.

'Your grandchild is due any time now. You should be here for that. Jaden and I can take care of this matter while you stay here,' Daniel replied.

'Thank you Jaden, Daniel,' Kyro said.

'We will let you know if anything happens,' Jaden replied. After saying goodbye to everyone, Jaden and his father left the waiting room.

'I hope they'll be ok,' I said softly.

'They'll be ok Luna,' Susan McCallister said. 'Like all of us here. My mate and our son will do what they have to in order to protect the pack,' she added proudly. I went to reply but stopped when I heard a nearby door open and someone walked out. I quickly stood up and saw that Doctor Veracruz had come out of the maternity room.

'Luna Levi, Former Luna Maevis. Tansy and Azalea are asking for the both of you. If you will please follow me,' Doctor Veracruz said.

'Of course,' Mum replied. Mum and I then followed Doctor Veracruz into the maternity room where we saw Tansy and Azalea laying on two beds with their legs propped up. Tansy and Azalea each had their mates standing by their side and it honestly looked as though their mates were in worse condition.

'Levi,' Tansy whimpered and I rushed to her side and grabbed her hand.

'It's ok Tansy,' I said to a tired Tansy. While I went to help Tansy, Maevis went to help Azalea. With two Lunas in the room, it seemed as though the birthing process went quicker and in a few short hours, three beautiful pups came into the world. As the pups were born, I felt the new links join them to the rest of the pack; it was a strange but wonderful feeling. Kingsley and Azalea welcomed twin daughters, while Rowan and Tansy welcomed a son.

'Oh, my goddess they are so beautiful,' Maevis said, a big smile on her face as she looked at the three newest members of the pack. After the pups were all cleaned off, they were given back to their mums, who looked exhausted.

'What names have you chosen for the pups?' I asked, eager to know the names of the little ones.

'Azalea and I had a few names picked but we have decided to name these little cuties Seraphine and Savannah,' Kingsley said proudly.

'Those are beautiful names,' Mum replied. You could feel the happiness rolling off of her as she continued looking at the pups. 'Tansy and I decided that if we had a son, we would call him Balthazar,' Rowan replied.

'Aww. Future Gamma Balthazar Matheson,' I said and Rowan nodded.

'I'm sorry to interrupt but Tansy and Azalea both need to get cleaned up and then get some rest,' Doctor Veracruz said gently.

'Of course. Why don't we go and introduce these little ones to the others while Tansy and Azalea get cleaned up?' Maevis suggested.

'Can you stay here please Levi?' Azalea asked.

'Of course,' I replied. Maevis nodded and then she along with Rowan and Kingsley each picked up a pup and left the room. I waited patiently as Tansy and Azalea were cleaned up and then I went and sat in-between the two beds. The midwives had moved the beds closer together so I could hold onto both Tansy and Azalea. By the time the pups were brought back into the room, Tansy and Azalea were both fast asleep. Once they returned to the room, Maevis and I left in order to give the new families some time alone.

Several hours after the birth of the pups, I was sitting in the waiting outside the maternity room with my mates, mum, dad, Kaito, Kode, Susan, Sakura, Mr Baker and Benson Baker. Jaden and his father had come back a couple of times to let us know how the patrol was going and so far, they had reported that everything was alright. Diomika and Aurora had also joined us a little while ago, after their shifts at the hospital had ended.

'Congratulations on the birth of the pups,' Aurora said, breaking the silence.

'Thank you Aurora,' Maevis replied.

'I am really happy that the mums and pups are safe,' I said. 'I'm glad nothing happened during the birth,'

'So are we Little Wolf,' Kyro replied.

'I love the names that they chose for the pups,' Maevis said and I saw she had a big smile.

'Yeah. Seraphine, Savannah and Balthazar, are quite nice names,' Kode said happily. A few minutes later I heard someone coming and when I turned around, I saw Emerald walk into the waiting area.

'Hey, Emerald. How is it going out there?' Denton asked as Emerald sat down.

'It's going good. So far there haven't been any signs of attacks but we are keeping our eyes open,' Emerald replied. 'Jaden said since I have been on patrol for the last fourteen hours, I should go and rest,' she added.

'That's a good idea,' Maevis said.

'Why aren't you resting then?' Sakura asked. 'You look tired,' she added, concern in her voice. 'I tried to rest but I couldn't relax so I came here to see how things are going,' Emerald replied. 'Are you ok?' I asked Emerald. I was worried about her, she looked very tired.

'I'm ok Levi,' Emerald replied with a tired smile. I was going to say something else but was cut off by several loud howls. Moments later the patrol wolves reported that a large number of rogues were coming at the pack from multiple directions. A moment later, Kingsley, Rowan and Doctor Veracruz rushed out of the maternity room.

'Doctor Veracruz get Tansy, Azalea and the pups ready to move the safe room. Mum, Diomika, Aurora, you three give her a hand,' Kaiden ordered Doctor Veracruz. Mum, Diomika, Aurora and Doctor Veracruz nodded and then the four of them went into the maternity to prepare to move Tansy, Azalea and the pups.

'Dad, Rowan, Kingsley, Emerald you four will come with Kaiden and I to help take care of the rogues,' Kyro began, 'Levi once Tansy, Azalea and the pups are ready to move, I want you to lead them to the safe room. Kaito, Kode, Sakura, Mr Baker, Benson, you five go with them,' he added, his tone serious.

'I will get them there,' I promised my mates. Kyro and Kaiden smiled at me and then they, their father and Emerald left the waiting area. 'Ok, everyone wait here while I see if the girls and pups are ready to move,' I said before heading into the maternity room. 'Is everyone ready to move?' I asked as soon as I went inside.

'Almost Levi,' Diomika replied.

'We might need someone to help push the beds,' Doctor Veracruz added.

'Kaito, Benson, Mr Baker get in here,' I called out and the three quickly entered the room.

'What do you need Luna?' Mr Baker asked.

'I need you three to help push the beds,' I replied. The three of them nodded and then they moved to the beds. Mr Baker and Benson went to Tansy's bed, while Kaito went to Azalea's bed. Doctor Veracruz said she would help move Azalea's bed. 'Ok, let's get going,' I said once everyone was ready. I then left the room with Tansy, Azalea, the pups, mum, Diomika, Aurora, Doctor Veracruz, Mr Baker and Benson. We then headed to the safe room with those that were in the waiting area. On the way to the safe room, we heard a loud crash nearby and almost straight away we caught the stench of rogues. 'Everyone, go on ahead. Diomika, Aurora the three of us will stay here and fight the rogues. We have to give the others as much time as we can to get to the safe room,' I told everyone. I had chosen Diomika and Aurora to help hold of the rogues because I knew that they both had some fighting skills.

'Levi no. You can't stay here. You have to come with us,' Azalea said with a whimper.

'No. I made a promise to protect this pack and that is exactly what I will do. Now everyone get going. That is an order,' I said. I could see that they wanted to refuse but I had used my Luna voice which forced them to do as I had said. Once they were out of sight, I turned to face Diomika and Aurora. 'Ok let's get ready, remember we need to hold them off as long as we can,' I said before shifting into my wolf form, shredding my clothes in the process. The two ladies soon followed with both shifting into beautiful brown wolves.

Warriors the pack hospital has been breached. I want some warriors here now. We still have people to get to the safe room, I called out over the mind link.

Yes Luna. I heard several pack warriors responded.

Luna, I am close by with a few warriors. We are heading to you now. Hold on as long as you can, I heard another warrior say.

We will hold on as long as we can, I replied.

I'm so sorry Levi. Kaiden and I are on the other side of the grounds. We won't be able to get to you, Kyro said over private mind link to me.

It's ok Kyro. You two do your duty out there. I will do what I have to in here, I replied. I heard another loud crash and knew the rogues were getting closer. **I have to go. The rogues are close. I love you both,** I said.

I love you too, I heard Kyro and Kaiden both say as I came out of the mind link. A minute later, Diomika, Aurora and I spotted at least a dozen rogues coming down the corridor we were standing in.

Remember, we have to hold them off as long as we can, I said to Diomika and Aurora.

We will Luna, Aurora replied. I turned slightly and gave both ladies a nod of my head. When I turned back, I noticed the rogues looked stunned and if I had to guess it would be because of the fact that I was a white wolf. I took advantage of the rogues being temporarily stunned, to launch myself at the them, growling lowly as I did. Diomika and Aurora quickly followed my action and soon the three of us were biting, tearing and swiping at the rogues who dared to invade our pack.

These assholes aren't hurting any more of our pack, Alpin growled out as we tore into a rogue's throat and ripped it out.

Damn right they aren't, I replied as I moved onto the next rogue. Sometime later I heard a couple of whimpers and turned to see Aurora and Diomika collapse unconscious to the ground. Thankfully I saw that they were both still breathing.

Only four more to go Levi, Alpin said and I nodded.

Let's get these bastards, I said. I leapt towards one of the rogues and sunk my claws into his back. As I went to bit his neck, another rogue rammed into us, knocking me away from the rogue I had attacked. Before I could get up and keep fighting, one of the other rogues rushed over to me and hit my head. As I faded in and out of consciousness, I heard someone shift and then I felt myself get picked up and placed onto the back of one of the rogue bastards. The rogue that now carried me, took off, quickly followed by the other three rogues. The rogues headed out of the pack hospital and through the pack grounds. As the rogues raced through the pack grounds with me, I heard several of my pack warriors start chasing after us. Unfortunately, before the pack warriors were able to catch up to us, I felt myself get put into the back of a van. As the van started up, I heard two loud, sorrowful howls. I knew that they were from Kyro and Kaiden who had realised that I had been taken.

I love you both very much, I said as the van drove off. I didn't hear if my mates replied, as I was soon overtaken by darkness.

Shawline Publishing Group Pty Ltd

www.shawlinepublishing.com.au